KELIS
KINGDOM OF FAIRYTALES
SEASON ELEVEN

You all know the story of your favorite fairytale, but did you ever wonder what happened after the fairytale ending? Well we know. Not all afters end up happily, sometimes the real adventure starts much later...

Following famous fairytale characters, eighteen years after their happily ever after, the Kingdom of Fairytales offers an edge of the seat thrill ride in an all new and sensational way to read.

Lighting-fast reads you won't be able to put down

Fantasy has never been so epic!

URBIS PRISON
SHIPLEY
THE VALE
AZREN
BADALAH
DESERT
KISBU
DRACONIS
ZHORE
ELDER
MOSA
ABORIA
URBIS
AZURE
ENCHANTIA
AIRE
SKYLA
EMERALD CITY
OZ
FLORIS
TULIS
W
E
S
ARCADIA
RENAIS
THE FORGE
MELFALL
ATLANTICE
ANTLA
KINGDOM
OF
FAIRYTALES

ISBN: 978-1-989997-33-8
Enchanted Quill Press



Contaact the author at www.enchantedquillpress.com
Cover by Enchanted Quilll Press
Interior Formatting by Enchanted Quill Press
Editing by Rose Lipscomb

# QUEEN OF REFLECTIONS

# 7TH OCTOBER

The sun streaming through the window warmed my face, waking me from a dream so dark my heart was still thundering minutes later, even though the memory of it had already faded, like a déjà-vu unremembered. I shivered as though the room was cold, even though it was still cozy from the fire that had been lit the night before. The feeling that something was wrong was intense, but without anything to tether it to, I brushed it aside.

I swung my legs around, planting them on the floor, and heaved myself out of bed. Frightening dreams had been plaguing me for a while now, but the very second I opened my eyes, they would drift away, leaving me with a sense of unease and no recollection of what I was dreaming.

I pulled out a pair of leather leggings, tunic, and lace shirt—all in black—and dressed quickly, trying to rid myself of the lingering restlessness I felt at the forgotten dream. With only my hair left to do, I readied myself for the latest stand-off with my grandmother's mirror, an enchanted artifact that almost brought down the whole kingdom over eighteen years ago.

"What are you wearing?" The mirror huffed a sigh as though my very existence annoyed it...which it probably did. "It might as well be a hessian bag."

"At least, I don't look the same every day," I threw back, giving myself a wink in the mirror. It looked like an ordinary mirror, though with an ornately decorated frame, but I swear it had the soul of a demon trapped inside it.

"There's no need to look different when one's existence makes one perfect," it snapped back, always taking everything so personally. I gave a grin and picked up my wand to spell my unruly black curls into submission. I'd never really gotten into spellcasting like everyone else in Enchantia, but I liked this spell. Then again, I liked anything which made it easier to deal with my hair. The wand vibrated in my hand, recognizing me as its owner.

As an Enchantian, I was supposed to know magic inside and out, but the truth was, my hair spell was one of the few I'd mastered, and that was only because it was easier than working a brush through the tangles.

"Even with your hair spelled, you're barely passable," the mirror sniffed.

"Thanks for the barely," I muttered.

"Anytime!"

Ignoring it, I strapped my holster around my waist

and slid my wand into it, giving my hair a flick for good measure.

A knock sounded at the door taking my concentration away from my hair

"Come in," I called.

The door didn't make a sound as it opened.

"How are you, Kelis? Sleep well?" Mother asked as she swept into the room, her dark hair and red lips a striking contrast to the white suit and cape she was wearing.

"My dear queen, how glorious and regal you look today," the mirror spewed, with obvious delight. "You truly are the most magnificent woman in all the kingdoms. Might I even say you are the fairest of them all," it continued. Hopefully, this would be one of it's shorter tirades. I wasn't sure I could stomach more this morning. Once, it hadn't stopped praising her for over an hour. She'd ended up walking out of the room without telling me what she'd come for.

"Here we go," mother muttered, rolling her eyes.

I suppressed a smirk as she gave it the side-eye.

"You look more and more enchanting every day," it continued. "There is no doubt you are the most beautiful woman in all the land."

I snorted, unable to help myself.

"It's not funny, Kelis," she warned me. "You know I detest that thing. It's not natural."

"It kind of is funny," I responded, knowing we were going to have the same conversation as always about this but not being able to stop it.

"I don't know why you keep that old thing," she muttered. "It's a terrible nuisance."

"It was grandmother's." I replied as though that was the reason it still hung on my bedroom wall after all these years. The truth was the thing was hilarious. Plus, throwing away an enchanted object seemed to be asking for trouble. She should know, all of her troubles started with this same enchanted mirror too. Well, and a wicked step-mother who wanted to kill her. But that was beside the point.

"Look at all the trouble it caused." Mother sighed and dropped herself onto one of the many chairs I had dotted around.

"Only because someone else wanted to be the most beautiful woman in the land," I pointed out. "I know, I'm not. So it hardly matters; besides, it's funny."

She sighed again, and I knew what was coming next. Like with the mirror, it was always the same. "You're beautiful just the way you are, Kelis," she assured me.

"I'm not looking for flattery," I responded. "I don't need to be the most beautiful person in the land." I shrugged.

"I know you don't. The mirror makes me nervous, though." She looked over at it, her distaste plain on her face.

"Don't worry, I'm not going to fall for its charms. Not that it has any."

She opened her mouth before closing it again, clearly not wanting to get into the same argument we'd had dozens of times before.

My mother reached out a hand and tucked a strand of hair behind my ear, an act reminiscent of my childhood when she'd help me get ready for the day.

"How is the magic coming along?"

"You know I don't do much with it," I pointed out.

She sighed. "I know. But it would make your life easier if you did..."

"Didn't you once tell me that an easy life wasn't a life

worth living?"

She chuckled. "When did you become old enough to remind me of my own wisdom?" A small smile quirked at the corners of her lips, conveying the true pride I knew she felt for me.

"I remember a lot of the things you taught me. Mostly about being a leader. I don't need people to fawn over me to rule well. I just need people to respect and like me as a ruler." She'd been teaching me since the moment I'd been old enough to understand, and I'd soaked it all up.

"You'll make a great Queen someday." There was a sadness in her voice that I didn't understand, but I didn't want to say anything and make her more upset.

"Not for a very long time," I murmured. I hated it when she brought this up. It reminded me of the future and what I'd one day have to lose to reach my full potential.

"I don't plan on it." She smiled again, this time reaching her eyes. "I didn't come here to talk about some far off future, though."

"You didn't?" Curiosity pinged through me. "What's up?"

She shook her head. "Adam's coming to visit."

"He is?" My heart began to pound again, but for a very different reason. If my cousin was coming for a visit, there was every chance he'd be bringing Jake with him.

"He is," she echoed. "He's coming for Fright Fest."

"Oh," I said as nonchalantly as I could muster. The Fright Fest was the highlight of every Enchantian's calendar. On the 31st of October every year, the whole kingdom came together to celebrate with a big party. It was supposed to be a festival to celebrate our ancestors, but nowadays, it was an excuse to dress up, show off, and have fun. If I was right about Jake coming, maybe I'd get to have a little fun too.

"I believe he's bringing some friends with him. You remember Jake, right?"

I sucked in a breath to calm my heart from doing a circuit round my chest at the mention of his name. I nodded, trying to keep my excitement from spilling out.

"How long are they staying for?" Fright Fest wasn't until the end of the month, which gave me plenty of time to pluck up the courage and say something to Jake about how I felt. How I'd always felt about him. The last time I'd seen him, I'd been a girl, but I was over eighteen, a woman now.

"They're arriving tomorrow and staying until after the Fest."

"What time?" I asked eagerly then checked myself. "I mean, shouldn't we arrange to meet them?"

"They'll arrive in time for the banquet tomorrow night."

"That's perfect," I replied, not doing a great job of keeping my enthusiasm from showing. "I wonder what I should wear?"

My mother gave me an odd look but didn't say anything. I had no doubt she'd read enough into my words to know why I was suddenly fussing about things that didn't usually bother me.

"If you need any help with that, let me know," Mother said.

"Thanks," I muttered, turning back to my wardrobe and wondering where I should start.

"I'll see myself out then." She chuckled. The door clicked back into place behind her, leaving me alone with the mirror again.

I rifled through my clothes, trying to decide what was best to wear tomorrow.

"Why is none of this right?" I demanded out loud, almost ready to give up on finding something to wear. There was a reason I never spent this long deciding on an outfit normally. I just didn't have the patience or the aptitude for it.

"Because you have no measurable sense of style," the mirror mused. If he'd been a real person, he would have been studying his nails as he spoke.

"At least, I'm unique." It was true. The style throughout Enchantia was to wear white at all times. I never wore white, preferring my predominantly black wardrobe to the chagrin of the mirror.

The mirror scoffed. "And do you think your mother became the fairest in the land by being unique?"

"I'd have thought it was *only* possible to be the fairest if you're unique," I replied passively.

"You just can't pull it off," the mirror retorted.

I rolled my eyes. One day, it might say something nice to me. I snorted. Yes, right. The mirror would say something nice the day magic dried up in Enchantia.

Turning my attention back to my clothes, I pulled out a black skirt I hardly ever wore.

I held it up to my body and looked in the full-length mirror in my dressing area. No way was I letting my grandmother's mirror have an opinion on something I wasn't even sure if I was going to wear.

"I wouldn't even bother. That went out of style before you were born."

Darn. It was like the thing had eyes everywhere.

"I'm a Princess, I'll bring it back in style," I shot back.

"You put the name Princess to shame."

"A Princess is more than what she looks like," I

parrotted words my mother had been teaching me since I was little. "She is her actions and her intentions above all else."

"If you keep telling yourself that, it may become true."

I hung the skirt back on the rail and turned to the next item, before dismissing that one too.

"He'll not like you, no matter what dreadful outfit you pick. I don't know why you are bothering."

I shot the mirror a look but found myself staring at my own angry reflection. That was the downside to arguing with a mirror; you could only ever see yourself in it.

"Who won't like me?" I knew exactly whom he meant, but I wasn't prepared to admit it.

"That boy you've been mooning over since you were knee-high to a grasshopper. I swear, if I had a mouth, I would have vomited over all the times you used me to practice kissing him with."

I blushed at the memory. I was about thirteen years old. "That happened once!"

"Once was more than enough. You'd have to make a costume to entice the poor guy. Preferably, one that covers your face."

A smirk played at the corner of my lips. That's exactly what I'd do. I'd make a costume. I was going to design a dress that would blow people away, and if Jake happened to be impressed, all the better.

No one would have any doubt that I was Snow White's daughter, not even the mirror.

"Thanks!" I said, throwing a smile at the mirror.

"What did I do?" it huffed, clearly not used to being thanked.

I kept my mouth shut as I headed to the balcony

and looked out over the kingdom that would one day be mine to rule. White buildings stretched as far as the eye could see, and pristine white streets kept clean by magic were used by the people going about their day. A few were already walking in the sunshine, their immaculate white robes almost glinting. I pulled on a pair of glasses to stop the glare and headed back to my wardrobe, pulling out my favorite black jacket. The night of the Frightfest, I'd wow everybody, but today I was happy enough being just me. As I walked out the door to start my day, I heard the mirror sigh.

"Black again," it mumbled. I stifled a laugh and closed the door behind me.

# 8TH OCTOBER

A shudder ran through me, waking me from another restless night of dreams. My breath caught in my throat until I remembered where I was, safe in my own bed in the palace. Something had happened, something awful, but as usual. The dream had already floated away, the memory of it gone, but the fear it produced still evident in my pounding heart.

A quick look around told me my bedroom was the same. Absolutely nothing was wrong, and yet, it took me ten minutes of measured breathing to calm down enough to get out of bed. Once I was up, the trepidation dissipated, and Jake came to mind, chasing the last of the unease away. He was coming today. Jake was coming today!

I hummed to myself as I got dressed.

"What is that dreadful racket?" the mirror demanded from its spot in the corner.

I rolled my eyes. Just because he couldn't be happy in his life, it didn't mean I couldn't be in mine. And Jake was coming. That was enough reason to hum to myself. Maybe this time, he'd see me for the woman I was becoming, not the kid I'd been. That was the problem with crushing on a guy who was three years older. He'd already been in the adult world for three years, whereas I was just stepping into it.

I ran my fingers through my hair, giving it a tousled look.

Feeling brave, I made my way over to the mirror, readying myself for the onslaught.

"Where did the bird go?" it asked.

"Huh?"

"From your hair. it looks like a bird nested in it."

"Haha, very original."

"My job is to comment on appearance, not come up with original jokes. If you want that, then maybe you should find the clown who did your makeup," he taunted.

"I'm not wearing any." I ran my fingers over my cheek, feeling for the cosmetics I knew weren't there.

"More's the pity." The mirror sighed dramatically.

"I'm not looking for your approval," I sniffed.

"Good. You won't get it looking like that. What's with all the black lace? You look like a hired mourner at a funeral."

"Thanks."

The sting his previous words had caused eased slightly, but it was getting to me more than usual. Jake's forthcoming appearance was making me second guess myself, and the barbs the mirror was throwing at me were sticking more than usual.

I was going to harness this feeling. The inadequacy, the bad things I thought about myself, I was going to fuel my creative side with them and enchant Jake in the process. At least, that was my plan. And it all hinged on having the best costume for the Fright Festival.

~

"If you divert the water from here, how many villagers will be affected?" Mother asked.

The man, who appeared to be some kind of general if his uniform was anything to go by, grimaced, clearly not quite as at ease with mother's question as he should be.

"Just what I thought," mother murmured. "Kelis, how good of you to join us." She beamed at me while gesturing to a seat at her side.

"Father said you'd be in here," I responded as I took the chair that had been mine for years.

"Yes, I was just talking to General Charles about some improvements he wants to make to the southern barracks."

I nodded, knowing exactly the ones she was talking about. "Is the land free to expand on?" I asked.

"The land is empty, yes," the general replied.

A flash of a picture came through my mind—waterlogged fields and dead crops in the fields near where he wanted to build.

"But there's something you're not telling us, right?" I gave him a pointed look. Father had no time for people talking around things, and had taught me how to spot when people were holding back, and this man certainly was.

He looked at mother, clearly expecting her to reprimand me for speaking out of turn.

Instead, she just smiled. "General?"

A smirk lifted the corners of my lips. We'd played this game with a few of the men in power over the years, and all of them reacted the same. They were fine with Mother having a say in how the realm was run, but they had issues with me. Not one of them believed my parents would actually value my opinion on matters of state.

They were wrong. And underestimating me had led to a lot of them revealing more than they wanted to. Sometimes, I even got summoned to come join them just for that reason.

General Charles sighed, clearly defeated by the blunt question. "We believe there's a chance that it might destroy the crops. We won't know until five harvests' time, though, and that seems like a fair risk." He shifted uncomfortably.

If I had to put money on it, then I'd say he knew we weren't going to agree to something that put our people in danger.

"Are we under threat of attack?" I asked him. "Last I knew, the lands were all at peace, why do we need to expand the barracks at all?"

I caught sight of Mother's smile from the corner of my eye. She'd no doubt had the same thoughts but didn't have the same flexibility I did when it came to asking blunt questions. My youth was an advantage there.

"No, we're not," he admitted. The set of his mouth gave him away more than it should have. He wasn't happy at all about having to concede that.

It was almost understandable. Almost. He was only trying to do his job, one that was a lot harder to justify when there wasn't a war going on.

"I think that will be all, General," mother said. "We'll be in contact with our decision."

"I'd rather hoped to have a decision today," he grumbled.

"We take the well being of our people seriously, General. We can't just make decisions without properly investigating matters." Her tone was soothing, far more than mine would have been in her situation. I didn't know how she did it.

The general looked like he was about to say something, but stopped himself before giving the two of us a stiff bow.

I tried my best not to let my amusement slip through, but I wasn't convinced I managed. At least I wasn't the only one, my mother's upper lip twitched as she suppressed her own smile.

The doors banged as the general left, no doubt he was annoyed we hadn't given him what he wanted.

"Well played," mother told me.

"Thank you." A smug feeling flowed through me. While my parents had been teaching me to rule for years, I still loved the feeling I got when I made a difference.

"Were you told I needed you, or were you looking for me?" she asked me as she gestured to the guard to hold the next person coming to petition her so we could have a moment. I appreciated that.

"I was actually coming to find you." My clothing suddenly became a lot more interesting than normal, and I started to pick at my hem.

"Kelis? Are you alright?" Real concern lingered in her voice. Not that it was surprising.

"Can-I-use-the-seamstresses?" The words came out as a jumbled mess, revealing just how unsure of the whole situation I was.

"The seamstresses? You've never been interested in them before. Don't you go to your own tailor in town?"

"Normally, yes." They were the only person in the city who'd agree to making my outfits in black instead of the traditional white. Thankfully, they seemed to balance who I was and the unusualness of my request in the price.

"But not this time?"

"I want something for the Fright Festival," I admitted sheepishly.

"Ah." There was an all-too-knowing glint in her eyes, and any doubts I'd had about her knowing how I felt about Jake vanished in a second. At least, she should understand the need for me to get something nice to wear while he was here.

"Can I?"

"Of course, you can. They're always there for you if you want them. They'll probably make you black clothes, as well, if you ask them." There wasn't even a hint of judgment in her voice.

Affection for my mother washed through me. She understood me on a level that no one else did. "Thank you."

"Do you need any help with the sketch or the idea?"

I shook my head. "I think I have one. But you can come see it before I give it to them, if you want?"

"I'd like that. Why don't I pick it up and take it to them?" The smile she gave me was so genuine that no one would be able to deny her what she asked.

"I'd like that." While I did have an idea, she might be able to help me if I got stuck with the design of it.

~

I chewed on my lip as I lay on my bed, the sketch pad in front of me bringing my costume to life. My hand flew over the page as my idea took shape. I was going to stand out, but this time it wouldn't be for wearing black. It would be for wearing *white*.

A smile slid over my face as I thought about it. The entire court, and most likely, the city outside too, knew me as the girl in black. And I was aware of what that meant.

I stopped sketching and looked down at my design. The cape would sweep out behind me, causing a train that would drag along the ground. Under the cape, I'd wear traditional leggings and top, but over that, I'd wear a gauzy shift with threads of silver. It might not be white like the rest of the outfit, but the silver should glitter from the multitude of colored lanterns that would decorate the street for the Fright Festival.

I tapped the pencil against my cheek, trying to work out what was wrong with it. There was something missing.

"Perhaps a headdress," I muttered to myself.

"So that people are distracted from your face? I must say, that's one of your better ideas," the mirror quipped.

I rolled my eyes. I shouldn't have spoken aloud. The mirror didn't always answer when I spoke to myself, but it did often enough for me to have learned to be careful about it.

"That's a no to the headdress," I said with certainty.

"If you ask me..."

"I didn't," I cut it off and turned back to the drawing. Oh, a staff. That would be the perfect addition. The

Fright Festival was all about the costumes, and so far, mine was nothing more than a statement about myself.

With a few smooth strokes of a pencil, it started to take shape. I added a high crown with dripping gems.

A knock sounded at the door.

"Come in," I called.

The door clicked as it was shut behind the person entering, and Mother swept into the room.

"Your Majesty, all beauty pales in comparison to yours," the mirror started.

Mother's face fell for a moment, but her easy smile was back within moments.

"Are you ready for me to take the sketch?" she asked, ignoring the mirror. She sat down on my bed and ran her fingers through my hair.

"Not quite." I sat up and handed her my sketchbook. As our fingers touched, another picture flashed through my mind, not unlike the one earlier when I'd been speaking to the general. This time My mother was deathly pale, her eyes closed and her hands together as she lay on her bed. My father's glassy eye expression showed he'd been crying. Then as soon as it came, it was gone. I gave myself a little shake and let go of the sketchbook so my mother could look at it.

The moment she stared down at it, she gave a sharp intake of breath. "This is beautiful, darling."

"Not as beautiful as you are, Your Majesty. Even the moon dare not claim it is more radiant than you," the mirror gushed.

Mother shot it a disgusted glance. "You've said your piece, now be silent."

The mirror didn't respond; it wouldn't dare. Nothing was more terrifying than Mother using her Queen voice. I wouldn't be making a sound in the mirror's position, either.

"You really think it looks good?" I asked. "I think there's something not quite right about it."

"Hmm." She rubbed her chin with her fingers, studying the smooth lines of my drawing and the tiny notes I'd made about materials and how I wanted things to fall and look. "Can I make a couple of changes?"

"Of course." I handed her my pencil.

I watched as she made a few extra notes, and added some more details. A gem to the top of the staff, that her notes instructed should be a deep green. She thought for a moment and noted that the dress should be green too.

"Not white?" I asked, frowning.

She shook her head. "You want to stand out, don't you? Wear black, and you'll look like you always do. Wear white, and you'll be dressed like everyone else. Your eyes are a beautiful shade of green. Maybe it's time to spice things up with your wardrobe? You can still wear the silver over the top and you should wear a red lip paint to contrast. With your dark hair and green clothing, it'll be very striking." She swiftly drew a face onto the diagram and added what she'd just said to the notes in the margin.

The thought of adding color filled me both with dread and excitement. No one wore colors of any kind in Enchantia.

"What about in the crown too?" I asked. "If there's going to be a little bit of color in the staff, maybe there should be some there too."

She nodded and added a couple of larger jewels to the drawing of the crown. "I think you're right about that."

We spent a little bit longer going over the design,

dissecting every part of it until we were completely satisfied with how it looked.

"Thank you," I said once we were done.

A wide smile spread over her face, and she reached out to cup my cheek. I felt like I was five years old again, with her looking down at me like I was the apple of her eye.

"You're going to look beautiful in this," she assured me.

I snorted. "I wouldn't go that far."

I waited for the mirror to cut in with one of its attempts at a soul-crushing retort, but it didn't happen. Perhaps it was respecting Mother's wishes and staying quiet.

"Don't listen to that *thing* when it tells you you're not." She shot the mirror a displeased look. "Beauty isn't something that is skin deep. It's something that's etched in the soul and is shown in so many other ways. I've watched you grow into a strong, caring, and wonderful person, Kelis. That's what makes *you* beautiful. I'm proud to call you my daughter."

A tear threatened to fall, but I blinked it away before it could. There wasn't a reason to cry, not when she was being so lovely to me, but I couldn't shake the image I'd seen earlier. Her eyes had been closed in the vision.

"I know," I whispered. "I promise I listened every time you told me that growing up." And I had. I'd also realized that not everyone had the support I got from my parents.

"I know, darling. You're going to be a wonderful Queen."

"But only of the Fright Festival, right?" I deflected, not wanting to think about her *not* being the Queen any longer.

She chuckled, no doubt realizing exactly what I was doing. I could have sworn it was some kind of Mother-sense she had. "You'll be the best Frost Queen they've ever seen."

I glanced at the drawing, still clutched in her free hand. Frost Queen was the right description for it. But was it going to be enough to impress Jake?

"He won't be able to take his eyes off you," Mother said, reading my thoughts, a slight hint of amusement in her voice.

"How did you..." I trailed off, not sure how to phrase my question.

"I'm your Mother. I know these things." A wry smile slipped over her lips. "But we don't have to talk about it if you don't want."

I nodded. "That would be good, thanks."

"A word of advice, though, if you want it."

I laughed, unable to help myself. "You'd give it regardless, just maybe not so bluntly."

"That's true. It's a mother's prerogative." She took a deep breath. "Just make sure he returns your affections for the right reasons. You're a princess and the heir to the throne. People will try and take advantage of that if they think they can get power just by marrying you."

I winced. "But they don't get any power," I pointed out.

"I know it isn't how it works, but some people won't take that into account. Just be careful, Kelis. You're too good to be trapped into a loveless marriage by someone who doesn't care about you." She rose to her feet and smoothed out the cape she was wearing, though there wasn't a single wrinkle in it. "I'll drop this off at the seamstresses on my way to bed."

"Thank you."

She leaned in and kissed my forehead. "Sleep well," she said.

"You too."

"Your Majesty, are you leaving us so soon? The room will be dimmer without your beauty to illuminate it," the mirror piped up.

Mother cast a side-eye at it. "You should get rid of that," she reminded me.

"Maybe we should have a ceremony where we destroy it. We could call it a *mirror sacrifice* and have tea and cupcakes to go with it." I quipped.

She flashed me a disapproving look, clearly knowing that I wasn't serious. Though, the mirror didn't. I'd probably get some peace and quiet from it until tomorrow now.

"I'll think about it," I promised. I'd do just that, but as always, I'd come to the conclusion that I didn't want to get rid of it. There was something about it that connected me to my past and made me reluctant to just destroy it. Maybe that need would go away in time.

Or perhaps I just needed it to give me one compliment before I could let it go. I wasn't sure I wanted to explore that option very much.

Mother waved goodbye and shut the door behind her. As I expected, the mirror stayed silent as I got ready for bed.

Another knock sounded on the door, swiftly followed by one of the servants bringing me a steaming cup of peppermint tea.

"Thank you." I smiled at her, appreciative that they respected my night-time ritual. There was nothing like a soothing drink before bed.

"You're welcome, Your Highness." She dipped into a curtsy.

I turned away from her as she left the room and grabbed the book I'd started reading earlier in the week. A little light reading of the history of our people never hurt. I might not be all that interested in performing magic, but the past of it fascinated me, particularly how the people from the other Kingdoms saw us. They'd used just about every word they could—witch, sorcerer, enchanter, caster—they'd all been used. The irony was that we didn't really have a name for ourselves. Magic was far too much of a part of who we were to be defined.

I waved my wand slowly in a swirling motion watching the peppermint tea go round in the cup. Unlike pretty much everyone else in Enchantia, I barely ever used my wand. Most people couldn't function without it, but when using it, I feared dependency on it. Something about it took away my independence, the part of me that was just me. Plus, I wasn't particularly good at it. I lacked the aptitude for magic other Enchantians relied on. I guess I was just different in all respects. I finished my tea and put the book on my nightstand.

Closing my eyes, I felt a frisson of nerves wondering what terrors the night would bring and if I'd wake up tomorrow with the same sense of dread I'd been waking up with for months.

# 9TH OCTOBER

The haziness of dreaming was easy to recognize but difficult to escape from. I found myself in a forest with dark trees and imposing shadows. My bare feet barely made a sound as I walked down the path, but the stones beneath them didn't hurt. This was a dream, after all.

I looked around, trying to work out what I was doing here. My mind must have a reason for showing me this. Somehow, I knew this dream was going to be different. Echoes of it would linger long after I'd woken up. Real memories rather than the echoes of feelings. I knew I was in a dreamscape, so I held on to it, trying to keep every detail so it wouldn't float away as soon as I woke up.

Voices sounded from deeper in the woods, so I picked up my pace. I should run in the other direction, but the dream had a different idea and urged me further into the woods. My heart pounded in my chest, and my palms began to sweat. I wiped them on the ragged dress I was wearing. It didn't look like anything I'd normally wear, but that made sense. The woods didn't look like anywhere I'd ever seen in Enchantia. And yet, there was something about the place I recognized. I'd dreamed about this place before—many times. I'd just forgotten. There was something in the woods in front of me, something terrifying. I wanted to hold back, not to go any further, but my feet kept me moving forward toward whatever it was.

I came into a clearing to find a single coffin lying in the middle of it. There wasn't anyone around, which made very little sense. I'd heard voices; there must be someone here.

*A dream. This is a dream.* I had to remind myself of that. It didn't have to follow the rules of the world.

Dread pooled in the pit of my stomach as I made my way up to the polished wooden coffin with no lid. Something bad was waiting there. Worse than just a dead body at any rate.

I swallowed down my nerves as I reached it. I peered over the edge.

My eyes widened, and I stumbled backwards, tripping over a twig and landing flat on my back. I opened my mouth and began to scream.

The world around me shifted, the dream-like edge to what was happening disappearing and becoming less tangible.

I thrashed against an unknown threat, finding my arms and legs were getting impossibly tangled.

My screams continued to fill the space, and my eyes snapped open to find the dim light of dawn streaming through my windows.

*A dream. Just a dream.*

My heart pounded, and my breathing came rapidly as I tried to process what I'd just seen. What I'd been seeing every night for a long time, but now I remembered it. I remembered it clearly, looking down into the coffin. My breathing hitched as I remembered her face, serene like she was asleep except she wasn't.

*Mother.*

I wrestled the sheets off me and swung my legs around. My robe lay over one of the chairs next to the bed, and I grabbed it, throwing it on.

"If you're leaving the room like that, then it's almost an improvement," the mirror quipped as I passed it.

Instead of retorting, I ignored it and headed out into the corridor.

I banged on the door to my parents' room but didn't wait for either of them to answer. This was too important. Parts of that dream had felt far too real for me to be completely at ease until I'd seen Mother's face and heard her voice.

*She had to be alright. Had to be.* If she wasn't, then I didn't know what I'd do.

"Kelis?" Father asked, sleep clouding his voice.

"Is Mother alright?" I asked, moving around to her side of the bed.

Her chest rose and fell in the rhythm of sleep. Could this be enough? It would be cruel to wake her up when she was sleeping so peacefully. And yet, the echo of my dream was so strong it almost demanded that I did.

Father sighed and shifted in the bed so he was sat upright.

"Kelis, what's the problem?"

I glanced at the floor. It would sound stupid to say it out loud.

"I had a dream. Mother...she was in a coffin in the middle of the woods."

One look at his face and I knew it was the right thing to tell him. He understood the panic.

"I wouldn't have come here," I continued. "But it felt so real, and I just had to reassure myself that she was alright."

Father smiled and nodded, but it didn't do anything to hide the concern in his eyes. "I used to cast a spell that would wake me up every few hours so I could check she was still alive," he told me. "It took years for me to realize she was safe, and that nothing like that would ever happen again. It was a long time ago that she was cursed. Your dream was probably your subconscious remembering the story of it. Have you been reading our history books again?"

I nodded. "I was reading one last night." But it hadn't had the story of my mother's curse in it. Could that really have been all it was?

I wasn't completely reassured, even if Father understood how I was feeling. But she was sleeping soundly and plainly alive and well. "I'm sorry, Father," I whispered. "I didn't mean to wake you."

He chuckled softly. "I'm glad you did." He paused and studied me. "How about a distraction? I have to go to the train station to pick up your cousin and his friends in a couple of hours, Why don't you come with me?"

I perked up. That would mean a chance to see Jake earlier than planned. That was something I was on board with.

"That sounds good, thank you, Father."

"You're welcome. Why don't you go get ready, and I'll meet you by the front doors when it's time to go."

I nodded, relieved to have a plan that would keep my mind busy.

~

The racket of the train entering the station was almost too much to bear, but I stood next to Father with my best regal smile.

The train screeched to a halt. Nerves began to flutter in my stomach. Jake was onboard, and soon, he'd be a guest in our palace. As excited as I'd been up until now, a sliver of self-consciousness started to take hold.

*What if he still saw me like an annoying kid?*

I smoothed down my leggings, a habit I'd no doubt picked up from Mother at some point in my life. I looked good, or at least as good as I could. I would make more effort for tonight's banquet.

The door hissed as it opened, and my cousin stepped out, his thick dark hair slicked back with magic. One of the many advantages people had in Enchantia was that they could use magic to make themselves look good. Hair, makeup, keeping clothes hanging right, and most people used it to their advantage.

"Uncle." Adam reached out his hand to shake Father's.

"Did you have a good trip?" Father asked.

"We did, yes." He gestured to the four people who'd gotten off the train with him. "You remember, Jake, Your Majesty?" he asked.

"I do, good to see you again," Father said politely.

My heart skipped a beat. *Jake.* Tall, handsome,

completely put together in a way no girl would be able to ignore, and with a face that looked like it was chiseled by the gods.

He didn't even notice me as he stepped toward my father. I bated my breath, ready to say hello when he lazily draped his arm around the shoulder of a petite blonde girl.

"It's a pleasure to be here, Sir," Jake said to Father. "This is my girlfriend, Lyss."

The bottom dropped out of my stomach at the dreaded word. *Girlfriend.* What was I going to do with that?

"These are two of my other friends, Rhi and Topher," Adam said, gesturing to the other two people with them.

The other girl, Rhi, was just as petite as Lyss, but with dark hair and she was more pretty than beautiful. But it was Topher who took me by surprise. He was scruffy, a word that wasn't often used in Enchantia. His dark hair fell over his ears and into his eyes. He swept it away in one smooth motion, only highlighting the stubble on his cheeks.

He glanced up at me with bright green eyes, taking me off guard. I quickly looked away and set my eyes back on Jake.

"We'll get some more rooms set up next to yours in the palace," Father promised. "This is my daughter, Princess Kelis."

I didn't miss his use of my title and had to wonder what had made him use it.

The two girls dropped into pretty curtsies, while Adam just smiled, and Jake did nothing. Topher swept into a deep bow.

"It's a pleasure to meet you, Princess." His voice rumbled pleasantly, a little at odds with his appearance.

"The pleasure is mine," I answered diplomatically.

Adam saved me from saying anything else by swooping forward and taking my arm. "How are you, cousin?"

I laughed lightly. I wouldn't say Adam and I could ever have been considered close, but we'd always gotten on.

"As busy as ever," I responded to him. "What about you?"

"The usual. I'm taking the university by storm, fighting off the women throwing themselves at me because they forget I'm not royalty, and just living life to the fullest."

I snorted. Mostly because I knew he wouldn't give most of those women the time of day. He was far too interested in his studies for anything else.

"Are you keeping up with your magic studies?" he asked me.

I shook my head. "You know it's not my thing."

"You could be great if you just tried," he countered.

"My future lies in running a kingdom," I countered. "Magic is the least of my worries when there's politics and the right way to address the third son of an Earl to pay attention to."

"You're really something special, Kelis. You know that, right?" Amusement tinged his voice.

"Of course. I am a princess, not many people can say that about themselves," I quipped.

"And then there's your personality."

A smirk tugged at the corners of my lips. "Some of us don't have dashing looks to make ourselves memorable like you and Jake do," I pointed out.

"You think Jake is good looking?" he asked.

"Objectively, yes," I answered too quickly.

The knowing look on Adam's face was enough to let me know he'd caught me.

Oops. That wasn't what I wanted to happen.

I'd almost picked a white dress. My hand had been ready to pull it out of my closet, but I knew I was choosing it to impress Jake. He had a girlfriend, I reminded myself The coolly impressive Lyss, with her perfect body and perfect face and perfect red lips.

"Your face will stay looking like a duck's if you continue to pout like that."

I flashed the mirror some shade and pulled out a black dress.

I had no reason to impress Jake. None, whatsoever.

I pulled out my wand and waved it over my hair. Sparks flew out of it, lifting the dark strands and making them into bouncy curls sweeping over and pinned so they fell over my left shoulder. Remembering what Mother had said about my costume for the Fright Festival, I picked up a pot of red lip paint and smoothed it over my lips. The full-length mirror in front of me revealed the effect of my paying more attention to my appearance.

I didn't look half bad. My black, shimmering dress fell to the floor in one smooth line. The sleeves stopped at my elbows with a square cut neckline. I needed' to choose an appropriate necklace from the ones in my jewelry box, preferably one that had a matching wand belt and sheath.

Rummaging through the box, I found exactly what I wanted, deep rubies set in black metal. The only thing that would pull attention was the gems. The wand belt looked the same. It'd cinch around my waist, and the black leather sheath would hang against my left thigh. A matching bracelet caught my eye, so I slipped it on. There'd be no sense in leaving it behind.

I sighed and studied myself in the full-length mirror.

"Not too bad, Kelis," I said to myself.

"I have to admit, you're not wrong," the other mirror said.

My mouth dropped open. I spun around to face it. "What did you just say?"

"You look passable. Definitely better than normal, but that doesn't mean much."

I blinked a couple of times. Had it just given me a compliment? A back-handed one, sure, but it was still far more than it had ever given me before. I wasn't sure how to process what had just happened.

"Erm, thank you?" Was that the best way to respond to a mirror that normally insulted me telling me something nice? I wasn't too sure about that one.

I swept out of the room in a rush, almost tripping over the dress as I went.

The corridors were full of people dressed in their best clothes, all white, naturally, and heading towards the banquet. I stuck out like a sore thumb in my black dress.

The smells of roasting meat and baking bread filled the air as I neared the hall. My stomach rumbled as I thought about eating. I'd been too nervous to eat much of my lunch, and I was starting to regret that.

I slipped through the banquet hall door and stepped into the room full of chattering people. No one paid me any attention, which was something I was used to. I made my way to the opposite side of the room where two thrones sat waiting for my parents. A smaller ornate chair to my Father's right was waiting for me if I chose to use it, but my parents had always made it clear that I could choose to sit with my friends instead of with them during events like this. Normally, I didn't take them up on that, but tonight it would be different.

Adam and his friends stood in a semi-circle a few paces in front of me. I reached out a hand to tap Jake on the shoulder so they would know I was there.

"Where are we sitting?" Jake asked.

My hand dropped.

"Why don't you sit next to Kelis?" Adam suggested, though I didn't think he'd seen me.

"Why?" Jake sounded shocked his friend had even suggested it.

"She likes you. It might be nice for the two of you to spend some time together."

I was mortified. Why would Adam say such a thing?

Jake laughed, the booming sound filling the room and making more than a few people stop talking. "Why would I want to sit next to that kid?" he asked.

Pain lanced through my heart.

"She's my cousin," Adam warned him.

"That doesn't mean I'm going to fake interest in her," Jake snarled. "Besides, I'm with Lyss."

I stepped back, hitting someone and stumbling slightly. My clumsiness drew attention to me, and I was greeted by a horrified look from Adam and a scowl from Lyss.

"So sorry," I muttered to the person behind me, turning away so that none of the others saw the tears welling up in my eyes.

"It's alright," Topher's rumbling voice distracted me for a moment. "Why don't we go take a seat?" he suggested.

I wanted to tell him no, that I already had a plan, but Jake's words still rang in my ears.

Instead of running back to my room like I wanted to, I nodded once. "That would be nice. My chair's at the top of the hall. You can take the one next to me if you'd like." It was an offer most of the court would fight over.

"That'd be great." His smile reached his eyes. I looked him up and down, paying more attention to him than before. Which was how I noticed that he had a dark material lining the inside of his suit jacket, and his wand holster was similarly black. Maybe he could be the friend I so desperately needed.

"Unless you want to sit with your friends, I understand if you don't want to..."

"No need, I'd be honored to sit next to you, Princess." He shot a glance at Jake that was almost impossible to decipher. Was he just doing this because he'd heard what Jake had said about me and wanted to be nice?

Did I care?

I shook my head. I was being given a gracious way to exit the situation, and I was going to take it.

"I'll show you to our seats. But no one calls me Princess in the palace. Just Kelis is fine."

"I'll take that into account *Just* Kelis." He smirked.

I didn't wait for the others to say anything. I just led Topher up to the top of the banquet hall, gesturing to the chair next to mine.

"There's an unspoken advantage of sitting here too," I said to him.

"That you can always see when someone spills on themselves?" The amusement was impossible to miss in his voice, and I found myself relaxing and starting to forget the nastiness in Jake's voice as he'd spoken.

I chuckled. "Oh, better than that. We get the first

choice of all the dishes they send up from the kitchen. After my parents, of course."

"That does sound good," he admitted. "Which ones are your favorites?"

I thought about it for a moment. "It depends on the day, but I'll tell you what's good and what isn't," I promised.

Before Topher could answer, trumpets sounded. Chatter throughout the room died off as Mother and Father walked in, their heads held high despite the heavy crowns placed on top of them. Their white cloaks trailed along the floor, glittering with tiny crystals that caught the light of the candles as they walked.

They were a vision. No one would ever doubt that they were the ruling royals.

People bowed and curtsied to them as they made their way up to the two thrones next to me.

"You look beautiful, Kelis," Mother said once they reached me.

"Thank you. So do you." She always did. The mirror wasn't lying when it sang her praises. She had the kind of beauty that was impossible to ignore. And no one ever did.

Once they were seated, servants began to stream in with various dishes piled high. They'd bring them straight to my parents, who would gesture to tell them which of the dishes they wanted. After them, they'd turn to me and Topher.

"Not that one," I warned him as he asked for a soup made out of fish heads. I'd always found that dish to be wholly unappetizing even if Father loved it.

"Is it not good?"

"Not unless you particularly like fish eyeballs," I told him. "But you do want some of that bread." I gestured for the server with a basket of baked perfection.

"What's in it?" Topher asked as a roll was placed on his side plate.

"Some nuts and some kind of spice. It's delicious, especially when it's freshly baked." I picked up my own roll and broke it in half. The inside still steamed from the warmth of the oven.

No one paid us any attention as the banquet progressed. My gaze slipped to where Jake and the others sat. Just like the rest of the people in the room, they weren't paying any attention to me and Topher. Jake had his arm slung around the blonde girl. Lyss laughed and popped a strawberry in his mouth.

Jealousy bubbled up inside me at the sight. She was perfectly perfect with her long blonde hair and white gown giving her the appearance of an angel, albeit with a face that was a touch too angular.

"You really like him, don't you?" Topher asked.

"Sorry, what?" I turned to face him.

He frowned. "Never mind. Are you looking forward to the Fright Festival?" he said instead.

I studied him. His intelligence was a little intimidating in some ways. He'd already been able to see through my emotions.

"Yes. It's going to be a good year. Are you?" I put on the politest voice I could.

"It's not really my thing."

I frowned, unable to work out Topher. Why was he here if he wasn't interested in the Fright Festival and didn't seem to want to spend time with his friends? It made no sense.

"Can I ask you something?" he interrupted my thoughts.

"Of course."

"Why isn't there more magic in the room?"

"What do you mean?" There was magic everywhere. I could see it in the way people had styled their hair, and the way their jewels shone and the fact no one's white clothing was stained despite the soup starter.

"Everyone's wearing a wand, but no one is doing any spells. I kind of expected the whole room to be full of them," he admitted.

"Oh. No, that won't happen. Magic is banned at feasts. There have been too many accidents involving sparks, fire, and spilled wine." And a couple of assassinations a hundred or so years ago, but I keep quiet about that one. "Besides, if a job's worth doing, it's worth doing by hand."

"That makes sense." He glanced away, but not before I caught the disappointment on his face.

"There'll be plenty of magic on other days," I promised, even though I didn't know that for sure. I never paid much attention to what people were doing with magic. Like I'd told Adam, there were more important things for me to focus on.

"I hope so. I heard talk of there being spell competitions here in the capital." The excitement was back, though maybe it was just a front. It was hard to tell.

"I can find out and send you the information in the morning, if you'd like," I offered.

"I'd like that if you don't mind."

I smiled as I picked up another piece of bread. I needed something to do with my hands right now. "Of course, it's not a problem."

Even as I said it, I realized I had no idea how to find any of that information on my own. But I wasn't the kind of princess who went back on her promises. He'd have his information, no matter what it took for me to get hold of it.

The banquet ended much too quickly. I'd spent all day readying myself for the dance that would follow, but I'd not pictured standing at the sidelines watching Jake and Lyss dancing like they were made for each other.

"His left foot is not quite in step," Topher whispered in my ear as I watched a traditional Enchantian dance being performed.

The way Jake spun Lyss around was almost magical, but now as I lowered my gaze to their feet, I saw that Topher was right. He wasn't quite in step like the other couples were.

The music changed, and Topher took my hand.

"What are you doing?" I asked as he whisked me into a line.

"In this dance, we all change partners. Here is your chance." He winked at me and I swallowed back the trepidation I felt. I knew the moves. I'd had plenty of dance lessons over the years, but this was the first time I'd actually had to put them into practice.

Topher pulled me toward him as all the other men did with their partners. We circled each other, and then I moved back into line facing him. After a minute of dancing, I found I was enjoying myself. Topher was not the best dancer, but he made up for it in enthusiasm, sashaying me across the hall, intertwining through the other couples. I was almost sad when the men took a step to the side, and I found myself in the arms of one of my father's oldest friends. He was at least six inches shorter than me and spent most of the next minute face deep in my chest. The men took a step to the side again, and I came face to face with Jake. He stepped forward and took me in his arms. Further down the line, I caught Topher giving me a wink and a sly thumbs up as he danced with one of the ladies. I closed my eyes and rested my head on Jake's shoulder, inhaling his aftershave.

"You're not a bad dancer," he remarked as he spun me around. I opened my eyes and looked into his.

"For a kid, huh?" I couldn't help myself. When would I learn to keep my mouth shut and just enjoy the moment? I'd been daydreaming about it long enough.

"You heard that, huh?"

I nodded, not trusting myself to say anything else.

"You are a good dancer, period. You fit into my arms like you were born to be there."

My heart looped the loop, and I almost tripped over my own feet in shock.

"What about Lyss? You were dancing pretty well with her."

To my surprise, he shrugged as though I wasn't just talking about his girlfriend. "She's ok, I guess. She knows all the moves."

"Do I know all the moves?" I asked

He laughed and then spun me back into the line. My turn dancing with him had ended. I didn't get a repeat performance for the rest of the night.

# 10TH OCTOBER

The forest was back. The trees moved without any wind to cause it. I hugged my arms tightly around myself, trying to ward off a chill that didn't stem from the dream world itself.

"Why am I here?" I whispered to the woods, trying not to let the stress and oppression get to me any more than it already had. This wasn't the kind of place I wanted to spend my sleeping hours in.

My feet were still bare, and this time, the stones on the path tickled the underside of them. I carried on down the path, drawn to the same place I had been last night. At least, I assumed it was the same place.

A whistling sound filled my ears. It still wasn't the wind. I hugged myself tighter. I tried to turn back, but whatever was causing these dreams wouldn't let me go.

I sighed and sped up. If I had to go through this, then I was going to get through it as quickly as possible. There was no point in drawing things out.

The clearing came up before me, with the varnished wooden coffin in the middle of it. I gulped down my nerves and approached. This time, I'd keep my cool. I knew what I was going to find when I looked in the coffin. I was ready for Mother's pale face and weakened state.

*It was just a dream.*

Nothing could hurt us here. It was nothing more than stress causing me to dream of things I shouldn't. Mother was safe in her bedchamber with Father, not poisoned, and certainly not in a coffin.

I closed my eyes as I reached the edge of the coffin. I knew it was pointless, and that the dream wouldn't end until I saw what was waiting for me, but that didn't stop me from wanting to put it off.

"Come on, Kelis," I muttered to myself. "You can do this. One peek is all it's going to take."

My eyes snapped open. And that was when I started to scream, even if I'd promised myself I wasn't going to. It was Mother's body lying in the coffin, but her face had changed. Her face was wizened with deep wrinkles and grey hair that was falling out in clumps. She looked sick. Sicker than I'd ever imagined possible.

The dream started to throw me out, the images blurring in front of me and becoming far less tangible.

"Mother!" I screamed. "No, Mother, please, let me help!" I thrashed against the dream, but it didn't let me go. Of course, it wouldn't. This was exactly what had happened yesterday.

My eyes darted open, and I found myself tangled in

my sheets. The dim light of dawn streamed through the window. Huh. Exactly the same time as yesterday. That had to mean something, right?

I took a few deep breaths, trying to steady the worry building inside me. It was just a dream. Nothing more than my subconscious worrying about things it didn't need to. If I stayed calm, it would disappear, and I wouldn't have to worry about it any longer.

I drifted back to sleep, though not very deeply, I was still full of the worry and distrust the dream had left me with. How had this happened?

The next time I opened my eyes, more light streamed through the windows. It was time to start the day, even if the echo of the dream still haunted me.

I crept along the corridor, not wanting to be spotted. I didn't want to go into my parents' room again. They might start thinking that I was going crazy. Not when they were so patient with me after yesterday morning. But I did want to check that Mother was alright. The dream was etched in my mind, and I knew it wouldn't go away until I reassured myself that she was alive.

I flattened myself against the wall as one of the servants walked past. This wasn't my best plan, and I'd certainly have a hard time explaining it if I was caught.

Mother's laugh filled the hallway as the servant slipped into my parents' room. I breathed a sigh of relief. She didn't sound hurt. Or sick. She was fine. I could get on with my day and stop worrying about her.

Before heading to bed the night before I'd asked one of the servants to find some pamplets on the various spell casting competitions currently being held around

Azure, Enchantia's capital city and to place them under his door with a note to meet me in the front hall after breakfast.

I walked down the corridors, nodding to the servants as I passed. It never hurt to be on good terms with them.

The moment I stepped into the entrance hall, I stopped in my tracks. In the middle of the marble floor, stood Adam's entire group of friends, including Jake. I swallowed my nerves. There was only one way I could save face in this situation, and that was to walk up to them as if nothing was wrong.

I held my head up high and put on my best princess face.

"Good morning," I said brightly. "Was there anywhere you had in mind that you wanted to go?" I directed my question at Topher as he was the one I'd arranged to meet.

"We were just deciding whether or not we wanted to go to one of the competitions that are on today," Topher said.

"Which one is it?"

"One on Queen's Row," Adam answered, eyeing me up and down.

"That one is supposed to be good," I said, though it was more to impress them all than anything, I'd never been to any of the spell competitions, so I didn't really have an opinion on them. I knew that was bad of me, but I couldn't help it.

Lyss glared at me, her eyes narrowed with displeasure. Clearly, she wasn't going to become my friend overnight then. "I think it's stupid." She crossed her arms under her chest, revealing a little too much for my tastes with her low cut top. "I don't want to go."

"You don't have to come," Topher cut in. "But I'd like to go, if Kelis is willing to show us where it is." He looked at me for confirmation.

I nodded at him. "Of course."

Indecision warred over Lyss' face. Clearly, she didn't like the idea that I was going, but she couldn't backtrack and say she was interested now, or she'd look like an idiot.

"I'd like to go," Adam said. "We don't get much spell practice at the university. It'll be good to do some while we're here."

Jake nodded. "That's a good point. I'd like to go too."

Lyss' scowl deepened, but I chose to ignore her. It wasn't my fault that her boyfriend had decided to come with us instead of staying with her.

"What about you, Rhi?" Adam asked.

She jumped, clearly not having expected to be asked anything. "Yes, I'd like to come," she said after a moment, shooting a longing look at Adam.

"Alright, then." I clapped my hands together to get everyone's attention. "I'll go order one of the carriages to take us to Queen's Row."

"How long until it'll be ready?" Adam asked me.

I shrugged. "Five minutes at the most. But it'll wait if you want to grab anything from your rooms."

The boys nodded and disappeared back into the palace. Topher lingered a moment longer than the other two, but didn't say anything and finally disappeared into the palace too.

"Do you need to go get anything?" I asked Rhi.

She shook her head. "I can just come with you."

I nodded and gave a half-wave to Lyss. She shot me a look of contempt and stormed back into the palace. I clearly wasn't making any friends with her. I wondered what had got a bee in her bonnet. Probably me dancing a little too closely with her boyfriend last night. Ooops.

"Do you often take part in spell competitions?" I asked Rhi to take my mind away from Lyss.

"No. I just don't want to be stuck in the palace with only Lyss for company." She screwed up her face.

"You don't like her?"

"Do you?" she threw back.

I didn't answer; instead, I just led her out of the front door and towards the stables where we'd order a carriage.

"Can I tell you something?" she blurted.

"Of course."

"You have to promise you won't tell anyone."

I glanced over to find her staring intently at the floor, avoiding any kind of inquisitive look. "I won't."

"I-I kind of have a crush on your cousin," she whispered.

I blinked a couple of times. On Adam? That wasn't what I'd expected when she said she wanted to tell me something.

"Have you tried to do anything about it?" I asked.

She laughed. "Have you done anything about the crush you have on Jake?"

I was saved from answering by our arrival at the stables. "One carriage to Queen's Row, please," I told one of the stablehands.

*"Of course, Your Highness." He dipped his head before disappearing back into the stables to get it ready.*

I turned back to Rhi. "How did you know about that?" I asked quietly.

"It was written all over your face yesterday when Jake said what he said. He can be a total jerk sometimes."

Oh. I hadn't even realized she'd been in the banquet

hall when the whole thing had happened. I stayed silent, not knowing how to respond to her.

~

The competition was this afternoon, which meant we had until then to practice our spells and learn some new ones. Or in my case, learn anything at all. I wasn't about to admit to any of them quite how out of practice I was at spellwork, but they were probably about to find out.

Adam and Jake instantly got into position, setting up to spar with one another. I hoped they were just as good at defensive spells as they were attacking spells, or someone was going to get hurt.

*They've been doing this much longer than I have.* I needed to remember that. These weren't amateurs.

"Want to pair up?" Rhi asked.

"I haven't had much sparring practice," I admitted. "Perhaps, Topher would be a better bet?"

He stepped forward, dipping his head to the two of us. He might be a bit scruffy on the outside, but his manners were impeccable. If he ever wanted to stay at court, then I suspected he'd fit right in regardless of his appearance.

"I'd be happy to," he said to Rhi.

She smiled and withdrew her wand.

The four of them were soon firing spells back and forth, bright lights flashing as they attacked and defended one another. I didn't know enough about any of this to work out what they were doing.

For the first time in ages, I slipped my wand from its holster, feeling the firm wooden grip in my hand. It was both alien and completely natural, a testament to the craftsmanship of the tool. It was a shame that I didn't use it enough, with the way wands worked, no one else could use it either, meaning this beautiful creation didn't get the love it deserved.

It was time to change that. I lifted my arm, trying to ignore the tremor running through it. None of them were watching me; they were too busy with their own mock battles. No one else in the arena was watching either, and even if they were, they wouldn't necessarily know who I was.

I counted to three and let out a simple fire spell. The stream of fire that headed towards the target opposite me was stronger than I expected. "Not bad," I whispered to myself.

Before I could fire off another spell, my vision blurred, and I placed a hand to my head, hoping it would steady me. What was all that about? I glanced around at the others, all doing their spells, only to find everything had taken on a fuzzy quality that was almost impossible to see through. Had I been hit by a spell? Was this some side effect? My eyes locked onto a spell shooting in our direction from one of the other groups. For some reason, it was the only thing that didn't have the blurry quality to it. I wished I'd paid more attention to magic, then I might have known what was happening better.

The spell pulsed a dark red. I reached out as if to try and catch it the moment I noticed it speeding straight for where Jake was standing. I tried to cry out, but something held my voice back. This almost felt like the dreams I'd been having, where something else controlled what I was doing, and I just had to go along with it, helpless.

It flashed brighter as it connected with Jake's chest. His eyes widened, but it all happened too fast for him to be able to scream. His skin paled, and his eyes changed from vibrant to dull as he collapsed to the floor in a heap.

Adam was the first to react, at his best friend's side within moments, checking for a pulse.

"He's dead," he said to no one.

Topher and Rhi stood behind him, neither of them saying a word, and no one paying me any attention at all. It was like I wasn't even there to them.

I stood motionless, the pain ripping through my heart almost too much to bear. *Jake.* Even if he'd hurt me at the banquet, I didn't want him to be gone.

A wave of dizziness overcame me, and I swayed back and forth even as the fuzziness of my vision faded, and the world came back into focus. The sound of shouting voices and whooshing spells assaulted my ears. I hadn't even realized they'd been missing before. What was wrong with me?

My gaze locked on Jake, who was still very much alive and blasting off spells with Adam and Topher, just like he had been when my vision had gone funny.

In fact, he was acting *exactly* like he had when my vision had started to change.

Did that mean that the other parts of what I'd seen were going to happen too? Had it been a vision of the future?

I dithered on whether or not I should do something, or even just give a warning. Seeing the future just wasn't a thing people did. For that matter, it wasn't something I'd ever done before either.

"Jake, watch out," I blurted before I could overthink it all.

He turned at the sound of my voice, a scowl marring his perfect face. But he didn't move.

I stepped forward. "You need to get out of the way," I said, feeling slightly crazy.

"Why?" He didn't seem particularly bothered about my warning, other than annoyance for me even giving it.

I grunted in frustration. If he wasn't going to listen to me voluntarily, then I was going to have to make him. I leapt forward and pushed him to the ground, only processing how close I was to him after our bodies began to touch. He struggled against me, but the surprise of my attack was enough to knock him to the ground.

"Will you get off me?" he demanded.

He pushed hard with his arms, and I fell to the side, grunting in pain as I landed. That was going to leave a bruise. Jake got to his feet, dusting himself off.

"What are you doing?" he half-shouted at me. "You think that you can just jump on people, you weirdo?"

I bit my lip, trying to keep back the tears that were threatening to fall. I didn't like the way he was speaking to me, but on some level, I knew I kind of deserved it. I'd done exactly what he was accusing me of, and there was no getting away from it.

"I..."

A flash of red light streaked past us, saving me from having to come up with an explanation that didn't make me sound crazy. The last thing I wanted was for it to go around that the heir to the Enchantian throne had a few screws loose, there was already enough talk of that, thanks to my dark clothing.

"Was that what I thought it was?" Rhi asked, her mouth gaping open.

Adam nodded. "It looked like a stun shot."

I looked between them from my position on the floor,

hoping one of them would explain what that meant. Once we got back to the palace, I was going to spend some time learning about casting spells. I hadn't paid as much attention to it as I should have, and it was starting to catch up with me.

"I was standing right there," Jake whispered, his face as pale as it had been in my vision.

"It would probably have killed you," Topher said without any hint of sadness that his friend nearly died. "It was lucky the princess was there to save you."

Jake glared at him. Maybe he didn't like the fact he'd been saved by a girl? A small voice in the back of my head whispered that his problem wasn't because I was a girl, it was because I was *me*. I shook it off.

"Those kinds of shots should be banned," Jake grumbled.

"It would only have gained so much power because of the distance," Topher pointed out.

I listened raptly. This was all new information to me, though that just highlighted how badly I was doing in that part of learning about my kingdom. I'd thought the basics would do me. I was wrong.

"Still." Jake shuffled about, twisting his wand in his hand nervously. He was more shaken than he was letting on.

He needed someone to reassure him. I opened my mouth, wanting to make that person me, but Jake stepped away before I could.

Topher moved as well, planting himself in front of Jake and crossing his arms. "Aren't you forgetting something?" he growled at Jake.

"What could I be missing?" There was thinly veiled contempt behind Jake's words.

I glanced over at Rhi and Adam, who both looked

about as confused as I felt. I was reassured to know I wasn't the only person out of the loop in this conversation. I did have to wonder what was going on between the two boys.

"A thank you for the princess," Topher said. "She did save your life."

An apology for speaking so harshly to me before wouldn't have gone amiss either. I pushed that thought away. There was no reason to expect an apology. He'd reacted in the only way he could, given how random me pushing him over had been.

Jake's jaw ticked in anger, but he turned to face me, nonetheless. "Thank you, *Kelis*," he said, stressing my name. It was probably just a response to Topher always using princess to talk about me, but it made my heart soar nonetheless. He was talking right to me. He said my name.

"It was nothing," I mumbled. Great. Where had my confidence gone? I'd held my own against a general just a couple of days ago, but faced with a twenty-one-year-old guy, I was stumbling through my words and acting like I didn't know what to say.

Jake flashed me a twisted smile and turned back to Adam, pushing Rhi to the side. Hurt crossed the other girl's face. She'd probably hoped she could spend time with Adam, much like I hoped I could with Jake. I didn't think it was particularly working out for either of us. Jake was behaving like a jerk, and Adam wasn't much better.

Topher sidled over to me. "How did you know that spell was coming?" he asked, genuine interest in his voice.

"I don't know," I answered honestly.

"Has it happened before?" He brushed his scruffy

dark hair out of his eyes. The stubble on his cheeks only accentuated his jawline. While I wasn't used to seeing men without clean-shaven faces, I found it suited him.

"No. This is the first time." Other than my dreams, that was, but I wasn't about to talk about them with anyone after my father's reaction. Besides, I needed to hold onto the idea that what I was seeing in my dreams wasn't going to come true. The last thing I wanted was to have to see my Mother like that.

"Seeing the future is a rare gift indeed. Very rare. Hmm. If it happens again, will you let me know?" Topher asked.

I nodded. "Sure." I wanted to ask why, but that wasn't polite.

"I'm going to practice more," he said uselessly.

"Have fun." I waved him off, leaving Rhi and me alone.

"You alright?" she asked. "Jake really is a horses ass sometimes."

I gave her a grin. Horses ass suited Jake right down to the ground. Now, if only I could get my heart to stop doing the conga every time he glanced my way. I'd never had a proper female friend, but maybe Rhi could shape out to be one.

Her eyes strayed back to Adam. She had it bad for my cousin. I started to wonder if there was anything I could do to help her get what she wanted. If I could figure it out, then I'd certainly do it. She'd been nothing but nice to me since we'd met.

"It'll work itself out," she said softly.

"I hope so," I said. But did I? Jake had treated me like crap from the start, so why was it that I wanted him so badly?

# 11TH OCTOBER

The trees around me groaned, and the wind whistled. I closed my eyes, wishing myself away from the dream world where I knew I'd find my mother's almost dead body lying in a coffin again.

I opened them slowly only to discover myself still on the path through the woods. This time, the stones on the path dug into my feet. If this was real life, I'd have cuts all over the soles of my feet by the time I'd made my way to the clearing.

The memory of yesterday's stray spell and how I'd known it was coming flashed through my mind. This wasn't the same. I needed to remember that. There was no fuzzy edge like the premonition, This was only a dream.

The stones crunched, and I tried not to wince as I

walked over them. The trees continued to wave, and the wind carried on howling, each of them clearer than they had been the night before. If this was going to keep happening, then I was going to become exhausted. Maybe there was something I could take to ease me into a sleep with no nightmares.

When the clearing was in sight, I sped up. Or I tried to. The dream didn't seem to want me to control it, though, and I approached it just as slowly as the last couple of times.

Dread swirled in my stomach. What was I going to see this time? Mother had already been motionless and had already aged. What could be worse than that? Did it bear thinking about?

The clearing arrived just as it was supposed to. As much as I was relieved that the dream was nearly over and I could get back to a more peaceful sleep, I didn't want to see what was lying in the coffin in front of me.

I took a steadying breath, though it changed nothing in this dreamland. It was never going to. As far as I could tell, nothing I did would change anything in the dream.

I peered over the side of the coffin and felt some kind of relief pop up beside the constant fear. Mother was no worse than she had been the night before. The only difference I could see was a rosy red apple in her left hand. It wasn't that the whole dream sequence didn't worry me. It did. But I felt that if it didn't get worse, then there was less to worry about. My theory was flawed, that was for certain.

"I'm sorry this happened to you," I whispered to Mother. Feeling brave, I reached out a hand and stroked it down her cheek. Her skin was warmer than I expected, almost as if she wasn't dead. Hope bloomed within me, even though this was a horrible situation. "I'm going to figure out how to stop this," I promised her.

A woman's voice called out to me. Not my mother's, but someone else's. Her words were too distant for me to hear her, but it sounded like she was calling for help.

The dream faded, not as suddenly as it had the other times, maybe my acceptance of it was starting to help.

My eyes snapped open moments later, and I stared up at the ceiling through the darkness in my room. My heart raced, and my feet ached as if they really had been sliced open by the stones.

"It's just a dream," I reminded myself in a whisper. "A dream."

Sleep returned, and this time, the blackness was a welcome respite from the horror of my dream.

~

I sighed and pushed away the stack of papers I was working on. I rubbed a hand over my face. I might have managed to fall back asleep for a few hours, but I still felt the exhaustion from the night before.

Shouts came from the courtyard below, pulling my attention further away from the work on my desk. Father always insisted that I didn't need to do work for the kingdom like this, but I felt like it was the right thing to do. One day, I was going to be the ruler of Enchantia. I needed to prove that I was worthy of the title, especially because of the real circumstances of my birth. No one but my parents and I knew the truth, but they'd adopted me after trying to have a baby of their own. They'd told me when I was old enough to understand they'd still love me no matter what, and I appreciated that. I'd also never doubted it.

A loud crash sounded from outside. Startled, I scraped my chair back and rushed over to the window of my office. It looked down on one of the north courtyards, one that was barely used by anyone.

One glance down told me everything I needed to know. Adam and Jake were shooting spells at targets they'd set up at the opposite end of the courtyard. Topher watched them intently, while Rhi and Lyss sat in awkward silence. Perhaps Lyss was aware of how little Rhi liked her, and by the way they were acting, it appeared as if the feeling was entirely mutual.

"First one to fifty wins," Adam shouted.

"You're on," Jake responded.

I wasn't sure what they were doing, but they rearranged the targets and took their places once more. I watched in fascination as they started taking shots. This magic was different from the spells they'd been using before. It shot out from their wands, hitting the targets. After they'd hit, they went to write their scores on a chalkboard they must have brought with them. I couldn't tell who was winning from this distance, but I found it fascinating to watch, even so. They flung spells as if they'd been born to do it.

My hand began to itch with need. I wanted to take out my wand and do magic myself. It was a new feeling, and one I hadn't experienced before. I hadn't even done any magic while we'd been at the arena yesterday. I hadn't felt like it after my strange vision, so I had just watched.

Eventually, Adam cheered after what seemed like a particularly good shot. He must have won, then. Jake kicked one of the wooden planters we used to decorate the courtyards. It tipped over, spilling soil and flowers all over the ground.

A heated discussion followed, but they spoke so quietly that I couldn't make out any of it. And then they disappeared off back into the palace to do whatever it was they entertained themselves with during the day.

The girls followed them, but Topher stayed back and used his wand to reverse the damage that Jake had done to the planter. I wasn't sure if it would be enough to save the flowers he'd knocked out, but it was a nice gesture, all the same. Once he was done, he followed the others back inside.

I sighed and made my way back to my desk where the stack of papers still waited for me. I pulled the top one closer and began reading it until realizing none of it was going in.

A knock sounded on my door, pulling me from my fifth re-read of the policy I was supposed to be reviewing.

"Come in," I called.

The door creaked open and Father walked in. "Are you alright, Kelis?" he asked, taking a seat opposite my desk.

I smiled at him, hoping it would reassure him. "Yes."

"You look tired." He looked me up and down, no doubt trying to work out what was causing it. He wasn't nearly as good at reading me as Mother was, though.

"I've been having bad dreams." I waved it away.

"The one about your mother?"

I nodded, feeling almost ashamed to admit it.

"Have you tried a sleep syrup?" he asked.

"No."

"I'll have some sent up to your room."

"Thank you." If I'd thought about it, I would have arranged for it myself, but I'd been distracted by thoughts of Jake.

"Kelis, you really should take some time for yourself," Father said, a stern look on his face. "There's plenty of time for you to have to run the country. You're young, you should act like it."

I chewed on my lip. Maybe he was right. I was overdoing it.

"You know what? I think that's an excellent idea." I got to my feet and smoothed out my clothing.

Father looked on, surprised by my sudden acceptance of what he was saying.

"I'm glad. You should have more fun," he said, still a little dazed. "Maybe you can start making some friends. That girl who came with Adam seems nice."

"Rhi?" I checked.

Father nodded.

"She is. I like her."

"You'll need some ladies-in-waiting soon. If you two get on, it might be worth asking her."

I winced. It was something I was aware of, but had been putting off for a while.

"I will, Father. Promise."

"Good. Now go have fun." He flashed me a doting smile.

On a whim, I leaned in and kissed him on the forehead. He closed his eyes, enjoying the affection I was giving him. I loved my parents and needed to make sure I showed both of them more love while I still could. And if my dreams were to be believed, then Mother didn't have much time left.

I glanced around the courtyard, anxious to check that I was alone. I wasn't sure why I didn't want anyone watching me, other than it had been a long time since I'd practiced magic, and I was worried that someone would see me doing badly and find it a source of amusement.

And by someone, I meant Jake.

The targets the boys had been using stood as bright red and white reminders of what I was going to try to do. This might be a bad idea, but if I didn't at least try and foster an interest in magic, then I doubted Jake would ever look at me with anything other than contempt.

I shifted uncomfortably from one foot to the other and withdrew my wand. It didn't feel as alien as it had yesterday, which was something. When I'd gotten back to my room, I'd spent some time holding it to try and get used to the feel. It had paid off. It was a lot more natural than before.

My arm shook as I raised my wand to point at the target. I was far too out of practice. A little well of guilt threaded through me at that. There was no real reason why I'd avoided magic for as long as I had. It was a part of our society and the very way Enchantia ran, it was something I should understand and use in my daily life.

"Stop stalling," I muttered to myself. At this rate, I was never going to get a spell out. I decided on a light spell, just something to improve my aim.

I flicked my wrist and a streak of yellowish light flew from my wand towards the target.

And missed.

My arm dropped to my side. Why had I thought it would be as straight forward as just *doing* a spell? I needed to try harder,

I sent off a second shot. It missed. As did my next three.

I let out a grunt of frustration. "Why can't I do this?"

I half-yelled at myself.

"You're just out of practice, that's all," a voice said from behind me.

I spun around, pointing my wand at the intruder.

"I'd rather you didn't point that at me if you're not sure how to use it," Topher joked.

"Sorry." I dropped my arm to my side. I didn't want to hurt him; I'd just been taken by surprise at his presence.

"Can I ask you something?" He sat down on the same bench Lyss and Rhi had been using earlier. Seeing nothing else for it, I went over to sit by him.

"Sure. But there are some things I can't answer."

A wry smile slipped over his face. "You're not an average princess, are you?" he asked.

I let out a short laugh. "Is that your question?"

"Just an observation."

"Hmm." I waited for him to say what he was really thinking.

"Why is Enchantia's princess so out of the loop about magic?"

"Oh, that." I shrugged. "I guess I was too busy with all the other things I needed to learn to ever practice much. There was always something more important to do."

"But, you want to learn now?"

I nodded. "When I saw you all using magic yesterday, I realized how much I wanted to do it myself. How much I was missing out on by not having learned. Then earlier..." I trailed off. Should I admit that I was watching Jake and Adam through the window? "That's my office," I added, pointing up at the window I'd been watching through earlier.

He nodded, clearly realizing what I was getting at.

"Do you want me to teach you?" he asked after a moment.

"Would you do that?"

"I don't have anywhere to be. You want to learn, and I know a thing or two about spells and magic. Don't tell anyone, but I'm the president of the society of magic at our university."

"Why can't I tell anyone?" I cocked my head to the side. "Surely, they're aware of it?"

"They are." He shrugged again. "But if people are reminded, then their egos get bruised, and I don't want to have to deal with that."

The memory of Jake kicking the planter came to mind. I glanced over at it. No one would have guessed it had been almost ruined a few hours earlier.

Topher chuckled. "Exactly my point. I like my things *not* broken. Now, magic. Stand up, please."

I did as he instructed, which included the proper way to hold my wand. Thankfully, it wasn't far off what had felt right to me anyway.

"Have you ever done archery, princess?" he asked.

"I thought I asked you to call me Kelis?" I responded.

"You did, but that isn't polite."

"Isn't it *less* polite to continue talking to me in a formal manner when I've asked you not to?"

He thought about that for a moment before brushing his hair out of his eyes and flashing me a winning smile. Behind the scruff, there was no doubt, he was handsome. The long hair and stubble potentially enhanced that. I pushed that thought aside. I already had one crush to deal with. My brain didn't have space for any more.

"Point taken, Kelis."

I smiled, enjoying the way he said my name. There

was no judgment or expectation in it. Despite the fact he used my title to refer to me, I wasn't just a princess to him. I could appreciate that. No, more than that, I needed that from someone.

"You didn't answer the question," he pointed out. "Have you ever done archery?"

I nodded. "A traveling fair came once, and they had a range." Most people didn't bother with weapons training in Enchantia. There was no need to when we could all use magic. I wasn't sure if it came from the water or something we ate, But I had yet to meet an Echantian who *didn't* have magic, even if some people were like me and chose not to use it much.

"Do you remember what the proper stance was when shooting?" Topher asked.

I nodded.

"That's what you need when you're shooting at a target with magic. If you're dueling, you need to be more relaxed and able to move, but we'll get onto that another time."

"You're going to teach me more?" I didn't hide the excitement in my voice. Maybe if I'd had a teacher like Topher before, I'd already know some of this.

"If you want to. Yes."

"Thanks." I shuffled myself around, standing the way he'd described. Instantly, I noticed the difference. I could focus on the center of the target in a way I hadn't been able to before.

"Now, lift up your arm so you can look down it," he instructed.

I did that. "This is so much better," I whispered, excitement coursing through me.

"It's still not quite right," he said. "Do you mind if I move you into a better position?" he asked.

I shook my head. If it would make me better and give me the skills I needed to impress Jake, then I'd do anything.

Topher moved into my personal space, bringing his scent with him. I'd expected him to smell a little earthy, perhaps because of his looks, but that was wrong. The only way I could think of describing the way he smelled was like apple pie, cinnamon, and hot, flaky pastry. Delicious and comforting at the same time. Just like his scruffy dark hair, it suited him.

His arms wrapped around me as he gently moved my head into a better position and lifted my arm slightly. "Your left foot needs to go back a little still," he said, his breath tickling my ear, though I knew he wasn't doing that on purpose.

I shifted, bringing us even closer together.

"Alright, now fire your spell. Use a marking spell. That way, we'll see where you hit." He stepped back, giving me the space I needed to cast my spell without hurting him.

I took a deep breath and focused on the center of the target, letting the magic fly out of my wand. Unlike before, the spell hit exactly where it was supposed to, leaving a shower of sparks in its wake.

"I did it?" Even to myself, I sounded surprised. I turned to Topher, who was grinning broadly.

"You did. But the question is, can you do it again? Without me positioning you."

"I can try," I said eagerly. I wanted to impress him. He was a wonderful teacher, and I needed to make sure he knew that.

I got myself back into position, feeling confident as I shot off a spell. It didn't quite hit the center of the target, but it came close enough that I was going to call it a win.

"Excellent, now we just need to practice more," he said, pulling out his own wand.

The more we practiced, the more confident I felt, no doubt, because Topher didn't once make me feel like I was the weird princess the world saw.

Exhausted but exhilarated from training with Topher, I trudged back into the palace. The stairs almost seemed too much for me, but there was no other way of getting around. With one foot in front of the other, I made my way back to my room.

I was about to turn into the corridor where the royal chambers were situated when I heard voices. Intrigued, I changed my direction and crept towards the source.

It was coming from one of the hallways the servants used to get around without being seen.

The voices were louder in here, and the cobwebs were thicker. This part must not be used anymore.

"Please, Michael, don't do that," one of the voices said.

I froze in my spot. I recognized the voice. *Lyss.* And someone called Michael? I didn't know any Michaels.

I peeked around the corner, my eyes widening as I took in what was in front of me.

Lyss pushed her jacket sleeve so it covered her shoulder once more, then leaned up and kissed Michael deeply. I vaguely recognized him, but couldn't place from where. Perhaps he was the son of one of the minor lords or knights. Most of their children spent time at court. When I was younger, I suspect they hoped I'd build a special friendship with some of them that could then be used to gain the monarchy's favor. I wasn't so easily swayed, and they'd stopped after a while.

"We could get caught," she whispered after ending their kiss.

"Isn't that part of the fun?" Michael responded. "Life here was so dull before you came along. That princess they have..."

I stumbled backwards. I'd seen enough, and had no desire to find out what a nobody thought of me. I exited the passage as swiftly as possible and half-ran back to my room, slamming the door shut behind me as I did.

"You shouldn't run; a red face makes you blotchy," the mirror said as soon as it noticed me.

I scowled but ignored it. I wasn't in the mood to enter into a verbal sparring match with it right now.

What should I do about Lyss? I couldn't just ignore what I'd seen. Jake had introduced her as his girlfriend. Surely, she wouldn't want to pass up someone as amazing as Jake for some random lordling?

*Jake.*

Should I tell him? Let him make his own mind up about what to do with Lyss? But no. There was a chance he wouldn't believe me, or worse, that he'd think I was trying to break them up and being extra weird in the process.

I took a deep breath. This wasn't something I should rush. I'd keep Lyss' secret for now, and only tell anyone if it became relevant.

With that decided, I headed over to my dressing room to get into something different to wear for dinner. *Not for Jake's benefit,* I reminded myself, *but he might be single soon...*

A small bottle caught my eye, and I walked over to find a note from Father next to it. He'd sent the sleeping draught up for me, just like he said he would. I closed my hand around the tiny bottle. Around the only chance I had at getting a decent night's sleep. I hoped it worked because otherwise, I was going to end up dropping dead from exhaustion.

# 12TH OCTOBER

I rubbed my hand over my face, chasing away the veil of sleep. There'd been no dream. I'd slept through the night without anything disturbing it. Relief flooded through me, Father's sleep syrup had worked.

I had planned morning tea with Rhi, and then I had some work to do before I spent more time with Adam and his friends. I found Rhi in the sitting room already waiting for me.

One of the maids brought a pot of freshly brewed tea and poured a cup for each of us.

"Thank you, Delilah."

"You're welcome, Your Highness." She dipped into a curtsy.

"You can leave now," I said. "We can see to ourselves."

"Yes, Your Highness." She curtsied again and left the room.

Rhi slumped back in her seat and sighed loudly. "I don't know how you do it."

"Do what?" I racked my brains for what she could be referring to and came up blank.

"Have the servants around all the time. I've only been here a few days, and it's driving me crazy already," she admitted.

"Oh, that." I let out a good-natured laugh. "You get used to them. But if you don't want them to do certain things, you just have to tell them."

"It's that easy?" Her eyes widened.

I picked up my teacup and blew across the top of it. "The staff is here to make everyone's lives easier, that means doing what you want them to, even if it's leaving you alone."

"Thanks." She picked up her own cup and took a drink before setting it back down. "And for inviting me here this morning. It's nice to just sit."

"The boys don't give you much time for that?" It tracked with everything I knew about them. Adam had been bringing Jake with him to the palace for years, and they were always all go, all the time. It was one of the reasons I hadn't spent that much time with them until this visit. I just didn't have the time to join them when I had all of my work to focus on. The crush I had on Jake hadn't been enough to tear me away from my duties.

"They never stop. I know Lyss is with them this time and while we were at university, but..."

"But?" I prompted. My heart pounded faster at the mention of the other girl. Should I tell Rhi about what I saw last night? From what she'd said, I didn't get the impression the two of them were close, but that didn't mean it wouldn't be dangerous to tell Rhi secrets like that.

"I don't know. She's changed. We used to be best friends before we went to university, but she's become someone different in that time."

"Different how?" I picked up a finger cake and took a bite to stop myself from asking more. I was intrigued to learn more about Lyss.

"I can't explain it. She stopped caring about her academic work and our friendship. All her attention switched to boys and how she looked. Just watch, within a week, she'll be the most fashionable girl in the palace." She grimaced, even thinking about it. "None of it will be anything like what you wear. You always look so good."

"Oh, erm, thanks." I glanced down at my plate, suddenly interested in the crumbs there. I wasn't used to people complimenting my clothing choices if they mentioned it at all.

"I wish I had the confidence to wear something black, It stands out so much. And I'm sure it looks more slimming than this." She gestured down at the lacy white dress she was wearing. Admittedly, it wasn't the most fashionable piece as far as I could tell,

"Why don't you?" If I could do it, then there was no reason she couldn't. I could lend her something of mine. Maybe a costume for the Fright Festival.

"I don't know. I think maybe I'm just too worried about what Lyss will say..." she trailed off. "Wait, why am I caring?"

"I'm not sure," I admitted. "I know you said she used to be your best friend, but I don't see it."

She grimaced. "I know."

"You can't tell anyone this, but I'm certain she's only dating Jake because of how close he is to the throne. A lot of girls at university are like that. They forget that you're the heir to the throne, and yet, they cozy up to Jake because he's best friends with Adam." Rhi's eyes widened. "But that's not why I'm interested in Adam, I swear, I couldn't care less that he's technically royalty. I promise."

"Don't worry; I know you're not." I wasn't sure why I was certain she was telling the truth, but I was confident about that. "Are you saying she doesn't really love Jake?"

"Love?" She raised an eyebrow. "I don't think she's capable."

"I may have seen some proof of that," I said quietly.

"You did?" She leaned forward, looking at me expectantly.

"I saw her kissing someone last night," I admitted, whispering the words.

"That doesn't surprise me." Rhi leaned back in her seat, an oddly satisfied look on her face. "They're as bad as one another," she added, crossing her arms over her chest.

"What do you mean?" She couldn't be suggesting that Jake was also going around kissing other people.

"Just that they're a good match. Both of them care more about what things look like than how they feel about one another. Lyss might be dating Jake to get close to royalty, but he's dating her because she's the hottest girl in our class. I'm not sure why Adam hangs out with them," Rhi continued. "Topher either. Though, I they wanted Topher to be their friend rather than the other way around. He just went along with it."

I perked up. Was this a chance to find out more

about Topher. Despite all the time I'd spent with him yesterday, I still knew next to nothing about him. "What makes you say that?"

"He's the best at magic at the university. Jake wants to rule the school, so to speak, and Adam always goes along with him. I never understood why Jake was the ringleader..."

I could. There was something about Jake that attracted attention more than Adam did. It was one of the things I liked about him.

"Topher was one of those people who didn't seem to care about friends, but then Jake decided he wanted someone with power by his side. That's where Topher came in."

I nodded. A standard power play. If you made sure the people who were well known for something were seen around you, then other people who respected that thing would also respect you.

"That makes sense," I said aloud.

"But I think he's fed up with them." The expression on her face said she was almost as fed up with them herself.

Perhaps, Father was right, and I would be able to form a bond with Rhi that could make her one of my ladies-in-waiting.

She took another sip of tea. "We're heading down to the Cider Festival in town this afternoon. Do you want to come with us?" she asked.

I nodded. "I'd like that, thank you. I wasn't aware there was a Cider Festival, though."

"Oh, I don't think it's very big, but Adam found out about it and wanted to go."

"It sounds fun." I smiled at her. I wanted to spend more time with her, as well as talking to Topher about doing more magic lessons. I should have done that yesterday before we were done, but I hadn't thought about it.

"We're meeting at two in the entrance hall."

We chatted about all kinds of things, but the conversation didn't come around to Jake again, much to my disappointment. I knew there was a lot more for me to learn about him, and Rhi seemed like a good source of that information. But I couldn't force it, especially not if I wanted to make her a true friend of mine.

The atmosphere was electric. I'd never heard of this Cider Festival, and from the size of it, I wasn't surprised. Festival was probably a generous term for it. There were several different stalls in a courtyard at the center of the city, but nothing more than that. Everyone had a drink in their hand, and all of it was cider.

I blew across the top of my spiced cider. The warmth coming from the mug seeped into me and was welcome in the slight fall chill.

"Have you tried the honeycomb yet?" Topher asked.

I shook my head. "I haven't tried much of anything yet."

"Want to come get some?"

I glanced at Jake and Adam, trying to work out what they were going to do. I didn't want to say yes and lose a chance to hang out with them, but I also didn't want to say no when Topher had knowledge that I needed. Plus, he was fun to hang out with too.

"Sure," I said. "Should we ask the others if they want to?"

Topher shrugged, though his expression soured a

little. Perhaps Rhi was right when she'd talked about how he felt.

I turned to the others. "We're going to go get some honeycomb, want to come?"

"I love honeycomb, count me in," Rhi answered, bouncing over to the two of us.

Lyss pulled a face. "You don't want to eat too much sugar; it'll cause breakouts."

I rolled my eyes. "I find sugar is worth it. You coming, Jake?" I asked, my heart pounding in my chest.

A smirk crossed his face. "Why don't you bring me some back?" he responded.

"Of course." I gave him a smile then turned to Topher and Rhi "Shall we?"

They nodded, and the three of us set off towards the stand Topher had pointed out.

The scent of sticky sweet honey filled the air as we got closer. I held my mug tighter, not wanting to spill any of it. The cider smelled delicious, and I was looking forward to tasting it once it cooled to the right temperature.

The selection of honeycomb was bigger than I'd imagined, though I failed to see what it had to do with cider. Then again, I supposed if a farm grew apples, then the chances were that they had honey bees.

"This one looks nice," Rhi said, pointing towards the one at the far end.

"They all do," I responded, wondering which of them Jake would like. I didn't want to take him the wrong thing.

"Why don't we get a bit of all of them, and then, we can try them all?" Topher suggested.

Rhi let out a small laugh. "Perhaps that works for you and Kelis, but I don't have the money for that kind of purchase."

"Sorry," Topher muttered, glancing away with reddening cheeks.

I looked on with confusion. Rhi didn't have a lot of money? I supposed that made sense. If she was studying at the university, then that was where most of it was probably going. But why did Topher have a lot of money? I didn't recognize him as the son of any of the noble families around

"I can get them." I dug into my pocket and pulled out some gold coins. "For everyone." I flashed a smile at Rhi, who visibly relaxed after my announcement.

That made me even more sure that I should offer her a position as one of my ladies-in-waiting. The position came with a hefty allowance and a lot of prestige. Once she was finished with university, she could come back to the palace and be my confidante. After this morning, I was certain I could trust her.

I handed the coins to the merchant, instructing him on what I wanted. He quickly bagged up the honeycomb and handed the bag to me.

"Keep the change." I flashed him a smile. It was almost certain that he didn't know who I was. Without an entourage, there was no way of telling I was a princess. But on the off chance, it was important that I be generous. Plus, it meant less time fumbling with coins and more time chatting with Jake about the different kinds of honeycomb we'd purchased.

We made our way back over to the others, though I didn't miss the sour look on Rhi's face at the idea. I was starting to see just how far her friendship with Lyss had deteriorated.

"We got one of each so we could all try them," I announced as we rejoined them.

Adam grinned easily. Jake did the same and slipped an arm around Lyss' shoulders. It didn't escape my notice that neither of them looked as if they felt anything towards the other except mild friendship.

I had a chance. I held out the bag, and everyone grabbed some of the honeycomb. I took a bite of my own piece, letting it bubble on my tongue.

~

I deflated the moment I realized the courtyard was empty. I'd hoped that Topher would be here and that we could do some more practice. Never mind. I could do things on my own. The better I got, the more likely it would be that Jake would take notice. We needed to have more in common, It was no wonder that I hadn't managed to make it work with him so far, we had nothing in common at all.

I shuffled my feet into position, lifting my arm so that my wand was held out in line with the target, just like Topher had shown me. I shot off a couple of spells, each of them hitting the target, but not quite the center.

I scowled at it, trying to figure out what I was doing wrong and how I could fix it without instruction.

"Kelis, you're early," Topher said.

I jumped and turned around to face him. He was leaning against one of the columns watching me.

"How long have you been there?" I asked.

"About a minute," he answered honestly. "I was held up talking with Jake." Distaste dripped from his words even as my heart jumped at the sound of Jake's name.

"Sorry, I should have waited."

"Why? This is your home, you're a princess, we're your guests. You're entitled to do whatever you want."

I scrunched up my nose. "I don't like that word. I'm not *entitled* to anything. That's not how being royal works. If anything, we have a duty sacrifice for the good of our country not an entitlement to get our way."

His eyes bored into me, as if trying to work out how much of what I was saying was the truth.

"You really believe that?" he asked.

"Yes, of course. It's something I've been working towards my whole life. My parents have done everything they can in order to prepare me for the life of a queen and its not anything to do with fancy dresses or looking good. We do far more than any of our people ever know. And more importantly, they don't need to know."

"You're going to make an excellent queen," he said. ,

"Thank you. But I think that's still up for debate. And if I want to do the title justice, then I need to learn more about magic." I glanced at the ground, feeling a little guilty that I'd been thinking about Jake as much as my role as queen when I was considering learning more about magic.

But I should put that first. The Jake thing was just a helpful by-product, and I would do well to remember that.

"Is there more you can teach me?" I asked him.

He chuckled, taking my change of subject in stride. He'd make good royalty too.

No. Wait, that wasn't the kind of thought I should be having.

"There are plenty of things I can teach you. That wasn't looking too bad, though." He gestured towards the target.

"Thank you. But I don't feel like I'm good enough."

"How long have you been practicing for?"

"Today and yesterday," I muttered. "I had some

lessons when I was younger, obviously, but they were a long time ago, and I don't remember all that much of them."

"So, a few hours, and you're already this good?" He whistled appreciatively and pushed away from the pillar he was leaning on.

"Erm, I suppose." I wasn't sure how to take any of this.

"You have real talent, Kelis. With a few weeks of practice, you can probably take the title at the competition the day after the Fright Festival."

"You think so?" I asked, my eyes widening and excitement blooming in my chest. This wasn't what I expected when I started practicing magic, but for some reason, that was what caught my attention now.

"Definitely. If it's something you want."

"I do." The words were out before I even thought them through.

"Good. Then we need to get to practicing. Your stance still needs a little work. Do you have any chalk?"

I shook my head. "But, I can get some for next time we practice?" I hoped he'd agree, that would mean we got to do this again. And if I was honest with myself, it was only partly to do with the magic that I wanted to meet. I also found myself enjoying Topher's company. He was easy to get along with.

"Yes, that's a good idea. But for now..." He pulled out his wand and gave it a wave. Two markers appeared on the floor, presumably, for where he wanted me to put my feet.

"Why do you need chalk if you can just do that?" I asked.

"Relying on magic to do everything is as an easy way of becoming complacent. Magic is a useful tool, but it isn't something we should use for everything."

"I thought you were supposed to be the president of the magic society at the university," I quipped.

"I am. But I got there from understanding things like that. From what I've seen, you're the kind of person who'll see the same things."

I nodded. There was no denying that what he was saying was true. It was one of the reasons I'd never used a lot of magic myself. Other things needed my time, and that made them more important. My parents were the same. In fact, while I'd seen them use magic on a lot of occasions, it had never been to solve a major issue.

"Right, get into position. Right foot on the front line, left foot on the back one. We'll work on your wand holding angle," Topher said.

"What was I doing wrong?" I frowned but got into the position he'd instructed anyway. He knew what he was talking about, and I was going to make the most of it.

"Nothing, there's just a better way for you to do it."

"Alright." I lifted my arm. "Up? Down? To the side?" I needed to be careful, or I was going to start babbling.

"Up slightly, and to the left. You're thinking too directly. While the wind won't affect the direction of your spell like it would an arrow, you still have to adjust for your own bias."

I nodded.

I did as he said. "How is this?"

"Better. But try firing a spell, and then, we'll see."

I shot off some magic. The golden streak headed for the target. It seemed like it was going to hit the center until it came into contact, just to the right of where I wanted it to be.

I groaned. "Why can't I do this?"

"You've been practicing for two days, and you're

frustrated because you can almost hit the target perfectly?" Topher joked.

"Well, when you put it like that, maybe I'm being a little ridiculous. But I just want to make sure I do it right."

"I know that feeling. My parents pushed me to be perfect too."

"It's not my parents," I defended. "They've never been anything but supportive. I just don't want to let them down." And some of that came from my insecurity about the fact I was adopted. The last thing I wanted was for my parents to regret taking me on.

"Ah, well, mine aren't like that. They wanted me to be the poster boy for the Enchantian middle class. Good at spells, win the most competitions, you know the deal."

Ah. That made some kind of sense with what I'd seen of him. "And you don't like that?"

"It's been helpful." He shrugged. "Now I'm at university. I get to keep a lot of my winnings for myself. And I can start being myself a little bit more."

"Hence the hair?" I asked before I could stop myself.

He chuckled. "Exactly. But you understand that, right?" He gestured to my black dress.

I smiled and nodded. "Being me is more important than conforming," I said. "It's nice to find someone else who feels the same."

# 13TH OCTOBER

After a morning of paperwork, I found myself having lunch with Adam and his friends. Both Rhi and Topher had invited me, and it had seemed rude to refuse. I reached over and grabbed one of the small finger sandwiches from the tray in the middle of the table.

"Are you all sorted out for what you're going to wear to the Fright Festival?" Adam asked the group.

"I found this dress; it's got panels cut out of it here and here." Lyss gestured to her body with a smile on her face.

Jake scowled at her, clearly unhappy with what she was suggesting.

"It sounds lovely," Rhi said with a little too much

enthusiasm for her to be telling the truth. She glanced back and forth between the couple, clearly trying to defuse the situation. I didn't blame her. I could already feel tension radiating from the two of them.

I picked up the teapot and poured myself a cup rather than enter the conversation. Lyss already didn't like me. There was no need to make it worse.

"Not drinking, Kelis?" Adam joked, trying to help Rhi out.

"I have work to do this afternoon," I reminded him. There was no point in explaining that I didn't drink much anyway. It wasn't my thing. I had the odd glass of wine at official dinners, but I didn't like the way it made my head hazy. Not unlike the situation at the arena the other day. I repressed a shiver, just thinking about it.

"Work?" Jake scrunched up his face. "Why are you doing work?"

"I'm a princess; it comes with the job description," I joked, only a little offended that he didn't think I did anything useful with my time.

"But why? You have all these servants to do things for you."

"That's not how it works. Some things only the royal family can deal with. We have the whole of Enchantia to look after."

Everyone's eyes were on me, causing my nerves to spring to life. I wasn't sure what was putting me so on edge.

I met Topher's gaze across the table, and he gave me a reassuring nod. I sucked in a breath, steadying myself.

"It's not something anyone but me needs to worry about," I said, putting on the best imitation of Mother's queen-voice that I could. If this wasn't going to convince them, then I wasn't sure what would.

Luckily for me, they seemed to find it uninteresting and moved back to talking about the Fright Festival. I didn't want to admit that I felt relief to be out of the spotlight, but I couldn't help it.

"I was thinking about putting some of that glitter here," Lyss said, running her fingers along her neck and collarbone. She was the center of attention again, just where she liked to be.

"You can't do that," Jake fumed.

I frowned. Why couldn't she? I might not like Lyss, but the part of her body she was indicating wasn't exactly provocative. I actually thought it would look pretty good under the lights filling the street during the Fright Festival. Not that I said any of that, I didn't want to get between them, especially not when they were fighting.

"I can." Lyss narrowed her eyebrows at Jake and picked up a cupcake.

Rhi pushed a crumb around her plate, and Adam turned to Topher to strike up a conversation. None of them wanted to be part of the argument that was no doubt brewing. I didn't want to be either.

Lyss and Jake exchanged heated whispers. I tuned them out, not listening to whatever it was they were arguing about. Even if I'd seen her with Michael, it wasn't really any of my business.

I gestured to one of the servants, knowing that if I wanted to get out of here before they started screaming, this was my chance.

One of the footmen shuffled forward, eyeing the couple cautiously.

"Your Highness." He dipped his head and waited for my orders.

"Could you clear the food plates and bring a pot of coffee to my office, please. I'll be heading up there shortly."

"Of course, Your Highness." He gestured to the other servants, and they swarmed the table, clearing up the food and plates.

Rhi flashed me a grateful look, clearly pleased to be getting the excuse to leave.

I rose to my feet and opened my mouth to say that I was excusing myself for work.

"You don't know what you're talking about," Lyss half-screamed, tears in her eyes.

"I do! You've been acting ridiculously since we got here," Jake growled.

"What do you know? You don't pay me any attention at all."

I shot a look at Rhi, who seemed about as confused as I was. Perhaps Lyss wasn't just using Jake after all.

"Lyss..." Jake's face softened a bit. A harsh voice in my head whispered that he was only acting that way because he knew the rest of us were watching now.

"Don't Lyss me!" she hissed, jumping to her feet even as she eyed up the glass of wine by Jake's hand as if debating whether or not she should throw it on him. A small part of me wanted her to do it, if only because it would be one more thing that might help Jake see that she was all wrong for him.

"Lyss..."

Adam sucked in a breath from beside me, no doubt, realizing that his best friend had said completely the wrong thing.

"Argh." Lyss didn't pick up the wine glass, but stormed out instead, her long blonde hair flicking behind her as she did and adding to the drama. At least, she'd appreciate that. She seemed like the kind of girl who cared about making a scene.

"What did I do?" Jake asked, looking straight at Adam.

My cousin shrugged, as clueless as the rest of us.

Darkness shrouded Jake's eyes as he scraped his chair back. The sound went right through me, setting my teeth on edge. I held my tongue. He was angry, and like a beast, he didn't need prodding.

He grabbed his wine glass and downed it in one, before leaning into the center of the table and snatching up a full bottle of the stuff.

"No one wants this, right?" He looked between us as if daring one of us to contradict him and tell him he couldn't have it.

I shook my head. "The servants can bring us more if we want it," I said evenly. Though from the expressions on the others' faces, they wouldn't be partaking themselves.

"Good." Jake strode away, the bottle in hand. At least, he'd left the glass behind so the servants could clear it up.

I slumped back into my seat, relieved that was over with.

"Do you want to head out to do some magic practice?" Topher asked, looking straight at me, though I was certain he meant the room in general.

"I think that's an excellent idea, it'll take all of our minds off things," Adam blustered, getting to his feet.

"I'd rather go read a book," Rhi said softly.

"We have an excellent library," I assured her.

"Alright then, Rhi will go read a book. Topher and I will go cast spells. You coming, Kelis?" Adam asked.

I shook my head. "I really should get some work done,

but I'll come down in an hour or so." I wasn't sure I was ready for him to see how unpracticed I was at magic. Topher might be a risk in that too, but he'd never made me feel bad about my lack of magical training.

Topher's face fell, but he covered it up the moment he noticed me watching.

"I'll be down later," I promised with a smile. I wanted to practice as much magic as possible, especially with Lyss and Jake's relationship falling apart in front of me.

Much later, I shrugged off my jacket, freeing my arms from the stiff confines. I didn't mind this time of year, but the chill in the air was too much to go out without one.

"Your hair is a disaster," the mirror said moments later.

"Thanks," I muttered. What did I care what it thought? I'd been outside practicing magic, and a fall wind had swept through the yard.

"That wasn't a compliment," it retorted.

"I didn't think it was."

I slipped off my holster, and put my wand back on the stand. I wasn't planning on leaving my room again tonight, so there was no need for me to keep my wand strapped to me.

A knock sounded on my door, and I startled.

"Coming," I called.

The door opened before I reached for the handle.

"Jake?" I said surprised. He was the last person I'd expected to see staggering into my room as if he owned the place.

"One of the servants told me where your room was."

His words slurred together, but I could still work out what he was saying.

"They did?" That was surprising. But, Jake was charming, so perhaps that was it.

"Yes." He pushed past me and into my rooms, letting out a loud whistle. "Wow, they give you nice digs here, don't they?"

I wasn't sure what was the best way to respond to that. This wasn't the way I expected Jake to end up in my room, and I wasn't sure how I felt about that.

"Can I help you?" I asked, trying to keep my cool, but it wasn't easy.

"You can explain how you have so much room when all I have is a one-bedroom with a tiny window that barely lets in any light."

"I live here," I pointed out. "This is my only room."

"Other than your office," he slurred, stumbling towards my dressing room. I hoped he didn't go in there.

"Yes, this and my office. But I only use that for work," I insisted.

"That's no fun." He stumbled towards the mirror.

"So, you said." I couldn't relax enough while he was that close to it. What if it said something? Magic was normal around here, so he shouldn't find it too strange if the mirror started talking to him unless he'd heard the stories about Mother. Then he might have some questions.

"You still haven't told me what you're doing here," I reminded him.

"You're nice. Did you know that?" He swiveled around and faced me, his eyes roving up and down me.

"I try to be," I responded.

"How have I overlooked you?" he murmured.

I stood in the middle of my rooms staring at him.

How did I respond to that?

"I shouldn't have said that."

"It's fine," I whispered, looking down at the floor. It felt like it was less likely to put me in a weird situation.

Every thought in my mind faded away as Jake closed the distance between us, his footsteps all I could focus on. I'd thought about this moment so many times. Dreamed of it and hoped that it would become real.

And now it was.

I opened and closed my hands, resisting the urge to wipe them on my skirt to dry away some of the nervous sweat that seemed to have formed on them.

Jake reached out and placed a hand under my chin, lifting my face so he could look into my eyes.

I blinked a few times, trying to determine if this was real or if my imagination was running wild with some fantasy.

His breath smelled like the wine he'd taken from the table, but there was no way he was still under the effects of that. He must have gotten some more from one of the servants. I didn't like the sour scent of it, but I wasn't about to let that ruin my moment with Jake.

He closed the gap between us by circling an arm around my waist and pulling me closer. The smell intensified with him being closer, so I started breathing through my mouth to help against that.

"I want to kiss you, Kelis."

It sent a shiver down my spine, and not in a good way.

"What about Lyss?" I whispered.

"She's sleeping with one of your staff, I believe," Jake snorted.

He knew about that?

There was no more time to think about it, as his

mouth crashed down on mine. My eyes widened before I realized what was happening and closed them. I was finally getting the moment I'd always craved with Jake, I was going to enjoy this, no matter what.

So why did I have the urge to push him away? This wasn't right. I wanted to enjoy this. More than that, I needed to enjoy it.

But his hold was too tight, the kiss was too wet, and the stench of alcohol was too strong. More importantly, I was able to think. That shouldn't be the case.

What did I do now?

I needed to stop this. It was wrong. He was drunk, and this wasn't how I wanted our first kiss to go.

With as much strength as I could, I pushed Jake away from me, breaking our kiss. This definitely wasn't what I expected to happen.

"Kelis?" He frowned, a fleeting look of anger crossing through his eyes.

"I'm sorry, I can't." I shook my head. "It isn't right."

"What do you mean, it isn't right? I thought you had a crush on me?" he demanded.

My mouth dropped open. I knew he was aware of my feelings, Adam had told him while I'd listened. But that didn't mean he got to take advantage of the fact while he was drunk..

"I want you to leave," I said softly. "If you want to pick this up tomorrow once the wine has worn off, then you know where to find me. But right now, you need to leave." There was more strength in my voice than I expected, but that was good right now.

"I'm sorry, what?" Confusion was written all over his face.

"Leave," I instructed again.

He seemed to start to say something but thought

better of it. He didn't say anything else to me as he left my rooms, slamming the door behind him.

A small part of me wondered if I'd just ruined my only chance with Jake. But no, if he was the person I knew he was, then there was no way it would be.

I crossed the room to my bed and sat down, covering my face in my hands. What had just happened? What was going on? This wasn't how I expected my evening to go, and I didn't know what to make of it.

I ran my tongue over my teeth, tasting the stale wine leftover from the kiss. I should brush my teeth, whatever it took ito get it out of my mouth.

I must have dozed off, as another knock startled me awake.

"Go away, Jake," I murmured, not loud enough for the person on the other side of the door to actually hear.

The knock sounded again.

"Coming," I half-shouted, rolling off the bed and trying to smooth down my hair to at least look semi-presentable. I wished I hadn't fallen asleep in my clothing, as it was all wrinkled from sleep.

I padded over to the door, relieved that this time, the other person was still on the other side and not just barging into my room. Potentially, not Jake then. It was bad that I was thinking this way when just yesterday I'd have relished the opportunity to spend alone time in my room with Jake.

"Mother?" She was looking tired.

"Are you free? I know it's late...are you still dressed?" She looked me up and down, shocked to find me completely clothed.

"I fell asleep before I could change," I admitted sheepishly. At least I'd managed to brush my teeth first. That was something.

"Can I come in?" she asked.

"Yes, of course. Do you want some tea, I can ring for one of the maids." I gestured to the ring pull by the door.

She shook her head as she moved past me. "Let's not bother them. No doubt, they'll be shutting down for the evening. I was just coming to ask you about your outfit for the Fright Festival." She swept into my room and past my bed.

The mirror stayed silent. I frowned. She'd walked right past it, why wasn't it smothering her in compliments that she didn't want? She should be rolling her eyes and telling me I should get rid of the thing right now. Instead, she hadn't even noticed that it was quiet.

"Is there a problem with it?" I asked, a little nervous about what she was going to say. I wanted my Fright Festival outfit to be the best it could possibly be. Especially now that Jake had expressed interest.

"No, of course not. The seamstresses had some questions and suggestions, though." She pulled out the original sketch and handed it to me.

I sat next to her on the bed and studied the new annotations, nodding along with what I was reading. "Did you really need me to approve this?" I asked, handing the sketch back to her.

Mother chuckled. "No, of course not. But I've barely seen you since your cousin arrived, and I wanted to check if you were alright."

"Thanks, it's all fine. I'm just tired. One of Adam's friends is teaching me about magic," I said.

"I know. I saw you the other day."

"Oh." It hadn't crossed my mind that my parents might have been watching me while I practiced with Topher.

"He seems like a good teacher," she said off-handedly.

"He is."

"And perhaps more than that?" She raised an eyebrow.

"Topher? No. We're just becoming friends," I assured her.

"Mmhmm." She didn't seem convinced, but I knew she wouldn't press me on the matter until I was ready to talk about it.

"Are you feeling okay?" The question slipped out before I meant it to, but she was looking more tired than normal, and it was starting to concern me.

She reached out and stroked a strand of dark hair behind my ear. Even if I was adopted, we had that in common. It was probably why none of the Enchantian people had questioned the circumstances of my birth.

"Your father said you were worrying about my health."

The fact that wasn't an answer didn't escape me.

"I'm fine, Kelis. I promise. I just don't think your father and I understood how much you'd been doing for us. It isn't fair for us to have relied on you so much."

"I'm sorry, I hadn't realized I was letting my duties slip. I'll put some time aside tomorrow," I promised. It had only been a couple of days, and I'd spent time in my office on both of them.

"Oh, Kelis, that's not what we're getting at. We're both glad you're getting to spend some time with your cousin and his friends. You need to be with people your own age sometimes."

I opened my mouth to protest, but she held her hand

out to stop me.

“I don’t want to hear about you being in your office for at least a week,” she instructed.

“But...”

“Kelis,” she warned.

I chuckled. “You know me too well.”

“I do.” She rose to her feet and leaned in to kiss me on the forehead. “We love you. We want what’s best for you.”

“And for Enchantia,” I prompted.

“Yes, and for Enchantia,” she acknowledged. “I’m heading to bed now. Sleep well.”

“You too.”

I watched as she left to return to her own bedchambers.

The moment the door had closed behind her, I made my way over to the mirror. There was something off about what had just happened. Why hadn’t it fawned over Mother? That wasn’t normal, and I wasn’t sure what to do about it. First things, first, I needed to check on whether the mirror was working. And the easiest way to do that was to get it to insult me.

I sighed loudly. “Mirror, mirror on the wall,” I muttered, remembering the words Mother had told me was part of her story.

“He had to have been drunk to have wanted to kiss you,” the mirror taunted.

“They do say that your true feelings come out when you’ve had a bit too much to drink,” I mused.

If it were capable of it, then the mirror would probably have chuckled. “Keep telling yourself that.”

The mirror was working just fine. It insulted me as if it were any other day, potentially, even worse. So why didn’t it say anything to Mother?

I half-wanted to ask the mirror what was wrong with it, but I didn't think it would give me an honest answer, so there was no real point. But that only left one explanation.

If the mirror no longer plied Mother with compliments, then that meant that she was no longer the most beautiful woman in all the lands.

# Heiress of Mirrors

## 14TH OCTOBER

I absent-mindedly pulled apart a bread roll, thinking of the mirror and its lack of sucking up to mother. She, like a few of the courtiers, was having breakfast at the huge dining table. I'd pointedly tried to keep my eyes away from her as if looking at her would make whatever was wrong real. She didn't need me watching her every move and worrying about her anyway. If she knew I was, then I was certain she'd have a lot of words for me. Most of them revolving around making sure I lived my own life.

I surveyed the rest of the dining hall, seeing who was about.

Adam and his friends were seated opposite me, having come in after I was seated. Jake laughed at something Lyss said, clearly back in her good graces after their fight the other night. They were a weird couple. He knew she was sleeping with someone else. He was coming to my room and kissing me. And yet, here they both were, seemingly happy together at this moment in time. His eyes flickered over to me, and I looked away, trying to seem interested in my bread roll. When I looked back, he was deep in discussion with Lyss again. She was giggling over something he was whispering in her ear. Something vomit-inducing, no doubt. I moved my line of vision to the others to give the thoughts of last night rushing through my mind a break.

Rhi caught me staring and gave me a grin, which I returned. When Topher saw her looking over at me, he gave me a small wave. Something about the gesture calmed me.

I responded in kind but found my gaze slipping back to my parents at the head table.

Mother reached out to the fruit bowl and picked up the single rosy red apple in it. My breathing hitched. Something about the action made me shudder. Probably, due to the fact she was almost killed by one many years ago. My own grandmother had poisoned her. The story went that she had actually died, and my father had brought her back to life with love's true kiss. Ludicrous, of course, but then again, the Enchantian newspapers did like to sensationalize everything.

From the corner of my eye, I spotted Jake throwing small chunks of bread at Topher, who sat and did nothing in return. A tiny slither of doubt about Jake crept into my mind. I pushed it away. Everyone had moments like he was showing. It was carefree, something I could stand to learn more about.

On the top dais, Mother raised the apple to her lips

and took a bite.

I held my breath as Mother chewed, clearly not affected by the apple in the slightest. This was ridiculous. I was eighteen, a grown woman, more or less, and a princess. I shouldn't let myself be as freaked out by a piece of fruit like this. Mother was fine.

"Kelis?" Rhi's voice startled me out of my thoughts. I hadn't realized she'd left the other table. "Oh, sorry, I didn't mean to make you jump."

I smiled at her. "It's no worry. I should have been paying more attention. Are you all right?"

"I was just wondering if you wanted to go to the library with me? The others are going into town because Lyss wants to find something different to wear for the Fright Festival." She grimaced. I couldn't say I disagreed with her facial expression. I wouldn't want to spend my day with Lyss, either.

"That sounds great. There are a few things I wanted to look up anyway." I could do some research into Mother's story and see if there was something I was missing. I'd grown up knowing the story of how my parents got together, but I'd always taken it at face value, never digging deeper.

"Great. I was hoping you could have some tea delivered..."

"You know you could just ask one of the servants for that; you don't need me," I assured her.

"Oh, I know. But I always feel so awkward doing it. I'm still glad you're coming with me," she said softly.

I glanced over at my parents one last time, checking that Mother was still fine. The apple core sat discarded on her plate. The apple hadn't done anything to her. I needed to pull myself together.

"Let's go." I scraped my chair back and hooked my

arm through Rhi's.

~

"What did you want to come here for?" I asked Rhi as we entered the library.

She shrugged. "I haven't decided yet. I should do some work for university, but I'm tempted to find something more entertaining instead." A half-smile spread over her face.

"We have some good novels in our fiction section. Or there are some works on folklore that are fairly interesting, depending on what you fancy," I suggested.

She sighed. "Anything on battle maneuvers of the late fifth century?" she asked.

I raised an eyebrow. "If that's the kind of thing that interests you, then I'm sure we can find something." It wasn't something that had ever sparked my interest, and I had no idea if we had it. But our library was extensive. We'd probably have something on the matter somewhere.

"Not really, but I need it for my coursework."

"If it doesn't interest you, then why are you studying it?" As the only heir to the throne, I learned everything I needed to know here at the palace. Which meant tutors and experts visiting the palace to teach me. And not having to study things I didn't particularly want to.

"It's one of the things I have to do to get onto the next stage of my course."

"That sounds dire," I muttered.

Rhi chuckled. "It's not the best situation, but if I want to make something of myself, then this is what I have to do. Not all of us are born princesses."

*Neither was I.* "I suppose that's true," I said instead.

"I'm sorry you have to study things you don't like."

"That's all right." She shrugged. "It's just the price I have to pay."

"We can see what we can find to help you," I offered. "There's the librarian. She's called Vita."

The small wispy woman had worked in the palace library for as long as I could remember. She stood at the desk, checking a stack of books. If anyone could find what Rhi was looking for, it was Vita. She knew the library inside and out.

"Then I'll just go talk to her. You can find your own books while I do."

I smiled at her. "I'll grab us a table. And some tea," I promised.

She nodded and disappeared off to talk to Vita.

I motioned for one of the servants, ordering the tea that Rhi had wanted. The man hurried away to fetch it, and I went over to the shelves filled with the history of Enchantia.

I trailed my fingers along the spines of the books, enjoying the touch of the leather bindings with gold text and accents. I closed my eyes, letting the sensations seep into me.

I pulled a few of the books from the shelf, starting with the ones I thought were most likely to have the answers I needed. It made sense to start with the easy stuff and move on to the more complicated texts, once I'd exhausted them.

I dumped the stack on one of the tables by the biggest fire and settled myself into one of the high backed chairs. At least, whichever of Mother's ancestors had designed this room thought about the comfort of people reading. Certainly, one of the scholarly kings rather than one of the warriors.

I shuffled back into the chair, half-wishing there was a blanket I could drape over my legs to add to the coziness I was feeling. The heat and crackle from the fire soothed me in a way I hadn't expected. I leaned my head back on the headrest. My eyes fluttered closed as the darkness of sleep began to descend, it wasn't called for, but there was nothing I could do about it.

I tried to pull myself back from the edge, not wanting to let sleep take hold. I had a whole day ahead of me, and I couldn't waste it with sleep. But my body had other ideas, and I slipped into an uneasy haze, despite the memory of the books waiting to be read.

"Kelis?"

Rhi's voice shocked me to attention.

"Sorry, what happened?" I mumbled, the words barely coming out right.

"Were you sleeping?" She frowned as if trying to work out what had happened.

"I don't know." I rubbed my eyes, chasing away all threats of unconsciousness.

"Are you all right?"

I shrugged. "I've not been sleeping well," I admitted.

"Any idea why?" She dropped down into the chair opposite me.

"I don't know," I admitted. "Bad dreams." It was the only explanation I had.

"Have you tried a sleeping tonic? My mother used to use them when I was younger."

"Yes, Father gave me one." I waved away her concern, the threat of sleep vanishing from me. How odd. I had to wonder if it was something to do with the same illness that was taking over Mother. "Did you get the books you wanted?" I asked, noting she didn't have any of them in front of her.

"Yes, but apparently, they're in the storeroom because no one ever wants to read them. Your librarian is fetching them for me."

The servant arrived back at our table with a tray filled with a pot and two teacups. He set it down on the table between us and poured tea.

"Thank you."

"Is there anything else I can do, Your Highness?" he asked.

"No, thank you." I nodded to him, effectively dismissing him.

The librarian appeared moments later with a stack of books, putting them down by Rhi. The two of them exchanged some quick words, but I didn't pay any attention to them. I pulled the top book off the stack I'd gotten for myself toward me and flicked it open.

"What are you reading?" Rhi asked.

I looked up. The librarian was gone, leaving the two of us alone again.

"It's a history of Enchantia. Something came to light the other day, and I want to check it out." It was a vague explanation, but I hoped she wouldn't ask too many questions. It wasn't that I didn't want her help; it was more that I didn't want to drag her into this mess.

"Sounds dreadfully dull," she admitted.

"About as dull as the battle tactics you're studying," I pointed out.

She chuckled. "You've got me there. Do you think they'll keep the tea coming for us while we study?" She glanced wistfully at the teapot as if hoping it would never run dry.

"They will if we ask them to." I smiled at her. She really didn't seem to understand what living in a royal palace meant. Getting extra tea was hardly out of the realm of possibility. She could have as much as she wanted.

We lapsed into silence, the two of us studying our own texts. Rhi made notes as she read, writing in a loopy script in a notebook she'd brought with her.

I flicked through the pages of my book, trying to find the information I was looking for. The book was filled with all kinds of things, from treaties to minor battles, and the marriage vows of various princes and princesses.

And then I found it, "The tale of Princess Snow White." It was written in a different hand to most of the book, no doubt because it had been added after most of it. This was recent history, just eighteen years old. No one who saw her today would believe Mother was only thirty-six years old.

I'd been told this story since the day I was born, but I'd never read it, always relying on what my parents had told me. Perhaps, there was something different in the written version. I had to hope that was the case. There must be something in it.

There had to be.

~

*Once upon a time, there lived a King and Queen who ruled Enchantia with a fair and noble hand. The day they had their daughter, there was rejoicing in the land, and everyone celebrated the birth of the beautiful princess, Snow White.*

*But all was not well in the kingdom, and an evil witch had decided to turn her attention to the kingdom and wished to seize power from the beloved royals. Soon after the princess's seventh birthday, the queen fell sick.*

*Healers were called from across the land, but none of them were able to save her. Soon, the queen succumbed to the sickness and passed away, leaving the child to be raised by her father.*

*For several years, the two of them lived the best they could, with Snow White growing into a beautiful woman.*

*Around the princess's fourteenth birthday, the king decided to take another wife. The powerful witch saw this as a chance to seize control of the kingdom and enchanted the king. He became infatuated with her almost instantly, and married her within days, giving Snow White the mother she needed.*

*Except that all was not well between the Queen and the princess, for the powerful witch had a magic mirror. Each day she would ask it who was the fairest of all in the land. In reply, the mirror would tell her that she was, but that Snow White was going to grow more beautiful still. The Queen hated that and decided she had to do something about it before Snow White indeed became more beautiful.*

*One day, when the princess was eighteen, the king died during a hunting accident, leaving the poor princess an orphan, and his wife the new ruler. When the queen next asked the mirror who was the fairest, it replied with the one answer she'd been dreading. Snow White was now the fairest of them all. With the king out of the way, the queen used her huntsman to take Snow into the woods, with the promise that he'd bring back her heart as proof that she was dead.*

*The huntsman did as he was told, but at the final moment, he wasn't able to deal the fatal blow. Instead, he told Snow White to run as fast as she could and find the tiny house in the woods within which lived seven dwarves. He returned to the palace with a deer's heart and presented it to the Queen. She discovered the deception and sentenced the huntsman to death, not wanting anyone to discover what she'd done.*

*In the woods, Snow White stumbled upon the small house, with its cozy brick facade and smoke rising invitingly from the chimney. She reached out and knocked on the door, waiting a moment before it swung open, revealing a dwarf standing there. He invited her into the cottage and introduced him to the six others he lived with. None of them had names and simply referred to themselves as a number. Snow White found this strange at first, but soon got used to that and other oddities.*

*Once the Queen learned of Snow White's location, presents began to arrive. A too-tight corset and a poisoned comb were among many evil tricks the Queen used, but all of them failed.*

*As a last attempt, the Queen disguised herself as an old crone and snuck out into the woods, knocking on the princess's door. She swung it open and invited the old woman in to rest her feet. The woman was so grateful, she offered Snow White an apple. Delighted, for it was her favorite fruit, Snow took the apple, eagerly biting into it. That was when the witch's plan took shape.*

*Snow White collapsed into a puddle on the floor, unconscious and unmoving. The queen let out a loud cackle, revealing the true nature of her heart. She left the princess where she lay, not needing to do anything else to her.*

*When the dwarves came home from their work, they found Snow on the floor. Devastated, they placed her in a coffin in the middle of a clearing. They mourned the beautiful woman who'd become like a daughter to them.*

*And then, a prince arrived. Handsome and youthful, he wasn't ready to let the princess go. He leaned in and kissed Snow, saying goodbye in the only way he could. The princess's eyes opened almost instantly, true love having done its part to defeat the evil plans of the witch.*

*Snow White and the prince returned to the castle with the dwarves in tow. The queen, terrified by Snow being awake, fled the castle. The dwarves chased her, reaching a cliff. The witch fell to her death, leaving Enchantia in peace for the first time since she'd taken control.*

*The prince and Snow White married soon after. Then, a child was born of them, the heir to the kingdom, Kelis.*

I grimaced at my name, and the amount of information the history of our kingdom seemed to skip. And none of that helped me much. Unless I counted knowing the dwarves lived in the woods, but I'd known about them for years. I even had vague memories of them coming for birthdays and Yuletide when I was younger. I wasn't sure *why* they hadn't been in the past couple of years, but perhaps it was time for a change.

Wait. That was it. I knew what I had to do. The dwarves were going to be key to all of this. I had to go into the woods and find them.

I glanced over at the window, disappointed to find the sky darkening with ominous clouds that echoed my thoughts. There was no way I'd be able to go today.

I rose to my feet, looking around for Rhi, but it seemed she'd left already. I vaguely remembered her saying goodbye while I was reading through the books. Something was going on in Enchantia. It had to do with Mother and her history. If I wanted information, I needed to go right to the source, Mother herself..

~

Our family dining room was a much more intimate affair than the banquet hall, which suited us when we wanted something like this. When I'd left the library, a servant had told me that I was expected for a family dinner.

"Kelis, are you all right?" Father asked.

"Oh, sorry, I was lost in thought." More like I was planning to find the dwarves tomorrow, but I thought it was best not to say that out loud yet. Something told me Mother wouldn't approve of it, even if the dwarves were her friends.

"A penny for them?" Mother joked, but I could see from the pained expression on her face that even this quiet dinner was too much for her. I wasn't surprised. Her face was drawn and pale. One look at her should be enough for anyone to realize how sick she was. And yet, no one seemed to think it was worth doing anything about.

"Nothing important," I responded. "I was just wondering about how the two of you met?" I cringed inwardly at the lie, though perhaps, the answer would give me more of the information I needed to persuade the dwarves to help.

Father smiled and set down his fork before leaning back in his chair. "It was at a ball when we were both fifteen."

Mother laughed. "And I hated him. He was the most pompous prince I'd ever encountered. It was only years later that we met again when he kissed me and saved me from..." She shivered. "Let's not talk about this."

"Sorry, Snow." Father reached out and placed a

hand over hers, giving it a reassuring squeeze.

Unbidden, I found my gaze flashing over to the empty seat next to mine. Perhaps one day soon, that would be filled. Over the years, I'd often imagined Jake seated at the family table with us, eating, laughing with my father, and complimenting Mother. Memories of the past couple of days swam through my mind.

I pushed the thoughts away, not wanting to dwell on them in case they led me down a path I wasn't ready to travel.

Mother coughed, pulling my attention back to the present.

"Are you sure you're all right?" I asked.

Mother shook her head. "I'm fine. Just a cold."

"It's more than that," I protested, worry twisting in my gut from the pained look on her face. "You're not well..."

"Kelis, that's enough." Her words should be sharp, but they weren't.

"Sorry," I muttered. I spent the rest of the meal in relative silence, only speaking when one of them asked me a question. There was no way Mother was all right. She was getting sicker by the day, and I had to prove it to her. The answer had to lie with the dwarves, and I was going to find it. Even if Mother would be angry at me for it.

# 15TH OCTOBER

The door in front of me was more intimidating than I wanted to admit, even to myself. This was ridiculous. I was a princess in my own palace. I shouldn't feel nervous about visiting people, especially when they were guests. Technically, they were here to see me. I scoffed, knowing that wasn't true. The only reason Jake, Topher, and the girls were here was because Adam had come. But I already knew my cousin was busy. He had duties with the royal guard to attend to, something to do with him having to have a royal post. I wasn't sure of the exact details.

"Come on, Kelis," I muttered to myself..

I raised my fist and knocked three times, firmly enough to be sure that whoever was on the other side would have to hear me. The last thing I needed was to be ignored because of something as simple as being too timid.

The door swung open seconds later, revealing a harried-looking Topher. Though it was hard to tell. His normal appearance did tend towards the scruffier end of the spectrum.

"You're wearing something white," he said, shock clear in his eyes.

I smoothed down my dress, trying not to feel self-conscious about my choice. The white shift dress had black lace over the top, but the white still poked through.

"I thought it would make a nice change," I muttered, hoping he wouldn't pick up on the lie. While I hadn't been able to completely leave my black wardrobe behind, the white was a way for me to try to fit in with Adam and his friends.

"You shouldn't dampen your own flame because of others," Topher said. "There's a lot more to be said for people who tread their own path."

I flashed him a smile, which I hoped would hide my hurt. "I'm not dampening anything." I refused to be cowed, even as the heat rose to my cheeks.

"Who is it, Tophy?" Jake asked, swaggering into view and dropping an arm around Topher's shoulders.

"Please don't call me that."

"Why not?" Jake didn't look like he cared that he was insulting poor Topher. Actually, something seemed off about him full stop. Perhaps it was the stench of wine, not dissimilar from when he'd visited my rooms the other day. I repressed a shudder at the memory. It was best if I didn't focus too much on that kiss. It hadn't been anything like what I'd hoped or dreamed of, and it was better for both of us if we pretended it hadn't happened.

"Because it isn't my name," Topher said levelly. "And Princess Kelis is here." He pointed to where I was stood, watching the scene in front of me unfold without any clue of what to do about it.

"Ah, Kelis." Jake flashed me a lopsided grin. "What do you want?"

Should I tell him? Right now, it didn't seem like the best idea to include Jake in my plans, especially with Topher right next to him. But then, I needed to get over myself and at least pretend the kiss hadn't weighed heavily on my mind since it had happened. Jake certainly didn't seem fazed by me, so why should I let him bother me? A little voice told me it was probably because he didn't remember the other night, let alone the kiss after all the wine he'd consumed, but I batted the thought away and plastered a smile on my face.

"I was going to go into the forest today, to find some family friends and invite them to the Fright Festival." That wasn't a complete lie. If they came back, then there was a chance they'd stay that long. "I was wondering if you wanted to join me?"

"The forest?" Jake winced. "That sounds dirty."

"If we stick to the paths, it doesn't have to be," I pointed out, despite not knowing whether the paths went deep enough for what I had planned.

"I'll pass." He shrugged and walked away, not giving me a second glance.

I tried to ignore the pain lancing through me at his dismissal. He hadn't seemed to care about what I wanted.

*You aren't his girlfriend,* the little voice raged. It was something I should remember.

"If you still want company, I'll come," Topher said.

I nodded, unsure what else to say, given the circumstances. Having not specified which of the two I'd been inviting, I had to respect his decision to come with me. "Thanks."

"I'll just grab my wand. Do I need anything else?"

I shook my head. "The kitchens have already packed a picnic of sorts. We're all set. Oh, maybe a cloak? It's cold out." My own was slung over my arm.

"Perfect. Want to come in while I get them?" He waved a hand into the room.

I stepped inside, trying to remain calm at the idea of being in the space he shared with Jake and Adam. The room was a mess, with clothes strewn everywhere, despite it being a receiving room rather than a bedroom. I swallowed the lump that rose in my throat when I recognized the dress Lyss had been wearing the night before crumpled in a heap.

Topher went over to the dresser and pulled it open, revealing rows of neatly folded clothes within. That must be where he kept his own things. A small part of me was relieved to discover he was tidier than the others despite his unruly appearance. He pulled out a cloak and placed it over his arm like I did. He placed his wand into the holster on his left leg and smiled broadly at me.

"Ready when you are."

"Great. We just need to collect the food, and then we're on our way," I responded. My gaze almost slipped in the direction of Jake's bedchamber, but I stopped it. I wouldn't let him consume my thoughts. Not when he didn't want to spend any time with me. Instead, I'd enjoy hanging out with Topher and talking about things that interested both of us.

~

I lay back on the picnic blanket, full from the delicious food the kitchen had provided for us. Just because all of it had been cold, didn't mean it hadn't been delicious. Between the bread baked this morning, the creamy cheese, and the perfectly cured ham, I was full to bursting.

Topher laid down next to me, the two us of staring up into the forest's canopy.

"It's beautiful here," I said after a few moment's silence.

"It is," he agreed. "Have you been here before?"

I shook my head, which didn't work all that well, considering we were lying down. "Never this deep."

"What are we really doing here?" he asked, showing his usual level of observance.

"What I said. We're going to visit some old family friends so we can invite them to the palace."

"You don't have to lie to me, Kelis. I'm not going to tell anyone." The earnestness in his tone was too much for me to ignore. Something about Topher invited me to confide in him in a way I'd never felt with anyone before.

I sighed. "I don't know where to start."

"I've found the beginning helps," he teased.

"Hmm." I paused, using the time to think of the best way to say all of this. "Have you noticed anything weird about my mother?"

"She's been looking a little ill the past few days," he admitted. "But I thought nothing of it. People get sick, even in Enchantia."

"She's refusing to see anyone about it," I said. "And

I'm worried. It's not just her health. I've...I've been having dreams about her story. You know the one?"

"Everyone knows the story. It's one of the greatest love stories in the world, according to several women I've been on dates with," he responded.

A pang of something went through me at the mention of other women, but I pushed it to the side. I'd explore what *that* meant later. For now, I'd focus on what I was telling him. And the fact that I didn't have to explain any of the backstory. That was always a good thing.

"I've been dreaming of seeing her in a coffin, unable to move. Completely dead to the world. I've been struggling to sleep despite using a sleeping draught."

"Oh, Kelis, I'm so sorry. But..." he trailed off.

"But?" I prompted.

"I'm not sure what this has to do with the two of us trekking through the forest," he said quickly as if he didn't want me to hear the words.

"Oh, that. We're going to find the dwarves. I haven't seen them since I was a child, and I was hoping they'd have some answers for me that I couldn't find in the history books. I'm not foolish enough to think it'll definitely work, but I have to do *something*."

He nodded. "That makes sense. Do you know where they live?"

I shook my head again. "Not exactly. Just a vague direction."

"Then we should set off as soon as we're able to walk again."

"Though, that's not quite yet." I placed a hand on my stomach, shocked by how full I felt. It had been a long time since I'd been out hiking, and I should have remembered not to eat so much at first.

"There's plenty of space in the clearing. We could do

a bit of spell practice if you'd like?"

I was on my feet in seconds, withdrawing my wand and nodding eagerly. "I think I've been getting better, but I could always do with more practice."

He smiled up at me before climbing to his feet. "That's the thing about spellcraft, you can always get better, and you have to practice in order to stay good at it."

"That's what I like about it," I admitted. "I'm not sure why I didn't pay more attention to it before you, Jake, and the others arrived at the castle."

He flinched ever so slightly at Jake's name, and I made a mental note to be careful of that in the future. Topher was turning out to be a genuine friend, and the last thing I wanted to do was ruin that by saying the wrong thing at the wrong time.

"Where do you want to set up targets?" I asked, partly so I could distract him from the conflicting emotions he clearly felt, and partly because I wanted to know.

"Why don't we try something different?" he suggested.

I cocked my head to the side, trying to work out what he meant. "Like?"

"I'm going to cast moving targets for you. All you have to do is try and hit them," he explained.

Excitement bubbled up within me at the idea. "That sounds like fun."

"Good." He took off his cloak, dropping it on top of the blanket.

I did the same, leaving me standing there in my long-sleeved dress and leggings. The air was crisp and just on the verge of being too cold without a cloak. But I needed my arms to be less restricted so I could cast better, and the cloak wouldn't help with that. I withdrew my wand from its holster, opening and closing my hand around it as I remembered the feel of the wood again. There was something reassuring about having the wood in my hand. This was what it meant to be an Enchantian. And as their princess, I needed to master magic and wandcraft. I couldn't believe it had taken me this long to work it out.

"Ready?" Topher asked, cutting through my thoughts.

"Yes. At least, I think so."

"Don't worry, if it doesn't work for you, we can go back to doing simpler things," he reminded me.

I bit my lip, not wanting to admit that fear of failure was going to stop me from asking him to change the task we were working on. I wanted to be the best, and I was determined that would be the case.

Topher raised his wand and shot out a couple of spinning red disks. Without thinking, I zapped the two of them with my own spells. They broke apart in a shower of red sparks, filling the clearing with an eerie glow for a few seconds before everything went dark again.

"Good. Ready for a few more?"

"Mmhmm." I widened my stance, feeling more confident now that I'd proved to myself that I could destroy two of the light disks he'd sent.

More followed. He varied the amount he put into the air, as well as the colors and shapes of them. It was hard work keeping up with them all, but I was determined, and spells flew from my wand with a surprising amount of speed and accuracy.

"I don't understand how I can do that," I admitted to him during a short break. Magic was coming to me much more naturally than it ever had before. For years, I'd wondered if I was an Enchantian at all, what with being adopted. Magic was as natural to the Enchantians as flowers were to the Florians, and Dragons were to the people of Draconis. It was only recently that I'd begun to believe that I really could have been born here after all.

"It's because you're not overthinking it. A lot of people, even those living in Enchantia who have grown up with performing magic like this, think all it takes is knowing the right words and the right way to cast the spell. But they're wrong. The truth behind unlocking the true potential of magic is to trust in your own abilities and to *feel* what's possible. When you have so many disks to keep track of, you don't think about what order to take them out in, you just make a decision in that moment, choosing as you go and making them explode. It's your gut instinct that answers the magic call," he explained.

"Huh, I never thought about it like that."

"Most people don't." He shrugged. "I know a lot of decent magic users who don't subscribe to that way of thinking. But each person has to make their own path. I can tell as many people as I want, but not all of them will believe me."

"I do," I assured him. I'd felt exactly what he was describing while sending my spells at the disks. I wasn't going to stop listening to him now.

"I know." He paused, looking as if he wanted to say something else, but didn't dare. "Do you want to try something a bit different?" he asked.

I nodded eagerly. "But then we need to get going again. It'll get dark soon, and I don't know what'll happen if we're out in the woods when it does."

"Probably nothing," he assured me. "Especially as we're both protected." He gestured with his wand.

"True. But I don't imagine I can be gone from the palace for too long without my parents noticing."

"You didn't tell them you were coming?" He raised an eyebrow.

I glanced at the ground. "I thought it best they didn't know. Neither of them has been taking this very seriously, and I thought it was best not to worry them more than I had to."

"I get it. I've done the same a few times with my parents," he admitted.

I smiled. It was nice to know I wasn't the only one who could see the truth when my parents couldn't. "You were saying about trying something different with magic?" I prompted.

"Oh, yes." He pulled a small item from his pocket and placed it on the ground.

"What is that?"

"A training tool," he answered instantly. "I haven't dared to use it at the palace. I thought it might attract the wrong kind of attention."

"What does it do?"

"It's a bit like the disks I sent at you, but for more than one person. There'll be two colors; you'll go for the red ones ,and I'll go for the green ones. The idea is to work together so we don't get in one another's way."

I nodded.

"It might not be easy," he said honestly. "You'll probably miss some of them."

"That's fine. Like you said, no one can get good without practice."

"It's refreshing having someone like you around."

I cocked my head to the side. "What do you mean?"

"It doesn't matter. Want to try?"

"Definitely." I changed my stance, readying myself

for more of the disks. This was going to be a challenge; there was no denying it. But I would do my best to hit all of the disks I needed to.

"Ready?"

"Yes."

He pressed a button and then stepped back, raising his own wand and readying himself to do his own spells.

Within seconds, colored disks spun through the air. I fired off spells, hitting as many of the red disks as I could, though some of them still hit the ground, just like Topher had said they would. I pushed aside the disappointment as each of them hit the ground and exploded. I hoped the box wasn't keeping count, or I was going to be at least a little embarrassed.

From the corner of my eye, I caught sight of Topher firing off spells left, right, and center, each one hitting its target with precision. My wand arm dropped as I watched, entranced by the way he was performing them. It hadn't hit me until now just how good at this he was, probably because he was trying to hold back for the others.

The last disk shattered into hundreds of sparks.

Topher dropped his wand arm, looking at me with a grin on his face.

"I now know how to destroy magic disks, but what about other magic? All I really know how to do beyond this is a spell to make my hair curlier, which isn't much use."

He leaned forward and touched my hair. It was such a small act, and yet, my heart flipped as he looked into my eyes.

"I like your hair."

I felt the blush rising to my cheeks. "Thank you."

"Sit!" he commanded.

I did as he asked and sat on the ground. He kneeled down next to me.

"See that flower?" he asked. It was a daisy, one of many. I nodded.

"Change its color."

I lifted my eyebrows. "It's white."

"I know. Make it so it isn't white. The spell is nothing like you've learned. I've been teaching you how to defend yourself. It's the kind of magic that I do in the spellcasting competitions. This requires much more precision. You can't fire out all your energy like you do when firing at the disks. You have to kind of feel the flower. Make it want to change color."

Make a flower want to change color. Hmm. I closed my eyes and pointed my wand at the daisy. I had no clue how to get a flower to want anything let alone to want to change color. I concentrated on the color yellow in my mind and imagined the inner part of the daiy seeping out into the leaves.

"Anything happening?" I whispered, not wanting to open my eyes and break my concentration. Topher placed his hand on mine.

"Feel the color moving. You have to really want it."

My concentration was broken. All I could think about was Topher's hand on mine. And then my Fright Fest dress popped into my mind. The green my mother had talked about filled my mind, almost consuming me. I felt it drain down to my hand and then into the flower.

"Take a look," Topher said. I opened my eyes to see one green daisy in a sea of white ones.

"I did it!"

Topher smiled. "You did. It's not an easy spell to work. One day, once you've got the hang of combative magic, these more precise spells will come easy, but I'd concentrate on your aim and defense spells first." He waved his hand, and the daisies all changed color until it was as though we were standing in a rainbow.

"You're amazing," I sighed.

"I've had a lot of practice," he muttered, kicking at a stone.

"Why don't you seem happy about that?" Perhaps, I was reading him wrong, but I didn't think so. Something about the situation upset him.

"Why don't we collect up all the stuff, and I'll tell you about it as we walk?"

I studied him. "Are you saying that to distract me?"

He shook his head. "No, I promise, I'll tell you while we pack up. But we should be on our way again."

I wanted to tell him no, but he was right. Even through the thick canopy of trees, it was possible to see the sky was darkening and night was drawing near. If we didn't find the cottage soon, then the two of us might have to make camp for the night and make do with the food we had left in our basket.

We made our way over to the site of our picnic, and swiftly packed everything away into the basket. With our cloaks over us once more, we set off back out into the woods.

"So," I prompted. "You were saying?"

Topher chuckled. "I promise, I wasn't trying to avoid the conversation."

"Good."

"I used to enter a lot of competitions. I used to win them too. There was something exhilarating about taking part. I'm sure you'll find out soon enough."

I nodded, remembering the spell competition before the Fright Festival.

"Why did you stop?" I asked.

"The egos." He smirked. "I couldn't hack them anymore."

"The egos?" I echoed. "What about them?"

"Oh, you'll get to know the type. Boys who think they're men just because they won a competition or did a more complicated spell. I'm not in the game for anything like that. I want to hone my craft and become the best caster I can be."

I nodded. "That makes sense." Even as I said it, I couldn't help but think of the way Jake and Adam had been acting in the courtyard the other day. I shifted uncomfortably as I walked. Not liking where that thought train was going.

We lapsed into silence as we walked, but I didn't find it uncomfortable at all. Topher was easy company, and that wasn't something to take for granted.

Night had almost completely fallen when we finally passed through a small tunnel of trees and found a small cottage waiting there, with warm light streaming from the windows giving it an inviting glow.

"Is this it?" Topher asked.

"I think so," I admitted. "Though, I'm not all that sure. I've never been here before. They always came to the castle when I was younger."

"What do we do now?" he asked.

I shrugged. "I guess we knock on the door and see what happens." Though now that we were here, I didn't feel so certain of my plan. What if the reason the dwarves had stopped coming to our castle was because they didn't like my family anymore? Or perhaps someone had insulted one of them?

"I can see you're worrying."

"How..."

"We've just spent an entire day together. I'd be concerned if I couldn't get a general sense of your emotions by now. But this won't go as badly as you fear it will."

"I hope you're right." I took a deep breath, not waiting for him to say anything else.

I stepped forward and rapped on the door firmly.

It swung open moments later, revealing Two standing there.

"Princess Kelis?" Two asked, startled.

"I was worried you wouldn't recognize me," I said.

"You're the image of your Mother at your age," Two said. "Save for the eyes."

I raised a hand and touched the skin next to my eyes. I knew what he meant. The golden rings around my irises were nothing like either of my parents. Of course, that made sense to me, given my adoption. But no one else knew the truth about that. I supposed it was simply lucky that I looked like a less beautiful version of Mother.

"Who is it?" Six asked, coming into view. "Princess Kelis!" A smile spread over his face as his gaze locked on mine.

"Six," I greeted.

"What are you doing here, Princess? It's almost nightfall," he said.

"My friend and I were traveling in the woods when it got dark." I gestured to Topher, who waved awkwardly in the direction of the dwarves as if he didn't know what to do with himself.

"Come in, come in. Why have you kept her waiting outside?" Six asked Two.

"They didn't say they wanted to come in," Two responded.

"Don't be silly; it's nearly dark out. Come in, Princess. We're about to have dinner, why don't you join us?"

"I'd like that, thank you," I answered for Topher too.

The dwarves moved out of our way, allowing us to enter the cottage. The warmth of their fire and the delicious scent of food overwhelmed me. I didn't realize how cold I was until that moment.

I greeted the rest of the dwarves, smiling throughout. It was good to see them. I'd missed them in the years they hadn't visited.

"You'll have to stay the night with us," One said. "You and your friend both."

"Are you going to introduce us?" Seven asked.

"This is Topher. Topher, these are the dwarves." I introduced them, starting another round of hellos. "Thank you for your hospitality. We'll gladly stay the night." It would give me the time to properly talk to them rather than just a quick conversation over a hurried meal.

"Excellent," Five said. "Sit down. We'll have the meal ready in just a moment. It's a long walk from the palace. You must be exhausted."

"Thank you." I gladly sat down, resting my feet and my body. Now that they mentioned it, the long day of walking and spell practice had taken its toll on me. Topher dropped down next to me.

"Wait, the basket. There's food in there. Please, take it as a thank you."

"Thank you, Princess." Three picked up the basket and began to unpack it, placing everything in its proper place on the table.

I relaxed, knowing this was going to be an easy meal,

with enjoyable company. I could wait until the morning to get the answers I needed. Tonight, we would just enjoy ourselves.

# 16TH OCTOBER

"Ouch," I muttered as I banged my hand against the wooden bedhead. How had I managed that? I didn't normally hurt myself on my bed. It took me another moment to remember *why* that might be. I wasn't at home in the palace. I was with the dwarves in the bedroom Mother had used while she'd lived with them.

The room was spacious, with a comfortable, albeit small, bed and a small dresser covered in trinkets Mother must have collected during her time here. I made my way over to the dresser and sorted through the things on it. None of it seemed to have any true value with most of it being sentimental. I hadn't considered the fact she hadn't come back here after Father had kissed her.

A small wooden pendant called to me, and I picked it up, turning it over in my hands. It was intricately carved in a style I recognized. I was reasonably certain Mother had made this herself using her wand. The small apple was barely the size of my little fingernail.

On a whim, I placed the pendant in the pocket of the shift I'd slept in, before grabbing the rest of my clothing and dressing swiftly.

A rap sounded on the door. I smoothed down my dress, hoping I was presentable.

"Coming," I called as I pulled open the door to find Four standing there.

"Breakfast is nearly ready if you are," he said.

"Oh, definitely." I plastered a big smile on my face and set off down the stairs after him.

"How did you sleep?" Four asked.

I frowned. "Like a log. I didn't even have any dreams." Though, I hadn't realized that until he'd asked.

"Is that a good thing?"

I nodded. "I've been having nightmares recently." I didn't say any more for fear of sounding crazy. I'd already told Topher and my parents about the dreams, I wasn't ready to tell the dwarves too, not if I didn't know whether or not they'd help me.

"You won't have nightmares here," he assured me. "There's a spell on the cottage that stops them from coming through."

My heart skipped a beat. That was possible? Was it something I could use to stop the dreams of Mother from returning? "How?" I asked, unable to hold the question in. "Is it something I can do for myself?"

Four shook his head. "It's strong magic, ancient in nature. It's not something we placed here. The only thing I can suggest is that you take something from the house and store it under your pillow when you sleep. I can't promise that it will work, but it's worth trying."

I nodded, thinking about the wooden pendant in my pocket. Perhaps that was why I'd had the urge to take it? My first night of decent sleep in over a week. "Thank you, I'll choose something of Mother's."

"That is wise. A connection to her should make the enchantment stronger, if it works."

"I hope you're right."

Our conversation was cut short by the two of us arriving in the main eating area. Four scurried off to do whatever he needed to, and I stood there, feeling like an idiot without a single thing to do.

"Can I help?" I asked.

"No, no. Take a seat and have some tea," Five told me.

Not sure what else to do with myself, I did what he suggested. As I picked up the pot to pour tea, Topher appeared on the stairway, his eyes still full of sleep. He looked so at peace. I almost forgot I was doing anything. The whole world was nothing more than him.

"Morning."

His voice rumbled through me, more enticing than I wanted to admit.

"Hi," I squeaked back.

"How are you so awake?" he asked, rubbing a hand over his eyes.

Two chuckled as he placed a ramakin full of freshly churned butter on the table. "She's a morning person, like her mother. You should get used to it if you're going to spend more time with her."

My cheeks flamed red at the implication, but I didn't do anything to dispute it. My heart might belong to Jake, but I still wanted to spend time with Topher. He was my friend, and I wanted to keep it that way.

"Do you want some tea?" I asked instead of saying anything else.

"Please. One sugar and a dash of milk." His smile could have lit up a dead fire.

I busied myself making the two of us tea, trying to ignore my errant thoughts.

With Topher downstairs, the dwarves seemed to decide that it was time to eat, and bustled towards the table with an assortment of food, including the bread I'd smelled baking when I woke up.

They sat down with us, chattering about nothing of consequence. I joined in, making sure I filled myself on the delicious food as I did. We had the long walk back to the palace after this, whether the dwarves joined us or not. I should make sure I had enough fuel for that journey.

One banged on the table when he was done eating.

The other dwarves stopped talking and turned in his direction.

"Why did you come to us, Princess?" he asked.

"Please, call me Kelis," I tried.

"We couldn't, Princess. Your mother was the same, but we must give you your proper title," One said.

I dipped my head, acknowledging that it was his right to do that. I didn't want to make anyone uncomfortable.

I took a deep breath, thinking through the best way to explain what was going on. "I need your help," I said eventually.

"If we can assist you in any way, then we shall," One said. The others nodded in agreement.

"Thank you." I took a deep breath and then launched into a full account of what had been happening, skipping my nightmares for the moment. I didn't think they needed to know that, especially when I already thought things were suspicious.

"That is very concerning," One said once I'd finished.

Seven raised his hand, though I wasn't sure why. Despite the way they'd named themselves, they didn't seem to have a hierarchy. One was just the most outgoing, so often led the conversation.

"Yes?" One said.

"I thought I felt *her* returning," he admitted.

"I felt it too," Three added. "Something is wrong in the air."

"What am I missing?" Topher whispered to me, his hot breath hitting my skin.

"They're talking about the witch who caused all of this," Four said from beside me.

My breath hitched in my throat. My step-grandmother was dead. Everyone knew that.

"And you all think she's back?" Topher asked.

"I'm not sure she's back," Two said, cutting over everyone else. "But something has happened with her magic."

"Agreed. I sense it too," One said. "We only have one option..."

I crossed my fingers under the table, hoping they'd come out in my favor. I had no way of being able to understand dwarven undertones. I hadn't spent as much time with them as Mother had.

"We have to go to the palace," One announced loudly.

I sighed with relief. They were going to help.

"Thank you." The words came out as barely a whisper, but I knew they'd all heard me.

If Mother wasn't going to listen to me, then hopefully she'd listen to the people who'd given her a home when she needed it the most.

~

I wiped the sweat from my forehead, though, it probably didn't make a difference. The dwarves had set a hard pace, and I was certain my face would be red and blotchy from the effort of the walk. Topher looked to be suffering just as much beside me, which was reassuring in some ways, but not in others. We couldn't reappear in the city this way.

"We need to stop for a moment," I informed the dwarves.

Five flashed me an inquisitive look.

"We can't go into court looking like this," I gestured to Topher. "We only need a moment."

I grasped Topher's arm firmly and pulled him to the side.

"Can you clean us up?"

He frowned. "Yes, but why?"

"We can't go in looking like this."

"I thought you didn't care much about your looks?" he asked.

I sighed. "It's not the most important thing to me; that's true," I admitted. "But I'm still the Princess of Enchantia, and what I do reflects on my parents and the whole kingdom. I have to be careful."

He nodded. "Sorry, I hadn't considered what it meant to have a role like yours."

I shrugged. "No harm done. I doubt anyone but another royal would understand it." A tinge of loneliness came through my words, but I pushed it to the side. Now wasn't the time to think about that.

"I'm sorry..."

"You don't need to be," I assured him. "I'm truly not

insulted. Now, can we…" I gestured to myself.

"Yes, of course." He pulled out his wand and waved it over me, and then himself, cleaning us both in the process.

I ran my tongue over my teeth, overjoyed to find his spell had also included them. "Thank you."

"No problem. Do you want your dress changed too?"

"You can do that?" I was certain my mouth fell open, and I must have looked like a fool.

Topher chuckled. "If you want me to."

"Please? I don't think I want the questions about wearing yesterday's clothing until I'm ready."

"Ah. Good point. I'll sneak away once we're inside the castle, too, protect your reputation and all that." There was a twinkle in his eye that filled me with amusement.

"Thanks. You can come with us if you want…"

He waved my concern away. "It's fine. You can join me for some spells later to make it up to me?"

"Can we play the disk game again?"

He chuckled. "If you want."

"Then you've got yourself a deal." He held out his hand, and I took it, giving it a firm shake as I tried not to think about how warm and welcoming it felt.

How right, even.

He waved his wand again, and my dress changed, this time into a black and red lace one.

"Nice," I whispered.

"I thought it'd suit you. I know red isn't normally your color…"

"It can be now." I smiled at him, enjoying the friendship growing between us.

~

I tried to ignore the nerves bubbling up within me as I waited for my parents in our small audience chamber. At least, I'd thought about asking them to meet us here, rather than in the main audience chamber. The last thing I needed was to panic the nobility who lived here by the arrival of the dwarves. I was certain if word got out that they were here, there'd be a lot of prying eyes.

"Kelis, what's the matter? Is everything all right?" Mother asked as she entered the room.

My eyes widened at the sight of her. It was like she'd aged ten years in the day I hadn't seen her.

"One? Is that you?" she asked instead, ignoring me now that she'd spied the dwarves.

"Yes, Your Majesty." He dipped into a low bow, the other dwarves following suit.

"What are you doing here?" she asked again, once they'd stopped.

Father placed a hand on her back, a gesture I'd seen him do countless times, and one I assumed offered her some kind of comfort. Thoughts of Topher flashed through my mind. What I wouldn't give for his unwavering support right now.

Oh. Wow. That was unexpected.

"Your Majesty, are you feeling all right?" Five asked.

"I'm fine," she assured him, shooting me a not-so-happy look. "But you haven't told me why you're here," she reminded them.

"Princess Kelis came to us," Two said. "She told of what was going on, and we had to come to see for ourselves to ask how we might assist you."

Mother's lips pursed together.

Uh-oh. I was in trouble now.

"Now that we can see you for ourselves, we're certain the princess is right," Three added.

"I'm not sure what Kelis has been telling you," Mother said softly. "But nothing is the matter."

"We're not convinced that's true, Your Majesty," One said. "We've all felt a shift in the magic recently. As if *she* is coming back. Something is wrong here, and..."

"I don't want to hear any more of it," Mother announced, standing up straight and giving everyone a withering look. It didn't work, but that was only because we all knew her too well for that. "You're welcome to stay at the palace for as long as you wish, but please don't interfere when nothing is wrong." She turned on her heels and stalked from the room, her long white cloak trailing out behind her.

At least, it was only her physical body that seemed to be suffering from the effects of the magic and not her personality.

"I'll see that your normal chambers are prepared for you," Father said, nodding to the dwarves. "Daughter," he added, a sad smile on his face. He gestured for me.

I stepped forward so that we could speak with the illusion of privacy. He knew the dwarves would be able to hear him, which I assumed must have been a purposeful thing.

"I fear you might be right. But your Mother will hear none of it. Be careful what you say."

I nodded. "I didn't mean to upset her."

Father reached out and cupped my cheek in his hand, looking at me with a mix of sadness and pride in his eyes. "I know. She'll come around in time."

"I'm worried we don't have any," I admitted.

He sighed. "I'll try talking to her tonight. If she thinks I'm as worried as you are, then perhaps we'll get lucky, and she'll agree to seeing a doctor just to keep the two of us quiet." He chuckled, though it was a hollow sound.

Concern for Father bubbled up to sit alongside the worries I already had. If I wasn't careful, it was going to become my defining quality.

"I'll go to her now," he promised.

"Thank you," I whispered. "For believing me."

"You're my daughter, Kelis. No matter what, I'll always believe you."

A tear threatened the corner of my eye, like it always did when he talked to me like this. For me, it was impossible to ignore any time Father treated me as if I was his own flesh and blood instead of adopted.

He left the room without saying anything else, leaving me with the dwarves.

"This is much worse than we first thought, Princess," Two said to me.

"We need to go to our chambers and decide on the best way to help. Will you be all right if we leave you?" Four added.

"Of course." I smiled at the dwarves, trying to cover my increased concern. "I'll be fine." Or fine-ish, as the case might be.

I fired spell after spell at the targets on the far wall, but none of them made me feel any better. That wasn't too surprising, if magic was as simple as raw power, then it wouldn't be as competitive as it was. The only reason it worked in the competition setting was because power and wands made no real difference to how good someone was.

"Are you trying to destroy them?" Topher asked from behind me.

I jumped ever so slightly, but only because I hadn't

realized how much I'd missed the sound of his voice after our day spent together yesterday. I turned to face him.

"You came."

"I did." His smile made my heart skip a beat.

No. This was wrong. I liked Jake. I had to keep my focus on what was important.

"I'm glad you're here."

"Me too. Did everything go well with the dwarves and your parents?"

I grimaced. "I'm not sure *well* is the way to describe it," I admitted. "More like acceptable."

"That doesn't sound too bad." He put out some markers as we talked, though I wasn't too sure why.

I shrugged. "Father is going to talk to her, and hopefully, Mother will see reason soon." I needed her to, or else I had no idea what the next step should be. Were there people other than the dwarves I could turn to for help? I honestly doubted it.

"I'm sure she will. My mother's the same. Even if you told her hundreds of times, she wouldn't believe it until she thought the idea was her own."

I chuckled. "You've got that right." I watched as he placed a couple more markers. "Is there anything I can do to help?" I asked.

"No, nearly done."

"You haven't even told me what you're up to," I pointed out.

"Taking your mind off everything." He turned and flashed me a grin that would more than manage the feat.

"And how are you going to do that?" Excitement filled me. The raw show of power I'd been doing before hadn't been a challenge, far from it.

“Stand here, please.” He pointed to one of the markers he’d put down.

“All right.” I did as he asked, turning my wand over in my hand and readying myself for what was to come.

“I’m going to start sending disks up like we did in the woods…”

“Um-hmm.” I’d hoped he’d do that again.

“You need to hit them in a certain order. Red, green, orange, blue.”

I repeated the list of colors under my breath a couple of times, trying to remember it the best I could.

“When you’ve hit the first set, you need to move to the next marker,” Topher explained.

“Ah. Got it.”

“When you’re ready, we can go. But don’t worry…”

“If I don’t manage to get them all,” I finished for him, remembering his words from yesterday. It had been surprisingly easy to listen to that advice. Probably because Topher never made me feel like an idiot when I didn’t manage something the first time.

He was a good teacher. I was about to tell him that when the first disk flew into the air, swiftly followed by the second. I resisted the urge to fire spells at them without thinking and focused on the order.

The red one first. Where was it? Ah, yes, to the right. A quick spell sent red sparks flying, but there wasn’t any time to celebrate. I hit the green one next, followed by the orange and the blue. Colored sparks filled the air around me.

I spun around, finding the next marker on the ground and moving to it. The next set of disks was already in the air. I didn’t have much time before I needed to start sending spells up again.

I had no idea how much time was passing while I

flung spells into the air, hitting disk after disk. Sweat beaded on my forehead, and blood pumped in my ears. The only word I could think of to describe how I was feeling was exhilarating. I'd never done anything like this before, and I enjoyed it far more than I'd ever expected to.

The last disk at the last marker fell before me, but Topher didn't give me a break and fired another setup. Trusting my instincts, I moved back to the first marker and began the sequence over again. He was sending them up even faster than before, providing me with a challenge. I liked that he wasn't going easy on me just because I was a princess. Too many people had tried to do that in my life, and I didn't like it.

I fired off one final spell, and the disk Topher had sent up for me to hit, exploding into thousands of showering sparks.

Slow clapping sounded from behind me, and I spun on my heels to find Jake leaning against one of the courtyard's walls, clapping his hands together. I waited for my heart to skip a beat like it usually did when he was around and was surprised when the sensation never came. Perhaps it was simply the adrenaline of doing so much magic so constantly.

"Not bad," he mused.

"Thanks." Heat rushed to my cheeks at the compliment from him. "I've been working hard on my casting."

From the corner of my eye, I noticed Topher crossing his arms. Should I say something? Or go over to him? It felt wrong to ignore him when he'd done so much for me, but at the same time, Jake was paying me proper attention, and I didn't want to waste that.

"It shows. I'd never have guessed you'd turn out that

good."

I frowned. Was that a compliment or an insult? I wasn't entirely sure.

"We're going for dinner now," Jake said. "Do the two of you want to join us? We didn't see you at the table last night?"

This time, my heart did skip a beat. It must have been the adrenaline before. Now it had calmed down, and it was doing what it was supposed to.

"I'll pass," Topher said. "I have things I need to do." He sounded unhappy, which decided me.

"Me too," I said, passing up on Jake for what must have been the first time in my life. "I spent most of yesterday away from the palace. I have work to catch up on."

Jake shrugged, apparently, not caring that we both rejected him. "Suit yourselves." He walked off, not even pausing to say goodbye.

"What is it that's more important than dinner?" I asked Topher, once he was gone.

"Not spending over an hour listening to false reports of how amazing he is," he muttered.

"You can join me in one of the private dining rooms if you'd like? We can talk more about spells?" I wasn't sure what made me offer or why I wanted to spend more time with Topher but not with Jake, but the words were out, and now I had to honor them.

"I'd like that," he said.

"Good. I'll just go request the food sent there, and then I'll be back." I smiled at him before hurrying off into the palace and trying not to overthink what had just happened. It was like I wasn't the same Kelis I always had been.

# 17TH OCTOBER

The natural light streaming through the windows woke me earlier than I wanted it to, but at least there hadn't been any dreams during the night. I reached under my pillow and closed my hand around the carved pendant of Mother's I'd brought back with me. Perhaps it had worked and given me a break from the dreams. A princess could hope. I let it go and shifted onto my back. I blinked a couple of times, trying not to let the empty feeling of my large room make me miss the coziness of the dwarves' cottage.

Not that I really wanted to go back there, anyway, there was too much to do here.

I threw off the covers, anxious to start going about my day and check to see if Mother was all right. I hadn't stopped worrying about her since we'd returned, especially as Father hadn't sent me a message with how his conversation with Mother had gone.

As if my thought had summoned it, a knock sounded on the door.

"One second," I called to the person on the other side, grabbing a robe from the end of my bed and wrapping it around me. As far as I could tell, dawn had only just happened. No one would be about other than the servants.

I pulled it open to find a messenger waiting on the other side.

"Your Highness." He swept into an elaborate bow that wasn't entirely necessary.

"Is everything all right?" I asked.

He nodded. "Their Majesties request your presence for breakfast in their rooms in half an hour."

I nodded. "Thank you. I'll be there. Is there anything else?"

He shook his head. "No, Your Highness, just that."

"Thank you." I shut the door as he turned and walked away.

I tried not to let the concern over them asking me to come to their room get to me. What was it about? Had Mother worsened during the night, and this was their way of letting me know without outright saying it? Or perhaps they were angry with me and didn't want to tell me off where the servants could overhear.

"You look *awful*," the mirror said.

Eurgh. I'd wondered when it would pipe up. "Thanks," I muttered.

"Seriously, you shouldn't leave the room looking like that."

"I wasn't planning to," I retorted.

"Though, I don't know if anything could improve the

bird's nest that is your hair."

"You need to get some better insults, you used that one the other day," I muttered, walking away from the mirror's vicinity. Just because it couldn't see me, didn't mean it would be any nicer to me, but it increased the chances of silence, and right now, that was what I could hope for.

I threw on the first half-decent outfit I came across, hoping it would do me for the rest of the day as well as the breakfast with my parents. So long as it covered me, I didn't think I had anything to worry about.

I grabbed my wand from my side and spelled my hair, having it fall in simple dark waves. It wasn't anything fancy, and it wouldn't be good enough for most of the women in the court, but I who was I trying to impress, really? Perhaps Jake.

Which reminded me... I tapped my dress, giving it some white panelling as well as the black. I wasn't ready to walk around wearing all white, but I could concede some of the way toward fashion for now.

"Marginally better," the mirror said.

"And that's marginally polite for you," I threw back. "Are you feeling all right?"

"I'll be better when I don't have to see your face, Princess."

I rolled my eyes, already done with the mirror's attitude. "Whatever. Have fun in a room by yourself for the rest of day." I gave it a half-wave as I headed for the door, letting it swing shut loudly behind me, drowning out whatever the mirror was muttering about as I left.

I hurried down the corridor, reaching my parents' room in no time. It was only once I was standing outside it that I recalled how nervous I'd been about coming for breakfast with them. I didn't want to be in trouble, even if it was for a good reason. Nothing was going to convince me that what was happening to Mother was natural. Something nasty was going on. They had to believe me.

"Stop it, Kelis," I muttered to myself. "They're your parents, and they love you." I might have been worried that they weren't all that happy with me, but they weren't going to throw me onto the street just because I was paranoid about Mother's health.

I knocked lightly before pushing the door open, knowing they were expecting me.

"Kelis, is that you?" Father called, his voice tired and full of an undefined emotion that I didn't want to think about too much.

"We're in the bedchamber," he added.

I frowned. Why were we having breakfast in there? The only time any of us had breakfast in our rooms was when...

Oh no.

It didn't take me longer than a moment to work out what was happening. He'd convinced Mother to take her illness seriously, but it had also somehow got worse.

I rushed in, mentally preparing myself for what I was going to find. Except nothing could.

Mother was propped up against the headboard with pillows, the blankets of the bed up to her chin, and a fire raging in the grate. Despite that, she looked cold.

"Mother." I rushed forward and sat on the bed, reaching for one of her hands and holding it in my own. "What happened?"

She shook her head. "I'm not sure. Your Father talked to me about your concerns last night, and I dismissed them."

I shot a look at Father, but he just shrugged. Concern

grew within me. Despite the noncommital gesture, I could see the fear in his eyes. This wasn't a little thing to him; this was dangerous. The dwarves' warnings that they thought the witch was back rattled around my head. How did that fit in?

"What happened then?" I asked, realizing I'd gotten sidetracked from Mother's story.

"I fell asleep, like normal. But then things changed. I had a dream." Her eyebrows knit together as if she was trying to recall what had happened. "It's all so fuzzy now. I couldn't tell you what happened in it. But I woke up and..."

"You were so cold," Father whispered."I thought..." He choked on his words. The man who'd raised me and who had always been the fearless King of Enchantia was broken. I could see it in his eyes. If something happened to Mother, he wouldn't be able to continue.

I stroked Mother's hand. "Will you let us call for the doctor?" I asked.

She nodded. "We've already done that," she admitted.

Relief crashed through me. At least, they were taking it seriously now. A doctor should be able to tell us more about what's happening to her and what we can do to change that.

"He'll be here mid-morning," Father added. "But we needed to see you first."

"We need you to perform royal duties today," Mother said.

My eyes widened. There wasn't anything specific that needed doing today, but that didn't change the immense responsibility this would put on my shoulders.

"A-Are you sure?" I stammered.

Mother flashed me a weak smile. "You've been training for this your entire life, Kelis."

"I know. But I've never had to do it without the two of you." And I'd never been in a rush to change that. I knew a lot of people my age probably couldn't wait for their parents to hand over the reins to them. Not me. We were a team. I wanted it to stay that way.

"You can do this, Kelis," Father assured me. "And it's just for a day."

One look at Mother's face suggested it *wouldn't* just be a day, but I kept quiet about that.

"All right. But I want to be here when the doctor comes," I specified. I needed to hear what he said for myself.

"I'll make sure you're sent for," Father promised.

"Thank you." I was certain my smile didn't reach my eyes. "I'll get going to breakfast downstairs. Please don't overdo it." I leaned in and kissed Mother's forehead.

"I'll try." Her chuckle turned into a cough. Father rushed forward and helped her drink from the goblet that had been placed on the sideboard for her.

I took that as my cue to leave. The two of them didn't need me here right now. They needed me in the main banquet hall presiding over everything.

"Do you want to come casting with us today?" Jake asked, dropping down into Father's chair.

I resisted the urge to shoo him out of it, not liking that he was sitting there. He didn't deserve to sit on Father's seat. My eyes widened with the shock of my thoughts until I pushed them away to focus on his question.

"I'm sorry, I can't," I told him.

Anger flitted across his face, but he smoothed it

down into a frown fast enough that I wasn't completely sure of what I'd seen. "Whyever not? I thought you were enjoying it."

"I am, but I need to work today."

His frown deepened as he watched me. "What's more important than spells?"

*The healthcare system. Education. Equal rights for everyone.* I didn't say any of those out loud. Something told me he wouldn't be particularly pleased about any of them.

"Royal stuff. Being a princess isn't all tiaras and ballgowns." I was certain we'd had this conversation before, but clearly, he'd decided not to listen to me when I'd told him any of it. I couldn't even bring myself to be insulted. I had too much on my mind today.

"Fine." He got up and stalked away, not even bothering to say goodbye.

"Can I sit?" Topher asked from my other side.

I jumped in my seat, not having realized he was there. I turned and smiled at him, not the forced one I'd had to put on while I was talking to Jake. Though, it also wasn't one that completely reached my eyes.

"Of course."

"Are you all right? You seem distracted. And don't get me started on what happened there." He waved in the general direction that Jake had wandered off in.

Despite myself, a small chuckle escaped. "*That* is him being upset that I have more important things to do than practice magic with him today." I sighed loudly before remembering who I was talking to. He knew most of what was going on with my family. "Mother's agreed to see a doctor."

"That's great news. I hope he can help," Topher said.

"I hope so too. But it's come with the admission that

she can't do anything around here. Hence..." I waved to myself.

"Hence you're running the palace for the day," he finished for me. "It makes sense."

"One of the drawbacks to being a princess. Sometimes, it isn't possible to spend the day having fun."

"I think it's admirable," Topher said firmly.

A blush rose to my cheeks, but I chased it away before it could linger for too long.

"Thank you. I want to try my best to live up to them. Sometimes, I don't feel like I ever can."

"I don't think they feel that way," Topher assured me.

I cocked my head to the side. "What makes you say that?"

"Because they've trusted you with this, now. When your Mother isn't in any position to pick up the pieces if you do something wrong, and your Father is looking after her. If they didn't trust you, or thought you'd let them down, then he'd be the one here, and you'd be the one at her side."

"Huh. I never thought about it that way."

"Of course, you didn't. You don't have an unreasonable ego." He glanced down the hall.

I followed his gaze and caught sight of Jake flirting with a serving girl in front of Lyss. Annoyance flared up within me. I might not want him to stay with her, but that didn't mean he should be treating her like that.

Where were all these negative thoughts about Jake coming from? He'd been the only guy I'd thought about for years. Really, it had been since before I'd understood what a crush truly was. Yet ever since he'd arrived here this time, something had been *off* about it all. He wasn't setting my heart racing like he had before. No doubt I was overthinking it, and it was nothing more than me being preoccupied with what was going on with Mother.

"Your Highness," a servant interrupted.

"Yes?"

"The doctor has arrived," he said.

I jumped to my feet. "Thank you." I turned to Topher. "I'm so sorry. I have to go..."

He reached out and took my hand, giving it a squeeze. My heartbeat increased, but that was just the adrenaline from knowing the doctor was in the palace. It had to be. "I know you do. Don't worry about me."

I relaxed and smiled at him. It was so different from the way Jake had responded to me earlier. I didn't have time to ponder on that, though. I needed to get back to my parents' room as soon as possible.

~

I had to hold myself back from running down the corridor, but I managed to maintain a quick but acceptable pace. The last thing we needed was anyone getting suspicious about why I was running up and down corridors instead of walking serenely like a princess should. Sometimes, I hated being royal. It was only when I reminded myself of all the good things I could do that I stopped feeling that way. As the heir to the throne, I could make a difference in people's lives, and that was something I'd be forever grateful for.

I turned down the corridor that led to my parents' chambers and picked up my pace. But it must have been too much for me as my vision began to blur and a pain shot through my head. I steadied myself against the wall with one hand, while pressing my other to my temple to try and relieve the pain, all the while trying to make sense of why I had a strong sense of deja-vu. This had happened before, but I couldn't focus enough to grasp at the memory of when.

The edges of my vision stayed that way, but the rest of it sharpened, giving me a clear view of the doctor next to Mother's bed. If possible, she looked even worse than when I'd left her a few hours ago. I tried not to let it get to me too much, but I could feel the worries creeping up inside me again. If we didn't do something soon, Mother was going to get even sicker, and then potentially die.

"If you would please lie back, Your Majesty," the doctor requested. "I need to examine you."

Mother nodded and shuffled in the bed. Father rushed forward to help her. I tried to lurch forward, forgetting that I wasn't in the room and only watching via a weird vision thing.

The doctor studied her intently, moving around and muttering things under his breath. He pulled away from Mother, a concerned look on his face. Oh no, that wasn't a good sign.

"Things aren't good," the doctor said.

"Is it treatable?" Father asked.

The doctor nodded, but his expression said there would be conditions to that. "She's being poisoned, slowly. The best way to treat it is to find the source and cut it off there. Once you've done that, plenty of rest and water and the issue should clear up."

My vision cleared, and I took a moment to catch my breath again. I had no idea what was causing these weird visions. Were they linked to the dreams I'd been having? Perhaps they were caused *because* I hadn't had the dream.

"Snap out of it," I muttered. Now wasn't the time to

spend working this out. I needed to go to my parents' room and see how the doctor was getting on. Hopefully, he'd have more answers than in my vision. I wasn't going to be satisfied with it simply being poison. I wanted to know what it was, how it worked, and how we were going to find out who was behind it. People didn't start dying from poison naturally.

I pushed open the door, knowing they were expecting me. If it was only Mother and Father in the room, then I would have knocked, but it wasn't worth disturbing the doctor while he did his work.

"Things aren't good," the doctor said as he pulled away from Mother. Ah, I'd missed the first part of his consultation. Wait, that was what he'd said in my vision in the corridor. That meant that my vision had come true.

"Is it treatable?" Father asked, his brow furrowed with worry.

"She's being poisoned, slowly. The best way to treat it is to find the source and cut it off there. Once you've done that, plenty of rest and water and the issue should clear up," the doctor instructed.

I tried to focus on what he was saying rather than the terror filling me about my visions. This wasn't the first time I'd had one, but it had taken me a little while to work out where I'd felt the dizziness before. It was the same thing that had happened while we were practicing spells before the mini-competition. The vision that had saved Jake's life. Not that he seemed particularly grateful for that. Huh, seeing the future would be a neat trick, if it wasn't so death-focused.

But what did that mean? Should I ask the doctor if he knew anything about what was happening with me? Would he know? No. I shouldn't share it with him, not until I understood more about it myself. And how my dreams fit in with it. The last thing I wanted was to be branded as the crazy princess of Enchantia. That wouldn't do anything good for my reputation.

"Thank you," Father said, picking up a purse of gold that hadn't been in the room earlier. He must have had one of the servants deliver it from the treasury. He pressed it into the doctor's hand. "Your discretion would be appreciated."

"Of course, Your Majesty." He dipped his head, taking the gold from Father. "You have a true and loyal subject in me."

"Our gratitude goes with you, doctor."

He dipped his head again before grabbing his bag and hurrying out of the room.

Father sighed loudly. "We probably have until nightfall."

"For what?" I asked, confused by everything, but that could be because I'd been too focused on my own problem.

"For news of your Mother's illness to spread."

"You think he'll tell people?" I glanced at the door, a frown on my face.

"Of course. He's one of the best in Enchantia, but he's also known to have a drinking problem. He might intend for this news to get out, or he might let it slip once he's had a few too many ales, but we should move quickly to ensure we're ready when it gets out."

I gulped, ridding myself of the lump which had formed in my throat. "What do we do?" I asked.

Soft snores came from Mother. I hadn't realized she'd fallen asleep, but the reclining position must have lulled her into unconsciousness. So long as no more harm could come to her in her dreams, this was probably the best state for her to be in.

"We need to get rid of all the food. Then we can get more in from the surrounding farms..."

"That's a lot of food to be rid of, especially with all the guests we have at the moment," I pointed out.

"We can't take any risks with her life." The pained look he shot Mother would have convinced anyone to do his bidding. Even to this day, I still found myself in awe of the love and devotion my parents shared. It could move mountains if it had to.

"It's only Mother who is sick," I whispered.

He shot me an intrigued look. "What are you thinking?"

"We don't need to throw out all of the food, just the apples."

Understanding dawned on his face. Mother was the only one who ate apples. Some of the merchants or other common people who lived outside the palace might eat them, but no member of the nobility did as a sign of respect to Mother's story. But without fail, she had a dozen apples delivered every week, and she ate them all.

"I think you're right," Father admitted.

"And we shouldn't get rid of them in the kitchen," I added. "That'll reveal to the person behind this that we know how they're doing it. We don't want them to suspect that."

"If they suspect we know, then they'll stop," Father suggested. "I hope."

I shook my head. "They'd only look for another way to achieve their goal." I thought for a moment. "What were the other parts of Mother's story again? The ways her step-mother tried to kill her?"

Father frowned, most likely because he was trying to

work out where I was going with my questions. "Corsets and combs."

"Hmm." I knew that anyway, I was only thinking aloud. "I think we should make a grand show of removing all the hair combs from the palace. That way, the person who is doing the poisoning will think the apples are safe to carry on."

"And we'll have them delivered up here, where we can get rid of them ourselves," Father suggested.

"Which will work particularly well if we tell people that Mother is unwell, but the apples seem to be helping."

Father's smile reached his eyes for the first time since I'd seen them both early this morning. Relief flooded through me at the sight. It made me believe we could get through this as a family, even if it wasn't going to be easy.

"Let's hope it's enough," he said, glancing back at Mother, his face falling. "I couldn't bear the thought of losing her."

I placed a hand on Father's back and moved it up and down in what I hoped was a soothing motion. "I can't either," I admitted. "And neither can the Kingdom. She *is* Enchantia."

I had no idea how long we stood there, the two of us watching for the rise and fall of Mother's chest. Her rattling breath set me on edge, and I dreaded to think how much more poison it would have taken to push her over the edge.

# 18TH OCTOBER

"How is she?" I asked Father the moment I was in my parents' room.

He sighed loudly. "No better, no worse. She was conscious for a small amount of time in the middle of the night. I told her what was happening, but I'm not sure if she understood or not." His crestfallen face broke my heart.

"Is there anything I can do?" I worried the hem of my dress with my fingers, hoping he'd say yes, and he could get some rest.

"No. Other than being around the palace in case anyone wants an audience with one of us. I've already instructed the servants to find you."

I nodded, both pleased and terrified that my parents were trusting me with this. I knew they'd been grooming me to take over since I was a small child, but somehow, it felt different with everything that was going on.

"Please sleep," I begged him. "You need rest too."

Father sighed. It didn't take a genius to see he was exhausted. He might not be the one who'd been poisoned, but it was taking a toll on him too. When I found out who was behind this, they were going to pay. They'd threatened the one thing that meant the most to me. My family had chosen me, and I would do anything for them as a result.

"I promise. I'll sleep."

"Thank you." I smiled at him, and he tried to return it but failed.

"Promise you'll have a servant wake me if you need anything."

"I promise, Father." I leaned in and kissed his cheek before leaving the room. If I stayed any longer, then I'd end up camped out on the floor watching over both of them. While that sounded appealing to the daughter side of me, the princess in me knew it wasn't an option. Just because we were facing family problems, didn't mean the kingdom had to suffer.

I leaned back in the library chair, not paying any attention to the conversation going on around me. It was odd for everyone to be here and not out doing their own thing, but a rainstorm had hit overnight, which probably made them reluctant to venture outside. Which meant they'd all ended up in the library along with me. Once I'd left Father, I figured this would be one of the best places to be. I'd even told several of the servants where I'd be, so I knew they'd find me if they needed to.

The warmth of the fire soothed me, and lulled me into a false sense of security. The bad dreams had stayed away, whether it was simply a coincidence or if it was because of the carving from the dwarves' house, I didn't know. But that hadn't made a difference to how well I'd slept. The stress of what was going on with Mother must have taken its toll because I hadn't managed to stay asleep for longer than an hour.

My eyes were half-closed, and it was all I could do to keep them open.

"Kelis," Rhi said. Jake, Adam, Lyss, and Topher were with her.

"Huh?" I shook my head, clearing it of the drowsiness. Or I attempted to. It didn't work very well, I had to admit.

"The weather's started to clear up, and if it stays that way, we were thinking of practicing some spells later, do you want to join us, or do you have royal duties?" There was no expectation in her question, which I appreciated after Jake's sullenness yesterday. He hadn't even talked to me today. At least, I didn't think he had. There was a chance I wasn't paying enough attention to notice. I pushed that thought aside. If he wanted to engage with me, all he had to do was say my name. That was what Rhi had done.

"I'd love to. But if something comes up, I might have to drop everything and go deal with it." I hated telling my new friends they came second, but at the same time, if they didn't understand that, then perhaps they weren't the best people to be friends with a princess in the first place.

"Does your royal duty always have to come first?" The snideness poured off Jake's question.

"As it should," Topher answered for me.

My heart leapt at him protecting my position for me. His respect for my position, and more importantly, for *me*, was one of the main reasons we'd become friends so easily. At least, as far as I was concerned, it was.

"She can speak for herself," Jake snapped.

"She shouldn't have to on questions like that. Her kingdom would always come first..."

I tuned them out as they bickered. Which was a nice way of me thinking that I was too tired to keep up. My eyes drifted closed without me wanting them to, and sleep called my name.

*I waved my arms around, trying to dispel the forest around me.*

*"Go away!" I shouted.*

*My words echoed around the woods, an unnatural sound to go along with the rest of the dream. I tried not to focus on that too much. There was enough to terrify me in this dream, I didn't need to add anything else.*

*Knowing I had no choice, I started walking down the path. The stones dug into my feet, though this time I was wearing shoes. Instead of being reassuring, that had the opposite effect. I looked down and found myself wearing the same black and white dress I had on in the library. I gulped. Perhaps it was simply my brain projecting the clothes I knew I was wearing onto me, but somehow, I knew that wasn't the case. This wasn't the kind of dream people had just because. This was brought on by magic.*

*I tried to run but found I couldn't. Whatever was powering the dream seemed to want me to do things at a certain pace. How annoying.*

*"Wake up," I muttered. "The others are watching you, wake up."*

*Unsurprisingly, nothing happened.*

*"Rhi? Topher? Adam? Jake? Lyss?" I knew calling out their names was useless, but I still tried. Perhaps, one of them would sense my distress and wake me up. I snorted. Even inside this terrifying dream, I knew that was pointless. In all likelihood, they were still arguing among themselves and not paying me any attention.*

*The clearing appeared, and relief flooded through me. I'd go up to the coffin, see Mother a little worse than last time and then wake back up and be able to go back to the rest of my day. Now that I knew what the problem with Mother was, it seemed less terrifying to see her in the depleted state. Not that I wanted to see her like that at all, and once I was up and about, I was going to wear the carving from the dwarves' house in case I fell asleep in the library again.*

*I had to wonder if even the act of sleeping was being caused by the magic surrounding Mother's poisoning. My dreams and visions had to be coming from somewhere. It wasn't completely unreasonable to think it was the magic.*

*The coffin loomed before me. I took a deep breath and closed my eyes, readying myself for what I'd find within. I might know what I was going to see this time, but that didn't mean I wanted to see it. Kind of. I did want to look, but only because it meant this dream would be over.*

*My eyes snapped open, and I stared down at Mother. She was paler than before, without a speck of life in her. Unsure what else to do, I placed a hand on her forehead. My eyes widened at how cold she was.*

*No.*

*This couldn't be happening.*

*I put my hand over the place where her heart and lungs should be working.*

*They weren't.*

*I opened my mouth and screamed.*

~

"Kelis, you have to wake up," Rhi's worried whisper cut through my haze.

I tried to open my eyes but found them stuck. I was still trapped in the end of the dream, despite the fact I couldn't see anything.

"Here, try this," Topher said.

A strong-smelling smoke filled my nose and mouth. I gagged, my eyes snapping open and bugging out of my face.

Topher waved his wand, collecting up the smoke. "Sorry, I couldn't think of another way." Guilt shone through his face.

"It's fine," I murmured.

"It isn't..."

"What happened?" Rhi asked, cutting him off.

Lyss, Jake, and Adam sat back, none of them saying a word as my two friends tried to help me.

"I had a bad dream," I admitted.

Concern replaced the guilt on Topher's face. "Like the other ones?"

Rhi shot him an odd look as if she had no idea why he'd know about my dreams. I'd fill her in on that later.

I nodded. "Just like those."

"Do you normally wake up screaming?" Rhi asked.

"I screamed out loud?" I frowned. That was bad.

"Didn't you in your dream?"

I nodded. "I did. But I didn't realize you could hear

it."

The two of them exchanged worried glances.

"I sent the servants away," Adam said, finally speaking up. "When you started to get agitated. We didn't want word to get around you weren't well."

"Thank you," I croaked. Though I doubted it would make much difference while Lyss had witnessed it all. She'd go and gossip about it to her lover the moment she could. Of that, I had no doubt.

"Is there anything we can do?" Rhi asked. "Do you need tea or anything to eat?"

"No, it's all right," I promised. "I need to get something from my room, but I'll be fine after that." It was a lie. I'd never be fine again. Two of my visions had already come true, and that was if I didn't include the original dreams of Mother getting sick. What if this one was going to as well?

"Kelis, you're trembling," Topher said.

I glanced at Lyss and Jake, both of whom were watching with distaste on their faces.

"Sorry, I'm fine." How many times would I have to say it before the two of them believed it?

This time, it was Topher who looked at Jake, imploring him to do something with his eyes. I wasn't too out of it to miss that exchange.

Jake sighed loudly and got to his feet, coming towards me and crouching down so he could look me in the eye. "Princess, you have to tell us what's wrong, then we can fix it."

"Since when do you care?" Lyss demanded, disdain dripping from every word.

"We should all care," Rhi snapped. "She's a person. That should be enough."

Lyss' chair scraped back. "Why does everyone think

she's so special?" she sneered. "Oh, poor Princess Kelis had a nightmare, let's all flock around her and pretend no one else matters at all. It's disgusting," she spat.

Topher stood up straight, facing off against his friend's girlfriend. "As you pointed out, she's your princess, that should be enough, even if common decency isn't."

Anger flared in Lyss' eyes before she stormed out of the library, leaving the rest of us behind.

"I'm sorry about her," Rhi said softly.

Of course, it was Rhi apologizing for her. There was no chance of it coming from Jake. I knew enough about him to be sure of that. I tried not to think about what that said about him as a person.

"It's not a problem."

"What happened in your dream?" Topher asked again.

I shook my head. "It doesn't matter." I couldn't admit I'd seen Mother dead. Not when she was as ill as she currently was. Perhaps if Jake and Adam weren't here, I'd tell them, but a small part of me didn't trust the two of them completely.

"Is there anything we can do?" Topher reached out a hand, but decided against it partway through and held it steady.

I stared at it, unsure what I wanted him to do.

He seemed to sense my hesitation, as he let it drop and didn't say anything about it.

Unable to deal with it all, I rose to my feet swiftly. "I have some work to do," I said, my voice shaking with the lie. "I'll join you all for practice later."

I didn't wait for them to reply, I couldn't. Tears were stinging my eyes, and I didn't want them to see me cry. Especially not Jake. I wasn't a weak little princess who needed protecting, and I wasn't going to act that way.

~

No matter how much I tried to forget the carved pendant, nothing could take my mind from where it lay against my skin. I had to hope its powers would work while I wasn't in my bed. Or that they worked at all. I still had no real proof of that beyond a dreamless night and my nightmare only taking over once I was in the library and away from it.

I sighed. This was nothing but superstition, and I needed to be careful with that. If it got out that I believed in talismans, it could cause a minor scandal. Right now, that was the last thing our family needed.

I snapped my fingers, hoping to chase away the thoughts in my head. No one else needed me, so it was time to practice magic. And for that, I needed a clear head.

The courtyard was filled with shouts and small explosions of color as everyone did their thing. I smiled at the sound. It'd be good to do something that would take my mind off the worry in my head.

I stepped through the archway and out into the open space. As Rhi had said, the rain had stopped earlier, and it had dried up enough for us to be outside. Saying that, the sky was still thunderous as if it could rain at any moment.

Rhi spun around and fired a spell at one of the targets hung over the plants at the other end. It hit right at the center. Huh. I assumed she didn't do as much magic because she wasn't as good as the others at it, but if what was in front of me was to be believed, that definitely wasn't the case. I'd have to ask her about that in the future.

Adam clapped, and her face lit up. She needed to do something about her crush on him. I was surprised he hadn't noticed it.

"That was a good one," he said.

She flushed and bowed her head to hide it.

Oh, no! Was that how I looked when I was responding to Jake's compliments? I needed to work on that if it was.

"Hey," I said as I approached Topher.

"You came," he observed.

"I did. I hope that's all right."

"Of course. We're always glad to have you around."

"You're only saying that because Lyss isn't here," I pointed out.

He chuckled. "Even if she was, most of us would feel that way."

"Good to know."

"Did you get everything you needed to?" he asked.

I touched the fabric of my dress where it covered the pendant. "I think so."

"So now you can have some fun?" The twinkle in his eye said he had a plan.

"Of course. What did you have in mind?"

"There's a game we can play with the disks."

"Like your machine?"

"Not really. We don't need that when there are five of us," he assured me. "But why don't you get warmed up first, then we can play?"

I nodded, eager to get going. If this was going to take my mind off what was going on with my parents, then I needed to get on with it. When I was thinking about the next spell I was going to cast, then I wouldn't be imagining Mother's pale face and the coldness of her skin.

I repressed a shiver and walked over to where Jake and Rhi were both shooting at targets. I joined in but soon grew bored of nothing more than firing in a straight line. There was no challenge in this. And that was what I was here for.

When Topher called for us to start the game, relief flooded through me. *Now,* things could get exciting.

"How about Kelis and Jake go first, then the rest of us can take turns after," Topher suggested.

"Sounds good to me," Rhi said, bouncing off to stand by Adam.

"Good to go," I said, getting into position behind the start line Topher had drawn while we'd all been hitting the targets.

"Good. Adam and I will fire the disks," Topher said.

The three of them stood to the sides, their wands out in front of them as they readied themselves to cast disks up into the air for Jake and me to hit out of the sky.

My heart pounded in my chest, adrenaline flooding through me. I never realized how exciting this could be. Now that I'd discovered doing magic like this, I wasn't going to stop. I cursed myself inwardly for not trying it sooner, especially when it was such an important part of the Enchantian culture.

"Ready?" Topher asked us, cutting through my reflections.

"As ever." I grinned broadly.

He nodded and looked at Jake.

"Whatever," my opponent muttered.

Was this a good idea? To go up against Jake? I wanted to spend time with him, but that didn't mean I needed to compete against him. Oh well. It was far too late for that now.

"Kelis is going for green, Jake for red," Topher said.

"Got it." I flashed him a smile, getting one back in return.

"On your marks," Rhi shouted.

"Get set," Adam added.

"Go!" Topher's word rang through the air, and a cascade of brightly colored disks flew into the air from Topher and Adam's wands.

Rhi was controlling the counters with hers, which would go up whenever we managed to hit one of our targets. I wasn't too sure how it worked, just that it did. I might be getting better at magic, but that didn't mean I knew everything there was to know.

I stopped thinking and let my instincts take over, picking up targets left and right, doing my best to avoid hitting any of Jake's.

He was doing the same beside me, his eyes ever so slightly feral as he dashed his wand through the air, slashing at the red disks and sending showers of sparks into the air.

One of mine nearly hit the floor. I flung my wand out, sending a bolt of magic at it. The disk exploded seconds before it would have hit the ground. Triumph flowed through me, but I squashed it down. The game was far from over, and I needed to focus on the rest of the green disks floating around. I fired off some more spells, causing three disks to explode in quick succession.

I didn't even look at the counter. As far as I was concerned, it didn't matter which of us was winning. I needed to hit all of my disks for *me.* Besides, Jake was by far the more experienced of the two of us. It was a given he'd be winning. But if I wanted to get better at this, then practicing with people who were better than me was the way to do it.

My next spell speared through two disks at once, shattering them one right after the other.

Huh. Could I cast a spell that recreated that on purpose? I had to try. Even if it failed, if I broke at least one of the targets, it wouldn't be a waste. I readied the spell, thinking about it curving through the air and hitting all of the green targets.

"One minute left," Topher called out.

It was now or never then. All right, that wasn't accurate. I could always try it at another point. But I was playing the game *now* and wanted to try this. I closed my eyes and took a steadying breath before letting the spell loose.

Rhi gasped. Worry filled me. What if the spell was hurting her in some way? Or doing other damage? I needed to know. My eyes snapped back open in time to see my spell doing exactly what it was supposed to. It whizzed through the air, shattering each green disk with startling precision. It caught one just before it hit the floor, then bounced up into the air and sliced through two more.

"Wow," I whispered. My wand hand was limp by my side. Even if I'd wanted to, I wouldn't be able to tear my eyes away from what was happening. It was amazing. And perfect. And nothing like I'd have been able to do if I hadn't been in the middle of a game.

My spell shot through the last disk just as Topher's buzzer rang.

"Time," he whispered, but he didn't seem interested in the game at all. His gaze was locked on me as if he was trying to work out what had just happened. He was welcome to try. I didn't have any idea myself.

"Kelis won," Rhi said brightly, a hint of smugness in

her voice.

"In the last minute, too," Adam added, though he didn't seem as happy about it as she did.

"It was amazing," Rhi gushed. "Jake was ahead the whole game, and then you shot out that spell."

"I've never seen anything like it," Adam agreed.

"She only won because Topher cheated," Jake muttered.

Topher sighed loudly, and I could understand why. It was a ridiculous accusation at the best of times.

"He didn't cheat for me," I said.

"He must have. He was the one controlling the disks." A dark look crossed Jake's face.

"Along with Adam."

"There's no way you could have won without his help."

I blinked back the tears that stung the corners of my eyes. Why was he being this way?

"I don't cheat," Topher said darkly, hatred bubbling behind his eyes. Huh, how hadn't I noticed how he felt towards Jake before? I knew he didn't like him sometimes and found him arrogant, but actual hate? Somehow, I'd missed that.

"Then how did she win?" Jake demanded.

"Because she's talented," Topher pointed out. "Didn't you *see* what she just did?"

"A spell you must have taught her."

"I didn't. I wish I knew how to do what Kelis did. But even if I *had* taught it to her, there's nothing wrong with that." Topher crossed his arms, his wand sticking out almost comically from beneath one of them.

"Then she cheated in another way." Jake shoved his wand into its holster so hard I was surprised the leather didn't split. Then, he spun on his heels and stalked off, only stopping so he could kick a stone out of the way.

The four of us watched as it clattered off the side of the stone building, confused about what had happened.

"I should go after him." Adam's grimace suggested he wasn't as keen on that idea as he felt he should be. "Good game, Kelis," he said more kindly.

"Thanks," I murmured, not feeling the glow of my victory nearly as much as I should be.

Once he was out of earshot, I turned to Topher and Rhi. "What happened there?"

Rhi shrugged. "He's a sore loser. That's all there is to it."

"Hmm."

Topher looked about as convinced as I was, but I didn't feel like I could prod him further on it. Jake was a topic that hung between us, not something we talked about a lot. Perhaps, I needed to think about why that might be.

"We should clean up and go in for dinner," I said weakly.

The two of them nodded, no doubt being able to identify my change of subject for what it was.

# 19TH OCTOBER

I stared up at the canopy of my bed. Another night without the dream. Though, having had it during the day yesterday, I wasn't going to discount the idea that it might still be coming. It was best if I didn't think about that too much.

I pulled the pendant out from under my pillow and sat up so I could put it around my neck. The click of the clasp settled me, especially because I'd slept better than I had in a few days. I stretched, glancing at the window and trying to work out what time it was. Still early, if the amount of light was anything to go by. That was good. It meant I could go see Mother and Father before I started going about the daily tasks I needed to see fulfilled. I should probably talk to my parents about making an official list and schedule if this was going to last longer. I knew they didn't want me to forget to have fun, but they also couldn't let the kingdom go to ruin.

The air was crisp, once I'd thrown back the covers, but that was a good thing. It took me from half-awake to fully alert within seconds.

"What is *that*?" the mirror asked.

I groaned. It was starting already? "A pendant."

"You know that princesses are supposed to wear precious metals and things that sparkle?"

"Not all that sparkles is gold," I retorted, pulling on my robe so I could fend off some of the cold.

"Then you need teaching about the value of things," the mirror said offhandedly.

I snorted. "If gold is the only valuable thing, then aren't you in trouble yourself?"

The mirror stayed silent.

"I'll take that as a yes. I'll talk to the steward about moving you to the scrap heap."

The following silence filled me with triumph. That would teach it to criticize something useful like the pendant. I hummed a pretty tune as I got ready for the rest of my day. A part of me was tempted to do my hair in front of the mirror and try and taunt it, but I thought better of it. Today was going to take a lot of energy as it was, I shouldn't waste it on an inanimate object.

I pulled out a white dress I'd never wanted to wear. It almost sparkled under my touch and looked as if it was made of magic. That would do. I wasn't about to wear all white, and I had a sheer black lace cardigan I'd wear over the top. It likely wasn't going to be what the nobility truly wanted from me, but it was my concession for fashion. Plus, Jake seemed to like it more when I conformed this way.

Giving myself a once over in my definitely-not-going-to-talk full-length mirror, I decided I'd do fine and set off to start my day. First stop, my parents' room.

~

The moment I saw Mother, relief washed through me.

"Kelis," she said, her lips turning up into a smile that even managed to light up her eyes.

I rushed forward and perched myself on the bed so I could be close to her. I picked up her hand and clasped it between my own. Her skin was warm, not like the coolness from my dream. Not that I was going to tell her that. If she was starting to get better, then the last thing I wanted to do was worry her with the directions my dreams had been taking.

"How are you feeling?" I asked, desperate to hear it for myself.

"Better. Your Father has been looking after me." She glanced over at him, a smile full of love on her face.

A warm fuzzy feeling slipped over me as I watched my parents. This was the way things were supposed to be. Mother not as sick, the three of us being a unit. It was perfect this way.

"How are things in the kingdom going?" Father asked me.

"Yes, tell us, Kelis. I've heard how you've been taking care of everything." She reached out with her free hand and cupped my face. "I can't believe how grown you are. It feels like it was just yesterday you were barely walking. Now, look at you, running Enchantia..."

"I'm hardly running it," I countered. "I'm only making sure I'm about while you're not well. You'll be able to take back control in no time." I smiled, but I wasn't sure it was convincing.

"Never undervalue yourself, Kelis. It only gives other people the right to undervalue you," she said. I couldn't ignore the ever so slight hitch in her voice as she spoke. It was clear she still wasn't well, but I didn't want to say anything. The last thing sick people wanted was to be reminded of their state.

"I'll try not to," I promised. "But I need a list of things that need doing and seeing to today," I told them.

"Good idea," Father nodded. "I'll get the steward to write it all down and bring it to you later."

"Thank you. I don't want anything to go wrong," I admitted.

"And it won't," Mother said. "You're far too smart for that."

"I might be, but I'm also only eighteen," I pointed out. "And people my age make mistakes."

Father chuckled. "You're too serious sometimes, Kel."

I closed my eyes and basked in his use of my old nickname from childhood. He barely ever used it anymore.

"I have a job to do, I have to be serious," I pointed out.

Mother sighed. "I'm glad you're spending time with Adam and his friends. Are any of them going to stay after Adam goes back to university?"

"I don't know," I admitted.

"Do you want any of them to?" Father asked. "We can always formally invite them to be part of the court if you'd like."

"Let me talk to them first," I said, thinking of Topher and Rhi. I didn't think either of them would want to take up a position here if it meant they couldn't complete their educations. But I would like them to come back here once they had. Oh, and Jake. I should consider making him an offer at court too. Or maybe he'd got one from Adam already, But knowing that would mean I had to talk to Jake, and I wasn't sure he was going to do that after yesterday. He seemed incredibly annoyed I'd beaten him. I hoped his problem had simply been that he'd lost, and not because it was me.

"Who would you ask to stay?" Mother asked, leaning back against the headboard.

"There's a girl that came with them, Rhi. I think she'd make an excellent companion. She's intelligent and kind. Just what you want from a companion." I smiled as I told my parents about her. "I didn't realize it would happen at first, but she's becoming a genuine friend."

"She sounds nice," Mother said.

"What about the boy you went to find the dwarves with?" Father asked.

My eyes widened. "How do you know about that?"

He chuckled. "Do you really think you can leave the palace and go off hiking in the woods without word getting back to me?"

"Oh."

"Plus, the dwarves told us when they visited me yesterday," Mother said.

"Traitors," I muttered under my breath.

She laughed lightly. "They didn't betray you. Six said something about how nice he was, and how much you seemed to trust him. And then, we asked more questions about it." A knowing smile slipped over her lips. That was reassuring. It felt like she was getting back to her normal self.

"His name is Topher," I told her. "He's been helping

me with magic. I like him." He'd make a good advisor too. I should keep that in mind, the older I got, the more I'd need people like him around me.

"I've heard reports of you practicing," Father said.

"Does everything get back to the two of you?" I asked him, more amused than insulted.

"Of course. That's the only way to run a kingdom. You'll realize that soon enough."

I sighed loudly. "Then you'd better make sure all the reports and information comes to me too. Then Mother can get the rest she needs."

"I see you're a doctor now too," Mother quipped.

A servant entered the room and placed a bushel of apples on the side table.

"Thank you, Martha," Mother said.

Father and I exchanged glances. Had he told Mother what we were going to do?

Martha left the room, and none of us said anything until we heard the click of the door shutting behind her.

"What are you going to do with them?" Mother asked after another moment.

Ah, at least, she knew they weren't here for her to eat.

"I thought we'd burn them," Father said. "It's the only way I can think of that won't leave a trace. And if it does, we can say you threw the cores in there."

Mother nodded, then watched in trepidation as Father and I threw each of the rosy red apples into the flames. They fizzled as they burned, probably because of the juice inside them. A foul smell came up from them.

Father pushed me back. "That's the poison," he said unnecessarily.

Behind us, Mother burst into a fit of coughing.

Father was in action mere seconds after she'd started, bringing a cup to her mouth and having her take small sips from it. I took that as my cue to leave, especially as neither of them would be paying any attention to me right now. This was time for the two of them to spend together. And if the servants were delivering apples already, then that meant the rest of the palace was up and about. It was time for me to get to work.

"I'll be back to visit later," I promised.

Father waved me away. It crossed my mind that neither of them wanted me to know the truth about how bad Mother's illness was. But that wasn't likely. I'd been in the room when the doctor gave his diagnosis, and I was here now, seeing that Mother was better than before. That was enough for me. My parents didn't lie to me, and I didn't lie to them. There was no reason for any of us to start doing that now.

"Kelis."

I twirled around at the sound of my name, especially because of the person saying it. "Jake? Is everything all right?" I was heading towards my office and hadn't expected to see him.

"You weren't around for practice this morning."

"I was with my parents," I said.

"And they're more important than magic?" His shock was readable on every part of his face.

I cocked my head to the side. "Why wouldn't they be?"

"It's just a bit strange to choose something boring over having fun."

"Running a country is hardly boring," I pointed out.

"And that's what you're doing?" He frowned.

"Yes." Had he missed all of the other times I'd talked about it? Or even the times Topher or Rhi had? Both of them seemed to understand why this was important to me.

"Are you coming out to do some casting now?" he asked, gesturing in the direction of the courtyard.

I grimaced and did a half-shrug to highlight the papers in my arms. "I have to go to my office and look through some of these reports."

"Can't you put it off?"

There was a fleeting urge to tell him I would, but it was smaller than I expected, almost as if it didn't matter to me that it would mean more time with Jake. Topher and Rhi would likely be there too, but they wouldn't be insulted if I skipped the session to do some work. Both seemed to appreciate I was more than the average eighteen-year-old.

"Sorry, not today," I said after a moment's consideration.

"Can't your work wait?" he tried again, an ever so slight whine in his voice.

Understanding dawned on me. This wasn't because he wanted to spend time with me. He wanted me to go outside so he could beat me and prove yesterday was nothing more than a fluke. And now he was getting frustrated because he wasn't getting his way.

"Not if we want to eat."

I turned away from him, mostly to save my resolve from breaking. I didn't want to give him what he wanted. He struck me as the kind of person who'd keep demanding more and more things.

"Kelis," he snapped.

"Yes?" I raised an eyebrow. Not that he could see it while I was faced away from him.

"Please, reconsider."

"I'm sorry, Jake. My kingdom, and my family, will always come first." With that, I walked away, my heart pounding in my chest.

Had I just ruined any chance I had of a relationship with Jake? I hoped I hadn't, but feared the worst. Then again, no matter how much I liked him, I would never put anyone before my duty. He'd have to come to terms with that if anything should happen between us.

A knock sounded on my door. No doubt, it was one of the servants delivering another missive or report about something.

"Come in," I said even as I signed my name at the bottom of a document ordering the release of a prisoner whose sentence had been served. I didn't see why I needed to be the one to do that, but it was on my desk, which meant I needed to deal with it.

The door opened, and I glanced up, expecting to see a servant there, but finding Rhi instead.

"Is everything all right?" I asked her. While I hadn't made a secret of where my office was or banned anyone from interrupting me, I hadn't expected anyone to come here.

"Yes, but I was wondering if you could spare a few minutes for me."

"Of course. Why wouldn't I?" I put down my pen and turned all of my attention to her.

She laughed lightly as she took a seat opposite me. "That's not what you said to Jake."

"Oh, that." I pressed the button on my desk that would bring one of the servants in. Rhi would likely want some tea, and I wanted to make sure she knew she was welcome here. If I was going to convince her to come back after she graduated, then this was the least I could do for her.

"You don't sound particularly happy."

"He was being pushy," I admitted. "And I didn't like it."

"Ah. That's why he was in a bad mood."

My eyes widened. "Oh, no."

Our conversation was stalled by one of the servants coming inside.

"You called, Your Highness?" the servant said, dipping into a bow. "Lady Rhi," he acknowledged.

Rhi shifted uncomfortably in her chair, not used to being called a Lady.

"Could you bring us some tea and cakes, please?" I asked.

"Of course, Your Highness. Is there anything else?"

"Do you need anything?" I asked Rhi.

She shook her head quickly. "No, thanks."

"That'll be all," I said, dismissing the servant.

He hurried from the room, and I knew he'd be back shortly. There were miniature kitchens on every floor in the palace to ensure the servants could always provide people with the refreshments they needed quickly. It was too far to the kitchens each time otherwise.

"What were we saying?" I asked.

"We were talking about Jake's bad mood." She smirked. "I don't think I've ever seen him that worked up over a girl."

"Does he have a lot of experience with girls?" The question was out before I could even think it through.

"I think a lot is an understatement," she murmured. "He has a new girl each week. I'm surprised Lyss has lasted as long as she has, though they'll be done by the end of the week."

I perked up at that. "Why do you think that?"

"You seriously don't? Not only are they terrible together, but he's set his eyes on someone else."

"He has?"

The servant bustled back in with a tea cart and all the trappings. Why was their timing always the worst? "Would you like me to pour for you, Your Highness?" he asked.

"No, thank you, we can do that." I dismissed him with a wave of my hand.

The moment the door clicked shut, we turned back to one another.

"Haven't you noticed? Jake has taken a fancy to you."

"He has?" I tried to make sense of what she was saying and how it made me feel. "If anything, he's started finding me more annoying, not less."

"Oh, don't worry, Jake loves nothing more than the chase. He likes the girls who say no to him."

"Oh." I didn't see why that would work. I'd never understand men. "And you think he likes me?" I picked up the teapot and began to pour the two of us tea.

"No. I don't think it, I *know* it. I heard him talking to Adam about you. He said now he'd seen how you do at magic, and now you're wearing white, he's more interested."

I focused on handing her the cup, rather than responding to what she'd said. A large part of me didn't like the conditions he'd placed on liking me. But then, I supposed there was always something that had to spark something between two people.

"I didn't expect that," I said eventually. I picked up the plate of cake and offered her one before taking one for myself.

"Do you still like him?" she asked, taking a bite of her cake.

"Is it bad to say I don't know?"

"I don't think so. You've spent more time with him since you admitted you liked him. That's going to change how you feel about him."

"I suppose."

"Kelis?"

"Hmm?"

"I'm not going to judge you for anything you say," she said softly.

"I know." I took a deep breath. "That's why I want to offer you a place here once you graduate." I hadn't made the decision to reveal that to her until the words were coming out of my mouth.

Rhi froze, not saying or doing anything. I sipped my tea and waited for her to break through her shock.

"Are you serious?"

"Of course. I know it's sudden, but..."

"I'd love to," she cut in. "I'm sorry, was that rude?"

I chuckled. "Technically, it broke protocol, but that's one of the reasons I want you to come back."

"What would I be doing?" she asked.

"Officially, you'd be my Lady-In-Waiting. At least, that's the title you'd have. In reality, you'd be my eyes and ears in the court and be a confidante and advisor to me."

"Lady-In-Waiting?" she repeated.

"Yes, I'm assuming you've heard of it..."

"Of course, I have. It's one of the highest honors,

especially since the Queen reduced the position down to only one position." The shock and disbelief on Rhi's face hadn't faded over the conversation.

"Yes, she didn't want to be surrounded by women constantly. But she does have one, a woman she's known since the two of them were girls. She's not at court at the moment because her father is sick," I explained. Which reminded me, I should send a letter to Dorris and bring her up to speed on what was happening at the palace. Of course, I'd downplay what was going on with Mother so she didn't worry, though.

"And you want me?" she asked.

"Yes." It was as simple as that. "If I'm honest, I've never thought much about the position until I got to know you. You're the first person who made me feel like I even wanted to fill it."

"I can't tell you how much I appreciate that."

"You don't have to say yes," I assured her. "I won't be angry if you don't."

"I know. I want to say yes." Excitement came through every word. "I didn't know what I wanted to do after university, just that I wanted to do better than a meaningless job. But I've loved it here. Coming back would be an honor."

Relief flooded through me. Perhaps I should have waited to ask her, but the response she'd given reassured me. "I'm glad. We can sort something out for the rest of your time at university, too, if you'd like. You could study during term time and work here during the holidays. With time off to visit your family, naturally."

"Thank you." If I wasn't mistaken, there was a tear in the corner of her eye.

It was time to change the subject. I didn't want to upset her.

"Do you think Topher would take a similar position?" I asked, taking another sip of tea and trying not to care about the answer one way or another.

"I don't think he'd suit the dresses a Lady-In-Waiting should wear," she said without skipping a beat.

I snorted; the mere thought of Topher in a dress somewhat amusing.

"Seriously, though, I suspect he would, especially if it got him away from the others at university."

"He doesn't like them?" I asked, though, I knew it was the case. He'd said he didn't like dealing with the egos and the inflated self-worth.

"I don't think it's that. I think there's something he likes here more." She gave me a knowing glance before eating another bit of cake.

"There is? What?" I leaned forward, eager for her answer.

Rhi raised an eyebrow. "You don't know?"

"I don't think so..."

"If you don't think so, then you definitely don't know." She chuckled and leaned back in her chair.

"Are you going to tell me?"

"Not this time," she said, a wide grin on her face. "But only because it isn't my answer to give. If I'm going to be your Lady-In-Waiting, then I need to know when to keep my mouth closed."

I chuckled. "That's true. And I guess I'll find out when I make him the offer."

"When will you do that?" she asked.

"I'm not sure. Before you all go back to university, I guess." I shrugged. "I didn't even plan to ask you today. It just slipped out."

"For what it's worth, I'm glad you did. What do I need to do?"

“We’ll get one of the stewards to draw up a contract with the terms of employment, and then we’re good to go. It might be best for you to wait until after this visit is over to start acting in the position.”

She tapped her chin. “Not necessarily,” she countered. “I can still be your eyes and ears now,” Rhi said.

“That’s true. Perhaps you should start by working out what’s going on with Lyss. I caught her with one of the nobles, and I’d like to know what’s going on there.”

“You mean if she’s cheating on Jake?” Rhi checked.

“Oh, no, that’s certain. Even Jake knows about it, but sometimes there’s more to affairs like that, and I want to know if this is one of those situations.”

Rhi nodded. “Jake knows?.”

“He said he knew. He didn’t seem to care that much.” I rolled my eyes at the thought of it. “Would you like more tea?” I offered.

“Yes, I’d love some, so long as I’m not keeping you from work...”

“I have time,” I promised. “There’s plenty of time, and so long as the reports know how to find me, it isn’t a problem.”

I had no idea how long the two of us sat there talking to one another, but I knew that the more we talked, the more certain I was that she was a good choice for the position of Lady-In-Waiting. I could see myself reigning for a long time with Rhi as my closest friend.

# 20TH OCTOBER

I was in a forest, but it was different from the one I normally found myself in when I was dreaming. For a start, there was sunlight. And not the murky kind which had been clouding the nightmares. This was clean, crisp, sun. Like it was the height of summer and not the middle of October.

"What am I doing here?" I asked the forest around me. There was no answer, not even the wind rustling through the trees. In a way, this was almost *more* eerie than the scary forest. Perhaps, that was all this was, an alternative narrative so that I'd get too caught up in the new area and let my guard down.

I stepped forward, trying not to overthink this too much. Like with the other dream, I'd simply have to do what the dream wanted me to and hope it wasn't as bad as the ones I'd been having before.

The path didn't hurt my feet like in the other dream, which I took to be a good sign. Perhaps, I wouldn't wake up from this dream screaming.

Birds began to sing through the woods, and I was certain I could hear the burrowing of other creatures.

One word could describe this scene. *Alive*. This was nothing like the other dreams. I should trust that.

The path opened up into a familiar clearing, though, this time, there wasn't a coffin in it, something I was glad for.

"Mother?" I called. It stood to reason that if the coffin wasn't here, and the whole tone of the dream was different, that Mother would be here and awake. I knew it wasn't *real*, but it was enough for me. My dreams and visions had been coming true, and if she was up and about in the dream, then it would be a good sign for the morning.

That was the theory anyway.

"Mother?" I called again.

There wasn't an answer. I stepped further into the clearing, determined to get to the middle and look around. She had to be here. She'd been in all the other dreams.

Even when I could see all the paths into the clearing, I couldn't see any trace of another person.

"Mother?"

A chuckle sounded from behind me.

I spun around. "Jake?" My brow furrowed as I tried to make sense of what I was seeing. How was he here?

"You seem disappointed to see me," he observed.

"Not disappointed, just surprised," I countered, though even as I said it, I knew I was lying. I wanted to see Mother, not him. Of course, I didn't say that out loud. Topher was right. He had an ego, and the last thing I wanted was to inflame it for no reason.

Wait. These dreams had been coming true, Did that mean we were going to have a meeting like this while I was awake? Perhaps, I should see how this played out before I got too excited about it.

"What are you doing here?" I asked him.

"You tell me, Kelis, it's your dream."

"Oh. Right." The dream that knew it was a dream. Though, I supposed dream-Mother might also know it was a dream, but she hadn't been able to talk to tell me that.

"So, what am I doing here?" he asked.

"I'm not sure. I normally let my dreams tell me what they want to happen," I told him.

"Then I shall too. What would you like me to do?"

I frowned. "I'm not sure. We can sit and talk if you want?" Though now that I'd said it out loud, it sounded ridiculous.

"I have a better idea," he assured me.

"You do?" What could be better than the two of us finally spending some time together? Even if it was in my dream. I suppose that the fact my others had come true was lingering in the back of my mind.

"Yes." He stepped close to me, the heat of his body radiating to mine. I tried not to let myself get too distracted by that.

He reached out a hand and cupped my cheek, smoothing a thumb across my skin as he did. For a brief moment, I imagined Topher in his place, but the image was gone as soon as it had arrived. What was with that? I pushed the thoughts away and focused on the guy standing in front of me.

"You're the most beautiful princess I've ever laid

eyes on," he said.

"Have you seen many princesses up close?" I asked. He'd never said anything like this before, but that didn't mean anything. This was a dream, after all. It could be telling the future and not the past.

"Admittedly not, but I've seen you. I have no doubt you are."

It was a lie, and we both knew it. I was far from the most beautiful person in Enchantia, nevermind the most beautiful princess, but I wasn't going to say anything about it.

Before I could say anything else, he leaned in and pressed his lips against mine. It took me a moment to realize what was happening and to respond.

He pulled me closer, deepening his kiss. I pushed my body against his, knowing this was how the kiss should go. I'd read enough romance books before my work for Enchantia had taken over. This was how a first kiss was supposed to go.

Wait. This was a second kiss. He came to me in my room last week. I wasn't convinced I was enjoying this kiss any more than the one that tasted of stale wine. I hoped our kiss in real life would be better than this one.

We broke apart, and I smiled up at him, unsure what else to do. I couldn't tell him that he was a disappointing kiss. Especially because it was all happening in *my* mind, so this was what I thought kissing him would be like.

Before I could do or say anything else, the dream faded into darkness, and sleep became my friend once more.

~

I stretched across the bed, waking up at a leisurely pace. I hadn't felt this rested in weeks, and it was nice to finally feel like I'd managed a decent sleep despite the weird dream. I wasn't sure if I wanted that to be prophetic or not, given my confused feelings towards Jake. Perhaps, I needed to call for Rhi and ask her what she thought about the situation. But then, what did it matter. Other than Rhi's assurances, I had no proof at all that Jake even wanted anything with me.

I sat up and put the pendant around my neck, pleased with how it was performing so far. Though perhaps, Mother's recovery yesterday also had an effect on my sleep. It had nothing to warn me about. Yes, that was what it had to be. Mother was better, so my dream had nothing bad to say. Though it seemed my strange new visions weren't going to stop despite that.

It didn't matter, it was later in the day than I'd been getting up in the past few days, and I had too much to do to waste time. I threw the covers off and got out of bed, padding over to my wash station and using a cloth to give myself a quick wash. I should try and get up earlier so I could have a bath tomorrow. I could keep myself clean enough with magic, but nothing could beat the hot water in front of a fire.

"You seem perky today," the mirror observed.

"And you look the same as ever," I replied instantly.

"It's unnatural. I don't like it."

"You don't like anything." I went off to my closet to pick out some clothes, not letting the mirror get to me.

"I like plenty of things. *Beautiful* things," the mirror insisted.

"Oh, yes, and you're the perfect judge of beauty. How is it you can tell what's beautiful and what isn't?" I asked. "Is it part of how you were enchanted?"

"That's none of your business," it retorted.

I picked out a black velvet dress, feeling more confident after the dream I'd had in my choice and my own individuality. I wanted Topher to see me being me.

No. Wait. Not Topher, Jake.

The oddest part of my dream came back to me. What was I going to do with that piece of information? Did it mean anything? Or had it simply been a moment of doubt? Topher and Jake were opposites in many ways. It was only my confusion over Jake coming to the front; I was convinced of that.

I changed into my outfit for the day, happy with how it turned out. This was one of my favorites, and I knew it would give me the confidence boost I needed.

Perhaps, I'd take the afternoon off after getting through my work today. I could go cast spells in the courtyard, or take the others on a picnic. That would be nice. A chance to relax and have a good time with friends.

Yes. That was what I was going to do.

I collected my wand, then looked into the full-length mirror. I lifted the wand and spelled my hair. It twisted into two long braids of shining black. Adequate. I was certain other people could do more elaborate things with their magic, but I didn't care, this was what I liked, and I wasn't going to change myself anymore.

"That hairstyle is more befitting of a cowherd than a princess," the mirror said the moment I was back in view.

"Then it's practical, just what I need from my hair," I pointed out.

"Practical is another way of saying you have to work hard for your living."

"I *do* work hard," I pointed out.

"Not that I ever see."

"That's because you're stuck in my room all day and can't see the rest of the palace," I said offhandedly.

"But I know what time you leave your room."

I shrugged. "I'm eighteen, barely even an adult. Did you do *your* job straight away?"

"I'm an enchanted mirror. What do you think?" it quipped.

I laughed despite myself. "I don't know what to think. You never tell me anything about yourself." And yet my relationship with the mirror wasn't the most one-sided one I had at the moment.

"And nor will I. It is none of your business."

"Then I don't want to know." I slipped my wand into my holster and went over my day in my head. Perfect. "I've enjoyed our little chat, as always, but I'm afraid I need to get on with things that don't concern you." Satisfaction went through me at that one. It was a cheap shot, but the mirror deserved it.

I left the room and signaled to a passing servant.

"Your Highness," the girl said, dipping into a curtsy. "How may I help you?"

"Can you send a message to my cousin, Adam, and his friends asking whether or not they'd join me for a picnic lunch?" I requested.

"Of course, Your Highness." She paused for a moment. "Would you like me to alert the kitchens too?"

"I'd appreciate that, thank you."

"It's no problem, Your Highness." She curtsied again and then hurried off to do what I'd requested. That would give me something to look forward to after I'd finished working.

~

The corridor was deserted, but that was to be expected. The rain of a few days ago had given way to glorious sunshine, and everyone who could be was outside enjoying it. I would be, too, later. But before I could go on a picnic with my friends, I needed to get some work done.

"Princess Kelis," a servant called. They were out of breath from running through the palace. Dread flowed through my veins. This couldn't be good.

"What is it?" I asked, turning around and walking towards him.

"Your Father sent me. He said there's been a complication, and you're needed in your parents' room immediately."

"Did he tell you what it was about?" I asked, trying to keep my voice steady. The last thing I needed was for the servants to think I was worried about what was going on. There was far too much at stake for that.

"No, he simply said that it didn't matter what you were doing or who you were with, but to tell you he needed to see you immediately."

"Thank you. Would you tell the steward I'm with my parents and am not to be disturbed? Anything that needs my attention can be left on my desk, I'll see to it as soon as I can," I instructed.

"Of course, Your Highness. I'll see to it."

"Thank you." I didn't wait for him to say anything else and headed to the closest set of stairs.

I jogged up them, heading to my parents' room as fast as I could.

As soon as I was there, I pushed open the door, not bothering to knock. Father had sent for me, which meant he knew I was coming.

"What's happened?" I asked as soon as I was in the

room.

I stopped in my tracks the moment I saw the red rings around Father's eyes.

"She won't respond to me," he whispered, his voice hoarse.

"No." I shook my head and stumbled back, knocking myself against a wall. "Is it just a deep sleep?" I asked, though, I knew deep down that wasn't the case.

"She's not waking up."

"I'll call for the doctor," I promised, knowing from the way Father was acting that he was barely able to send a servant after me, nevermind the doctor.

I popped my head out of the room and called out to a nearby servant. After I'd sent them off to find the doctor, I turned back to the room to go to Mother's bedside. Before I could, seven small figures came rushing towards me.

"What's happened, Princess?" One asked.

"Mother's taken a turn," I admitted, letting them in so we could talk more privately. The last thing we needed was for the wrong person to overhear the truth and cause more problems.

"What kind of turn?" Six asked.

"She's unconscious. Not responding. It's like the stories..."

Even before I'd finished, the dwarves rushed into the room to see her. I didn't even try to stop them. These men had been by Mother's side for most of her life, caring for her and keeping her safe. They'd want to do the same now.

"How did you know something was wrong?" I asked Four, who was the last one to pass me.

"We can sense it in the air. Like we could feel the return of the witch's magic."

I shuddered at the thought. I hoped Mother's situation didn't have anything to do with the woman from her stories. The last thing any of us needed was to go up against her again.

And so we started our vigil at Mother's side, nobody saying much. Anyone who walked into the room would know there was something bad going on. Mother would hate this. She'd want all of us to carry on as normal with smiles on our faces. But that wasn't going to be possible. None of us had her talent for turning everything good.

~

I paced back and forth, hating the wait for the doctor. I'd have to see if he'd take a retainer to be more accessible for us. Nothing was too much when it came to getting decent care for Mother.

Finally, the knock knocked on the door. I rushed over and pulled it open.

"Thank you for coming, doctor."

"No problem, Your Highness. Is everything all right?"

I shook my head. "Unfortunately not. Mother has taken a turn for the worse."

"Then show me in; we have no time to waste," he insisted.

I moved out of the way and waved toward the bedchamber. The doctor hurried into the room and began his examination. I resisted the urge to bite my nails, knowing that it wasn't a very princess-like thing to do.

"Is her food being tasted?" the doctor asked.

Father simply sat by Mother's side, holding her hand in his and staring into her face.

"Yes. Everything. And we've gotten rid of what we

thought was the probable cause too," I answered when it became clear Father wouldn't.

"That's good. What happened when you destroyed the poisoned food? I assume you did destroy it and didn't just throw it away?"

"Of course," I assured him. "We burned it."

"Excellent. What happened when you did that?" he asked.

"A noxious smoke came from it."

"Hmm." He nodded. "Definitely poison then." He checked Mother's pulse and did a few other visual checks. "As far as I can tell, nothing has changed from last time. I have no explanation for why this has happened. I could suggest a few remedies, but..."

"Write them down anyway, please," I requested. "We want to try everything we can."

"I can understand that, Your Highness. I'll write it all down." He dipped his head and went back to where his bag was packed and started scribbling down.

I stood there for a moment, staring at Mother's unconscious form on the bed, and Father's distraught figure leaning over her. He was a desperate man. He'd do anything to bring her back from this state. And he'd take her place in a heartbeat. Then again, so would I.

"Here you are, Your Highness," the doctor said, handing me the list of things to try.

"Thank you, doctor," I responded. "Please see the steward for payment. You can negotiate a retainer from him too, so long as you agree to be summoned to the palace at short notice."

"Of course. I'd be honored to serve the royal family in such a way."

"Thank you." I dismissed him with a wave of my hand.

He hurried out, no doubt, to get his money, as well as escaping the stifling atmosphere in the room. The tension was mounting by the moment, and I wouldn't want to be in here any longer than I needed to be either.

"I have something that might help, Princess," one of the dwarves said.

I turned to find Seven standing next to me. The dwarves had appeared a couple of minutes before the doctor did, making it very crowded in here, but they refused to leave. I could understand that. I didn't want to leave Mother's side either, but I knew I'd have to. It was somewhat reassuring that the dwarves were going to be here instead of me. They'd stood vigil last time, and Mother had woken up, I was going to take that as a good sign.

"What is that?" I asked, gesturing towards whatever it was he was holding.

He held out the tiny charms for me to look at properly. "They're called *protectors of poison.* It's an old wives' tale. If you hang them above the bed of someone who is suffering from a poisoning, then they'll get better."

"Will it work?" I didn't want to get my hopes up, but even one glance at my unconscious Mother was enough to convince me to try anything that had a chance of helping.

"I don't know," Seven admitted. "Your Mother is the only person I know who has been poisoned. I looked into old wives' tales after the last time, just in case..." He choked on his words, clearly unable to think about the disaster losing Mother would cause.

I placed a hand on his shoulder, giving it a squeeze. "With all of us watching over her, she's going to come through this," I promised him.

How had I ended up being the strong one in this

situation? Inside, I was torn apart. I couldn't lose Mother. She was everything to me.

"Can I place them above the bed?" I asked Seven.

"Of course, Princess." He handed me the charms, and I took them gladly. I wasn't sure if they were going to work, but considering the dwarves had been right about the pendant I was wearing, I was willing to take a chance they were right on this too.

"Thank you." I hurried towards the bed and hung it above Mother's head, before turning to watch her and see if there was any difference in her. There wasn't a single movement.

"I don't understand," Father said, pain lancing through every word. "We've treated our people so well. We've done everything right. Why is this happening to her?" He looked up at me, his eyes filled with terror.

I leaned in and pressed a kiss against his forehead. "We'll find a way of fighting this," I promised. "She'll wake up."

"I don't know what I'd do without her."

"Me neither," I responded, trying my best to hold my own despair back. "Have you tried kissing her?"

He frowned. "Do you think that will work?"

"You haven't tried?"

"I can't say it crossed my mind," he admitted. I hated how dazed he sounded. This wasn't the man I was used to. "All I could think about was how much losing her would hurt."

Was the magic that was causing Mother's illness and my dreams affecting Father? It had to be, especially after kissing her had worked the first time. That would have been the first thing Father tried under normal circumstances.

"Why don't you try now," I suggested.

Father nodded. "I just can't believe I didn't think of that."

"You've had other things on your mind," I pointed out.

"I know, but..."

"Father, please, don't blame yourself. Something bigger than us is going on here," I assured him. Even if that wasn't true, I'd have told him as much. Right now, Father needed reminding that this wasn't his fault. None of us could have seen it coming.

He nodded and rose to his feet. He sucked in a deep breath as he stared down at Mother.

"I love you, Snow," he whispered. He leaned in and kissed her on the lips.

I held my breath, waiting for something to happen, even though I wasn't sure what that would be. I was the only person in the room who hadn't been through this exact situation before, and I didn't dare to ask.

Father pulled back, staring down at Mother with a forlorn expression on his face. "Snow?" he asked.

Nothing happened.

"Maybe you should try again?" I suggested.

"Yes," he agreed. "That's the only thing I can do."

Father kissed Mother again.

Still nothing.

The realization of what that meant sunk in the moment Father let out a keening cry.

My heart broke. For Mother, who was going through the pain of a poisoning again. For Father, who had to watch the love of his life slipping away and be unable to do anything about it. For people of Enchantia, who were facing losing their Queen.

But most of all, my heart broke for me. For the loss of my Mother and the person who'd always believed in me. The woman who'd taught me right from wrong.

In that moment, I forgot I was a princess. I was simply a girl who was about to lose everything.

# THRONE OF WANDS

## 21ST OCTOBER

I pushed the fork around my plate, not wanting to eat, but knowing I had to. No one else in the hall seemed to be having the same problem, though that made sense. They had no idea that Mother was on her deathbed, or that the future of the kingdom was at risk. At times like this, it was easy to hate being a princess.

"Is there anything I can do to help?" Topher asked as he dropped into the seat next to me.

"I don't think so." I smiled at him, but it felt forced. I was certain he'd be able to tell. I was normally better at keeping my expression steadier.

"There hasn't been any change?" He reached out and grabbed one of the soft bread rolls from the basket which had been placed in front of me by the servants, no doubt they'd hoped they'd entice me into eating. Father had probably encouraged them to do it.

"Not a good one," I admitted. "I'm not sure what we're going to do next."

"We can look into things in the library later if you want?"

I shrugged, though time with him wasn't to be sniffed at. "If you want. But I understand if you have better things to do."

"There's nothing better than helping you, Kelis."

My heart fluttered despite the pressure with Mother. Wasn't this the kind of thing I was supposed to do when Jake was around, rather than Topher?

As if he was called by my thoughts, Jake dropped down onto the chair on my other side. He looked fed up, despite it being so early.

"Why does everyone here insist on getting up so early?" he muttered.

"I think it's so they can get things done," Topher suggested. "There's plenty of things that take all day."

"But *I* don't need to do them," Jake countered. "I could have breakfast later."

I took a deep breath, not wanting to snap at him.

"I'm sure you can," Topher said lightly. "Just ask the servants to bring you some food, and they will."

"It isn't as good as the food served here," Jake responded, throwing his legs over the side of the chair.

Embarrassment flared to life inside me. I hoped no one was paying too much attention, this wasn't the way I wanted them to see my friends act. Could I say something to Jake about it? No, I couldn't. Not if I wanted him to take me seriously.

What was I thinking? Between my kingdom and a boy, I should be choosing my kingdom every time.

"Can't you make breakfast later, Kelis?" Jake asked.

"No." The word came out more curtly than I expected. "It's been at this time for my entire life, it won't be changing."

"That's a shame." He waved towards one of the servants. "Coffee."

I waited for him to say please, and when he didn't, my lips curled into a grimace of distaste. What did he think he was doing? No one deserved to be treated that way.

Someone said my name from somewhere close by, pulling me from thoughts of Jake's attitude. I looked around for the person, but couldn't work out who had spoken. It wasn't a voice I recognized. I tried not to stare too much. Whoever it was would no doubt introduce themselves when they were ready to. All I had to do was sit still and make sure everyone knew where I was.

At least, Jake had stopped complaining, though I was still dimly aware of him muttering under his breath. I rolled my eyes. Was he ever going to stop? I didn't understand what his problem was. Breakfast would continue for another hour or so, he could have come down then.

"Kelis," Topher said under his breath.

I turned to see him nodding toward a spot in front of me. A woman in long dark green robes strode towards me with all the confidence of someone who didn't care that their clothes weren't white. I understood that. My own black dress went against all the conventions of Enchantia. I'd already stopped trying to include more white in it. It wouldn't make any difference to how *some* people would see me.

"Your Highness," the woman said, dipping her head.

"Welcome to Enchantia," I said smoothly, guessing

from her dress that she wasn't a local. The smile on her face told me I'd guessed right. "I hope you're being made at home."

She chuckled. "Everyone has been pleasant so far," she admitted.

"When did you arrive?" I asked pleasantly. I should have asked for her name first, but I was distracted and hadn't thought about that. Father would have, though.

"This morning. The moment the guards heard I was a healer, they were very insistent that I meet you."

I perked up at that. "They were right to," I assured her. "What is your name?"

"You can call me Vanessa," the woman said.

I cocked my head to the side. "Is that not your real name?" I asked, more curious than insulted.

A knowing smile crossed her face. "Not much gets by you, does it, child?"

Jake scoffed from beside me. I threw him a dirty look, but he missed it as he went back to eating. He was going to start causing problems if he kept acting this way. I couldn't have Enchantia looking bad because of how an unofficial representative was acting. I didn't want to have the awkward conversation with him that might lead to Jake hating me forever.

"No, it isn't my real name," the healer admitted. "But you wouldn't be able to pronounce it."

I frowned. She didn't have an accent. But if she wasn't from a different land, then why would I have any problems saying her name? I pushed the thought aside. It was possible she used a different sort of magic to the ones we did in the rest of Enchantia, which resulted in some kind of unusual name. If that was the case, then I didn't need to press her about it. She was entitled to her privacy.

"Thank you for heeding our call to aid. You'll be taken to the appropriate rooms when the time is right," I assured her.

"I am at your service." She dipped into another bow and then stepped back.

"Do you think she can help?" I asked Topher quietly.

"It's worth a try," he said. "Though I don't know enough about any kind of healing magic."

I nodded. I was in the same boat. Well, I didn't know a lot about any kind of magic. I was trying to fix that now, but it was taking more time than I liked. If only I'd paid more attention as a child.

Jake started laughing from my other side, pulling our attention to him.

"Yes?" I asked, raising an eyebrow. He was getting on my nerves, which I hoped was only temporary. I'd liked him for so long, and now, it was all slipping away.

"You're inviting all these people here and expecting them to make a difference. Who are they even supposed to be treating? The town crazy woman?" Jake got out through his laughter.

I narrowed my eyes, not knowing where to start with that one. As far as I knew, there wasn't a town crazy woman anyway. We prided ourselves in looking after the health of our citizens in Enchantia, including things that only seemed to be wrong in people's minds.

"You know, Jake, you should really try empathy one day. You'd be surprised how far it can get you," Topher said, louder than I liked. He scraped back his chair. "I'll see you in a bit, Kelis."

Topher didn't wait for me to reply. Instead, he walked off. I followed him with my gaze, feeling as if my main back-up had left along with him.

"You should lighten up, Kelis. Have some fun," Jake

said, bumping into me with his shoulder.

I scowled at him. What was wrong with him? I was clearly presiding over breakfast, which meant my parents weren't able to. He should be able to work out that something serious was going on, but apparently, he couldn't.

"I have things I need to be getting on with," I said instead of one of the multitudes of insults going through my head. "But if you need anything, I'm sure the staff would be more than happy to see to your needs." I stood up and brushed off my skirts. Feeling more confident than I perhaps should, I walked off, leaving him to watch me go...potentially.

I had no idea if he actually cared enough for that.

I closed my eyes and took a deep breath, leaning against the wall outside my parents' bed-chamber. I knew I had to go in there and not only out of duty. I *wanted* to know Mother was all right. But that doesn't stop the whole situation from being exhausting. I wanted her to be well again. I was doing the best I could at keeping the kingdom going without my parents' guidance, I was feeling lost. Plus, it wasn't like there was anything pressing I should bother them with. All they had to do was focus on Mother getting better.

If only it was that easy.

"Come on, Kelis," I muttered to myself. I pushed away from the wall and checked around me to ensure I was alone. I supposed it wouldn't matter if I was or not, the servants knew more about what was going on than the nobles did, and they were keeping their mouths shut for the love of my family. If they saw me taking a moment to myself, then they'd turn the other way and pretend they hadn't seen anything at all.

At least, that was my hope.

Slowly, I made my way to the door and rapped three times. I didn't wait for a response. I didn't need permission to enter, but I felt like I should announce myself beforehand. It was only fair; this was my parents' safe space.

"It's me."

"Kelis," Father's voice came through the room, laced with exhaustion. I wished I could take offer him some relief, but I wasn't in much better shape.

I closed the gap between us and sat down on the second chair in front of the fire, trying not to think about it as being Mother's. It was better for all of us if I kept thoughts like that to myself.

"How are things in here?" I asked.

"The same," he admitted. "The dwarves are still doing their vigil, but I don't think it's going to achieve anything." He looked as tired as he sounded, something I wasn't going to mention to him.

I nodded. "Have you tried kissing her again?"

He sighed and rubbed a hand over his face. The movement caused the small grey hairs at his temple to stand on end. I could have sworn they weren't there before all of this started.

"Every day. I've barely slept from trying. I don't know what else to do."

My heart broke for him. Father had been a pillar of strength for as long as I could remember, and now, he was reduced to sitting and worrying about his wife like this. I had to wonder if this was part of whatever was going on. Perhaps whoever it was that caused this was doing it on purpose to weaken Enchantia. We didn't have any enemies that I knew of, but for all I knew, my parents had been keeping one from me.

"Have any more apples arrived?" I asked, wanting to assure myself that the threat of new poison was over.

Father shook his head. "Though, you'd know better than I do. You've been the one checking the inventories."

"I know, but if someone was determined enough to try and harm Mother, then I figured they may be intelligent enough to get apples in a different way."

"I hadn't even thought of that. I'm sorry, Kelis. I should be protecting you..." For the first time in my life, I could see tears threatening to fall from my Father's eyes.

I reached out and placed my hand over his. I gave it a reassuring squeeze, hoping Father would accept my comfort.

"I'm fine," I promised. It was only partly a lie, and if it eased his mind, then that was all the better.

"Are you, really?"

"Father, I'm fine. I have friends here..."

"Ah, yes, the ones who came with Adam. How are they getting on?"

I shrugged, not wanting to get into the complications that were my budding friendships with Topher and Rhi. Nor my complex feelings about Jake. Even I couldn't make them out. "Fine. They're keeping themselves busy." Perhaps I should have told him about my worries regarding how Jake was acting in front of the guests, but father didn't need any more worries added to his plate. And certainly, not ones that I could deal with on my own.

"That's good. We haven't been very good hosts to them."

"No one is thinking about that," I assured him.

"Everyone who knows about the situation hopes for Mother's swift recovery. They're not focusing on the fact we're not paying them much attention." Then again, I had no idea what the people around the palace were saying, in general. For all I knew, most of them hadn't even noticed my parents' absence and were carrying on with their normal lives as if nothing at all was wrong.

"I hope you're right. But we should prepare for some hard questions when all of this is over," Father said.

"The people of Enchantia won't think twice about it," I assured him. "They love Mother, and would do anything for her. If they knew she was sick, they'd be out in the streets singing for her." Which was one of the many reasons we *weren't* telling them. It would bring the whole kingdom to its knees.

"I have faith in them. But a good leader prepares for all of the possibilities in front of them."

I nodded, knowing father was right. My parents hadn't gotten the respect they had by running the kingdom badly. "Do you think it'll be all right if I go in and see her?" I asked, gesturing towards the room where Mother still lay prone and unresponding. Even the thought of it was choking me up.

"She'd like that," father said. "I don't know if she can hear us when we talk to her, but I hope so. If we're lucky, perhaps it would help her find her way back to us."

I forced a smile to my face, though I suspected it didn't reach my eyes. "We can hope."

I got to my feet and leaned over to kiss Father on the forehead. A brief peace flitted over his face. At least, I was able to bring him some. With everything going on, it was a relief to see he could still feel positive emotions. I squeezed his hand, before turning to head back into the bedchamber where mother lay.

The walk between the fireplace and Mother felt far longer than it should. It was almost like the dread weighing down on me was making it harder to go in.

Torches flickered on the walls, illuminating the bed surrounded by dwarves. They looked up at me as I entered, and my heart broke for them. I'd never seen them look so sad before.

I made my way over to the bed, slipping in between Seven and Two and perched on the sheets. I leaned in and took Mother's hand in mine. I stroked it gently as I tried to hold back my own tears at the sight of her. She was deathly pale, and if I hadn't been assured that she was still alive, then I'd doubt it.

"Hi, Mother," I said, sniffing to hold back the tears. Even if it was only the dwarves who could see me, I didn't want them to see me break down. Part of my training to be the future queen was to make sure people couldn't see what I was feeling when I didn't want them to. It was something I could put to use now.

"I know you might not be able to hear me right now, but we're working as hard as we can to find out what's happened and how we can fix it. I promise, we're not going to give up until we have the answer."

One of the dwarves placed a hand on my back, offering me comfort through his touch. I appreciated it. Out of everybody in the whole palace, they were the ones who understood what we were going through the most. They'd been the ones who had stood by mother as she'd gone through this the first time, after all.

"Have any of you had any ideas about how we might be able to fix this?" I asked, knowing what their answers would be even before they said anything. It would take a miracle for them to say something they hadn't for days.

"We're sorry, Kelis," One said. "We've done everything we can think of. Even the things we tried the first time that didn't work."

I nodded solemnly, trying not to let it get to me. This whole situation was beginning to feel as if we'd never find a solution to it at all.

"It's all right. I knew that would be the case." I took a deep breath, knowing I had to remain calm.

A knock sounded from the outer door, but I ignored it. Voices rumbled in the other room, though it wasn't until I heard Father's join them that I paid any attention. The conversation grew nearer, making it clear that they were coming into Mother's room. I looked up to see Father standing in the doorway with the healer from breakfast.

She looked different. Now, she was wearing the clothing I assumed she was most comfortable with. The bright colors of her scarves and beads stood out among the white-clad Enchantians. It was a good thing it was just the dwarves who were there. I knew they wouldn't do anything to make her uncomfortable.

"This is my daughter..." Father started.

"Kelis, yes, we met at breakfast," Vanessa said. "She's a credit to you, Your Majesty."

A real smile spread over Father's face at that. I was glad of it.

"And this is the Queen?" she asked, gesturing to Mother unnecessarily.

"Yes. She's been like this for days, and nothing we've tried has worked," I said.

Vanessa nodded. "May I get closer so I can examine her?"

"Of course," Father responded. "Kelis can stay with

you to help." The expression on his face begged me not to contradict him. Though, of course, I would never even have thought of it. I'd do anything for mother.

"I will help in whatever way I can," I promised.

"Good." The older woman set her bag on the bed as the dwarves made their way out of the bedchamber and into the outer room with Father.

Vanessa rummaged through her bag and pulled out a small packet of something.

"What would you like me to do?" I asked, hoping she'd explain what it was she was doing. There was certainly something magical about her as there had been about a lot of the healers who had come to visit us and tried to give a diagnosis. But this wasn't like the normal magic I saw in Enchantia. And it *definitely* wasn't like any magic I'd ever performed myself.

"Put this on the fire, please." She handed me the packet.

"Of course." I paused as I took it, wondering if it was impolite to ask too many questions.

"It will purify the air of any evil magic. Some people say it's nonsense, but I've never had a spell go wrong after using it, so better safe than sorry," she answered before I even had a chance to voice my query.

"How did you know..."

"What you'd ask?"

I nodded.

"Nothing fancy, dear. It's a question I get asked almost every time I do something like this," she explained as she laid out a few things on the bed next to Mother.

"Oh." I took the packet over to the fire and dropped it in.

After a moment, the flames flickered from orange to blue. My eyes widened.

“Stand back, dear. I need to examine your mother and need the firelight,” Vanessa instructed.

I did as she instructed and watched awestruck as she lifted her arms. The beads dripping from her sleeves clanked against one another as she waved them above Mother’s prone form. There was something beautiful about it, even if I didn’t understand any of the movements she was making, or the words she was saying.

The room grew hotter as she progressed. Although, that could have just been me. I wiped my sweaty palms on my skirts, grateful I’d already gone back to wearing my black clothing and didn’t have to worry about leaving stains that people could see.

Vanessa blinked rapidly as if something was happening to her. Should I step in and wake her up from her trance? I didn’t want her to hurt herself because of me or my family, even if it was getting me the answers I needed.

The temperature increased again, and I had to tug at the collar of my dress to try and get some cool air flowing around me. I was distracted moments later by Vanessa’s entire body beginning to shake. I stepped forward and reached out, wanting to stop whatever was happening to her.

“Vanessa?” I whispered, hoping it would rouse her without any damage. I should have asked about what would happen to her while she was doing her thing. That way, I could have been prepared.

She gasped, and her eyes snapped open. The tension in the room slipped away, and the heat died down around me. Huh. Perhaps, I hadn’t been imagining it, after all.

“Is everything all right?” I asked.

"With me, yes. But with your mother, I'm afraid it isn't quite so simple," Vanessa answered in her normal voice. Somehow I'd expected it to be laced with power and the ancestors, or something like that.

I needed to do more research into other magic users so I could avoid being so judgmental in the future.

"What's wrong with her?" The question we'd been asking ourselves almost constantly came out before anything else. I cursed myself for not asking about *her* health first.

"I don't think this will be news to you, but the Queen has been cursed."

A lead weight dropped in my stomach. We'd suspected it all along, but it felt different to have someone else confirm it.

I crossed my fingers and hoped for the best while fearing for the worst. "Is there anything you can do to help her?"

"Unfortunately, there's nothing *I* can do."

Her stress on the word "I" didn't go unnoticed.

"Does that mean there's something someone else can?" I asked.

"Yes. And I think you know it has to be you."

# 22ND OCTOBER

I clutched the carved apple necklace I kept from the dwarves' house and hoped it would ward off the dream I could feel was coming. I'd hoped that I was past this now that I knew what the problem was, and that mother had succumbed to whatever curse had been cast on her. What else could I see now?

The dream began to take shape, and I found myself in a dark corridor lit with torches. There wasn't anything defining about the place, so I suspected it was nothing more than a construct of my dream, and a way to get me where I needed to go. But then again, what did I know about how these things worked? Mother hadn't followed the path of my dreams. But that didn't change that I'd seen what was coming.

Which meant this might not be literal, but could

simply be a representation of something to come. Either that or I was reading too much into this. I had no idea how my dreams worked, and I doubted anyone could tell me.

The dream propelled me down the corridor. The lack of fear was odd. In the dreams with Mother, I'd always felt as if I was heading towards something bad. Perhaps I'd get lucky, and I'd enter a room and find Mother standing there with flushed cheeks and lustrous hair, rather than the sickly pale imitation of herself that I'd left behind.

When I came to a door, I didn't even hesitate before pushing it open and stepping inside. It was brighter here, although I didn't think that had anything to do with the torches around the room. Despite it being underground, and me having no way of *knowing* how I knew that, it almost seemed as if it was lit by natural light.

My heart sank as I realized that, even though they all had their backs to me, none of the people were Mother. So much for that theory. It had been more wishful thinking to begin with.

"Hello?" I said, hoping to gain their attention. Actually, that was a lie. I had no control over what happened to me in the dream, even if it was easier to pretend to myself that I did.

When the people in the room didn't respond to my questioning, I decided the only thing I could do was move into the middle of the room and try to find out more about them. I moved between each of the people, looking them up and down and trying to make sense of what was happening.

I sucked in a breath without thinking about it as an odd sensation of familiarity flooded through me. Why did it feel like I knew these people?

I studied one face after another, trying to work out if I knew any of their names. The harder I looked, the more certain I became that I'd never met them before, or certainly not in my living memory. Perhaps, this was a past life or something like that?

"We're waiting for Kelis," the girl at the front, with long golden brown hair said.

Well, that theory went out the window. They knew my name. Which only left the option of this being more of the future. I tried to find the words to answer the girl, but instead, I found myself transfixed by her eyes.

Something about them caught my attention, but I couldn't put my finger on what it was. This was getting annoying. What was the point of having dreams that gave me hints about the future if they weren't going to explain things to me. The only thing I knew with any certainty was that I wasn't going to dismiss this one as merely a dream.

Before I could work out what it was, the whole dream began to fade, and sleep overcame me again. Despite being disappointed, I was also a little relieved that nothing worse than a mystery had happened. Memories of the prophetic dreams I'd had about Mother still haunted my mind, and I had no desire to experience anything like that again, even if it gave me useful information.

~

I brushed a strand of dark hair away from Mother's face. She looked even paler than before, but perhaps that was more in my imagination than anything else. Vanessa had left some of her packets of purifiers for us to use on the room when we felt like it needed it, along with instructions on how to reach her if we needed more. I appreciated that, but I wished she could have done more to help Mother than give me the cryptic suggestion that *I* was the only one who could stop what was happening to her.

Had I tried true love's kiss? I knew that was normally a romantic thing, but it would work between a mother and child too, wouldn't it? Especially when the child was adopted like me. I knew mother loved me with all her heart, and she knew I felt that way about her. Why wouldn't it work?

But surely, I'd tried to kiss her before?

I racked my brains to work out whether I had or not, but it was hard to tell in the haze of all the things that had happened in the past couple of weeks. I sighed. There was only one way to find out if I had or not. I leaned in and brushed a kiss against her forehead, putting all of the love and affection I could muster into the one gesture.

Unsurprisingly, nothing happened.

A fat tear rolled down my cheek and splashed against her cheek. The sight of it was enough to break the dam, and a swift flood of them broke free. I wasn't sure how long I cried, or even if anyone saw me doing it, but oddly, it helped me feel a bit better.

As the sobs subsided, I started to focus on what had me so upset. To my surprise, my sadness turned into a smile.

"Do you remember when I was seven, and I broke the teapot in the kitchen?" I asked Mother. She might not be able to answer me, but that didn't mean she couldn't hear me. In fact, I hoped she *could* hear me. It meant that she'd be able to hear everybody else who took the time to talk to her daily too.

"I'd been trying to take it off the shelf so I could practice holding a tea party for the ladies of the court." I chuckled at the memory. "I overstretched and knocked it off the shelf instead, and it smashed into hundreds of tiny pieces. I thought you and Father would be so angry. But when I told you, all you did was take my hand and guide me back into the kitchen. You taught me how to pick it up and made sure I knew to always clean up after myself, even if there were other people whose job it technically was. E*specially* when it was someone else's job. That way, I'd learn that I shouldn't take advantage of other people. And then Father told me that it was a good leader's responsibility to know how to do even the lowliest of jobs in order to better understand their people."

I closed my eyes, enjoying the warm feeling of happy moments. Now that the floodgates had opened, memory after memory came back to me, and I told Mother about every single one. None of them were particularly important in the grand scheme of things, but they meant a lot to me, and for that reason, they'd mean a lot to Mother too.

"And then there was the time you taught me to ride. At first, I was scared of the horse, but you showed me how to feed the horses apples and how to talk to them." I'd only been ten at the time, which was older than most noble girls learned to ride, but I'd been busy with a lot of the other lessons my parents had started for me. They wanted me to have a well-rounded education so I could become a good leader when my time came. I'd forever be grateful for that.

Eventually, I drifted into silence, doing nothing more than stroking mother's hair and settling into the comfort of being in the room with someone who loved me, even if they couldn't say anything.

A soft knock pulled my attention away from Mother. I looked up to find Father standing in the doorway, an apologetic expression on his face.

"Is everything all right?" I asked.

"Yes, I just didn't realize you were still here," he admitted.

I leaned in and kissed Mother on the forehead again, before slipping off the bed. "I can leave you alone."

"You don't have to..."

I flashed him a reassuring smile. "You're not getting a lot of alone time with her either. You should get some in while you can."

"You've become a wonderful young woman, Kelis. I'm proud of you. And your Mother is too."

"Thank you." As I passed him, I went up on my toes and kissed him on the cheek. He was shorter than I seemed to think he was, though I wasn't sure if that was because so much had changed for me in the past few weeks, or because of how much pressure there was on Father. "I told her stories," I said.

"She'll have liked that," he assured me.

I reached out and squeezed his hand. "I'll be back this afternoon..."

He shook his head. "Come back tomorrow, Kelis. Spend the afternoon with your friends or doing something fun. Don't let your life stop just because your mother is in this position."

I glanced at the bed, guilt flooding me. "But..."

"There's no but," he countered. "You have to look after you too. You've been spending all of your time with us or doing things for the Kingdom, you should spend some time for you."

"I've still been doing those things," I pointed out. "I've been learning more about magic."

"Then that's what you should do. Forget about all of this for an afternoon. The problems will still be waiting for you when you wake up in the morning."

A short laugh escaped me. "That's not what you told me growing up."

"You have to learn what you *have* to do before you can learn when not to do it." The serious look on his face told me all I needed to know. "You should go practice being the best spell caster you can be."

"All right. I promise I'll go and practice some spells." Hopefully, that would reassure him that I was coping just fine with everything going on. And perhaps he was right, and casting some spells *would* make me feel better about the whole situation. It was worth a try, at the very least.

My stomach rumbled. Clearly, it was time for lunch before I did anything else. I said goodbye to Father, and left him to have some alone time with Mother. He'd take comfort in spending the time with her, just as I had.

~

The courtyard had been empty when I arrived, and I wasn't sure whether or not that was a good thing or not. On the one hand, it was almost easier to practice when I didn't have anyone around to distract me. On the other, I had a lot of thoughts spinning around my head, and not a lot of ways to distract me other than firing off spells.

I reset the game Topher had given me to practice with the other day, grateful that he'd thought to give me something I could do on my own.

The disks of light began to fly out of it. One after the other, I threw a spell at them and watched them dissipate into a shower of sparks. Normally, I found this fun, but something felt off today. Perhaps it had to do with my dream or what had happened with Mother.

Still, if I wanted to become good at this, then I needed to practice. Topher might think I had a natural flair, but nothing beat practice when it came to getting better at something, and I was determined to become the best.

The disks sped up, and so did I. It got harder the longer I was playing, but that was the point of the game in the first place. This wasn't only about casting the spells, but also about the dexterity and speed at which I could get them out of my wand. It was an aspect of spell casting that I'd never considered before, and I liked it. If someone had told me about this when I was younger, perhaps I'd have shown more interest in magic.

I was panting loudly by the time the game ended, but it still didn't satisfy me. The burn in my muscles was a welcome distraction, though, which left only one solution. I had to use the faster setting on the game so that I could challenge myself more.

It took a couple of moments for me to finish setting it up. I flexed my fingers around the handle of my wand as I waited for the disks to start flying. The slowest setting was at the same speed as the fastest one on the last round, which meant I was already moving at lightning speed. It was enjoyable to see each of the disks explode into sparks. Soon, I was moving fast enough that I even managed to forget all of the things I was trying to run away from.

Three disks fell to one spell, filling the air with light and blinding me to the next disk as it flew to the side.

I twisted around, almost falling in the process. A spell shot from my wand without me fully noticing where it was going.

A loud crash pulled my attention away from the game.

"Huh?" I looked around for the source. Was there someone else here with me that was breaking things?

I dismissed the rest of the disks with a wave of my wand. I supposed that technically meant I'd completely won the game, but it felt like cheating, so I didn't like doing it. But if someone was watching, then I wanted to know.

It only took a second for me to realize it was me who'd broken one of the plant pots that decorated the courtyard. The sight of it brought back memories of the teapot I'd told mother about. I slumped to the ground, leaning against one of the taller pillars that encircled the courtyard. I hugged my legs to me and rested my head on top and let the tears fall. This hadn't done anything for me like it was supposed to. All it did was put off the inevitable emotions. If I was going to deal with what was happening, then I was going to have to try and do something about it.

I sniffed, having reached a decision about my next course of action. But first, I had to fix the broken pot.

~

It wasn't until I was knocking on the door that I realized I was hoping Topher would answer instead of Jake. But then again, after the way he'd behaved at breakfast yesterday, perhaps that was a good thing. Jake hadn't exactly proven himself to be the most supportive of my cousin's friends, whereas Topher had been there at every turn. He was exactly what I needed to support me...

*No.* I had to push that train of thought away. I had enough going on without working out what that could mean.

"Hello?" Topher asked as he pulled open his door. "Kelis, are you all right? Have you been crying?"

Oh. Was it that obvious? I wiped away any leftover tears, but if he'd already noticed, then it was too late.

"I'm fine. I, just, eurgh." I sighed. What was wrong with me? I wasn't normally this useless when it came to talking to people. At least, I didn't think so. "Are you busy?"

He shook his head. "I'm never too busy for you."

"Pfft. I know that's a lie. I hope you *are* too busy for me sometimes."

An odd emotion passed through his eyes, but I didn't try to decipher what it was.

"What did you want to do?" he asked. "We can do some spell practice, or we could go for something to eat..."

I shook my head. "Could I come in instead?"

"Of course." He stepped back to let me into the room.

I took a deep breath and entered. Just like before, it was easy to tell which part of the room was being used by Topher, and which by Jake. The fact that they were sharing a suite only made it stranger that I'd come so certainly to see Topher instead of the guy I'd had a crush on for years. I supposed a crush seemed to pale in comparison to the scale of the things that were happening now. I couldn't even begin to think of something as trivial as a crush right now.

"Is there a reason you're still standing in the entrance?" Topher asked as he stepped back into the room.

"Sorry, it felt like I was snooping if I went into the room without you," I admitted.

"Isn't this your palace?"

"Well, yes. But that doesn't mean I can just barge into other people's rooms and snoop around. We'd lose the support of a lot of people if we did that, and it's important that it *doesn't* happen."

"Ah, a wise and valiant leader," he teased.

A small snort escaped me at that. "I don't feel like it at the moment."

"Why don't you take a seat and we'll talk about it?" He gestured to a table with chairs on either side.

I sat down on one of them at the same time he sat on the other one.

"Thank you, Topher." I reached across and placed my hand on his, then gave it a squeeze. "I really appreciate the time you're spending helping me get things right."

"I promise, it's not a hassle," he said. "I've enjoyed spending time here. It's different from being at the university."

All that did was remind me that he'd be leaving me at some point. I wasn't sure what would happen when he was gone, especially if Mother's situation hadn't changed by that time. Not that I was going to say anything like that directly to him, it would reveal far too much.

"What's on your mind?" he prompted me when I'd let the silence go on for too long.

I sighed. "How long have you got?"

"As long as you need," he promised. "Though we might get some funny looks if we're here until dawn."

I raised an eyebrow. He wasn't normally so forward, I wonder what had made him so bold? "So basically, what you're saying is that so long as I'm back in my bed before midnight, then it would be acceptable?" Was I flirting with him? I couldn't really tell. I'd only ever tried to do that with Jake, and it hadn't ended very well.

Topher turned to me with a serious expression on his face. "What upset you earlier?"

"I-I-" The words didn't come like I intended them to, and instead, I started to cry again. If this continued, then I'd be able to provide water for the entirety of Enchantia during dry season. Not a classic role for the reigning monarch, but I supposed it did perform a service.

Topher left his chair and came around to mine. He put his arms around me. At first, I thought it was going to stop me crying, but instead, it only made things worse. But he continued to hold me, which did help, even if it made the tears come faster.

When things slowed down, I finally managed to get out everything that had happened, while Topher listened patiently. I had to hand it to him, he was good at that.

Eventually, the tears faded, and I was able to properly collect my thoughts.

"I'm sorry this is all happening." He rubbed a hand up and down my back to reassure me.

At least, he'd known about most of what was happening to begin with.

"Didn't you say that the people love your mother?"

I nodded. "I've never heard of a single person in the whole of Enchantia who doesn't. Ever since she rid the kingdom of the previous queen...her stepmother, she's been seen as some kind of savior."

"I wish I could have gotten to know her better," Topher admitted. "She sounds like a wonderful woman."

I took a deep breath. "Can I admit something you can never tell anyone?"

"Of course." He stepped back.

I wanted to ask him to carry on holding me, but I knew it wasn't appropriate.

"Sometimes, I worry about what will happen if I can't live up to her legacy." I'd never admitted that to anyone, but it was something I'd thought about a lot. Admittedly, not in the past couple of weeks. My mind had been on other things.

Topher poured me a mug of tea and handed it to me. I smiled in thanks, wrapping my hands around it and letting the warmth seep into me.

"I have no doubt that you'll live up to your mother. I have no doubt about that at all."

"You're sweet to say it, but that doesn't make it true. I'd have to do something crazy like save the entire nation from a war, or..."

"Break a curse," he supplied, a wide grin spreading over his face.

I cocked my head to the side, trying to work out what about that had him so excited when it was bad news.

"I don't think I understand." I took a sip of my tea to keep myself busy.

"The healer from breakfast said that what was afflicting your mother was a curse, right?"

I nodded. I should have known he paid enough attention to have picked up on that.

"And that she implied *you* were the one who could break her curse."

"Huh. She did." Somehow, that fact had slipped my mind during my crying session, though it did appear that I'd managed to at least *tell* Topher about it.

"Then that's the solution to all of this. You can

break the curse on your mother, and live up to her achievements in one go."

"Oh." I hadn't looked at it that way.

He knelt down on the floor in front of me, before setting my mug on the table again and taking my hands. "I promise to do everything I can to help you make that happen. You'll break the curse, I'm certain of it."

"Thank you, Topher." As silly as it sounded, I *did* feel better for having talked to him, and I was glad it was him I'd set out to go see rather than Jake.

I never thought I'd choose someone else over my cousin's best friend, and yet now, I did it without even thinking twice about it.

# 23RD OCTOBER

People were dancing all around in a whirl of colors and music. I couldn't make out exactly what was happening, which was a good thing as it probably meant that this wasn't part of a prophetic dream. Just a normal one.

I stepped onto the dance floor and looked around for whoever it was I was supposed to be dancing with. Given the direction of the dream, I wasn't even sure I'd recognize the person, whoever it was.

When a man held out his hand, my heart skipped a beat. It must be someone I wanted to dance with, even if I didn't know who. We spun around, joining the other dancers as we all moved through the fence. I lost myself in the dream, enjoying that it didn't mean anything.

None of the people around me had faces, which made it easy to forget how serious some of my other dreams had been.

I spun away from my dance partner, then back again. But this time, he had a face.

And it belonged to Topher.

Before I had a chance to work out what the dream might mean, it faded into darkness, and I drifted off into a peaceful sleep.

~

I sat bolt upright in bed, woken by loud knocking at my door.

"I'm coming," I called.

With nothing else for it, I swung my legs out of the bed and grabbed hold of my robe. I tied it tightly around my waist and headed to the door, smoothing my hair as I went. It was almost certainly a mess, but it could wait until after I found out what the person on the other side of the door needed.

I swung it open, completely oblivious to who might be on the other side.

Topher flashed me a reassuring smile, sending me back to my dream. I pushed the thought to the side and focused on the man in front of me.

"Is everything all right?" I asked.

Indecision warred on his face as if he didn't know whether to say yes or no to me. I supposed it didn't matter.

"Do you want to come in?" I gestured into my room without thinking about it.

"If you're comfortable with that. If not, we can go to breakfast or somewhere else."

"It's fine," I said, stepping back so he could enter.

He hesitated for a moment, but then came in. With one glance at my unmade bed, he turned his attention back to me.

"Is there somewhere we can sit?" he asked.

"Over here." What was he here for? I hadn't invited Topher to my room at any point, and yet it wasn't weird to have him here, even when I'd only just woken up and was looking a little worse for wear.

He took a seat opposite me and leaned back in his chair. Should I order tea, or was that presumptuous? I didn't know what time it was or how long he wanted to stay.

"Have you seen this?" Topher asked, putting a scrunched up piece of paper on the table.

I picked it up and studied it, reading a description that was more familiar than I wanted to admit.

"Where did you get this?" I asked.

"From Urbis."

I frowned, trying to make sense of how he'd have gotten to Urbis and back so quickly. It had been late when I'd left his rooms last night, the trains had stopped running long before that.

"How?"

He chuckled. "I get newspapers delivered from Urbis every morning. This was included in the stack today."

"Did you..."

"Bring the newspapers?" he finished for me, a wide smile on his face. He plonked a bag onto the table between us. "I did. But I thought the wanted poster was the most important thing to show you because of your eyes."

A small thrill traveled through me at the knowledge he'd spent long enough looking to notice the golden rings around my irises. I thought it was one of my best features, even if I had no explanation for how it had come about.

"Why would the Urbis guard be looking for people with golden rings in their eyes?" I asked, as much to myself as to Topher. As far as I knew, there was nothing particularly special about me. Everyone in Enchantia could do magic, so I was far from alone on that front. I supposed there were the same dreams, but they hardly counted.

"I don't know. But I wondered if there'd be something about it in some of the papers." He patted the bag, then opened his mouth as if to ask something else.

"Yes?" I prompted when it became clear he wasn't going to manage to get the words out.

"I've never met anyone with eyes like yours before," he admitted.

"Neither have I. But, that isn't what you wanted to ask, is it?"

He shook his head. "Why do you have them?"

I shrugged. "There's no reason that I can tell. I asked my parents while I was growing up, but they didn't know the answer either."

"So, it wasn't something they did while your mother was expecting you?" His face screwed up in concentration as he tried to make sense of a mystery that had simply become part of my life.

"I'm adopted."

Horror flitted through his eyes. He must have thought he'd overstepped and upset me.

"Oh, no, don't worry. I've known for as long as I can remember," I promised. "My parents never hid it from me, though we haven't made it public knowledge for obvious reasons."

He nodded. "I doubt that would go down well with some people."

"Unfortunately, not. But they've never been able to have another child, so we all thought it would make more sense to keep quiet about my true parentage."

"Do you know what that is?" he asked.

I shook my head. "No idea. A woman delivered me to them in the middle of the night with no explanation, and that's all we know about it."

"Could these people be related to you?"

I considered it for a moment. "I suppose that could be the case, but I have no way of knowing for sure." Though perhaps that would explain the dream I'd had. Should I tell him about that? I'd mentioned the dreams about Mother's condition before, so it made sense that I should tell him about this one too.

"Perhaps there'll be something about them in the papers that will give us a clue," Topher suggested.

He started pulling the newspapers out.

"That's a good idea. But..." I took a deep breath. "I had a dream about people with golden rings around their irises," I admitted.

"Like the ones you had about the Queen?" Topher sat up straight, excitement clear in the way he was bouncing up and down in his seat.

"I think so, but it was hard to tell. I went into a room, and there were maybe ten people there. I didn't count. I should have, but I didn't realize this would be a thing." I waved at the wanted poster between us.

"Understandable. Did anything else happen?" he asked.

"Not really. I tried to get them to talk to me, but no one responded to me. It felt like I knew them and their eyes all had a golden ring around their irises like mine does.

"All right. We can work out what's going on with them. Even if it takes a little bit of research," he promised. "Did any of them look like you apart from that?"

"Not really. They all seemed different from one another. But I don't suppose that really means anything. I've met plenty of relations who don't look like one another. Mine and Adam's fathers are brothers, and they don't look much alike."

"That's true. Though, I suppose I understand why you look nothing like Adam."

I snorted. "I bet you were disappointed when you found that out." It was hard to keep the bitterness out of my voice. Adam was the perfectly handsome cousin who always played by the rules and looked the part. Whereas I was the quirky crown princess who never wore white and refused magic for a long time. I could imagine that seeing me was disappointing, to say the least.

"Far from it," Topher whispered.

I stared at him, unable to believe the words, even if I wanted to.

Topher seemed to sense my mood as his gaze met mine. The sincerity in his eyes was hard to ignore.

A lump rose to my throat as I waited for him to explain himself.

"You could never be a disappointment, Kelis. You're smart, loyal, and determined. You'll be an amazing queen when your time comes, and you'll live up to your parents' legacy. I'm certain of that." He reached over and gave my hand a squeeze.

For a moment, I thought he was going to say more, but it didn't come. I pushed the disappointment within me away, especially because I didn't have an explanation for it.

"Thank you," I said quietly. "I've never doubted myself as much as I have in the past couple of weeks. I don't know what's come over me."

"I do. You've had your whole world turned upside down. It was bound to happen."

"Perhaps that's not a good quality in a queen..."

"Please stop doubting yourself, Kelis. You can do this. But why don't we distract ourselves by looking through the papers?" he suggested.

I nodded. That sounded good, and not only because it would stop me from thinking about things like how good his hand felt in mine.

We grabbed one of the newspapers each and started to go through them. The first I looked at came from Urbis itself, and while there was a small article about the wanted poster I'd seen, it didn't include any new information. If they weren't going to tell us why the people with eyes like mine were wanted, then we couldn't make much of a decision about them.

I flipped through the rest of the paper, scanning for more news. An article about Enchantia caught my attention briefly, but it was only about the upcoming Fright Festival. Which turned out to be nothing more than a stark reminder that I'd forgotten about it. At least, my costume design was already with the seamstresses. Though, I wasn't sure I'd be going at this rate. It seemed insensitive to party while Mother was cursed.

"Do you have anything?" Topher asked.

I shook my head. "You?"

"There's some talk of unrest in The Vale. It doesn't go into detail, but it seems as if the ruling family was hit hard."

"Huh." I folded the paper from Urbis and started on

another.

This one was from Badalah. It only took me a couple of pages to find mentions of similar unrest.

"This one is talking about the same thing," I told him. Despite some time having passed, I knew he'd know what I was talking about still.

"Same here."

"Where is your paper from?" Was this going to be the same thing for all the kingdoms? A small part of me hoped so, because it might explain a few things.

"Floris."

It didn't take long for us to turn up reports from most of the other kingdoms. We ripped out each of the articles and laid them out side by side, before standing next to one another so we could see all of them. I tried to ignore how close Topher was to me, especially with the growing urge to take his hand in mine. I found it more reassuring than I wanted to admit to hold his hand.

"Is there a link?" I asked as we poured over each of the articles to try and work out what they had in common, and if there was any way the problems could be linked to the people with the eyes.

"There has to be," Topher answered. He pointed to one of the first articles. "This one seems to have the most information in it."

I leaned over and read the words on the page, soaking them in. Which was when it hit me.

"It's the happy endings," I whispered.

"The what?" Topher prompted, reading the article too, probably so he could try and work out what I meant.

"The happy endings. Don't you know?"

"No..."

"About eighteen years ago, there were a lot of happy endings across each of the kingdoms. Mostly the royalty.

It all looked so bleak, and then suddenly, something changed." I snapped my fingers as if to prove my point.

"Like your mother's curse?"

"Exactly." I took a deep breath, not wanting to say the next part, even if I sensed it was true. "And I think her current curse is something to do with this one too. Mother's first curse was broken at the same time as all the others..."

"So it stands to reason that her second one is happening for the same reason these others are," Topher finished for me.

"Exactly." Excitement built inside me at the thought. If we knew what had caused this, then we could do something about it. In theory.

"What caused it the first time?" he asked.

"An evil witch who tricked her way into being Mother's stepmother. That's her mirror over there." I gestured to the suspiciously quiet mirror. Why hadn't it said anything since Topher had come in? That was unusual. Though I was certain, it wouldn't last forever.

"That doesn't sound good."

"No. It isn't," I admitted. "Mother doesn't talk about it very much, but what she has said isn't very good."

"But that doesn't answer the question of what's caused it to happen this time. And how could it have affected all of the kingdoms at the same time?" Topher tapped a finger against his chin as he considered it.

"That's where I'm a little stuck," I admitted. "And I'm not sure how to change that."

Topher shrugged. "We can look over the articles here again, or I could put out some feelers with my contacts in Urbis."

I was certain my eyes lit up at that. "Would you?" I turned to him, completely oblivious to the fact I wasn't properly dressed. He made me so comfortable that it didn't matter.

"Of course." With his body turned towards me, we were closer than we'd ever been before. "I'll always help you in any way I can. That's a promise you can always count on."

The heat from him warmed me, and I had a surprising urge to step closer and press my lips against his. The shock of the thought made me stumble back.

"There's one other place where we can ask for help," I mumbled quickly.

"Your father?"

"Oh, no. He's told me everything he knows, there's nothing else he can tell us. But I was actually thinking about the mirror." I knew it had been too soon to think that the mirror had been quiet. Though this would be the first time I'd try to make it talk on purpose. I must have been losing it. There was no other explanation for what was happening.

"Do you think it'll know something?" Topher asked.

"I honestly don't know. But it was around the first time this happened. If we ask it nicely, then it might give us some clues." Even as I was saying it, I thought it was a silly idea. The mirror had never been my friend, and I doubted that was going to change now. But this was more important than the shreds of my ego. This was my mother's fate.

"Then we should give it a go," he agreed.

"I have to do one thing first." With how cruel the mirror could be, I didn't want to go in front of it without my hair at least partly done.

I walked over to the stand my wand sat on and picked it up. I waved it over my hair, fixing it within a moment.

Topher chuckled. "So, your appearance hasn't

bothered you until you have to look at yourself?"

"Nope." Should I have done this before I let him in? I hadn't thought about it until now, but perhaps he thought I was sloppy for not caring.

"I like it both ways."

My traitorous heart skipped a beat. What was it up to? I didn't understand how I was feeling about him, other than that I liked it.

"You might, but the mirror is another matter. It isn't the nicest."

He frowned. "What do you mean?"

"You'll see." Could I really do this in front of him? I could ask Topher to leave and then tell him what the mirror said after.

No. That was ridiculous. The mirror's insults didn't hurt me. I wasn't about to let that change now.

"How scared of this mirror should I be?" he asked.

"You, not at all," I assured him with a forced smile.

With nothing else for it, I strode over to the mirror and looked into it. Nothing happened.

"Is it supposed to do something?" Topher asked.

"Yes. Normally it simply interjects things into conversations where it's not wanted. I've never had to wake it up before." And if I was honest, I had no idea how. The only woman who probably knew how was unconscious in her room, cursed by whatever was going on.

"Does it have a name? Then you could call out to it the way you normally would to get attention."

I shrugged. "It's never told me one."

"Then make one up?"

With a sigh, I turned to look into it. My reflection stared back at me. Jet black hair, sleek due to the spell I'd just cast. But there were bags under my eyes.

My dreams must have been taking their toll on me. Topher's reflection comes into focus behind me. His hair seemed to have gone from scruffy to charming in my eyes. I shook my head ever so slightly to rid myself of the thoughts about him.

"Wish me luck," I muttered under my breath, but I didn't think he heard me. "Mirror, mirror, on the..."

"Is *that* what you wear for having company over?" the mirror asked.

Oh no. My eyes flickered to Topher's reflection, waiting for him to flinch away, given the insult. When he didn't, relief flooded through me. Along with a tiny amount of confusion. Shouldn't he be agreeing with the mirror? It was right, after all. My bedclothes and robe weren't the right attire for entertaining, though, I supposed that wasn't what we'd been doing. This had been about something far more important than our own enjoyment.

Which only made my outfit more inappropriate.

To my surprise, Topher seemed to sense my distress, and reached out, taking one of my hands in his and giving it a squeeze. Relief flooded through me, along with a shot of my normal confidence. If he didn't care, then I wasn't going to either. I didn't normally let the mirror's jibes get to me, I shouldn't let them this time either.

I took a deep breath before continuing. "This is Topher," I introduced.

"Hello." He gave a half-wave with his free hand but didn't let go of my other one.

So this was what having an ally against the mirror felt like. Mother didn't approve of me keeping it, so she never actually said anything against it, even when it was cruel to me.

"Shame on you for taking up such a fine gentleman's time with your nonsense, Kelis," the mirror said.

This time, I used my mother's trick and rolled my eyes.

The mirror huffed, clearly disliking my indifference. "You wanted me?"

Oh. Interesting. So indifference *did* work on it after all.

"It's about my mother," I started.

"Ah, the Queen. The fairest woman in all the land. No one can match the beauty of the true ruler." It paused, probably for dramatic effect or something. "Especially not you."

"Witty," I muttered, but then pushed my annoyance aside. Some things were more important than my feelings. "We need your help."

"Why should I help you?"

Topher looked as if he wanted to punch the mirror. I didn't blame him. I was starting to feel as if that was the right way to go in the whole matter.

"Like I said, this is about my mother. Not me. She's been cursed again."

"Oh, dear." I had to hand it to the mirror, it at least sounded a little sad. That was something, at least. Maybe.

"We want to know how to break the curse," I said.

"How should I know that?"

I closed my eyes and counted to ten, hoping I could regain my composure before I spoke to it again.

"You were there last time, we were hoping you knew what happened and how it was broken." I got the impression that this wasn't going to get us the answers we wanted. And not just because the mirror hated me for some reason.

The mirror laughed. An odd sound coming from something made of glass and metal, but unmistakable all the same. "You really think I know about that?"

"You're a magic mirror," Topher pointed out, breaking his silence.

"So?"

"Don't you have memories?"

"Of course, I do. I remember the beautiful queen before Snow White, and the even more stunning and magnificent Queen who now sits on the throne. It's a shame those women are going to be followed by this one."

I scowled, hating how it was insulting me in front of Topher, even though I appreciated how little he seemed bothered by what it was saying. It made me feel special in a way I never had before. Not even when Jake spoke to me.

"Do you know who cursed Mother before?" I asked the mirror.

"No."

"And you don't know how it was broken?"

"True love's kiss is my guess. But I can only know certain things," it pointed out. "Just like you have gaps in your knowledge about how to dress and make yourself look good, I don't know about things that happened outside of my direct line of vision."

I sighed loudly. "Fine." I turned away, pulling Topher back out of the mirror's line of sight.

"I know you're there," the mirror called after me.

I ignored it.

"Is there a chance it's lying to us?" Topher asked quietly.

I shook my head. "It can be nasty, but I don't think it's malicious. It would have gloated if it knew something that I didn't, but needed to." Despair filled me, no doubt showing on my face.

Topher reached out and brushed a strand of hair away from my face. "I promise, Kelis, we'll work this out. I'm with you the whole way." The earnestness in his tone was impossible to ignore.

My heart fluttered, filling me with hope. With him by my side, I could do anything.

# 24TH OCTOBER

The corridor with the torches was back again. At least this dream wasn't as stressful as the ones about mother. In the end, all that would happen was me ending up in the room with the people who had eyes like mine. None of them had been dead or cursed. No one had spoken about hurting anyone. In fact, none of them had really spoken at all other than to say my name.

I pushed through the door and into the room. I didn't bother trying to speak this time. There was no point. Instead, I walked among them, studying each of their faces and committing it to memory in case I came across them again. Perhaps a portrait of one of them would appear in one of Topher's papers. He'd promised he'd keep looking at them and tell me if anything of interest came up.

I walked up to the girl with golden-brown hair. *Azia.*

Huh. Where had that come from? Was my subconscious simply naming them so that it would be easier for me to tell them apart in the dream, or was it something more than that?

Where was she from? Was she related to me as Topher had suggested? My memory had suggested that none of them had looked much like me, but I hadn't been *looking* for similarities, so I hadn't noticed any. Other than the eyes.

Azia was nothing like me, though. She was beautiful. Stunning, even. No one would have thought twice about it if my parents said she was their daughter. Not because she looked like them. Simply because she was beautiful like they were, while I wasn't.

I moved on, coming to two boys. One looked as if he'd spent most of his life outdoors. *Castiel.*

How was this possible? I was so certain of their names, but I didn't know any of them. It made no sense.

The other one was called Jakon. And neither of them looked anything like me. This all made no sense. If it was the first time I'd had the dream, then I might have been able to dismiss it as nothing more than that. But this was the second time, and after the dreams of Mother, I wasn't about to take anything like this lightly.

And I was so certain about their names. Almost as if I knew them.

I turned around and looked at the others in the room.

*Fallon, Deon, Halia, Ivy*...all of them had names, and it barely took a moment to know them.

"Hello?" I said. I knew it hadn't made a difference

the last time I was here, but perhaps now things had changed.

No one responded. I shouldn't have expected them to, that would have made things too easy. I closed my eyes, hoping to give myself a moment to work out what was happening and what my next move should be.

After taking a deep breath, I opened them again but found only blackness on the other side. The room and the people in it were all completely gone.

All right, then. I supposed I wasn't going to learn anything else about them tonight. I drifted off into a deep sleep, one that wasn't plagued by people with golden rings around their eyes. Though, I knew they'd be in my thoughts when I woke up.

I grunted in frustration and dropped the book I'd been reading onto the stack I'd already searched through to try and discover how to break a curse. I wasn't surprised that most of the books didn't have any information on the subject. I imagined that most people wouldn't want it to become common knowledge, especially in a kingdom of magic users like Enchantia. But, we didn't really use our magic in order to curse people. Unless people had been hiding things from me, which seemed unlikely. My parents wanted me to be a good queen when my time came, and keeping important information about the kingdom from me wasn't good training.

I pulled the next book towards me and flipped through until I found a page about curses. One small paragraph was all that it gave me, and most of what it said amounted to *don't do them.* I rubbed a hand over my face, frustrated with the way this was going and wishing Topher was still here with me. We'd come to the library after breakfast to look into curses and what they meant, but he'd had to leave to go talk to some of his contacts. I knew he was doing it for me, but that didn't stop the pang of loneliness at him being gone. Somehow, having him around made the whole situation easier to handle, though I wasn't certain why.

The book thudded down onto the pile of useless ones. The stack had nearly a dozen books in it already, whereas the useful pile only had one slim volume, and that wasn't *much* use. All it did was detail the happy endings that had happened around the same time as my parents'.

A pang of guilt flooded through me at that. Shouldn't I be with mother right now?

No. I couldn't think like that. Doing this research was helping her more than staying by her side the entire time was. In fact, if I did that, I could imagine her getting particularly upset with me when she woke up. She'd want me to continue living my life. What I was actually doing lay somewhere between the two options, and for now, it was what I was comfortable with.

I sighed and pulled the next book towards me. It was going to be a long day if things continued this way. Unfortunately, this one didn't have a table of contents, which meant it was going to be a lot more difficult to work out what I needed to pay attention to, and what I didn't.

I summoned one of the nearby servants and asked her to bring me some tea before settling in to read the book in front of me. The words were cramped, and looked as if they were handwritten instead of printed, which was only going to make this even slower going. I tried not to think about that too much. The last thing

I wanted was to miss something important because I couldn't be bothered to determine what the words said.

Time passed, though I was only dimly aware of it. Mostly because of the cold teapot beside me. It had long since been emptied, but I didn't want to trouble anyone with bringing me a fresh one when it was probably around lunchtime. Most of the staff would be busy serving in the main food hall or taking food to those nobles who ate in their rooms. To my knowledge, that was a small number, but it still kept the staff busy.

I was only half aware of someone approaching my table. It must be Topher. He was the only one who knew where I was. Although, Rhi might have known me well enough to try it. I needed to make more of an effort to see her. It had been a few days since the two of us had managed to spend much time together. No doubt, that made me a terrible friend, especially as I knew how much she hated spending any time with Lyss.

"I was wondering when you'd get back," I said offhandedly as I flipped over the page.

"Back from where?"

My head snapped up at the familiar voice that didn't belong to my friend.

"Jake." His name slipped out without me meaning it to. "I'm sorry, I was expecting someone else."

"Don't tell me, Topher?" He pulled out the chair opposite me and flopped down into it without even asking if I could take a break from what I was doing. He had no way of knowing it was research and not some important business for Enchantia that I couldn't pause.

"Yes, he's just nipped into town to get something." I leaned back in my chair and crossed my arms. There was no point in paying any attention to my book now. Jake was the kind of person who demanded complete attention on him and no one else.

A smirk twisted at the side of his lips. "You sent him on an errand?"

"No." Guilt welled up within me, but I pushed it away. I hadn't *sent* Topher anywhere unwillingly. He said he wanted to help, and this was his way of doing it. And I appreciated it. That wasn't taking advantage of him, was it?

"Pity. I reckon you could get him to do anything you wanted."

"I doubt that," I countered instantly. "Topher is his own person, he'll do as he pleases."

Jake laughed bitterly. "Then, you haven't noticed how he's been following you around like a puppy?"

"No. Because he hasn't been," I snapped, anger on Topher's behalf welling up within me. Why was Jake being so mean about him? Oh. Right. Jealousy. I remembered now. He didn't like that Topher was more talented than he was. From what I'd seen, Jake didn't like that *I* was either, but he seemed to be able to push past that. Perhaps, because I had a crown attached to my name. Not that it should make a difference. But to someone like him, it would.

My feelings about Jake weren't the same as when he'd arrived. I wondered when they'd changed?

He sighed, bringing me back to the moment at hand. "I'm sorry. I didn't come here to talk about Topher."

"Oh. Did you need something?" It was the only explanation I could come up with. Other than the night he'd drunk too much, Jake didn't seem in the least bit inclined to search me out at all.

"Only to spend some time with you." He reached over and placed a hand on top of mine.

Sweat slicked his palms, and I itched to pull my

hand away. It didn't feel like this when Topher touched me.

Why was I thinking about Topher when the boy I'd been crushing on for so long was right in front of me and wanting to spend some time with me? I must be going crazy.

"I'm a little busy at the moment," I told him, unsure where the words were coming from. "But I could meet you for dinner or for spell practice if you want?"

A sneer replaced his smile, twisting his features unpleasantly. He pulled his hand back. "Neither of those involves us spending time together alone."

I could have pointed out that what he was saying wasn't true, but I knew that was pointless. Given his expression, he wasn't going to listen to reason, no matter what I said.

"I'm sorry, but I have important things to look into." I tapped the book in front of me. It wasn't a lie. What I was doing *was* important. But it could also have waited if I really wanted it to. But a part of me wasn't in the mood to put up with Jake's brand of conversation. Within minutes, it would devolve into talking about him and everything he wanted to be and stand for.

And he wouldn't offer to help me with the curse facing Mother. Of course, he didn't know about it either, but I wasn't about to change that. He wouldn't see why it was important to fix the problem, either for the kingdom or for me. My faith in him had been utterly destroyed at some point during the past few weeks, and I couldn't even pinpoint when that had happened or why.

"You used to be fun," he pouted.

I resisted the urge to point out he had no idea about that as he'd never actually spent any time with me. At least, it made my decision easier. He wasn't going to help, and I shouldn't expect him to.

"I'm sorry, there's too much going on in the kingdom that I have to attend to. But I was going to go to the courtyard later for some practice..."

"I'm going to go practice now," he huffed as he scraped his chair back. The feet of it screeched along the floor, making me flinch.

"Oh, well, if you're still out there, maybe I'll join you later."

"No need. I'll be done. But I have to get ready for the upcoming competition."

"Oh." They'd mentioned it a little while ago, but I hadn't done anything about it. Another thing the current events had taken from me.

"It's a shame you won't be competing, I'd have enjoyed beating you," he sneered.

I sighed. He was bad at being rejected as well as a bad loser when it came to games. I supposed that made sense, even if it made managing his ego harder. I felt sorry for the girl who ended up with him.

My eyes widened at that thought. When had I stopped imagining the person he ended up with being me?

"I'm sure you'll get some other opportunity to spell cast against me," I said offhandedly to cover the realization in my head.

He didn't respond and stormed off instead. I watched him leave as I tried to sort out what was going on in my mind. Perhaps, it was nothing more than a blip brought on by being tired and having too much to worry about.

And yet, something felt off about my emotions. I shook my head to clear it, determined to leave matters of my heart for another time. I had to find out more about curses first. Boys could wait. The only thing I was certain of was that things had changed, though I wasn't sure exactly what.

~

Despite several hours having gone by, the helpful stack of books hadn't grown at all, whereas my useless stack had now grown into three stacks. Mostly because I was trying to be sensible and not pile the books so high that they'd fall on top of me. That wasn't a good thing for anyone.

I picked up the only book I hadn't read yet and studied the cracked green leather cover. I had to hope there was something inside this one that could help. Otherwise, I'd be spending the next few hours walking up and down the library shelves trying to find more books that might be helpful, only for them to end up in the stack beside me.

This was ridiculous. There had to be an easier way than this.

I set the book down. Perhaps it was time for me to take a break. It was nearing dinner time, and the court would probably expect me to make an appearance after being missing all day. I tried not to let guilt overtake me again. I was struggling with it a lot at the moment, partly due to all the pressure I was feeling. I seemed to have to be something for everyone at the moment. A good daughter, a good ruler, a good friend...and I felt like all I was doing instead was letting people down.

"Do you mind if I sit?"

Topher's voice filled me with hope. I looked up to find him standing beside my desk.

"Of course. When did you get here?"

"About thirty seconds ago. Didn't you hear me?"

I shook my head. "I must have zoned out for a

moment."

"Or found yourself reading a particularly riveting book," he teased as he took the seat that Jake had sat in a few hours ago.

"Eurgh."

"That bad?"

"Terrible. These are the stacks of books that have no information we can use at all." I gestured to the huge piles of books next to me. "And these are the ones that are actually useful." I placed a hand on top of the much smaller stack.

"Ah. Let me guess, those aren't all that useful either?"

"Nope. They don't really tell us anything we didn't already know but in a slightly more flowery way."

"That's not good."

"It feels like I've wasted my entire day," I admitted softly.

"It was worth a try," he said reassuringly, reaching out and taking my hand.

This time, there wasn't an urge to pull my own away. I wanted him to hold it. His touch was comforting, almost like the calm in a stormy sea. He was the answer I needed, even if I didn't know the exact question.

"I don't know. I haven't done anything for the kingdom today, I haven't visited Mother since first thing this morning..."

"How was she?"

I shrugged. "The same. She won't respond to anything. Father and the dwarves are keeping her company." They were doing the same thing I did yesterday and telling her stories about their pasts together. I hoped Mother could hear through whatever hell she was going through and knew how much we all loved her. It was one of my only solaces in the situation.

"We'll figure this out, Kelis. I promise."

"Not if I spend all day looking at books that don't have the answers," I complained.

"But this *is* helpful," he pointed out.

I shot a dirty look at the books. "I'm not sure I'm following."

"Sometimes, it's good to work out what you do know, and what you need to find out. That's what you've been doing here. Plus, we can rest assured that the answer isn't sitting in the library right under our noses."

A small laugh escaped me at that one. "True. I've always hated it in stories when the hero has the answer right in front of him but never looks."

"And now, you've been looking. And you know that you haven't missed anything."

"I'd feel better if you read through the books too and made sure," I teased.

"Of course I will," he answered instantly.

"No, Topher." I placed my free hand over his, making an odd hand tower in the middle of the table. If anyone walked in and saw us, they'd think we were more than friends. "I don't want you to do that, I was only joking."

"Oh. Phew." He chuckled nervously. "That's a lot of books."

"It is. People might start thinking I'm a librarian and not a princess if I'm not careful."

"Then I suggest you start wearing a tiara while you read, that would solve the problem," he suggested with a cheeky grin.

I pulled my hand back and tapped a finger against my chin. "Ah, and here was me wondering whenever I was going to use my reading tiara. There never seems to be the right moment."

Topher's eyes lit up at the joke. My heart warmed at

the sight.

"Did you find anything out when you were in town?" I asked.

He shook his head. "I brought the papers for you." He gestured to the bag he'd dropped by the side of the table. "But there's nothing in any of them that's new. The ones we looked at yesterday were only a day old."

"Makes sense. I guess the press doesn't know too much about what's going on themselves, then."

"That would be my assumption. Or perhaps some of what's going on is being kept out of it? I have no idea. Without being in any of the other kingdoms, it's impossible to tell."

"Which leaves us exactly where we were yesterday," I finished. "This is something to do with magic and the happy endings, but we don't know what's causing it, why, or how to undo it."

Despite saying he wasn't going to, Topher picked the top book from my stack of rejects and started to flick through it.

"Basically." My own disappointment was echoed in his voice. At least he understood the gravity of the situation—unlike Jake.

No. That wasn't fair. The other boy had no idea what was going on. If he did, perhaps he'd be acting differently about it all.

Thinking of Jake reminded me of the other thing he'd mentioned. The competition.

"Topher..." I started.

"Hmm?"

"What happened to the spell casting competition we were going to enter?" I could hear the nerves in my voice and hoped he didn't, though, with my question directed at Topher, I knew he either wouldn't mention it, or he'd make me feel better.

Horror crossed his features. "Oh no, I'm so sorry, Kelis. With everything going on, I completely blanked on it. I didn't put our names down."

"It's all right." A kernel of disappointment grew inside me, but it wasn't as big as I expected it to be. I supposed he was one of the reasons I'd been enjoying doing magic anyway, and as I was still getting to spend time with him, it wasn't such a big deal that he hadn't put our names down.

"No, it isn't. I should have done it. I'm sorry..."

This time, it was me who took his hand in mine and gave it a squeeze. "I promise; it's not a problem. There's nothing to be sorry for."

"But, you were enjoying doing magic."

"That's true, but there'll be other competitions," I pointed out. I shouldn't even be thinking about something so frivolous with Mother's curse in progress, and I felt a little silly for considering it.

"There's still time," he countered.

I shook my head. "The competition is next week. They've probably closed sign-ups already," I pointed out. "It's not important. It'll give me more time to focus on this anyway." I tapped the leather-bound green book in front of me, knowing he'd understand this to mean the whole situation and not that one particular tome.

"It'll be good for you to do it still, though," he said. "It'll give you something to focus on and direct all that nervous energy you have building up inside you into something different."

"Hmm." He might be right there. A lot of nerves, frustration, and other similar sensations were part of how I was feeling at the moment, and it would be better if I got them out in a controlled way. Spell casting might be the right outlet.

"There's a trial you can take to enter. Most people don't bother, but given how close we are to the sign-up date, you can take it. They'll have to let you compete once they see how good you are."

"Don't you mean once they notice I'm the princess," I muttered. His idea had been a good one until I'd made that realization. I didn't want people handing things to me just because of who I am.

"We can give them a fake name. If you wear white, then no one will ever guess you're the princess."

"Hmm. Maybe." I wasn't completely convinced, though I was partway there.

"You do own white clothes, right?"

I laughed lightly. "Yes, of course, I own white clothes. Where's the fun of being shocking in black if it isn't a choice."

"Thought as much."

"What about our research, though? It's a lot of time we could spend looking into things..."

"How about we go to sign you up and take the trial tomorrow, and then we research again later?" he suggested.

Was that a good idea? Could I pause what I was doing in order to spend some time doing something fun? Father's words and advice drifted into my mind. He wanted me to still relax. And I supposed it would help if I was in a better mood.

"All right. Fine. We'll go sign up tomorrow. But after that, we need to try and find some actual answers."

"Deal," Topher said, a wide grin on his face. "Have you eaten, by the way? I'm starving."

I shook my head and let out a small laugh. "I haven't. But we can go down to the kitchens and get them to give us some cold cuts."

"Ah, finally, knowing the princess is paying off," he teased.

"You haven't seen anything yet," I returned, a genuine smile spreading over my face. It was so easy to spend time with him, and I wanted to make the most of each second.

## 25TH OCTOBER

After visiting with my parents to check on how Mother was doing, I made my way down the stairs two at a time. I was running a little late to meet Topher in the stables so we could take a carriage into town. There was only a limited amount of time before they wouldn't let me sign up anymore at all, and I didn't want to waste that. Especially as the two of us were already late.

I was out of the main door within moments and making my way to the carriage, which had already been prepared, so Topher must have thought ahead and requested one. I appreciated that. He was always looking out for the best thing to do.

He waved at me as I arrived, slowing from my half

jog.

"Sorry," I panted.

"Whatever for?" he asked, holding out the carriage door so I could get in first.

"For being late." Why wouldn't that bother him?

He shrugged. "I figured you were doing something important. Besides, it's only five minutes."

"Even so, I'm sorry." I climbed into the carriage and waited for him to follow me up before explaining. "I was visiting with my parents."

"Are they all right?" he asked as the carriage began to move.

I sighed. "As well as they can be, given the situation. Mother hasn't changed. She still isn't responding. Father must have tried true love's kiss on her dozens of times in the past day."

"Is he coping?"

"Not very well," I admitted quietly. I doubted the driver could hear what we were talking about over the noise of the road, but it was better to be safe rather than sorry. The last thing we needed was for rumors about what was going on to start spreading through the city. I didn't know what would happen under those circumstances, but I suspected it would be similar to the unrest going on in the other kingdoms.

"Is there anything we can do to help him?" Topher offered.

My heart swelled at the words. He was considering my parents' feelings as much as he was considering mine, for no real reason other than that he was a good person.

"I don't think so. He's sending most of the things for the running of the kingdom to my office. I think most of the staff know to send things there too."

"The staff knows what's going on?" He raised an eyebrow, clearly surprised by that.

"Not as such. They know Mother is ill, but that's about the extent of it. Haven't there been whispers around the court about it?" I knew I could trust his answer more than my own judgment. At the end of the day, I was still the princess, and most of the people living in the palace knew that. They'd be careful what they said around me. Topher, on the other hand, was an unknown. I doubted anyone had discovered how close the two of us were growing, especially because our one on one time had only been more recent. They'd still gossip in front of him. Or perhaps even to him.

"Not a peep."

I smiled. "That's the loyalty to Mother you're seeing there. I'm not sure how she did it, but the servants love her as if she was a member of their own family."

"I think you'll find they love you that way too," he pointed out.

I scoffed. "I doubt it. I'm just the annoying princess who always wears black." Except for today. I tugged on the edge of my white skirt uncomfortably. It was strange, but I felt like I was going to stand out *more* by wearing white, despite the fact that everyone else around me would be too.

"You're more than that. I've heard a few of the things the servants say about you. It's all about how well you handle yourself in bad situations, and that you've had a hand in running the country for so long, that when you become queen, it'll be natural."

My mouth fell open. "They really say that?"

"Of course. But I have to ask, how long *have* you been helping to run the kingdom?"

"No idea," I answered instantly. I'd think more

about what the servants said about me once I was on my own later. "My parents started teaching me as soon as they could, but I don't know how old I was. For as long as I can remember, I've had lessons in diplomacy and politics. To the detriment of some other things." I tapped the wand in my holster to remind him of the gaps in my knowledge. I didn't want anyone thinking I was all-knowing. I was simply lucky to have a good education.

"That makes sense. Will you do the same for your children?" he asked.

"I've never really thought about it," I admitted. "It seemed so far off. And I'd never put much thought into marriage. But I guess I would. I like the way I was raised. My parents made me feel that I was more important than what I looked like. It gave me the confidence to focus on the things that will make a difference to people."

"But not to magic?"

I chuckled. "No, not so much to magic. In hindsight, I should have paid more attention. And maybe my parents should have put more pressure on me to learn it, but I think they were just happy that I was paying attention to the more important things at the time."

"Plus, it's given you something to learn now," he pointed out.

"That's true."

The carriage slowed down, which I assumed meant we'd reached our destination. I flashed an inquiring look at Topher. He nodded, though there was the slightest hesitation.

Oh. That was probably because he'd spent more time in Urbis than here. He likely didn't know our city very well.

Once the carriage came to a complete stop, he

popped his head outside the door, then jumped down. All right, then. It was definitely the right place. I went to exit, only to find him standing there with his hand out.

"My lady." He dipped his head.

"Don't do that here," I hissed. "I don't want anyone knowing who I am, remember?"

"Sorry." He grinned in a way that made me think he wasn't being completely serious in his greeting.

I took his hand and stepped down from the carriage, mostly for the excuse to touch him rather than anything else. I wasn't sure when I'd decided on that, but apparently, I had. It was best not to think about it too hard.

"Where is it we're heading?" I asked.

He pointed to the right, where a large stadium was set up.

"Ah."

"Bigger than you expected?" he guessed.

"Yep. I haven't been here before." Which I realized sounded ridiculous, given how close the palace was.

"Neither had I until this trip, but I know the way in now." He held out his arm and let me slip my hand through it. "What do you want me to call you?"

"I thought you were comfortable calling me Kelis?" I checked. He'd used my name plenty of times, why was it suddenly a problem now?

Topher chuckled. "Yes, but you don't want anyone to know you're the princess."

Oh. Right. That. "Mmm. Kel, maybe?"

He laughed loudly. "You're seriously going to go undercover by dropping two letters off your name?"

"And by changing the color of my clothes," I added as he led me towards the doors of the stadium.

"Oh, sorry, you're right. You're a completely different

person now. I'd never have recognized you," he quipped.

"Haha, very funny," I teased back. It was nice to have someone I was comfortable with like this; it made everything so much easier to deal with.

"So long as most people in there don't know you, you should be fine," he assured me.

"Then, let's hope for that."

We entered a room that was empty save for two people standing behind a desk. That must be the registration desk. I pulled my arm away from Topher's, missing his touch almost instantly. I strode forward, trying to forget that I wasn't in my normal clothing, or feeling completely comfortable. It wouldn't matter once I'd managed to sign us up.

"Good morning," one of the people said, a stocky woman with a turned-up nose. The tall man who'd been standing with her had gone over to a chest at the other side of the room and was sorting through it for something.

"Hello," I answered brightly. "We're here to sign up for the tournament, please."

"Registration is closed," the woman said bluntly.

"It's what?" Topher asked. "I thought it wasn't supposed to close until this evening."

"Originally, that was the plan. But we've had so many applicants this year that we've had to close them early. You'll have to try next year."

Topher opened his mouth to speak, but I placed a hand on his arm.

"It's fine. We'll do it next time," I told him.

"That's not good enough, Kel." He turned to the woman with an angry look on his face. "My friend here is one of the best casters I've seen in my life. Please let her compete. It'll make things much more exciting."

"That won't be possible. Registration is closed. If you wanted a place, then you should have been on time," she said firmly.

"I'm sorry, but we were on time," I pointed out as my annoyance grew to match Topher's. I couldn't understand why they were being so difficult about this. Even so, I was going to continue to use my manners and speak calmly. That was the way I'd been raised. "If registration was supposed to be open until five, would it please be possible for us to still do so? We've come all this way to sign up, and it feels unfair to be told we can't now."

"We're at perfect liberty to close registration whenever we want. We're not going to reopen it because some brat wants to show off for her boyfriend."

I raised an eyebrow. That has to be the first time in my life that I'd ever been called a brat.

"Do you have any idea who she is? How dare..." Topher started.

I put a hand on his arm, effectively silencing him. My own anger was bubbling under the surface, but not for the same reasons he was. If they knew I was the princess, they'd be treating me very differently. But that shouldn't matter. They should treat everyone with respect, no matter their station.

"Yes, you do what she says, honey," the woman sneered at Topher, dropping all pretense of being reasonable.

I took a deep breath. I couldn't lose my temper. Not only because it was rude, but also because if it got out, then I could get our family into a lot of trouble, and I wasn't comfortable with that. "Would you please let us know your name and who we can contact about a complaint?" I asked through gritted teeth.

Before she answered, some voices came from the opposite side of the room. I glanced over to see a man and two women enter, all talking with one another in an excited manner. I had no idea who they were, but it would no doubt be a good thing to have witnesses to what was happening.

"Philip," the woman snapped at the man who had been standing with her. "Get over here. I need your help in removing these pests."

Another of the competition staff looked up at her barked tone and came over.

"Is everything all right, Marigold?" the new man asked, even as Philip rejoined her.

The woman's eyes widened as if she'd been caught doing something she shouldn't.

"Everything is fine, David, I was just asking these lovely young people to leave. They were asking about entering the tournament."

"Oh, jolly good," David replied. "I don't recognize either of you. Are you local?"

"From Urbis, sir," Topher answered. I stayed silent, letting his answer speak for both of us and stop myself from having to lie in one fell swoop.

"Excellent." He clapped his hands together. "That should liven up the competition. I don't think we have anyone else from Urbis this year..."

"Actually, we've just been told we can't register," I said.

David frowned, then looked at Marigold. "There are plenty of spots left."

"I..." We all waited for her to finish whatever it was she was going to say, but the words never seemed to appear. Instead, Marigold was turning a bright shade of pink.

"Marigold said we were to close registration after her niece...Ooof." Philip was cut off by a sharp elbow in the ribs from the woman.

"That is rather serious, indeed. May I have a look at the registration list, please?" He held out his hand, expectantly.

Marigold handed it over, a sour expression on her face.

David examined it for a moment and then sighed loudly. "Sealed with magic too. Oh, dear." He turned to the two of us. "Unfortunately, the list has been sealed. But there is still one way to enter the tournament."

"With the trial?" Topher suggested eagerly.

He nodded. "Yes. But we only have one spot available..." He set the list back down on the table.

"That's fine. Kel can take it. She's the better caster of the two of us." He pushed me forward. I stumbled a little but managed to flash the organizer a small smile in the process.

He clapped his hands together in excitement. "Excellent. Why don't you make your way through the double doors, and I'll have a word with Marigold here. I assure you, we don't take attempts to fix the tournament lightly, and will be looking into what happened to the two of you immediately."

We nodded and followed his instructions. I didn't want to be a part of whatever conversation he was going to have with Marigold. I couldn't imagine it would be very pleasant.

The double doors led to a surprisingly simple waiting area.

"What happens during the trials?" I asked Topher as I looked around. Now that I was here, this didn't seem like the best idea. But I had to go through with it now.

"I have no idea. I haven't entered a tournament in a long time, and never one that involved a trial to start things off. You'll be fine, though. I've seen how quick you are on your feet."

A blush rose to my cheeks at the thought of him watching me. Which was ridiculous. He'd been tutoring me in magic, he had to look at me in order to do it. Even so, the faith Topher had placed in me was enough to fill me with more confidence than anyone else ever had. Though I was also feeling more nervous than ever before too.

David swept into the room a moment later. Somehow, that had taken less time than I'd expected. Which was silly, as I hadn't known what he was saying to her or any other details about it.

"I'm so sorry about that. Please be assured that the rest of the tournament will be run with the utmost integrity. Marigold's niece will still be competing, but she will no longer have the advantages her Aunt was arranging for her." The dark look in his eyes convinced me of what he was saying.

"Thank you," I said, at a loss for any other words. I'd never been in this situation before.

"What was your name, please?" he asked.

"Kel."

"Of Urbis?" he double-checked.

"No, I'm from Enchantia, actually." I couldn't lie about that. The chances were slim that anyone would call me out on my real name, but if they did, then I didn't want to be caught in a lie, it wouldn't be a good look for the royal family in general.

"Excellent. May I see your wand, please? I must make sure it adheres to the requirements."

I frowned but pulled my wand from its holster on

my leg, all the same. Handing it to him was odd. No one ever touched my wand but me. Mostly because no one could *use* my wand but me. I wasn't sure how it worked, but whatever enchantment was placed on the wands in Enchantia, the only people who could use them was the owner. I liked the quirk, it meant that wand theft numbers were low. Without me, my own was nothing more than a fancy looking twig.

"This is excellent quality. From a good maker."

"Thank you." It was actually from the *best* maker, but I didn't correct him. That might draw more attention to me than I wanted.

"Good. This is all in order. Your trial will begin in a moment. Go through those doors at the end, take a right, and you'll find yourself on the field. Your aim is to score as many points as possible."

I nodded my understanding, the nerves in my stomach fluttering so hard that I was unable to say anything else.

"Can I watch?" Topher asked.

"Unfortunately, no. But you may wait here for Kel to return," David said. Turning to me, he said, "Once you're done, come back here and I'll let you know whether or not you've qualified,"

"Thank you," I got out.

With one final nod, he turned and walked away, probably so he could go somewhere to witness my trial score.

"Good luck," Topher said.

"Thank you."

He reached out and gave my hand a squeeze. My nerves settled down at the touch. If he believed in me, then there was nothing I couldn't do.

I took a deep breath and followed David's instructions.

I came out into what appeared to be a long tunnel.

"Keep calm, keep focused," I whispered. I opened and closed my fingers around my wand, trying not to grip it too tightly. The last thing I wanted was to snap it. Was that even possible? I had no idea. What I did know was that it would be harder to cast spells if I was holding it too tightly.

I looked around, trying to work out how I'd know the trial had begun. That was perhaps a flaw in David's instructions. I had no idea what I was supposed to be doing. Then again, the ability to accurately gauge what was going on around me might be one of the things they were testing. If so, then I hoped the beginning of the trial was obvious.

As if summoned by my thoughts, a flash of light caught my attention. I threw out my wand arm, a spell coming from my wand and crashing into the light.

After that, I lost myself in the flash of lights, the spells leaving me, and the movement of my body as I twisted and turned myself into the best position to get them all. It was harder work than the games Topher had me play, as I had no idea what was coming from where and when.

I ducked low to hit a red target, only to then have to jump and catch a blue one, which appeared at twice my height. I was out of breath and sweating from every pore in my body, but it was worth it. There was nothing on my mind but the determination to hit every target and prove that I was as good at this as everyone said.

I briefly found myself wondering what the actual tournament would be like, but pushed the thought aside. That was something to worry about later. For now, my main focus had to be on getting through this trial.

A shower of sparks came from a green target, and I spun around, looking for the next one. After a moment, the lights in the corridor dimmed. Ah. That probably meant it was the end of the trial.

I waited another moment to make sure no other targets would appear. If I'd been designing a test, then that was one of the things I'd make happen. It would test patience, as well as the ability to plan.

After nothing happened, I decided it was best to walk back to where Topher was waiting.

I stepped outside the door in time to see a woman lifting something red to her lips. My eyes widened. An apple? How had she gotten one of those? Without thinking about it, I let a spell fly, knocking it from her hand.

Oh, no. What had I done? I'd just deprived a random woman of something that almost certainly *hadn't* been an apple. No one in the kingdom ate them apart from Mother.

To my surprise, the woman turned and smiled at me before disappearing again.

I shook off my confusion and made my way back to Topher.

David stood next to him, a wide grin on his face. "Not many people get that last target," he said.

"The green one?" It hadn't seemed particularly difficult to me, but perhaps I'd simply been in the flow and not thought about it enough.

"Oh, no. That one is a false end."

I tried not to feel smug about that but failed miserably. It was nice to know I'd been right about the end of the trial. "Which one, then?"

"The red one in Julia's hand at the end," David said, excitement coming from every word. "Most people think she's eating something, normally, an apple. Which is odd, because no one eats apples here. But you know that."

"Mmhmm." I hoped he meant because I was from Enchantia, and not because he knew who I was. Though, as Topher had pointed out, my disguise wasn't exactly the most elaborate or well thought out.

"Anyway, congratulations, you've earned yourself a place in the tournament, Kel of Enchantia. Where should we send the welcome packet with all of the instructions?"

I exchanged a worried glance with Topher. It would be a bit of a giveaway if I asked for it to be sent up to the palace.

"I'm coming into the city tomorrow morning, why don't I collect it for you?" Topher offered.

I breathed a sigh of relief. He always seemed to know what to say. One of the many things I appreciated about him.

"That would be great, thank you," I said, "if that's all right with David?"

"Of course, of course. Let me just take your name and let the admin staff know."

"Topher of Urbis."

"Excellent. Thank you. I look forward to watching you in the tournament." He waved at us then left the room, leaving both Topher and I standing there and staring at his retreating back.

"I don't even know how to describe what just happened," Topher muttered.

A laugh escaped me. "That's one way of putting it."

"How was the trial?"

"Not what I expected. It was sort of like one of your games, but nothing was moving, and the lights popped up at all kinds of different heights and angles."

"That doesn't sound too bad."

"It wasn't," I admitted. "It makes me wonder what the tournament will be like."

"I guess we'll find out when I pick your welcome packet up tomorrow," he responded.

"Thank you for doing that."

He shrugged. "I'll be here anyway picking up the papers, I might as well come here too."

"That doesn't mean I'm not grateful," I pointed out.

He slipped an arm around my shoulders and pulled me in for a weird hug. "I know. You can pay me back by coming with me to collect *today's* papers, and then we can go back to the palace and do some more research."

"Sounds like a plan." I relaxed for the first time since I'd woken up. Knowing we were doing something to try and ease Mother's curse helped me from feeling too guilty about not being at her side all the time, even if I knew she'd hate that.

# 26TH OCTOBER

The moment I walked into the banquet hall for breakfast, I knew Mother's situation had become common knowledge. No one would outright say it to my face, but I could see it in the way they looked at me. And the way they stopped talking when I approached.

I pushed the food around my plate, trying not to dwell on what was going on around me. I wished Topher was here, he would have taken my mind off everything. But he was out collecting the papers and the welcome packet for my tournament.

"Kelis, are you all right?" Rhi asked as she dropped into the seat next to me.

Some of the tension left with her arrival, replaced

by a small pang of guilt that I hadn't been spending enough time with her. I should have been a better friend, especially if I expected her to come back here and work for me once she's finished with her studies in Urbis.

"I'm fine. I just have a lot on my mind," I said.

"No doubt. I'm sorry to hear about your mother. Is there anything I can do?"

"Not really," I admitted. "Unless you want to come to the library with me later and try to keep me distracted?"

"I can do that," she said brightly. "I've been meaning to go for a couple of days, there are some things I want to look up."

"Like how to get rid of unwanted companions?" I asked, nodding towards where Lyss was sitting on her own.

"Eurgh. I wish she'd go home already," Rhi muttered. "I don't know what she's staying for. Things are awkward enough as it is."

"Maybe she's hoping to meet someone at the Fright Festival?" I suggested.

"Ah. Possibly. I've heard it's *amazing*. I was actually really excited when Adam asked us all if we wanted to come for it."

"You've never been before?" I'd never thought of the Fright Festival as a particular draw. It was fun and colorful, that much was true, but I didn't realize people came from all over to see it.

"No. I've seen some pictures, though. It seems larger than life."

"It is, in some ways. We'll have a great time."

"You're going?" She almost bounced up and down in her chair with excitement.

"Of course. We always make sure one of us goes.

The people like to see their royal family. We normally go because it's fun, and hot apple cider is delicious."

"Those sound like good reasons to me," she responded. "And I bet that's one of the reasons people love your family so much. You're so in touch with your people."

I forced a smile to cover the concern that all that would change now that Mother was bedridden. "We try to be."

Rhi leaned forward and grabbed a bread roll, before tearing it in two and smothering it in fresh honey. It looked delicious, and I was about to ask her to pass me one of the other rolls when she squeaked.

I looked up to find Jake and Adam approaching. Confusion, the echoes of my crush, and annoyance all warred for attention inside me. Apparently, I had no idea what to feel when Jake was around anymore. My cousin was a different matter. It was almost a relief to see him. He'd been so busy with his duties, and some of the other small ones Father had asked him to pick up in his absence, that I'd hardly seen him.

Rhi had shuffled back in her chair, trying to make herself as unnoticeable as possible.

"Hey, Rhi," Adam said, shredding her thin cover with two words.

"Hi," she squeaked.

"Is the seat next to you taken?" he asked.

She mumbled something incoherent, making me smother a laugh. She was too cute if she thought this was going to fool him. Anyone with eyes would be able to tell she liked him.

"Morning, Kelis," Jake said.

"Good morning." Was he here to moan about how early breakfast was served again? I wasn't sure I could take much of that. I had enough on my plate without adding more to it. Plus, I was almost certain that some of the court would start asking questions about Mother soon, and I hadn't decided how I was going to answer them yet.

Jake didn't bother asking me if the seat next to me was free like Adam had Rhi and just plonked himself down into it.

Great. That was this morning off to an even worse start.

"We hoped you'd be here, Kelis," Adam said.

"Oh?"

"We went by your parents' room first, but Uncle said you'd probably be here."

My stomach dropped. He'd taken Jake to my parents' room? That wasn't acceptable, and I wasn't comfortable with it. But what could I say without looking like a spoiled princess?

"What happened?" It had to be something urgent if Adam had been trying to find me.

"We heard about your mother this morning," Jake said.

Adam coughed pointedly.

"Fine. I heard about her during a card game last night," Jake admitted.

I flashed a confused glance at Adam. He'd already known about Mother's situation as a family member.

He shook his head. "Not me," he mouthed, completely unnoticed by Jake, who was piling his plate with bacon and eggs while he waited for me to say something. Whether about Mother or about the card game, I wasn't certain.

"I didn't realize it had become common knowledge," I said.

"Yes. One of the healers blabbed."

"Blabbed?" How distasteful of them.

"You know, talked about what they saw in your parents' room," Jake explained.

"I knew what you meant," I snapped without meaning to.

He shrugged as he buttered a roll. I couldn't believe how unimportant he found all this. Didn't he realize that this was my *Mother?* The most important woman in my life. Someone who couldn't be replaced. For me, my father, or for the kingdom.

I glanced over at Adam, hoping he could offer some help, or at the very least, an explanation of what was happening. Unfortunately for me, he seemed to have struck up a conversation with Rhi and wasn't paying me any attention. I was glad for her. My cousin wouldn't find a better woman than Rhi.

"Well, after I heard about it, I decided I needed to do something about it," Jake said.

I snapped my attention back to him. Had he just said what I thought he had? I didn't want to ask in case I'd misheard.

"And I talked to Adam, and he promised he'd help too. Something about doing anything for his aunt. I don't know. I didn't properly listen." He stuffed the buttered roll into his mouth, chewing loudly. The sound went right through me—another thing I couldn't believe I had failed to notice. His habits were becoming less and less enjoyable as time went on. Not that I'd admit that to anyone.

"Oh?" Now I was interested, even if I couldn't think of anything he could do that Topher wasn't already doing. I was going to keep quiet about that. Perhaps I could leave Jake to whatever plan he had, and if it worked, then great, but if not, I wasn't going to end up hurt by it.

"We think we can find out who cursed your mother," he said proudly.

"You can?" A jolt of excitement shot through me. What had they discovered that I hadn't? I'd scoured most of the books in the library, as well as going over the daily newspapers with Topher, and putting out other feelers, and none of them had turned up anything. I doubted they could find anything we hadn't. Especially because I knew what I was looking for.

"Well, it's obviously her stepmother. It was her last time, and she's known for being evil." Crumbs spewed from his mouth as he spoke.

I sighed loudly as the spark of hope inside me fizzled out and died. "It's not going to be her," I countered. "She hasn't been seen for years, and the dwarves *dealt* with her then. She can't have come back." And if she had, then I was certain we'd have heard rumors about it. We had people on the lookout throughout the kingdom in case she did. My parents had taken no chances where the previous owner of my mirror was concerned. And with good reason.

Jake didn't seem deterred by my very real news and simply shrugged. "She might still be back. It's worth looking into. And if it isn't her, then we'll start at the beginning and try again. It's got to be someone."

I supposed he was right there. Someone *did* do this. At least, searching for them would keep him out of the way.

With nothing else for it, I leaned over and touched his hand. Disappointment filled me at the lack of thrill it gave me to touch him. Almost like it didn't mean anything. "Thank you, Jake, I really appreciate you looking for me."

"You're welcome. Perhaps after this is over, you'll knight me for it." He waggled his eyebrows.

"I can't decide things like that," I responded. Though, it was probably a lie. I'd never wanted to have anyone knighted before, so I hadn't asked Father. But I couldn't see him saying no if I did ask.

"Shame. Sir Jake has a nice ring to it."

I put a bland smile on my face. I should be glad he was taking more of an interest in the affairs of the kingdom, shouldn't I? This was all I'd wanted for so long. But then, why didn't it feel good?

Jake went back to eating his breakfast, and I went back to scouring the hall for signs that Topher had returned. Though, if anyone had asked me if that was what I was doing, I'd have denied it. I wasn't sure what it was about Jake's behavior at the moment, but all it did was remind me of how much better it felt to spend time around someone else.

It seemed best if I didn't dwell on that thought too much, especially when I had problems like the one facing Mother to deal with.

~

Later, In the early afternoon, a servant set down the tray of tea and sandwiches between Rhi and I.

"Would you like anything else, Your Highness?" she asked.

"No, thank you. We'll call if we do." I smiled my thanks and watched her leave.

"If we're eating lunch, does that mean we can take a break and talk about something that'll take your mind off everything?" Rhi asked.

"I'm sorry, I don't mean to be so one-track-minded..."

"Don't be sorry, Kelis," she interrupted. "I've never experienced what you're going through, but I do understand how terrible it must be. But I want to help. And right now, the best way I can see to do that is by distracting you from the horrible thoughts that are going through your mind."

"Thank you." I smiled at her, hoping it reassured her that my words were truly meant.

I picked up the teapot and poured cups for us both.

"What subject did you have in mind?" I asked once I'd finished.

She shuffled uncomfortably in her seat. "Can I talk to you about Adam?"

I frowned. "Of course. Things seemed to be going well this morning..."

Rhi let out a bitter laugh. "No, they didn't. He said that Jake wanted to talk to you, and we should talk in order to give you privacy. He was actually giving me a very detailed description of how he grooms his horse."

My hand flew to cover my mouth as an involuntary giggle escaped me. "I'm sorry, I don't mean to laugh."

She smothered a smile of her own. "It's fine. It *is* kind of funny. I now know far more than I need to about horse care."

"So, in what way *did* you want to talk to me about him?" I asked.

An oddly tense silence stretched between us as if she didn't want to say whatever she was thinking. I nibbled on one of the sandwiches, more for something to do than because I was hungry. It was past lunch, though, and we hadn't eaten anything, so I probably should.

"I think I should move on," she blurted.

"Oh?"

"It's not that he isn't a nice guy, he is. And he's always nice to me. But it's always so boring like he doesn't want to be talking to *me*."

"That's not true..."

"Isn't it?" She raised an eyebrow, then sighed. "If he was interested, then he'd do more to spend time with me."

"Didn't he invite you to come here in the first place?" I checked.

"Huh. I suppose he did, yes."

"Then perhaps he's more interested than you think he is?" I suggested.

She sighed. "Maybe, but I don't want to waste my time pining after him. On the off chance he *does* want to spend time with me. If he does, he's going to have to do something about it. I'm not going to be the one waiting for him anymore."

I nodded. "There are lots of eligible nobles around here if you're looking for someone else," I suggested.

"Good. I'll make sure one of them falls head over heels for me instead," she joked. She picked up one of the sandwiches for herself and took a bite.

"Any man would be lucky to have you."

She chuckled. "Of course, he would. I'm smart, pretty, and funny. Not to mention well connected. I'm a friend to the heir of the throne, as well as her cousin. And one of the best magic users in the kingdoms."

I picked up my cup and took a sip as I pretended not to be too interested in what she was saying. "Topher?" I checked once I'd swallowed my tea.

Rhi flashed me a knowing look. "I hardly meant Jake."

A wry smile stretched over my lips as I remembered

what both she and Topher had said about Jake's annoyance at *not* being the best.

She leaned back in her seat, studying me intently. "He's interested in you," she said.

"Topher?" I repeated, my eyebrows knitting together as I tried to work out what she was talking about.

"No..." She gave me a strange look, but I ignored it so she'd continue with what she was saying. "Jake."

"Oh." I waited for some kind of reaction from my heart, but nothing happened. I supposed that was to be expected. He'd been annoying me more and more with each passing moment. "What makes you say that?"

"You're all he's been talking about for the past couple of days. It's getting annoying if I'm honest."

I laughed lightly. "It's annoying to hear things about me? I've heard that one before."

"No, that's not what I meant," she answered hastily.

"I know, don't worry."

"It's the things he says that are annoying, not the fact they're about you. He keeps waxing lyrical about the shine of your hair and the beauty of your eyes."

There was no stopping my snort of derision. I doubted anyone would ever talk about me in that way. Well, perhaps about my eyes. The golden rings around my irises did look particularly stunning most of the time. "Has he hit his head recently?"

Rhi dissolved into laughter at that one. I waited for it to pass, knowing it would be over soon.

"I think it's because you've suddenly become good at magic," she answered.

"You're kidding me, right?" That was a ridiculous reason to suddenly start liking someone. "Are you sure it isn't because we have a shared interest?" That would make some sense, at least.

"Nope. Not because you've taken an interest in magic. Specifically, because you're *good* at it. Adam asked him outright at dinner last night just as Topher walked in. He didn't seem happy with Jake's answer *at all.* I thought he was going to punch Jake for a moment."

"I doubt he'd punch anyone," I said to cover up the small thrill it gave me at the thought of Topher wanting to defend me like that.

Rhi set her teacup down with a soft clink, a serious expression on her face. "Can I be honest with you?"

"Always," I promised. There would be no point in us being friends if we couldn't be honest with one another. It was one of the many reasons we'd become friends so quickly. At least, I hoped it was. I knew what was happening from my side, but it could be different for her.

But should I be worried about what she was going to say? Unless she planned to completely change the subject, it was going to be about Topher or Jake. I supposed it could also be about Adam, but she'd moved on quickly from him. Probably because she wasn't as ready to move on from him as she believed. I honestly hoped not. Whether she'd seen it or not, he *had* acted like he was interested in her at breakfast. And they'd be good together. Despite his sometimes suspect choice of friends, Adam was a good guy. One who put his family above his own entertainment as the last few weeks had proved.

She took a deep breath as if what she was going to say would be difficult. "I don't know what you see in Jake." The words burst from her so quickly that they ran together to form one giant one.

"Oh." How was I supposed to respond to that? I needed to think of something, though, I wasn't sure what.

"I know he's handsome, but that's about it for good qualities," she admitted. "Plus, there's the string of broken hearts he left behind at the university. It isn't a good look. Certainly not in the consort of a princess."

"He dates a lot?" I waited for jealousy to spring to life inside me like it had when he'd first arrived with Lyss, but it didn't come.

"A lot doesn't even begin to cover it. Between them, I don't think Topher and Adam would have even half the number of dates Jake does."

This time, the jealousy *did* rear its head. And it certainly wasn't aimed at my cousin.

"Topher dates?" I tried to keep my emotions out of my voice. Rhi was far too perceptive for my own good. But I had to know the answer to my question.

"You sound surprised." Her expression suggested I hadn't fooled her in the slightest.

Oops.

"He doesn't seem the type is all," I said quickly in an attempt to cover myself.

"Mmhmm."

She waited a moment, probably expecting me to deny whatever it was she was thinking. I wasn't going to bother doing that. If I didn't, then perhaps she'd do me a favor and work out how I felt about Topher for me.

"No, he doesn't date a lot."

I sighed with relief. Perhaps I'd explore the emotions I was feeling towards him once I was alone again.

"But Jake does. You said that he has a new girl on his arm, at least once a week," I said, not that I cared anymore. I just wanted to get away from the topic of Topher seeing other girls.

"Yes. A lot. Honestly, I've been surprised by how long

he's spent with Lyss. By my calculations, they should have broken up before they even got here."

"Oh."

"But he doesn't think twice about it. He's on to the next girl already, and then he'll only break her heart."

"And that's me?" I checked.

She grimaced. "I'm sorry, I spoke out of turn..."

"No, you didn't. I'm glad you feel like you can tell me these things. I need to know them." And every word she was saying only went towards validating how my feelings had changed.

"Admittedly, it was his idea to look into who cursed your mother. Which was sweet, and surprisingly thoughtful compared to what I've seen from him before. But I reckon you've already thought of that."

I grimaced and took a sip of tea to cover up my thinking time. "Yes, I already thought of that," I admitted.

"And do you have people doing anything about it?"

I sighed. "We always have people watching out for my step-grandmother. Nothing's been reported about her."

"And it was probably the first person you thought to look into."

"Yep. No doubt, Jake's going to come to me at some point in the next couple of days and suggest this can all be sorted with true love's kiss too." I tried to keep the exasperation out of my voice, but it didn't work.

"I imagine you've already tried that."

"Father has," I admitted.

"And you? I'd imagine true love also works between children and...ah, you have." She must have seen the expression on my face and understood the meanings behind it.

"Topher and I have been looking into a theory, but we

have nothing of use yet. I'm hoping that'll change when he gets back from his errands in the city." I didn't add that I'd hoped he would be back by now. That seemed too telling, to myself as well as to Rhi.

"You have? Interesting." She drank some more tea.

"Yes."

She gave me a knowing look, but it changed into an easy smile within a few moments. "In which case, I believe it's time to take my leave of you." She set her cup down and rose to her feet.

"You don't have to go..."

She looked over my shoulder at someone there, and my traitorous heart skipped a beat.

"Good afternoon, Topher," she said.

"Hi, Rhi," he responded.

I didn't look around. I couldn't until I had control over the rush of emotions within me.

"Do you mind if I pull up a seat?" he asked.

"Oh, you don't have to. I have something important to attend to, you can have mine." She stepped back and gestured to hers.

"Thanks, that'd be good." They switched places.

Was it me, or did Topher's eyes light up when they locked on mine?

No. They couldn't. And I shouldn't feel this way about it, anyway. Jake was finally interested in me. I should be making the most of that, not be getting confused by my feelings for someone else.

And yet, my entire day was brighter now that Topher was back in it. And I spent most of my meals searching the crowds for him.

No. I shouldn't think about this too much. I was going to sit here and research with my friend, and I'd decide what to do about Jake later. Because Rhi was right, he definitely wasn't a good consort for the heir to the throne. I supposed it would all depend on whether or not he had the ability to become one.

# 27TH OCTOBER

I was almost relieved when I found myself back in the corridor that led to the underground room. Unlike the dreams about Mother, each of these seemed to give me more information about what was going on. Though, I supposed the ones about Mother also did that, but only insofar as telling me about her illness getting worse, which wasn't a particularly fun kind of knowledge.

I half-ran down the corridor, hoping to get into the room more quickly. I stepped inside and looked around. The same people as before were there, each looking the exact same way they had before.

Good. The dream hadn't changed. Instead of staring at the people this time, I looked around the room itself. Perhaps there was some kind of clue about where they were. If I worked that out, then perhaps I could go find them and ask them to help me with my situation.

Was that a silly thing to do? I had no way of knowing if they'd help me. Or even if I could trust them. Other than the rings around their eyes, and an odd sense of familiarity that had nothing to do with that, I had no idea who they were or where they'd come from.

The girl at the front, Azia, coughed, and then called the rest of the room to attention. I wasn't sure why she was the one who was in charge, but just like I knew everyone's names, I also knew that too.

"We all have to work together if we're going to do what we have planned," she said, her voice ringing out through the room. "We know there's been a lot of discord in the kingdoms, and some of you want to get home so you can help your families sort it out and protect your people. I want that too."

Ah. That was it. Royal. She was royalty. As were several of the other people in the room. Though I suspected that, just like me, they'd been adopted at an early age.

"But if we want to do that, then we have to start at the beginning," she carried on. "We have to bring back the happy endings."

My eyes widened. Or my dream-self's eyes did. I imagined my real eyes were shut tight as I lay in my bed. But this was exactly what we needed. I couldn't wait to tell Topher about this dream. I knew he'd be as excited as I was about the fact other people were trying to do the same thing we were. There was no doubt that the happy endings they were referring to were the same ones that all the kingdoms were famous for. No wonder they wanted to find me. I had eyes like theirs and was the adopted daughter of Snow White, a woman who had one of the most famous happy endings of all. Though, I supposed I was a little biased on that front.

The dream started to fade before I could hear anything more of what she was saying, but that was fine by me. My dreams had finally given me information I needed, and I had no doubt that if the underground room returned at any point, it would tell me more information that I needed to know. In theory, at least.

I let sleep take me, knowing I'd have exciting news when morning came. I could go see Mother too and tell her about all the things that had been happening. I'd been so busy the last couple of days that I hadn't spent much time with her. Though, I had been dropping in to tell her I loved her and that I was trying to find a way to fix what had happened.

~

Mother's face was deathly pale, making her name of Snow White more appropriate than ever.

"Hi, Mother," I said to her, grateful Father and the dwarves had taken this opportunity to go and have breakfast. It was a relief not to have to be the royal in attendance like I had been for the past week or so.

"I'm sorry I haven't been here more. I know you're being well looked after, and I've had so much going on. My friends are helping me look into what happened to you, and we think we've worked it out. There are similar things happening in other kingdoms. The happy endings are all coming undone. I know you wouldn't approve of it, but I even asked the mirror for help. But it was useless. I'm certain you could have warned me of that in advance, but it was worth a shot."

A loud crackle from the fire made me jump. I glanced

behind me to find out what had happened, but nothing had changed. I scraped my chair back and got to my feet. I grabbed one of the pouches of purifying herbs Vanessa had left for us. She'd said we should use them whenever we felt the time was right, and as it stood, I felt like this was it.

I ripped the top off the packet and sprinkled the herbs into the fire. Just like last time, the flames flickered from orange to blue, then back again.

I breathed a sigh of relief and went back to my seat next to Mother. For all I knew, the herbs didn't actually do anything, but they gave me peace of mind, and that was worth it.

"Everyone's found out about what's going on now. But everyone is being nice about it. There are some people calling for the Fright Festival to be canceled, but I don't think that's a good idea." And not just because I had a great costume planned. It would give people a great outlet for their energy, as well as creating good cheer among them. "I think they're only asking for things like that because it's come as such a shock. But they've been through this before. I'm sure our people will be fine once you've woken up."

I hoped I was telling the truth. The people of Enchantia had always loved Mother, and I was certain they'd be happy when she woke up. But I hoped the situation wouldn't go on for too long. Worry could turn some people crazy. And then there was the potential grief to deal with.

"Adam and Jake have gone to Urbis this morning to try and find out who cursed you. I don't think it's as simple as that, but I appreciate that they're trying to help. Topher and Rhi are helping me by researching curses, and what's going on with all of the other kingdoms." I sighed. "I'm scared."

The moment the word was out, I realized how true it was. And that it encompassed so much more than I thought. I didn't want to leave home to go and find the other people with eyes like mine. Not when Mother was so sick. No, not sick. Cursed. But that didn't mean I wasn't going to do it, especially if it was for the sake of the kingdom. Add in how uncertain my feelings had become for Jake, and now Topher, and I was a mess. Not the kind of person anyone wanted running a kingdom, anyway.

"I can hear your voice in my head telling me that it's all right to be scared, so long as I do the right thing, despite that." A funny smile passed over my face at the thought. I missed her so much, and yet, here she was, loving on without saying a word. "I think about you all the time," I promised.

On a whim, I pulled the necklace of hers that I'd taken from the dwarves' house from my neck, and gently lifted her head so I could slip it around hers.

"I'd say this was a present, but it was yours to begin with. It was in your room at the dwarves' house. I was trying to use it to keep the bad dreams away, but it seems that isn't possible. Whatever it is causing me visions at night, I don't think it can be stopped by a small wooden apple." I touched the pendant.

Perhaps it was odd to feel so much affection for the symbol of something that had caused so much grief in our kingdom. But, it belonged to Mother, and that made it special.

"I don't know if you're dreaming while you're lying like this. But if you are, then maybe this can help keep away the bad ones. So long as they're not made from the same magic as mine, anyway." I sighed.

The clock in the other room chimed the hour, but I ignored it. Father hadn't returned yet, and the last thing I was going to do was leave mother alone. Just because she couldn't respond to me, didn't mean she didn't know I was there.

I filled her in on the rest of what had been happening but glossed over some of the finer details of my romantic feelings. I couldn't get those straight in my own head. It was best I didn't say them aloud in case the wrong person was listening. When I ran out of things to tell her, I slipped into a song she'd taught me as a child.

The lyrics were silly now. I was eighteen, but I didn't care. They'd make her laugh if she was awake, and that was what mattered.

At some point, I must have dozed off, as I woke to Father shaking my shoulder.

"Kelis," he said softly.

"Huh?"

"There's someone outside waiting for you," he said. "Topher."

"Oh." I must have been here longer than I thought. Topher would never come to my parents' room without good reason. He wasn't like Jake. He wouldn't intrude on someone's privacy like that. "Thank you."

"Are you all right? You look tired," Father said.

I nodded. "I'm as good as I can be."

"I know that feeling. But you're still managing to have some fun, right?"

"I'm trying."

"Good. I don't want you giving up on living your life because of this. She'd never forgive me."

We both looked at Mother. He was right. And more to the point, Mother wouldn't forgive me, either.

I leaned in and kissed Mother's forehead, before

doing the same for Father, once he'd taken my place.

"We love you, Kelis," Father said.

"I love you both, too," I responded instantly. "We'll get through this."

"I hope you're right," he whispered, but I didn't think I was meant to hear it.

With nothing else to say, I made my way out of their rooms to where Topher was waiting.

The moment I stepped through the door and saw him leaning against the wall, it felt as if a weight had been lifted from me. I longed to go up to him, wrap my arms around him and lose myself in the comfort of *him*.

"Is everything all right? I thought I was meeting you in the library after breakfast?" he asked without a hint of accusation in his tone. He truly wanted to know that I was safe.

"Yes. Sorry, I fell asleep." I frowned and glanced back at the closed door to my parents' rooms. What had happened in there? Was it Vanessa's herbs? Had they put me to sleep?

No. That wasn't possible. I'd been in the room when they'd been used countless times before. I'd used them myself before, too, and I'd never fallen asleep.

Perhaps it was to do with my dreams. I thought I'd had plenty of rest, but what if that wasn't true? I'd felt particularly tired after the ones about Mother, so maybe these new ones about the people with the eyes were no different.

"Let's go find a good spot in the library, and I'll tell you about my new dream," I suggested.

His eyes lit up. "Another dream?"

"Yep. And another one that included useful information, too," I promised. "But first, tea and a comfy chair." Sleeping while hunched over Mother's bed had left a crick in my back that I was desperate to get rid of.

~

"I meant to ask you, what was there in the papers this morning?" I asked Topher.

He grimaced. "Nothing much, but I was only able to get half of them for some reason."

"Which ones?"

"I'll have to check when I go back to my room. I didn't bring them because there wasn't much in them," he admitted.

I sighed. "I suppose a good source of information on what's going on was too much to ask."

He chuckled but didn't say anything. There wasn't much he could say. It wasn't his fault that the papers didn't arrive.

"Did you have a chance to look over your tournament information?" he asked, taking me off guard with the change of subject.

"I did, yes. Well, a quick one to see if there was anything interesting." I'd been too tired yesterday to read all of it in detail, but I had scanned it in case anything jumped out and needed more attention.

"Was there?"

"Not really. I'm not allowed to get a new wand between my trial and the tournament."

"Was that ever likely to happen?" he asked.

"No. The only reason someone gets a new wand in Enchantia is because they broke theirs. And even then, most people get it fixed rather than buy a new one."

"Because it's cheaper?"

I shook my head. "Because wands are too personal." A thought I'd never considered popped into my head.

"Don't you have a wand?"

"Yes. But it was an oddity that turned up in my grandfather's shop when I was a child. I never knew much about it, other than that it worked for me, and I enjoyed being able to do magic."

It was impossible not to smile at the way he spoke.

"Honestly, I hadn't thought about it until now. Wands are so personal, I assumed everyone knew about them."

"Which is why no one has ever told me any of this. They all assumed I knew."

"That's not necessarily a good thing."

"No, not at all," he admitted. "You'll have to tell me more about wand lore, unless there's a book about it?"

"I have no idea if there is or not. It's so much a part of our culture that most people are just expected to know it."

He started to ask another question but was interrupted by a loud crash at the entrance to the library.

We were both on our feet within seconds, our wands drawn, and ready to defend ourselves or fix the damage, whichever became the most important when we discovered the disturbance.

To my surprise, we rounded one of the bookshelves to find Jake standing in the middle of the library doorway, panting for breath. Nothing seemed out of place, which must have meant that the crash had been the doors opening with more force than they were supposed to be.

I sheathed my wand, and watched as Topher did the same. There was no need for the two of us to have them drawn at this point.

"What's going on?" I asked.

"Urbis," Jake panted but didn't get out any more than that.

"Where's Adam?" Topher asked.

Jake waved a pointed finger in the vague direction of the stairs. Sure enough, a moment later, Adam came up them, looking a lot less out of breath than Jake did.

"Would you mind finding a servant and getting some tea, water, and sandwiches brought here?" I asked Topher quietly.

He nodded, then disappeared out into the hall. Would Jake have done something like that so easily? Or would he have kicked up a fuss about it? I pushed the thought aside. I wasn't likely to find out any time soon.

"What's going on?" I repeated, looking to my cousin for answers this time.

"Why don't we sit down. I'm not sure how to describe what's going on," Adam suggested.

I nodded and brought them back to the table Topher and I had been sitting at. Luckily, there were already four chairs there, and with a bit of maneuvering on my part, I managed to keep Topher's next to mine.

The man himself returned from finding a servant moments later. He placed a hand on my lower back and leaned in. "They're bringing it up," he said softly, then pulled away.

A part of me wanted to ask him to return to that position, but it was probably better if I didn't think too much about it. "Thank you for doing that," I said instead.

"It's no problem," Topher responded. "I'm glad I could help."

I flashed him a grateful smile as we all sat down.

Jake glared at Topher, though I had no idea why. They weren't the closest of friends, that much was true, but they were on the same side. And had Adam in common.

"Now, will one of you please tell me what happened? Weren't you going to Urbis today?"

The journey itself wouldn't have taken long, but they hadn't been gone from the palace long enough to have gone there and back and discovered anything interesting. Not unless every person they'd ever met had been at the train station waiting with shorthand notes of what they'd seen since the last time they'd been there.

"We *did* go to Urbis today," Adam started. "But we only got as far as the train station."

"Not even there," Jake corrected. "The train approached the station, and then, the conductor walked down telling everyone that the Urbis gates were closed and that we couldn't enter the station."

"What?" I didn't mean for the question to sound rude, but what he had just said sounded so weird.. I'd never heard any reports of Urbis shutting down like that before.

"We tried to tell them that we lived there and studied at the university, but they said it didn't matter. If we were outside Urbis, then that's where we were going to stay," Jake said.

"I suppose that explains why you couldn't get all of your newspapers," I said to Topher.

"Newspapers?" Jake snapped, anger filling his tone. "If you're already getting news from *him*, then why did you send us to Urbis?" Anger and bitterness were both evident in his voice, though I didn't know how to deal with either.

"I didn't send you anywhere," I pointed out. "You wanted to go."

"But..."

"Not now," Adam shushed his friend.

I didn't say anything aloud, but I was glad of it. I didn't want Jake's ego getting in the way of finding out what was wrong with the kingdoms.

"Did the conductor tell you anything else?" I asked Adam.

He shook his head. "But I cast a communication spell with one of our friends who is still at the university, and he filled me in about some of the things he's seen. He's going to keep us posted too, though I'm not sure he'll be able to get any of the newspapers to us. Sorry, Topher."

"It doesn't matter. We were only going through them to try and find correlations, but I think we've got one," Topher responded.

I nodded my agreement. "It would be nice to have them, but it isn't that important." Even as I said the words, I felt a pang of regret. I'd enjoyed going through them with Topher and hated the fact we'd lost that moment of closeness now. "What did your friend say?"

"Nothing much of interest. A lot of people in Urbis are going about their days as normal. But there are two main things happening. The Urbis guard seems to be searching for some people in earnest, but no one knows *why*. It's very confusing. Especially because..." He gave me a knowing look.

I nodded but didn't say the words out loud. Adam knew I was adopted, as did Topher, but as far as Jake knew, I was the daughter of Enchantia's monarchs. And given his drinking and loose lips, I wasn't ready to trust his discretion.

"Didn't he say they had golden rings around their irises?" Jake asked, looking at Adam.

My heart sank. Had he worked it out already?

"Yes." Adam tried not to look at me.

Not that it mattered. Jake didn't seem to care.

"We should send out a decree in Enchantia to keep an eye out for them. How much of a reward are they offering? I might go out and find them myself," Jake said with a truckload of false bravado.

I exchanged a confused glance with Adam. Didn't Jake realize what he was saying? The most likely reason for his nonchalance was that he simply hadn't noticed the color of my eyes. That realization would have floored me days ago, but now barely registered. It was actually a good thing he hadn't.

"You said there were two main changes?" I prompted Adam, mostly so we could get off the topic of eye color. If the news about eyes like mine was spreading, then perhaps, it would be wise for me to change mine with magic for now. I didn't want to draw the wrong kind of attention.

"Yes. He said the other one was that there was a large build-up of magic over Urbis. I think that's why they've shut it down. It's not normal, and I doubt it would be safe," Adam said, clearly as relieved as I was to be away from the previous subject.

"Do they have any idea what's causing it?" Topher asked.

"No. But it could be that no one's told my friend, nothing more than that," he supplied.

"Hmm." Could this all be related to the things I'd seen in my dream?

If Topher was right, then the people with the golden eyes could be my relatives. If I wasn't born an Enchantian, which was looking likely, then perhaps they weren't either. And if that was the case, then maybe they had magic too. Mine had to have come from somewhere. I'd never put much thought into who my birth parents were. It didn't matter when I had the ones who chose to keep me, so I'd always assumed they were Enchantians.

And if that was the case, then were my relations causing the magic build up? It made a certain amount of sense, though I doubted they were doing it on purpose. And perhaps that was all linked to the curses, too. Azia had said they were trying to bring back the happy endings, so it seemed like that might be the case.

Only a couple of things were becoming clear to me now. The first was that I needed to talk to Topher alone. As much as I didn't want to admit it, a large part of me didn't trust Jake at all.

The other thing was that I needed to talk to the people from my dream.

# GODDESS OF MAGIC

# 28TH OCTOBER

I tried to restrain the hopeful feeling that came over me when I realized I was again having the dream about the people with eyes like mine. Each previous time I'd had it, I had learned more about Mother's curse and the problems in the other kingdoms. I hoped that tonight I'd learn enough to have a clue as to what to do next.

I'd take any information I could get right now. I had to. Topher would help me work out what it meant in the morning.

The torches flickered in the corridor, making the shadows dance. But I didn't pay them any attention. They weren't going to do me any harm. Instead, I rushed down the corridor, eager to get to the room.

I pushed through the door and stepped inside. It was emptier than before, with only a few of the people I'd come to recognize inside. Two of them were leaning over a map, moving small markers up and down. I frowned, trying to make sense of what I was seeing. How was this supposed to help me? They weren't talking about me, the curse, or Enchantia.

Gaia walked in, a newspaper in her hand. "Have you seen this?" she asked, dropping it onto the table with the map.

"Not yet. What is it?" Azia responded, looking up.

"Just read," Gaia said, pushing the paper closer to the other girl.

Intrigued, I leaned over to get a look at whatever it was that had Gaia all worked up. I scanned the paper, reading the front page three times to make sure I was understanding it correctly.

The paper was dated the thirty-first of October. That was still four days away. Shouldn't they be dismissing it as complete rubbish just based on that alone?

Azia picked up the paper and unfolded it. "What page?"

"Three," Gaia said.

She flicked through it and scanned the article in question. Unfortunately for me, Azia wasn't holding it in a way that enabled me to read it.

Neither of them seemed confused by the fact it was from the future, though. Had they got an advance copy?

No. That wasn't possible. The people behind the paper wouldn't be printing it that far in advance. It would be far too out of date by the time the thirty-first came around.

Which must mean that this *was* the thirty-first or

later. At a stretch, it was the thirtieth.

I was seeing the future. Not only in the visions I'd had, but in my dreams also. Everything I'd seen had come true.

Now that I knew what was happening, only one question remained. Could I do it on purpose?

Before I could spend much energy thinking about it, the blackness seeped in, and sleep took me once more. But that was all right. I could give it more thought in the morning.

~

Sunlight woke me from sleep. I hummed and stretched, not opening my eyes. Once I did, all the normal worries of the day would slip back in, and I wasn't ready for that to happen.

Memories of my dream from the night before began to slip back in.

My eyes snapped open.

*The future.*

That wasn't something I could ignore. I supposed the real question was, could I see into the future at will? Or was that thought nothing more an unconscious effort to make sense of the dreams I'd been having? Both theories made sense, but I didn't know which was the truth. When I could make magic fly out of the end of my wand, and do all manner of strange things, seeing the future didn't seem all that far-fetched.

But perhaps I should try to find someone to talk to about it before trying it out by myself. That was the most sensible course of action, even if I didn't know who to trust with it.

Topher's face drifted through my mind. I was almost

certain he'd know about this kind of thing. And if he didn't, he would know where to look to find the answers. He was good at that, and I was grateful for it. I wasn't sure what I'd do without him and the support he gave me. It made me feel different from how my parents' support did. Though, I couldn't put a finger on why. No doubt, the explanation was a simple one. It always seemed to be.

He was the most logical person to turn to, especially when I didn't want to worry Father with something like this. He probably didn't have the experience to answer any of my questions anyway. And even if he did, his attention was already taken up by everything that was going on with Mother.

My excitement waned a little at the memory of her unconscious form. I pushed away the guilt. If Mother could talk to me, I knew she'd tell me that I had to do things for myself. Not just to let go of some of the stress building inside me, but also, to distract people from the thought that anything was wrong in the royal family. That was part of what came with the job. Half the things we did were for appearances. While we had choices about some things like me wearing black most of the time, there were other things where we didn't have that freedom.

I'd seen Father sick and sitting in his chair presiding over a banquet before, despite the fact he should have been in bed. Or Mother getting back up after stumbling and putting on a brave face as she righted herself.

Besides, why shouldn't I feel excited about being able to see the future? If I could do it, then there might be a chance I could see something that would help us heal Mother, or break the curse hanging over her head. Of course, there were other things I wanted to know, but they could wait.

There was the slight issue of my not knowing *how* to see the future. All the times I'd done it before, it hadn't been intentional. I'd either been asleep or concentrating on something else.

Neither of those would make it easy to use the gift of being able to see the future if I had it.

I pushed a hand over my face as I tried to work out what to do. Should I stay in bed or get up?

Staying lying down was probably the best bet. I'd seen the future more in my sleep than when I'd been awake, which meant that I should probably be as relaxed as I possibly could. If this didn't work, then I'd write a message to Topher and get him to join me. He'd probably have some ideas on how to do it. Actually, once I got up, I'd do that anyway. If I managed it, then he'd love to hear about it.

I took a deep, steadying breath and counted to ten, trying to relax. It was more difficult than I anticipated while my palms itched, and my heartbeat raced a mile a minute.

I was thinking about this too hard.

So trying to relax wasn't going to work. But what could? Perhaps I needed to think about the future I wanted to see. Everything I was wondering about flooded through my mind at once. Mother's curse, the people with gold-ringed irises, whatever was going on in Urbis, whether or not Topher would be in my life for a long time to come...

Wait. No. Not that last one. I meant Jake, not Topher. Even as I told myself that was the case, I knew it was a lie. Somewhere along the line, my feelings for the two had started to get muddled, and I wasn't sure what the best way to sort them out was. Only a couple of weeks ago, all I'd wanted in the world was for Jake to notice me, and now, he had. But so had Topher. And he was the one I kept turning to when I needed help.

Those were thoughts for later if I wasn't sure how I really felt about either of them. But then, my love life was the wrong thing to focus on when I was trying to see the future on purpose. I needed something easier. Simpler.

An idea hit me. I knew what I should look for.

I closed my eyes and thought about my Fright Festival costume. When would it be ready? That was what I hoped my gift would tell me. It might have been a frivolous request, but I wanted to check out how things worked before I moved on to bigger problems that actually made a difference.

*My costume. The cape, the green stones.* Mother and I had worked on it together. Before she fell asleep.

Even with my eyes closed, the world around me swirled and slowed, just like it had when I'd seen the spell that nearly killed Jake. It was working. I focused harder.

My room came into focus behind my eyelids, but I knew it wasn't real. At least, it wasn't real *yet.* I saw myself sitting on the edge of my bed. A knock sounded on the door, and I sprang to my feet. I grabbed a dressing gown and slipped my arms into it before hurrying over to the door. In the vision, there was a maid waiting behind it with a garment bag in her hands and a smile on her face.

My eyes snapped open. I hadn't seen very far into the future, but that didn't matter. I'd done it. That was the main thing.

I swung my legs around and sat on the bed, wondering how long I'd have to wait for the maid to arrive. I hoped it wouldn't be long. Then I could focus on trying to use my gift for bigger things. Perhaps, I should use the waiting time to write a note to Topher. I needed to see him now more than ever. He could help me make sense of this and help me work out how to use it better. I was certain he'd have answers I needed.

Before I could make my way over to the dresser, the expected knock sounded on the door.

Excitement pounded in my chest. This was proof of what I'd managed to achieve. I bounced to my feet and put on my dressing gown. I didn't want to open the door wearing nothing more than my nightclothes.

I pulled the door open to find the smiling maid there, garment bag and everything. Relief washed through me. There'd been a small voice in the back of my head trying to tell me that I was crazy for thinking I could see things that were going to happen in advance.

"Good morning, Your Highness. I have your Fright Festival dress for you," the maid said.

"Thank you, would you bring it in?" I asked.

She nodded and entered the room, hanging the garment bag on one of the hooks on the wall by my dressing area.

"Is it done, or are there still alterations needed?" It was best to know before I got my hopes up too much and thought this was the finished thing.

"It's mostly done, Your Highness, but you have a fitting on Friday to make any changes you need and to make sure it fits perfectly. I think your friend has one at the same time," she offered.

Oh. That was good. I needed some time with Rhi, I hadn't talked to her enough in the past few days. "Thank you."

The maid stepped back. "Is there anything else I can

do for you, Your Highness?"

I was about to dismiss her when a thought came to mind. "Yes. I have a note I'd like delivered to one of the guests. Would that be possible?"

"Of course. Do you have it ready?"

"Just a moment." I rushed over to my dressing table and picked up one of the pens I kept scattered about.

It only took me a moment to scribble the note. I folded it over and handed it to her. Perhaps I should have sealed it too, but it didn't say anything particularly interesting. The maid probably wouldn't even look.

"Can you take this to Topher, please?" I asked, handing it to her. "He's one of Adam's guests." It was safest to tell her that in case she didn't know who he was. That was possible. He hadn't been at the palace all that long. Then again, he'd been spending a lot of time with me, so perhaps the staff had learned his name.

"Of course, Your Highness." She tucked the note into her pocket and dipped into an elegant curtsy that a lot of noblewomen would have envied.

"I'll deliver it right now, Princess." She curtsied again, then left the room.

As soon as the door clicked behind her, I retook my place on the bed and took a few steadying breaths. Perhaps, I should have gotten dressed first, but I was too focused on what I wanted to see to be able to concentrate on something so trivial.

This time, I was going to try and see when Mother would wake up. If I did that, then I'd be able to give Father some good news. I was certain he'd appreciate it with how worried he'd been over the past week or so.

I took another breath and closed my eyes.

Mother's face formed in my mind, and I tried to think of it the way it was when she was awake and uncursed.

It was difficult to focus on when I knew she was lying down the corridor, not responding to the world at all.

*When will she wake up? When will she wake up?* The statement whizzed around my mind, and I might even have been saying the words out loud. I had no way of knowing, considering that all of my attention was on the phrase.

My vision started to shift, even in the darkness, and excitement built up within me. Was I going to see the answer? I hoped so.

A room came into focus. I looked around, trying to make sense of what I was seeing even before it fully came into focus. Even through the haze, I vaguely recognized the room I was in. That was good. It was probably Mother's bedchamber. That would make the most sense.

The vision snapped into place, and disappointment welled up within me.

I was in the underground room. I waited for a moment, looking around to see who was in the room and if they were doing anything of interest.

Unfortunately, they didn't seem to be. None of them were talking to one another. Instead, they were glancing around, as if they were expecting something to happen.

I let the vision slip. This wasn't what I wanted to see, and they weren't doing anything of interest to warrant my staying

After it had gone, I settled and took a few minutes to compose myself again.

*Mother. Mother. Mother.* A question hadn't worked before, so perhaps one word would now. It wasn't like the magic could mistake anyone in the underground room for my mother. At least, I hoped it wouldn't. It seemed unlikely given that they all seemed to be about my age. But, stranger things had happened, and I didn't know anything about my real parentage. Perhaps it was time I asked Father about it.

Just as I was about to ponder more on the subject, my vision blurred again. Good.

As soon as everything was in focus, I cursed inwardly. I was back in the underground cavern. And even worse, nothing had changed. I let the vision slip again. The only positive in this was that I knew I was *capable* of seeing the future when I wanted to. But it seemed like I wasn't able to control what I was seeing, which wasn't so good.

Except, that wasn't right. I'd been able to concentrate on my Fright Festival costume and see what was happening there. It was just the more complicated things that seemed to be a problem.

No matter. I'd simply keep trying until I saw what I was looking for.

I let myself drift into another vision. The same thing happened. The underground room. The people shuffling around nervously. But nothing new.

I tried a few more times but didn't manage to see anything different.

Frustrated, I got up from the bed and walked over to the small table. The moment I was on my feet, a woozy feeling washed over me. I pressed a hand to my temple, hoping to ward it off. Was this a result of trying too hard to see something about Mother's future? I hoped not. I wanted to try again later.

"What have you been doing, Kelis? You're a mess," the mirror announced.

I groaned. Somehow, I'd managed to forget it was in the room. That was quite a feat, considering I hadn't left the room since the night before.

"I look fine," I grumbled.

"Ha. Have you seen yourself? You could pack half your closet in the bags under your eyes."

I scowled, not in the mood for the mirror's word games. Normally, I could give as good as I got. But not today.

"Whatever." I set my mug down and moved over to my dressing table. I gasped the moment I saw my reflection.

I hated to admit it, but the mirror was right. It looked as if I hadn't slept in three days. As if seeing it for myself caused it, a wave of tiredness rushed over my body.

The urge to return to bed hit me. I couldn't do that, though, right? I had too many responsibilities to waste my time in bed. But I knew that both of my parents would hate to hear me talking like that. They'd say my own health and mental well-being should come above anything else.

And a nap never hurt anyone. I was going to lie down, and when I woke up, I could try on my Fright Festival costume, then get on with the other things I needed to do with my day. Perhaps when I was done with all of those, I could try and see into the future more. Unless Topher responded to my message first.

I slipped off my dressing gown and got back into bed, pulling the covers tight up to my chin. Before sleep could take me, I thought back through all of the things I'd seen. The people with the golden irises had seemed restless, maybe even nervous. Like they were waiting for something. It was something to do with what was happening in Urbis, I was certain of it, though, I had no idea how or why.

Before I could come to any kind of conclusion, I found myself drifting off into a dreamless sleep.

~

I was about to leave my room when the garment bag the maid had brought earlier caught my eye, and I remembered how I'd promised myself that I would try it on before I went about my other errands. Now that I was refreshed after my nap, I should do just that. I needed to know what adjustments I'd need before I had my final fitting.

Slowly, I unzipped the bag, nervous about what I'd find inside. The soft green fabric slipped between my fingers. This would be a joy to wear. I pulled each of the pieces from the bag and laid them out on the bed. The leggings and undershirt were made of the same soft green material, while the silver thread and green embroidered tunic was rougher to the touch, but would look amazing. It would glimmer and shine under the various lights of the Fright Festival. The crown sat on a stand in my closet while the staff was propped up in there too. They'd been delivered while I slept. It sounded creepy, but I was used to them coming in and out. The staff had been doing it for as long as I could remember. If I wanted privacy for whatever reason, then all I had to do was tell one of them, and they'd give it to me.

I stripped out of my clothes, letting them fall to the floor. I wouldn't be wearing my costume for long, and then I could put them back on.

The undershirt and leggings went on without any fuss, fitting perfectly to my body. That wasn't a surprise. Even if I didn't use them very much, the seamstresses still had my measurements. They made all of my formal wear, which all had to fit like a glove.

The tunic was a little bit more fiddly. It was a little big, and no matter how I tried to put the belt on, I couldn't seem to get it right. After a few minutes of struggling, I seemed to get it right. Though, I suspected I'd need one of the seamstresses to make a couple of changes when it came to that part of my costume.

Satisfied with that, I pulled the cloak on, using the attached bright green gem to fasten it together. It swished against the floor, making me feel a lot more powerful than any cloak should. I finished by attaching my wand holster, just to see how it all felt together.

And now, for the best part. I lifted the crown from its stand and walked back into my main bedchamber where a full-length mirror was. I took a deep breath, then lowered the crown onto my head. The white metal twisted into elegant peaks with the green gems dripping from it, adding an amazing contrast.

I blinked a couple of times as I stared at myself in the mirror. I looked good. Like a frost queen about to rule her people.

"You look good."

I startled at the sound of the mirror's voice.

"Say that again?" I asked it, not believing what I'd heard.

"I said, you look good," the mirror repeated. "I admit it isn't likely."

I ignored it—kind of. But as I studied my reflection, I couldn't help but agree with its assessment. I did look good. And when it came time for the Fright Festival, I was going to leave an impression.

# 29TH OCTOBER

I hurried along the corridor, excitement coursing through my veins at the thought of seeing Topher today. He'd finally sent a note back to me last night before I'd headed to bed. He'd been out of the castle researching something but said he'd be around for all of today. And that meant I could go fill him in on everything that had happened. I *needed* to tell him about the visions, I was sure he'd be able to help me make sense of them.

I'd tried to see the future again once I'd gone to bed, but I hadn't managed to see anything new, just the same underground room, and the same people with the golden eyes doing nothing more than nervously sitting around and waiting for something. It might not be fun for them, but it was even less fun for me. I had no idea what was going on. Not with them, not with Mother, or in Urbis...It was like shooting a spell into the dark and still expecting it to hit a target.

It only took a few more minutes for me to arrive at Topher's room. Well, at the one he shared with Jake as Adam's guests. I hoped that Jake wasn't about. With everything going on, I wasn't in the mood for Jake's brand of dismissal towards just about everything that was important to me.

A hint of betrayal entered my thoughts. I'd spent so long hoping my future would be spent with Jake, and yet now, I wasn't even sure I wanted to be in the same room with him, especially if we were alone. Why wasn't I happy with the fact he seemed to know I existed now? A small part of me knew the reason but wasn't ready to properly think about it. For now, I simply had to accept how I was feeling and move on from there. I had bigger things to focus on.

I was only slightly out of breath from rushing through the palace, but it shouldn't be noticeable to anyone but me.

I knocked on the door and waited. Scuffling sounded from within. I clenched my hands together, trying not to let my nerves get the better of me. Why was I even feeling nervous? I wasn't usually one to get too worked up.

It swung open, squeaking a little on the hinges. I made a mental note to ask one of the members of the staff to do something about it. As far as I knew, it would only take a simple spell to fix it. I'd do it myself, but I wasn't aware of *what* the spell entailed. Offensive magic like I'd been using was different from magic that was useful around the house, and I had no idea how it worked.

"Kelis," Topher said.

Relief rushed through me at the sight of him standing in the doorway, his dark hair tousled as if he'd just got out of bed. But that wasn't likely. He was an early riser from my experience.

"Are you busy right now, or do you want me to come back?" I asked.

*Please don't send me away.* I needed his help, true, but I also wanted to spend time with him. Even if it ended up that he couldn't do a single thing to help me.

"I always have time for you," he responded. A little uncertainty danced in his eyes, but it didn't stop the smile which spread over his face. He really did want to see me.

I shuffled from side to side, trying to work out what to say next. I wanted to go into his room, where we would be away from prying eyes, but I didn't want to force myself into his life.

"Why don't you come inside?" he asked, as if able to read my mind.

I nodded eagerly

"I'll head downstairs and get us something to eat. You should make yourself comfortable while I do," he offered.

"Thank you."

He slipped past me and down the hall. I watched him for a moment, before shaking away my thoughts and stepping into his room to wait for him to come back.

Just like before, it was easy to tell which part of the room was being used by whom. And this was only the reception room they shared. Judging from the mess that led to one of the rooms, I didn't want to think about what lay beyond Jake's door. He'd left clothes everywhere. I was surprised Lyss had put up with him for so long.

Huh. That was one of the first times I'd been able to think about her *without* feeling a surge of jealousy. But then, Rhi had implied that Lyss wasn't a good person to begin with, which stopped me from feeling too bad about it.

The door opened once more and revealed Topher with a shaky tray of tea trying to balance it at the same time as entering the room without letting the door slam in his face. I rushed forward and took the tray from him.

"Thanks."

"No problem." I set the tray down on a table with two chairs on either side of it, before taking a seat.

Topher joined me, sitting while I poured us each a cup of steaming tea.

"You know they bring it to the room if you ask?" I checked with him.

"I do. But your note sounded urgent, and I didn't want to waste time that we could use for talking."

I nodded. That made sense. If we weren't interrupted by one of the maids, then we could get straight down to business. I was glad he'd judged correctly that what I had to tell him was for his ears and no one else's.

Topher, I could trust. Everyone else, I wasn't so sure about. And that was a problem.

"I'm sorry I wasn't around yesterday," he said. "I was trying to find out more about what's going on in Urbis."

"That's all right." It felt like I'd spent most of my day sleeping anyway. "Did you find anything out?"

"Not much. But we can talk about that after whatever it is you need to tell me. It sounded urgent," he prompted before picking up his teacup and blowing across the top of it.

"It is. Kind of," I admitted. "Do you remember when I told you about the dreams I'd been having?"

He nodded. "They sounded like they were a way for you to process what was happening with your Mother."

"They're not."

He raised an eyebrow. "Oh?"

"I think..." I trailed off, suddenly wondering why I was going to admit this out loud. Now that I was thinking about it, I sounded crazy.

Topher didn't say a word, waiting for me to explain what was going on. I appreciated his support. It felt similar to the way my parents had always looked out for me. It was unconditional. He wanted to help me in whatever way he could.

I took a deep breath. He wasn't going to tell me I was crazy. He'd help me work out whether or not it was true, and if it wasn't, he wouldn't judge me for believing it for a small amount of time. I knew him too well for that.

"I think I'm seeing the future," I blurted.

"In your dreams?" he checked as he set down his teacup.

I nodded. "But not just then. I think I can do it when I want to, as well. Kind of."

"Huh." He leaned back in his seat, processing what I'd said. "I hadn't even considered that as a possibility for the things you were seeing."

I sipped my tea, nearly burning my tongue in the process. Once I set it down, I shrugged. "I hadn't either until last night. But after what I saw, it all slotted together, and suddenly made sense."

"What did you see?" he asked.

"Remember, I told you about the underground room

and the people with the golden eyes?"

"Yes. You said they looked like yours."

"They do. I think....they have something to do with where I came from," I admitted. "But I have no idea why I think that."

He pondered for a moment. "I think that does make sense, especially because you don't know anything about your past. Is there any way we can find out more about your birth without asking awkward questions?"

I shook my head. "I doubt it. You're one of the only people outside my family who even knows I'm not my parents' child."

"How did they even manage to cover that one up?" he asked. "From what I've seen, the Enchantians are very into watching everything you royals do."

"I'm not sure. But a lot of Enchantian women hide their pregnancies with a glamour. I'm not sure how it works, other than it being a spell."

"I can think of a few that would work," he agreed. "But it does bring up the question of *why*."

Before I could help it, an exasperated sigh escaped. "Because magic makes it easier to look perfect, and that's what everyone wants. It's why you won't ever spot anyone with a wine stain, or gravy down their front despite the fact they all wear white."

"And your aversion to the color is because you *do* like to spill on yourself?" he teased.

An uncharacteristic giggle escaped me. "It's more to do with wanting to be able to be my own person. It's hard when everyone else is wearing exactly the same thing. So, when I was twelve, I decided I didn't want to go around in white all the time."

"You could have done that with color instead of just black."

I shrugged. “Maybe. But I liked the way all black looked.”

“It surprises me people haven’t copied your style yet,” he joked.

“Maybe no one likes it.” The thought hadn’t crossed my mind before, and it didn’t particularly bother me. People could copy my style if they really wanted to. It was no skin off my nose. Of course, there were other people at the palace who didn’t always wear white. Mostly, visitors or people who otherwise shunned magic. They stood out, but they were in the minority. Not that anyone treated them any worse for it. That wasn’t what Enchantia was all about.

“I’m sorry, we seem to have gotten side-tracked. You were telling me about your dream and seeing the future,” he prompted.

“Oh, right, yes.” I’d actually forgotten that was why I’d come here. It was so easy to get lost in conversation with him. He was like no one I’d ever met.

I leaned back in my chair and took a drink before carrying on. It wouldn’t do to let myself get dehydrated.

“I saw the room again, but they had a newspaper from Saturday.”

“That doesn’t seem likely.” Topher ran a hand through his hair, making it even scruffier than it already was.

“No. At first, I thought it was an early print, but that didn’t make sense. Why would I be seeing that yesterday?”

“It’d be too early,” he agreed. “Especially if it was overnight too...”

“I hadn’t even thought about that. But yes. Once I’d worked out that it wasn’t likely the paper was an early edition, I made the leap to it being the future.”

He nodded along as I spoke.

"That makes sense to me, too."

I glanced down at my knee, fiddling with the hem of my skirt as I thought about the next question I wanted to ask. It was hard to take this seriously, still. Even with Topher believing me.

"Have you heard about anyone else being able to do this?" I blurted. If anyone knew anything, it would be him. Topher seemed to know a little bit about everything. It was one of the things I liked about him. I could actually ask him stuff.

"No, but I can look into it and see if anyone I know has."

"That's all right. You don't have to. We have more important things to worry about," I reminded him.

"I'll just ask while I'm grilling them for other information." He flashed me a reassuring grin, and it was all I needed to know he was telling the truth.

"Thanks, I appreciate it."

"Have you managed to see the future while you're awake?" The curiosity in his voice was hard to miss, and I found myself smiling as a result. This was what I liked about spending time with him. He knew exactly what questions to ask and was genuinely interested in the way I answered.

I nodded. "I managed earlier, but I didn't see much. Only a maid coming to my room and more of the underground room." Neither of which seemed particularly interesting.

"Anything of use?" he asked as he refreshed our cups. I hadn't even realized I'd finished my tea.

"Not really. The people weren't really doing anything. They were nervous about something, but I had no way of telling what it was. After I processed it, I was certain it was something to do with what's happening in Urbis, but I don't know why." I picked up my new tea and took a sip.

It was a little bitter, having steeped for too long. But for this conversation, our privacy was too important to ask any of the staff members to bring more.

"Nothing about your mother, though?" he asked.

Sudden tears filled my eyes. I hated that I could be reduced to that by a mere thought. But it didn't matter. Topher had seen me cry before. If he saw it again, it wasn't the end of the world.

"I tried, but whatever is controlling my visions just kept taking me back to the people in the room." A tear splashed against the table. I wiped them away.

Topher reached out and placed one of his hands over mine. He squeezed gently. I couldn't explain why the action was so reassuring, but I liked it. It was nice to feel like I had someone completely on my side.

"I'm sorry," he said. "We can find a way that will show you more about her."

"Maybe." Even I wasn't convinced by the word. But I still appreciated the sentiment behind what he was saying. "But I don't want to try and see her again yet. I'll try once I have more control over it."

He nodded. "That makes sense."

We sat in silence for a moment, both of us thinking about what was going on.

"You said you had papers for today?" I asked, remembering that we'd pushed that aside for a moment.

A quick grimace flickered over his face, but he covered it almost instantly. "I do, but you're going to be disappointed. There isn't anything interesting in any of them."

He got up and walked across the room to a dresser where a stack of papers was waiting. I should have noticed them when I came in, but I hadn't been looking for them. Plus, it was rude to snoop, even if it was on something that was for me anyway. Topher had been bringing me papers from Urbis almost daily, and we went through them together to try and piece together what was happening.

Not that it had helped. We were still clueless. I just wished my visions would help fill in some of the blanks. So far, they hadn't, and it meant we were shooting in the dark when it came to any of it.

I sighed loudly.

"You all right?" Topher asked as he dropped the stack of newspapers on the table.

I shuffled the tray of tea slightly to the side so it was out of the way and picked up the first paper to flick through. It wasn't that I didn't believe him when he'd said there was nothing of interest, but more that I hoped I'd spot something he missed.

"I just wish we knew more," I admitted.

"Me too. Being cut off from Urbis sounds....not good."

He was right. It was all a very strange situation. But I was convinced it was all linked—the curse on Mother, the odd happenings throughout the kingdoms, and the people with the golden eyes. There wasn't another explanation that made sense. There were too many strange events for it to be completely coincidental.

I got to the end of the paper and refolded it before dropping it onto the floor. That would be the start of my new discard pile. I pulled the next one off the pile while Topher watched me patiently. No doubt, he understood why I needed to look at them all myself. Perhaps, he was hoping I'd find something as much as I did.

"There really isn't anything here," I muttered, throwing another paper down in frustration. I was most of the way through the stack already, and there was simply nothing to go on. If these papers were to be believed, nothing at all was happening in any of the kingdoms, which didn't seem likely.

"I know. Even the lack of news is suspicious," Topher agreed.

"So, what do we do? If no one's reporting anything, and we have no idea what's going on, even in Enchantia, then what are we supposed to do to fix it all?"

"I think we have to rely on the visions."

"I was afraid you'd say that," I half-joked. "But what if they don't tell us anything new?"

"They might not," he admitted. "But I think we have to try. Don't we?"

"I like how you're saying we, despite the fact all you're going to do is watch me while I try."

"So that means you're going to?" he asked.

A light laugh escaped me. "Yes. I will."

"Want me to go get a refill of tea while you try?" he offered.

"That would be good. And can you see if they have any cookies or cakes too?" I hadn't been able to eat much at breakfast while I worried about everything, and I was starting to get a little hungry as a result.

"Of course." He got to his feet, and hesitated, almost as if he wanted to say or do something else. Maybe he wanted to kiss me on the forehead? I'd like that.

I pushed the thought aside, a little confused about where the desire had come from, especially when there were bigger things for me to worry about.

"I'll be back in a minute. Why don't you try and see something else while I'm gone?" he suggested.

"Got it."

The moment the door clicked behind him, I closed

my eyes and thought of the golden-eyed people. It was the first time I was trying to find *them* on purpose, and I hoped that the other visions I'd had were a sign I'd be able to control this vision. Whatever magic was controlling things, clearly wanted me to see them.

My vision swam, and a scene around me started to take shape. I almost let out a scream of excitement as I realized I wasn't seeing the basement.

Trees swayed in the breeze, though they weren't dense enough to be a forest. I didn't recognize the exact location, but from the height of the sun and the kind of plants around, it looked as if the place I was seeing was close to Enchantia, or one of our neighboring kingdoms.

My attention shifted to the people in the vision. Bingo. They were the same ones I'd been seeing in the underground room. Though at first glance, it appeared as if there were fewer of them than before. It could have been a result of them being in a different environment, though. I knew a change of perspective could make things look different.

There was one big change I hadn't expected. The people weren't alone. Something flew along above them, but it wasn't moving in a way that resembled any birds I'd ever seen. I squinted against the sun and tried to will my vision to bring me closer. Unfortunately, it didn't work. Apparently, the magic didn't work like that. I hoped that would change in time. Being able to control which part of the vision I was focusing on would make a big difference.

It flapped its wings again and breathed fire.

Wait. Fire? Was that...no. It couldn't be. The only thing that made sense was that it was a dragon flying above them. I knew they existed, but I'd never seen one in person. I supposed that this wasn't in person either, though if my instincts were correct, that would change once they reached Enchantia.

I pulled my attention away from the creature with difficulty. As magnificent as it was, I wasn't going to learn very much from it. If I wanted to know more about why they were coming here, and what would happen when they did, then I'd have to find other clues.

"How long until we get to Enchantia?" one of the girls asked.

"We'll be there in a few days," Azia responded.

So they *were* coming to us. I'd felt like that was going to be the case for a while, but it was good to have some confirmation of it.

The vision started to swirl and fade, and I let it leave me. I'd already learned something from this vision, which was a start, and better than the other visions I'd managed to force on myself.

Topher's room came back into focus to reveal him standing in front of me, a concerned look on his face.

"Are you all right?" he asked. "You didn't respond to me."

I nodded eagerly. "I had a vision."

"Oh." He pushed a cup of tea and a plate with a small cake towards me. Good. I was parched.

I drank the tea down eagerly. Apparently, having visions took a toll on my body. That was a good thing to remember. It meant I should be prepared whenever I tried to do it.

"What did you see?"

"The people with the eyes," I responded eagerly. "They were coming towards Enchantia."

"Is that a theory or..."

I shook my head. "No. They said it. They said they were only a couple of days away."

"And you think they're coming for you?" He bit into one of the cakes while he waited for me to answer.

"I'm sure of it." And I was becoming more and more certain, the more I saw. "And I think they hold the key to saving Mother too."

Topher leaned back in his chair. "What makes you think that?"

"I'm not sure. It's only a hunch." I felt silly even saying it, but if anyone was going to believe me, then it was Topher.

To my surprise, he nodded. "Then it's a hunch we'll listen to. You said we have a few days, right?"

"That's what they said. Though I have no idea when the vision took place. It could be today, last week, next month..."

"I think it's the near future," Topher said. "From everything you've said, your visions seem to be imminent."

"That's true."

He reached out and grabbed my hand again and laced our fingers together, sending a flood of warmth through me. "Then, we'll prepare as if they'll be here this week."

"Thank you," I whispered. I hoped he knew how much I appreciated his support.

# 30TH OCTOBER

I knocked before slipping into my parents' room.

"Kelis," Father said, getting up from his seat and giving me a warm hug. I leaned into his embrace, accepting the comfort that could only come from him. The only thing better would be a hug from Mother, but that was impossible.

I pulled away and studied his face. He still looked tired, but it wasn't anything new. This had simply been the way he'd looked to me ever since Mother's curse had set back in, and he'd started sitting with her every night. I wasn't even sure where he was sleeping when he did. There wasn't another bed in the room, and the dwarves barely left her side unless they had to.

No wonder news of Mother's condition was starting to get around the castle. Father hadn't been seen in weeks, and food for eight was being sent here several times a day. It was only a matter of time before the press got wind of it and started sniffing around themselves. It wouldn't take them very long to work out the truth.

"How is she?" I asked, even though I could probably guess at the answer.

Father ran a hand through his hair, leaving it sticking up all over the place. My heart broke for him. This was hard enough on me, but must be even tougher on him.

"No better and no worse," he admitted. "I almost wished there'd be a bad change just so there could be one."

I nodded. It made sense. If something worse happened, then we'd be able to start processing it, potentially even start grieving. But at the moment, we were simply trapped between hope and despair. Neither could win out while nothing changed.

"You should come sit with me," Father said as he retook his place by the fire.

I followed him over and took a seat opposite him.

"I take it no one new has come forward with any more potential cures?" I asked.

Father sighed again. "No. But I suspect that without putting out a wider call and letting the public know exactly what's going on, we won't."

"Ah. I'd rather not get them involved."

"It might be time to," he countered. "Especially with the Fright Festival coming up."

I winced at the idea. While I'd been excited to get my costume a couple of days ago, the more I'd thought about it since, the more certain I was that I shouldn't be going to it. The thought of partying while Mother lay in her cursed state left a bad taste in my mouth, one I could easily avoid by simply not going.

"I don't think I'm going to take part this year," I said.

"But, your mother told me how excited the two of you were about your costume." He smiled fondly. No doubt, he was imagining the two of us talking and sketching as we designed.

"You should still go," he said. "You'll have fun with your friends."

"It feels wrong to go."

Father sighed. "I understand that. But she wouldn't want you to stop living your life."

"I know."

"Besides, the journalists *are* starting to suspect something's wrong. They'll only prod around in our business more if you don't go to the Fright Festival. Your mother and I not being there can be played off as us deciding to give you more responsibility, now that you're eighteen."

"Do you really think they'll buy that?" I asked.

He shook his head. "Honestly, I have no idea. Perhaps, they will for a bit, but it won't last long."

"That's what I feared." If the other people like me were on their way here and could help with the situation, then all I needed to do was buy us a little bit of time. "I'll go."

"I'm glad," Father responded. "And try to have fun while you're there."

I snorted. "You really think I won't?"

"I think you'll spend most of the day worrying about your mother."

"It's hard not to." I glanced at the doorway that led to their sleeping chamber.

"I know, Kelis. But we'll figure it out. We just need to give it a bit more time."

I sighed. "I know."

"Why don't you go in and see her?" he suggested. "You might feel better once you've reminded yourself she's all right."

"That's a good idea." I got to my feet and started heading in the direction of the door. When I was nearly there, I remembered that there had been something else I'd meant to ask him, but it wasn't something I wanted to discuss with the dwarves around, and members of the palace staff potentially walking in at any moment. "Father?"

"Hmm?"

"Would you mind coming to my room later?" I asked. "There's something else I wanted to talk to you about."

He frowned, probably as he tried to work out what it could be.

"Of course. Is anything wrong?"

I shook my head. Though, I supposed that technically wasn't the right answer. I wasn't actually sure if that was the case. He'd have to make up his own mind when I started asking about my birth parents. I hadn't pried into the subject very much before. Mostly because I'd never seen the need to. I had two parents who loved me, and there was nothing more that I needed.

"Just a chat," I promised him.

"All right. I'll be there. It'll do me good to get out of this room."

I didn't say anything, but he wasn't wrong about that. If the press was asking questions, then they'd be watching to see when we were all popping up. If they saw Father, then it might stall them for another day, and that was an advantage to us all.

"Now, go see your mother. You'll feel better for it," he instructed with a doting smile.

I returned it, sure he was right. I turned and then

disappeared into the room that held my comatose mother.

~

"Rhi!" Excitement filled my voice at the sight of the other girl waiting in the fitting chamber. Somehow, it had completely slipped my mind that she'd be here, despite the fact I'd been told a couple of days ago.

"Kelis, I haven't seen you in days," she responded, showing just as much enthusiasm as I had.

"I'm sorry, I didn't mean to desert you." I hung up the garment bag containing my costume so the seamstresses could get to it, and then turned to her.

She shrugged. "I figured you'd have a good reason for it, considering you're basically the one running the kingdom."

"I wouldn't go that far." I gave her a weak smile.

"That's not what's going around the palace."

"Eurgh, gossip?" I supposed I shouldn't be too surprised by that. Things were bound to get around eventually, and the nobles could be terrible when it came to keeping things under wraps. I wouldn't trust any of them to keep a secret, even if it was in their best interests.

Before Rhi could answer, one of the seamstresses bustled into the room. I thought her name was Josephine, but I wasn't completely sure.

"Good afternoon, Your Highness, Lady Rhi." She dipped her head at each of us in greeting, though, I knew from experience that she'd drop the formalities after this. Something about the seamstresses seeing us in next to nothing removed some of the necessary formality from the situation. It made sense to me.

“Good afternoon,” I responded.

“Is everything all right with your costume?” she asked.

“Mostly,” I confirmed. “The tunic is a bit loose, though.”

She nodded. “I thought that might be the case. We didn’t want to make it too tight and tear the fabric. Once we’ve seen to Lady Rhi’s fitting, we can sort yours...if that’s all right?”

“Of course.” I took that as my cue to take a seat. I had no idea what Rhi’s costume was going to be like, but it must have been more elaborate if they were going to do hers first. Or perhaps, it wasn’t completely made yet. I’d find out soon enough.

I kicked back and watched while Rhi was directed onto the stool in the center of the room. The seamstress had her strip down to her underclothes and then put on some kind of dress. The bottom of it was blue, and the top had a white base with sea life embroidered on it. Everything glittered and sparkled, even the red starfish perched on her left shoulder.

“You look beautiful,” I said.

Rhi beamed. “Thank you.”

“It’s a good fit,” Josephine said. “But there are a few places I can see where it needs alterations. Please hold still.”

“Got it,” Rhi responded.

“Are you excited about the festival?” Josephine asked.

“Yes. It’s my first one.”

A smile spread over my face at Rhi’s answer. I was excited for her. There really wasn’t anything like the Fright Festival. There was always so much color and life about it. And laughter. Though, I wasn’t sure how I felt about that this year.

“Oh, you'll have a wonderful time, dear,” Josephine gushed. “I always thought it was one of the most romantic events of the year. I met my husband there about ten years ago. We never miss one. It's a chance to celebrate finding each other there.”

“What are you going as this year?” I asked. It was nice to think about something that didn't matter too much in the grand scheme of things.

“We're going as a prince and princess,” she announced cheerfully.

Not a surprising choice. Royalty was always popular when it came to costumes. So were birds and other animals. For something called Fright Festival, it wasn't an event built on fear. I wasn't sure how it started, but now, it was a joyous celebration, almost like a carnival with music, dancing, food, and drink. The main aim seemed to be that everyone had fun. In a way, it made sense. People needed a way to blow off steam, and this was the one that had become Enchantia's tradition.

“Do either of you have dates to the festival?” Josephine asked.

Rhi and I exchanged knowing glances.

“No,” I answered for both of us. It was better that I didn't show up to a Fright Festival with a date until there was something serious in the cards, anyway. The people would take it far too seriously if I did.

“Surely two beautiful girls like you have the boys lining up to ask you to go.”

I rolled my eyes, but I doubted the seamstress noticed. No one called me beautiful, and I was fine with that. My parents had taught me to be. Just because my beauty was on the inside, it didn't make me worth anything less than someone like Lyss, whom everyone would find to be perfect, at least, on the outside.

"I think we'll have plenty of fun, just the two of us," Rhi answered. "Besides, someone might ask us to dance while we're there."

"Oh, that's true. Then you can have a beautiful story to tell your children." Josephine pinned a few things on Rhi's dress as she spoke.

Neither of us offered any comment on the clothes themselves, probably because we didn't know enough about them other than that they looked pretty.

"That should do it for you, Lady Rhi. If you'll excuse me a moment, I just need to go check your accessories before you take it all off."

"Not a problem," Rhi replied.

Josephine bustled out of the room, humming as she went.

Rhi swished her dress back and forth, the strips of fabric floating from her skirt swaying while she did. "Isn't it beautiful?"

"It really is," I agreed. "You'll catch people's eyes."

"Do you think..." she trailed off before completing the question, but I knew what she was going to say. She wanted to know if I thought Adam would notice her.

"He'd be crazy not to," I assured her. "And if he doesn't, then he's really not worth your time, and you can do better."

She giggled. "He's your cousin."

"So? He can be my cousin and not good for you. It doesn't matter that he's family." It was as simple as that for me. If Adam wasn't interested in Rhi, then she should move on and find someone who *was* worthy of her. It wouldn't make me love him less as my cousin, but I didn't want my friend to settle for him if he wasn't going to treat her right. I wasn't deluded.

"Thanks, Kelis. Sometimes, it's hard to remember that."

"It is." Romance certainly wasn't as straightforward as I'd believed when I was younger.

"Are you hoping a certain someone will notice *you* during the festival?" She raised an eyebrow.

Topher's face sprang unbidden to my mind, but I knew that wasn't who she meant. We hadn't talked about our feelings since she'd told me that Jake wasn't a good guy and I shouldn't go after him. Even then, I'd known she was right. But now, I was even more certain of it. Jake made me feel uncomfortable about myself, even if I had no idea why. And I couldn't put up with that for my entire life. I could barely put up with it for an hour. What I had said to Rhi was true. It didn't matter what someone was like. If he was no good for me, then I shouldn't end up with him.

~

I closed my eyes and thought about Mother, hoping it would lead to some kind of vision about when she'd wake up from the curse. Nothing was coming, no matter how much I tried. The future magic didn't even show me the people with the golden eyes. Perhaps, I'd broken it somehow.

More likely, there was nothing I was supposed to see yet. I didn't have any clue how it worked. I hadn't seen Topher yet today, so I had no idea if he'd managed to find anything out yet either. He most likely hadn't, anyway. It would take time to put out feelers and see what people came up with. Which was frustrating when I wasn't sure we even *had* any of that left. Ideally, it would be best if Mother was back on her feet before the end of the year. With only two months left, I suspected Father could keep things under wraps until then.

I sighed and gave up on trying to see anything. It wasn't going to happen, and it was better if I saved my energy for the rest of the day. Dinner was coming up, and there'd be a lot of people there.

Someone knocked on my door, startling me. Had Topher gotten back from his errands already? I wasn't expecting to see him until after dinner.

I bounced towards the door, happy even at the thought of seeing him. It was as easy to spend time with him as it was to spend time on my own, something I'd never experienced before in my life.

My heart fell as I opened the door and saw it wasn't Topher. But then, it lifted back up almost instantly when I realized it was Father standing on the other side.

It was strange to see him outside of his rooms. It had been so long since I'd seen him in a different environment.

"I'm going to go to dinner after this," he said as he stepped inside. "Unless I'll cramp your style, and you don't want me there."

I chuckled. "I want you there," I assured him.

A small part of me worried he wouldn't want to spend the time with me once he learned what I had to ask him about. One of the reasons I'd never pressed either of my parents for the truth about my birth was because I didn't want to hurt them. It wouldn't be fair after everything they'd done for me—a loving home, an education, more love than I could possibly have imagined. I was under no illusions about the possibility of me having a better life under other circumstances. No matter who gave birth to me, these were my real parents.

"You seemed to be a bit worried about something earlier, is everything all right?" Father asked.

"Why don't you sit down." I indicated the table Topher and I normally used. I winced slightly at the stack of old newspapers by the side of it. I should have gotten rid of them, especially as they didn't have any kind of useful information in them.

"You're starting to scare me, Kel." Despite his words, he took a seat.

I sat down opposite him and took a deep breath, wondering what it was best to say first. I needed to remember that this was Father in front of me. He'd never made me feel small or dumb, and I needed to trust that he'd listen to me with an open mind—because he would.

"I need to know about my birth parents," I blurted.

A shocked look crossed over his face. "That wasn't what I expected."

"I'm sorry," I said quickly, not wanting him to hurt. "I wouldn't ask, but some weird things have happened recently, and I don't know what's caused them."

He frowned. "What things?"

It was a fair question. But that was fine. He'd believe me, just like Topher would. That was one of the things I liked about Topher, anyway, the fact he made me feel the same way my parents' did when it came to supporting me. Perhaps it was weird to feel that way. But then, they did say people ended up falling for their parents.

Huh. Falling for? Where had that come from? I pushed the thought to the side, needing to focus on other things first.

"I've been seeing the future," I blurted, not seeing a better way to tell him. I should work on that in case more people need to know what's happening.

"Well, that's not what I expected," Father admitted, a hint of amusement in his voice.

"I can't say I expected it, either," I said. "But there's no doubt what it is. I've tried to see what happens with Mother and when she'll wake up, but nothing is coming to me."

"You shouldn't worry about it," Father assured me. "If you're meant to see things, then they'll come. So long as you haven't seen anything bad happen...."

I shook my head. "Nothing, so far."

"You saw your mother lying asleep in your visions a while back," he reminded me. "Is this the same thing?"

I'd seen her like she was dead, not that I wanted to point that out.

"I guess so. I didn't know that was an actual vision of the future. Those dreams just made me uneasy."

"I should have paid more attention to you back then."

"I don't think either of us could have stopped this," I answered. "What do you know about my birth parents?"

"I can't really offer much help in that regard, I'm afraid," he said evenly.

"Oh." I tried not to let my disappointment show.

"It's not that I don't want to tell you," he added quickly. "But I don't know."

I frowned. How was that possible? Surely, he knew where they'd gotten me?

"It's time we told you," he started. "The only reason we didn't is that there really isn't much to tell. After your mother woke up and everything was starting to look good, there was a knock on the door, and an old woman had you in her arms. She gave you to us, and we were so taken aback that we took you and didn't ask any questions. We should have, but it didn't cross our minds until there was no one to ask anymore."

I nodded, but otherwise, stayed silent. He was on a roll, and I didn't want to disrupt that.

"Now, I see that perhaps we failed you in that regard."

"But not in any others," I assured him quickly. "I promise, I'm not asking for any other reason than a practical one."

"I know," Father responded. "I can understand what's going on must be scary. You want information that might help, and you hoped I'd have it."

"Yes," I admitted. The corner of the wanted poster Topher brought last week caught my eye. Perhaps something in that could jog Father's memory. I leaned down and picked it up. "Do you recognize these people?" I asked, handing it to him.

He took the wanted poster from me and then frowned down at it. "Their eyes are like yours."

"I know. It's one of the things that got me thinking about my birth in the first place," I admitted.

"Understandably. I'm sorry that I can't help on that front. Do you know why they're wanted?"

"No. But I've seen them in the visions I've been having. They're heading here, and I think they're going to help us save Mother."

"Then I promise I'll let them straight into the castle when they arrive. So long as they get here before the Urbis guard does. If they're here, then there won't be much even I can do," he said.

I nodded. "They should be here before the Urbis guard," I assured him. "I think they'll be here in the next few days."

"Then I'll make preparations for them to be welcomed. If you trust them, then I do, too," he promised.

"Thank you."

He reached out and put his hand over mine. "I'm

sorry, I can't tell you more about your birth."

"It's okay. I understand." I smiled at him reassuringly. "I love you, Father."

"I love you, too, Kelis. Never doubt that."

"I don't." And I meant every word. No matter what happened with the golden-eyed people, I was glad this was where I'd been brought as a baby. I couldn't have asked for anything more than my parents had given me.

# 31ST OCTOBER

Lights flashed, and magically enhanted music filled the air. It was impossible to ignore the din of people chattering and singing along. I closed my eyes and drank it all in. This was exactly what the Fright Festival was all about. People having fun, dancing, letting all of their cares slip away, if only for an evening.

"This is amazing," Rhi said beside me.

I opened my eyes and turned so I could see her face. There was a childlike wonder on her face as she took in everything, and even the glimmer of scales on her costume couldn't outshine the lights in her eyes.

I scanned the scene in front of me, trying to see it with new eyes. It had been so long since I'd seen the town look so alive.

"Your costume looks amazing," she said.

"Thanks. Yours does, too."

Even though we'd both seen one another in our costumes, it was still different with the atmosphere around us.

"What are we going to do first?" Rhi asked me, almost bouncing up and down on the balls of her feet.

"That depends. What do you want to do? We can go grab a drink and something to eat, then head over to the dancing platform?" I suggested.

"That sounds good. Is there anything else I should see?" she asked.

I laughed, but the sound got lost in the noise around us. "You should see all of it. There's truly nothing like the Fright Festival."

As if on cue, a drum started beating, and the crowd parted, revealing a group of acrobats tumbling through the people.

Rhi clapped her hands together, and I found myself pulled along with her excitement. I liked it. It gave me something to get lost in.

The tumblers passed us, moving on to the next part of the crowd.

"Is it all going to be like that?"

"Pretty much," I said. "Almost anyone who makes any kind of art comes out for the Fright Festival." It probably wasn't originally meant that way, but that was how it turned out. I liked it simply because it showcased the talent we had here.

"I expected more magic, though," she admitted.

"It's coming," I promised. "And there's more of it all around us than you think. All the lights and most of the music is created by magic. You'll probably see some people using magic for displays later." I patted my wand holster as a force of habit, checking that my wand was still there.

"I've never seen anything like it. Everything is so beautiful." It wouldn't surprise me if Rhi started dancing around at any moment. She seemed to be having the time of her life, and the night hadn't even properly started yet.

I chuckled. "There's more color than normal, that's for sure." Like me, many had opted for colorful costumes this year. I didn't stand out as much as I thought I would.

We made our way through the crowd towards the food area. I could do with some hot apple cider; I loved the spices they used in it. I could get the kitchens to make it for me, but there was something perfect about having it in the crisp October air. This was one of my favorite times of the year with the cool breeze.

Once we'd ordered, we stood by the side of the square. I wrapped my hands around the cup, absorbing the warmth from it.

"I'm glad you want me to come back after I'm finished at university. You have the best food and drink here," she said.

Relief flooded through me at her words. I hadn't spent as much time with Rhi as I should have over the past week or so, and as much as I wanted her to come back, I would have understood if she hadn't wanted to.

"Wait until you taste some of the stuff we make around the Winter Festival," I said. Now wasn't the time to get into any deep conversations, not when we could be interrupted at any moment.

"I can't wait," she responded.

A trumpet sounded, pulling our attention to the middle of the square. Within moments, a masque began in the middle of the square. It was a simple tale that was always told this time of year. It was easy to produce and didn't take up too much time.

"Kelis!" Adam's voice called through the crowd.

I turned in his direction, not missing the fact that Rhi didn't pull her attention away from the play. No doubt, she was trying to ignore Adam's appearance.

I was more interested in the dark-haired boy behind him. Topher's costume was emerald green with a sweeping coat and a tall hat.

"Hey, Kelis," Jake said, coming over and putting an arm over my shoulder.

I tensed, not wanting him to touch me that way, but not being sure how to get out of the situation without causing too much offense.

"How's it going, cousin?" Adam asked, stepping in between Rhi and me. I hoped it was so he could be closer to her, but I wasn't sure. I thought he was into her, but it was impossible to tell. Despite having known him my entire life, I couldn't get a read on the way he felt about her.

"Decently," I said. "I want to get a top-up of cider, though." I used that as an excuse to slip out from under Jake's arm.

"You look good in color," he said as I moved, not seeming at all disappointed about my move. "It matches your eyes."

"Thanks," I muttered, though I didn't completely mean it. I didn't like people telling me what to do, especially when it came to my clothing and how I expressed myself. "I'll be right back."

"Mind if I come with you?" Topher asked. "I could use a drink."

"Of course, the company would be good." Unlike

with Jake, I actually meant what I was saying when it came to him.

The two of us walked over in the direction of the stand in comfortable silence. No doubt, he was soaking in the atmosphere just like I was.

"Jake is right, you do look good," he said eventually.

"Thank you. You do too. I love the green." I reached over and touched the lapel of his jacket on a whim. We matched perfectly, almost as though it was planned.

He froze, and I did too. What was I doing?

I pulled my hand away, not wanting to prolong the awkwardness between us.

"Two ciders, please," I asked the vendor.

"Coming up," he responded cheerfully. He clearly didn't care who I was. Or perhaps, he didn't know.

Ultimately, it didn't matter which of the two was the truth. Some of the people who didn't spend much of their time at the palace might not know. But the press and the nobles did. I was perfectly safe. No one was going to try anything, especially while I was wearing a wand. People would take that to mean I could fight back. And I supposed that now, it was true.

I paid for the cider and handed one of them to Topher. My fingers brushed against his as he took it from me, and a tiny thrill went through me at the simple touch.

He coughed, then stepped away.

"Are you ready for the spell casting competition tomorrow?" he asked.

My eyes widened. "I'd completely forgotten."

"Understandable. There's so much going on at the moment," he assured me.

"I shouldn't have let it slip, though. It's important, and we worked so hard to get me a place in it." Horror was welling up within me at the thought of wasting the opportunity to show off what I'd learned.

"Kelis," Topher said, his use of my name shocking me from my thoughts. "You'll be fine. You're talented and know what you're doing. All you have to do tomorrow is trust yourself. And we'll be there, cheering you on."

"Except for Jake and Adam," I countered.

He chuckled. "Adam will still cheer you on."

We started walking back to the others, though, I couldn't help but notice how slowly we went. There was no rush to get back for either of us.

"So no pretense that Jake would ever want me to win," I muttered.

"He doesn't want anyone to win except himself. He's not a very good loser."

"I noticed," I agreed. "But I also don't care." I was surprised the words came out of my mouth and even more surprised that I meant them. I wanted to beat Jake at the competition for no other reason than I wanted to, and that he needed a lesson in humility.

Before Topher could respond, we reached the others. Rhi and Adam were in conversation, though, it didn't seem to be a particularly deep one. Even so, it was a good sign.

We spent the next few hours drinking, eating, and watching the shows as they came into the square while we waited for the dancing to start. Most years, I went home before it began. I hadn't had time to make many friends, and when Adam and Jake had been visiting, I hadn't worked up the courage to stay with them. Even to me, it sounded a little ridiculous. I was a princess, I should have been more confident than that.

But things were different this year. *I* was different. And I'd made friends with both Rhi and Topher of my own accord. Though that did nothing to explain the weird tension between Jake and me. It was best if I didn't dwell on that too much. Fright Festival wasn't the place to work out what my feelings for Jake were.

The square cleared as the night wore on, and some of the vendors returned home. Others would stay open the entire time. An orchestra set up in the corner opposite us and started to tune-up. After that, the dancing would start.

And I was hoping Topher would ask me. All I knew was that I wanted it, and if I had to be the one to make it happen, then that's what I would do.

The music started to play, more in tune than it had been earlier. It was almost as if this portion of the day was more organized than the early evening. I liked it. I should have stayed the other years, too. I missed out. At least, I'd figured it out at eighteen and not later in life when I'd already missed out on decades of these things.

I set down my empty cup on one of the many trays that had been set up for just that. They'd be cleared away by some of the workers once we stepped away.

"Let's dance, Kelis," Jake announced loudly, not giving me a chance to ask Topher.

I looked over Jake's shoulder, wondering how I could get out of this and manage to dance with the person I wanted to spend time with?

Before I could come up with anything, Jake was tugging me onto the floor. I kept my eyes trained on Topher even as he pulled me away. The look on his face made me feel sick. He looked as if he'd been kicked while he was down. In a way, it was reassuring. Perhaps, he felt the same way I did about me dancing with Jake, though it was too late for me to change anything.

Jake put his arms around me, and I pulled back

from him as far as I could without causing too many problems. He swayed me along with the music, but all I could think about was how I could get out of this and how quickly.

This wasn't how I should be acting. I'd wanted this for so long, and now that it was happening, I didn't want it. How had that happened? Was it because I'd seen what Jake was really like, or was it something else?

"You're becoming quite the catch, Kelis," Jake said.

"Thanks," I muttered.

"I can't believe I overlooked you for so long."

And yet, he'd ignored me for years and considered me beneath him until I was good at magic. Because it couldn't be down to me being a princess. I'd been one of those since the moment we met.

"Hmm," I said instead of anything else, mostly because I wasn't sure what was going on. Why did he suddenly like me? It made no sense.

We danced in silence for another couple of songs, and I tried not to focus on how awkward it felt to be in his arms and not where I wanted to be. There was nothing that made me feel good about it all, which was frustrating. It was confusing to feel one way about someone for so long, and then have things do an about-face.

"We should find the others," I said, eventually, unable to take any more of the silence. "Maybe grab something else to drink."

Jake leaned in, his hot breath fanning against my ear, but not in a pleasant way. "Why don't we go somewhere more private, instead?" he whispered.

Oh, no. How did I get myself out of this one? I didn't want to go anywhere else with him, especially if it took me further away from the people I wanted to spend my time with.

Before I could come up with a reply, Jake pulled away from me. The rush of cool air was welcome, as well as the space from him. At least, it was until he wrapped his hand around my wrist and pulled me along with him.

I tried to tug my arm out of his grasp without being too obvious about it. Enough people who would recognize me were around that I didn't want to cause a scene.

Thankfully, Jake stopped us when we were between two houses just off the side of the square. I could still see the dancers, and I could hear the music. At least, if he tried anything too far out, I could get away quickly. Though, the long cape and mass of accessories wouldn't help me.

"What are we doing?" I asked, trying to keep the accusation out of my voice. I didn't want him to freak out or anything.

"I thought we could use some time just the two of us," he said.

"Ah, right. Well, I'm supposed to be seen a lot at the Fright Festival, part of my royal duties. So if you don't mind, we should get back out there..."

"I thought you wanted this?" he murmured as he caged me between his arms.

The urge to duck out under his arm was almost too strong to resist. I didn't want to spend any more time with him than I had to, especially not alone.

"I'd like to go back to the others now," I repeated.

"We will, but first..." He pressed his lips against mine.

My eyes widened. What was going on? I didn't want

this anymore. It felt as wrong as it had the night he'd come to my room while drunk.

Knowing it was the only thing I could do in the circumstances, I pushed him away.

"What's wrong, Kelis?" he grumbled, not sounding in the least part like he cared.

He leaned in again, but this time, I was ready and knew what he was going to do. I moved to the side so our lips didn't even touch and then ducked out from under his arm. My crown tugged against my hair, falling off and clattering to the ground. I scooped it up, then rushed away back out into the main square.

It took Jake a couple of minutes to compose himself and follow me. By that point, I was already back on the square and scanning the place for my friends.

I tried to ignore the guilt mounting inside as I realized I'd simply abandoned them without a word. Not that I'd had much choice. And Rhi knew I didn't *really* want to be running off with Jake. At least, I hoped she did.

My eyes locked onto Rhi, who was dancing with Adam and laughing. My heart lifted for her. Perhaps, she'd get what she wanted, after all, Adam seemed to be paying her a good amount of attention. They actually seemed to be getting on well.

But Rhi and Adam weren't who I really wanted to find.

Topher's eyes met mine from across the square. Even from this distance, it was possible to see the hurt in them. My heart broke a little at the thought. The last thing I wanted to do was cause him pain after he'd been such a good friend to me.

I didn't waste any time, and hurried across the square, dodging between dancing couples and vendors.

"Are you all right?" he asked me once I arrived within

speaking distance. His concerned gaze trailed up and down. No doubt, I looked a mess, especially with the crown in my hand, and the rest of me in disarray.

"I will be," I assured him, before glancing over my shoulder to check whether Jake was still following me.

Luckily for me, he seemed to have gotten distracted by a pretty serving girl. I'd never been so glad for his wandering eyes. It was a good thing I was getting over him, or else, I would be facing a lifetime of getting my heart broken over and over.

"Do you want to get out of here?" I asked Topher.

"Wouldn't we miss the fireworks?" He didn't seem all that bothered, but I appreciated that he even asked.

"We can watch them from my balcony at the palace," I suggested. "It's a good view. It's where I sit every year to see them go off."

"I'd like that," he said softly. "But let me get some of the spiced cider for us to take with us."

"Oh, good idea." I could get used to the way Topher thought about things.

The whistle and bang of fireworks exploding above our heads formed a backdrop of one of the best feelings I'd ever experienced. The two of us leaned back in our chairs on the balcony of my room, sipping hot cider and enjoying the display. I'd have invited Rhi up too if she hadn't still seemed so caught up in Adam and their dancing. I knew my cousin was a good guy, and he wouldn't hurt her on purpose. And more importantly, he wouldn't take advantage.

"How come I didn't know this was here?" Topher asked.

"The balcony?"

"Mmhmm."

"There's a lot of my room you haven't seen," I pointed out. "But mostly because it's not hot enough at the moment, and I don't want to make the staff do the extra work to set up the brazier."

"But for tonight?"

"Fright Festival is special," I pointed out. "I always sit out here with the heater and a blanket. I've never..." I trailed off, unsure how much I wanted to admit to.

"You've never?" he prompted.

I sighed and ran a hand through my hair, managing to get it tangled in the knots caused by the crown falling. "I've never had anyone I wanted to share it with before.

Topher was silent for a moment, and I began to fidget uncomfortably in my seat. I didn't want to make things weird between us.

"Thank you," he whispered, almost too low to hear.

"What for?"

"For choosing to share it with me."

"I like your company." Maybe that wasn't the kind of thing I should be saying to someone, but Topher deserved to know how I was feeling, even if I didn't exactly have a name for it yet. All I knew was that there was *something* here between us.

"Are you sure you don't prefer Jake's?" he asked, his voice mostly level, but I could still hear a hint of bitterness.

"Definitely not," I answered instantly. "Why would you think that?"

And why would I ask that? As far as Topher was concerned, I'd just disappeared with Jake voluntarily and then come back ruffled.

He shrugged. "Everyone prefers Jake. He's better

looking and shows off more than I do. Girls seem to like that."

A snort escaped me without me wanting it to. "I want to deny that to protect womankind. But it's sort of true. I liked Jake in theory for a long time, but now...I don't."

For the first time, I realized my feelings about Jake weren't complicated at all. I'd just thought they were because of how I thought I was *supposed* to feel after liking him from a distance for years. But what I'd liked wasn't the person. It had been the idea of him as a slightly older, more worldwise person I didn't see very often.

But during this visit, I'd finally gotten a chance to get to know him. Or he'd finally deemed me worthy of getting to know him. And I found that I didn't like what I found. I wanted more from someone I was going to spend my life with.

I wanted someone intelligent, observant, empathetic, someone who would support me and help me with the tough decisions I'd have ahead of me.

Someone like...

I glanced to my right and tried not to think about the end of that sentence. I was only just coming to terms with the end of my feelings for one boy. I wasn't ready to put a name on what I had and what I wanted with another.

"I'm glad you've seen him for what he is," Topher admitted. "Not many people do."

Rhi's warnings about Jake sprang to my mind. "I think more people see through him than you think."

Topher huffed. "Perhaps. But somehow, I doubt that. He's too charming."

"Only when he wants something," I muttered, my words slurring together as I yawned.

“You need to get some sleep,” Topher said, rising to his feet.

“You don’t have to go yet,” I countered.

“I do. We have an early morning for the competition tomorrow, and it’s important that you get your rest in advance.”

Reluctantly, I nodded. I was feeling a little sleepy.

Topher swayed towards me, and I almost expected some display of affection, but nothing came. Much to my disappointment. But that was all right. We didn’t have to rush things. We could take them at our speed and not worry about the rest of it.

“Goodnight, Kelis,” he said softly.

“Goodnight, Topher.”

He disappeared, leaving me alone on my balcony. I took a couple of moments to compose myself, and then made my way back inside. I was already down to the undershirt and leggings of my costume, so it wouldn’t take me long to get ready for bed.

I stripped out of the rest of my clothing and put on my nightgown.

“You really should sleep more, Kelis. You’re looking very pasty,” the mirror taunted.

I rolled my eyes and dropped into bed. I no longer cared what the mirror said. And I was starting to think Mother was right about it. The mirror had to go. I’d see to it once we’d fixed Mother’s curse. It might still remember something useful until then.

# 1ST NOVEMBER

Nerves fluttered in my stomach. There were so many people here, and all of them seemed far more excited than I was. One girl was even bouncing up and down. Though, I supposed that could be from nerves too. I hoped so.

Rhi and Topher were chatting on the sidelines. Neither of them was taking part, which meant they were only here to watch. I looked around at the other contestants, but none of them were paying any attention to me.

Knowing there was nothing else for me to do, I made my way over to them. Topher's face lit up as I approached, an expression I was certain was reflected on my own. Even though I'd parted ways with him less than twelve hours ago.

"How are you holding up?" he asked.

I shrugged. "I'm not sure what to expect." That was as much as I was going to admit out loud. I didn't want any of the other players hearing how nervous I was and taking advantage of it. Though, as far as I was aware, there wouldn't be any rounds where we were doing magic against each other.

"And that worries you," Topher observed.

"Yes," I admitted. "I should have spent more time on the welcome packet rather than cramming it this morning." I hadn't meant to leave it until the last minute, but it had just slipped my mind with everything going on.

"Take a deep breath," Topher instructed. "And I'll run you through it."

"Thanks." I followed his instructions and breathed in and out a couple of times. To my surprise, I actually felt better once I'd done it.

"There are three rounds. One will test your control, one will test your dexterity, and then there'll be one that's something like the assault course you did to qualify. You'll have to act quickly and accurately if you want to win that."

"Are they all weighted evenly?" Rhi asked.

I frowned. "I thought you'd been to these competitions before?" Though, come to think of it, she'd never said anything about competing in them. I'd just assumed she did them along with the boys.

"I have, but I didn't pay that much attention. My family is from the other side of the border. I didn't grow up with magic like the rest of you. I had to learn about it since going to university in Urbis with this lot," she explained.

"Oh." I was being a bad friend at the moment, and I needed to change that. It wasn't fair to her if I didn't.

"No, they're not weighted the same," Topher said, answering Rhi's question from before I'd side-tracked her. "The first two make up half of the marks in total, and the third part counts for the rest of it. I've seen people win solely based on how they performed on the final part of the test, though it's a lot harder to do that. Really, you need to score in the top five during rounds one and two in order to have a chance at winning."

I nodded. "Right. So, lots of contestants that I need to do better than," I muttered.

Topher reached out and squeezed my arm. "You'll be fine."

"Maybe I should have registered under my own name after all."

He chuckled. "And then you'd never have been happy because you'd worry that everyone *let* you win because you're their princess. Don't think I don't know how your mind works."

"You have a point," I conceded.

Adam and Jake swaggered over, the latter of the two looking rather pale and worse for wear. My cousin didn't look too bad, especially not from the shy smile he flashed at Rhi. I guessed things went well for them after we left the night before. That was good. I was glad about that. Rhi deserved something bright in her life. And she'd be good for Adam.

Jake groaned and dropped an arm around me.

I grimaced and shrugged him off. Didn't he get the message when I all but ran away from him last night? I'd have thought that was a giveaway that I was no longer interested.

"How are you all so awake?" he whined.

"We didn't drink as much as you," Adam pointed out.

Eurgh. He was hungover. That explained the whole situation. But it wasn't good for me. I didn't want to beat him because he was at a disadvantage. I wanted to beat him because I was the best.

"Kel's going to beat you if you don't pull it together," Adam joked.

It was impossible to miss the amused smirk on Topher's face, even though he covered it up quickly.

Jake's face was like thunder. It was almost like he'd already lost. He really was a sore loser. How could someone be *this* upset by something that hadn't even happened yet?

"She's not going to beat me." His eyes narrowed at me before he stormed away. I had no idea where he was even heading to. The only friends he had here were the people he'd just walked away from.

"Don't worry about him," Adam assured me. "He'll get over it."

I shrugged. "It's his problem. It's up to him to sort it out."

Adam nodded but didn't say anything else about it. There was no need to. We all knew that what he was saying was true.

"I'm going to go say hello to a few people. Want to come, Topher?" he asked.

"Yes. If we're not back before you get called up, then good luck, Kelis."

"Thanks." We shared a smile, and I could feel his well wishes as well as hear them in his voice.

The two boys walked off in the same direction as Jake had gone, leaving me alone with Rhi—finally! It would be good to catch up with her.

"So, what happened last night?" I asked the moment they were out of earshot.

"I could ask you the same thing," Rhi responded a note of amusement in her voice.

"It's a really boring story," I promised. "Jake tried to kiss me, and I freaked out. Then Topher and I went and watched the fireworks."

Why did it sound so much more clandestine when I said it out loud? Nothing Topher and I had done would cause a scandal, and yet it felt like I was saying something gossip-worthy.

"And did he kiss you?" she asked.

I shook my head. "I think we've come close a couple of times, though," I admitted quietly.

She leaned in, giving us a greater sense of privacy. "Do you want him to?"

"Yes." The word was out of my mouth before I meant it to be. There was no doubt in my mind about what I wanted from Topher anymore, but it still felt weird to be admitting it out loud.

But this was Rhi. I'd already asked her to come back to Enchantia after she finished university for the express reason of being the person who knew all my secrets—and kept them. We could practice with this one. Though I supposed if I got what I wanted, it wouldn't be much of a secret.

"That's great. I'm glad you've moved on from Jake," she assured me.

I laughed lightly. "Me too. Who knew that all it would take was getting to know him. But you're changing the subject," I pointed out. "What happened with you and Adam last night?"

Her eyes lit up. "He asked me on a proper date while we were dancing. We almost kissed, too, but he stopped us just before we did and said we should wait until we go out together for the first time."

A small squeal of excitement escaped me. "When are you going on it? Where are you going? What..."

"Calm down, Kelis," she said, laughing along with me. "It's only a date. Not true love like your parents had."

"It's got to start somewhere," I pointed out.

"Yes, but do you know that you and Topher are the real thing already? It's complicated, this love stuff."

I snorted. "You're not wrong there." After all, I'd thought I'd never get over Jake and that he was the only person I could ever spend my life with, and I'd been wrong. More than wrong.

"Could all contestants present themselves for the first round," a voice boomed out before we could finish our conversation.

"I'm sorry, Rhi. I have to go. But we can continue this later if you want?" I said.

"Hopefully, we can do that while we're celebrating," she joked.

"Oh, I plan for us to be."

I was determined to win. No matter what it took. At least, so long as the tactic was above board. I didn't want to do anything that broke the rules. That would only tarnish the win in my eyes.

I glanced up at the leader board and tried to stem the disappointment within me. I was sixth at the moment, thanks to a poor showing in the first round. My lack of training had shone through while I was trying to prove my dexterity. With more practice, I was certain I could have aced that round.

Perhaps, I would next year.

But for now, I had to focus on the task at hand. Topher had said he'd seen people win based on the third round on its own, so I had to believe that it was possible.

I searched for him in the crowd, smiling when I saw him sitting with Rhi. He gave me a thumbs up, and I waved back to him, hoping he knew how grateful I was for him being there and supporting me.

"You don't stand a chance against me," Jake muttered from behind me.

"Sorry, what was that?" I asked, spinning around so I could face him.

I knew he was probably right. He was currently at the top of the leader board, well above me. Even if he was annoying me, I was a little bit impressed, given how hungover he was.

"I said well done," he lied. "Sixth is a great starting position for the final challenge. I've seen people get to second or third after that."

Hmm. Second or third wasn't what I had in mind.

"That wouldn't be so bad for my first competition," I said sweetly. "How's your hangover?"

"Gone. I got a potion off Stacey over there." He nodded to a girl standing to our left with a tray of potions held out in front of her.

I frowned. Were we allowed to get help like that? Surely, it couldn't be part of the rules. It certainly *felt* like cheating, which was enough of a reason for me to stay clear. Of course, it was easy for me to say that when I didn't have a hangover. I hadn't drunk nearly enough for that and had eaten a good breakfast. One of the advantages of being royal was that I'd had plenty of experience with the effects of beginning the day on an empty stomach. It had only taken three state events with a rumbling stomach to teach me the errors of avoiding food in the morning.

"I didn't realize those even worked."

"They do sometimes," Jake admitted. "But sometimes, they're not enough."

"Good to know."

"Hannah Blackthorne," the announcer called.

A blonde girl with twin plaits pushed past us and towards what looked like an entrance. That must be where we had to go to start the third test.

"Are we going in on our own?" I asked. I really should have read the welcome packet, especially when I now had to rely on Jake to give me the right information, and I wasn't completely sure he would. He wanted to win far too badly for that. Then again, I was in sixth, and that meant I wasn't a threat to him.

"Yes. The third test is always done blind," Adam said, reappearing beside us. I wasn't sure where he'd been, but I was glad he was back. "Worried, cousin?"

"More nervously excited," I countered. "It's the first time I've entered a competition like this. I don't know what to expect."

"You qualified, though, right?" Adam asked.

"She probably just used her name," Jake muttered bitterly.

I rolled my eyes. "For your information, I entered under a fake name so people didn't just hand it to me." Something he should be able to see from the leader board, but I doubted he was paying enough attention considering he was at the top at the moment.

"Smart. I did the same the first time I entered a competition here," Adam told me. "I use my own now. But that's because I already earned my place in the competitions."

And, potentially, because he wasn't doing so well overall. He was currently fifteenth out of twenty. Not a great start, but it wasn't last.

More and more people were called to perform their trial until Jake and Adam had both left me. I assumed they must have been calling people based on when they qualified, which meant I'd probably be last.

My gaze kept flickering towards the scoreboard, even though I knew it wasn't updating with each performance. They wouldn't update the final scores until everyone had competed, probably to keep stress to the minimum.

It wasn't working. Nervous energy filled every part of me, and there was no escaping it. Even so, every time I looked over at Topher and Rhi, one of them waved or offered some other indication that they were watching and supporting me.

Finally, I was called.

I stood in the entrance of the third test, taking deep breaths as I opened and closed my fingers around my wand. The only way I was going to crawl up that leader board was if I focused and did well on this task. Adam had said it would be like what happened when I qualified, which reassured me. He wasn't like Jake. He didn't have an ulterior motive when he said things like that to me. That was probably *exactly* what this test was.

A light flashed to my left, and I zapped it with a quick spell. My heart pounded in my chest as adrenaline coursed through me.

Another light. Another spell.

None of the other contestants had exited the same way they went in, and there hadn't been another exit, which meant I'd need to go through the course.

Hopefully, it was as straightforward as that, though I feared it might not be.

Each time a light popped up, I hit it with a spell. All of them hit, as far as I could tell, though, the haze of nerves surrounding me didn't help in the slightest.

*Focus, Kelis.*

If I reminded myself of that enough, then perhaps it would rub off. The only way I was going to do well at this was if I concentrated. Competing was all about pushing the worries to the side.

And that meant more than just how I felt about the competition itself.

I took a risk and closed my eyes to center myself. I pushed aside all thoughts of anything that had been weighing on my mind. Mother. The curse. The future. The people with the golden eyes. Jake. Topher.

Actually, the last one was a lie, even to myself. Topher was probably the easiest part of my life right now. He didn't deserve to be lumped in with all of those other things.

My eyes snapped open. I wasn't going to be distracted now. I could do this.

Two more spells left my wand, magic thrumming through me as it passed out into the air and hit the lights exactly the way they should.

When the next one appeared, I intuitively knew it was different. This one moved. I tracked it for a moment, not wanting to allow myself too much time to overthink what I was going to do. I had to rely on my instincts.

I shot down the next set of lights and moved closer to the exit. Other than the intensity of my nerves, this wasn't as hard as I had anticipated.

I turned the next corner and stopped suddenly in my tracks. I was at the end? Already? How much time had passed? It didn't feel like very long, but there'd been about fifteen minutes between each contestant being called to go through the maze.

What if I'd done it wrong?

I pushed that thought away and walked forward.

"Thank you, Kel," one of the officials said. "If you'll join the others, we'll tally your score, and then the winner will be announced."

I nodded, at a loss for words, then followed the instructions.

I found myself in a large tent. It was completely empty except for a number of large blocks. I turned around to ask one of the officials what I should do now, but he'd already gone.

The exit of the tent flapped in the wind. I walked through the tent feeling uneasy. The third test was meant to be difficult. People from all over the kingdom came to participate in these competitions and I'd managed to get through quickly without much problem at all. Something didn't sit right with me, but having never done one of these competitions before, I had nothing to go on. Maybe it was just that easy. Just shooting stunning spells at lights. It was what Topher had taught me after all.

I left the large tent and found myself in a smaller tent.

All of the other contestants were milling around while they were waiting, but unlike before the tests, no one was actually speaking to anyone else. It was as if the imminent results had sapped them of their conversational skills.

"You got through?" the girl with the braids asked me mechanically. She looked a little pale. "It was really hard wasn't it?"

"Err. I guess," I lied.

The others spoke in hushed tones, conversing with one another. I heard snippets of them talking about how difficult they'd found it and how it was the hardest competition they'd ever taken part in.

I thought back to what I'd just gone through. Sure, hitting the lights had taken lightning fast reflexes, but the spells used weren't complicated.

Jake found me before I saw him.

"I've never seen anything like that," he said, wiping his brow. He looked exhausted and more than a little sell shocked. "Phew. I'm glad it's over."

Now that I thought about it, they all looked pale. The other competitors looked like they'd just run the gauntlet where as I might as well have strolled through a park. I wasn't even out of breath.

"I think I did it wrong," I whispered to Jake. I knew he'd tell on me and I'd be disqualified if I'd messed up somehow, but I'd followed the course perfectly and couldn't for the life of me remember any other ways I could have gone.

"What do you mean?" he asked cheerily.

"It was easy. Ok, not super easy, but I got through it quickly. All I had to do was shoot stunning spells."

His grin widened to almost comic proportions as he flung his arms around me.

"You are so good at this. You'll win for sure."

Sweat dripped down his face wetting my cheek as he hugged me.

"Are you feeling alright?" I asked. This wasn't like him at all. Where was the bitterness, the sarcasm?

"I'm great. If you win, it will be a victory for all of us. You are wonderful."

"Huh?" He'd never been nice to me like this. Sure

I'd had my fair share of back handed compliments and he'd kinda been nice when he was drunk. I'd not seen any wine bars on the way through the course which meant something was wrong.

"Did you get hit by a spell during the course?" I asked, pulling out of his grip and checking his face.

"No. I'm nowhere near as good as you though. I probably should have been hit," he enthused.

He was still pale, unusually so. His pallor was beyond paleness. He was almost grey. Looking around, so were the others.

"Jake."

"Yes?"

"How's your hangover? Did the potion from Louise work well?"

"Yes. Louise is a star!"

"You told me you got a potion from a girl called Stacy," I said leveling my wand at him."

"Er what?"

I closed my eyes and let the spell shoot out of my wand. If I was wrong I was going to be the first Enchantian Princess to go to prison for murder.

I opened my eyes just in time to see Jake's head explode.

The scream

caught in my throat. What had I done? But then his body turned into a blue mist and evaporated into the air. A loud ping sounded out from somewhere, but I didn't have time to worry about the source of the sound. All the other contestants were now pointing their wands at me. Except they weren't contestants. They were part of the course.

Streams of blue magic from the fake contestants were shot my way. I ducked and rolled back into the empty tent I'd previously come from. Now I understood what the blocks were for. They were for hiding behind.

I ducked behind one at the far end as the contestants raced in. They spread out, shooting spells my way.

Shooting at them went way beyond my comfort zone, but reminding myself that they were not real helped. The real contestants were probably all enjoying a cider outside and wondering what was taking me so long.

I held my breath as I shot a spell at one of them, a young man who I'd not spoken to before. I'd picked him because I figured it would be easier to start with someone I'd not had any interaction with. Still, my heart almost bounded out of my ribcage as my spell hit its mark and he too exploded. Another ping rang out. It was all too real until the point where they dissolved into blue smoke.

Blue spells flew left and right as I weaved through the blocks, shooting my own spells at anything that moved.

The sound of the spells hitting the inside of the tent was deafening. There was no doubt the noise had been magically enhanced but it wasn't helping my nerves. I was pretty sure the magic they were shooting out wasn't fatal. It probably wouldn't even hurt me if they scored a direct hit, but I knew I'd have points deducted if they got me. Maybe it would be game over and I'd have to leave the tent.

I quickly got into a rhythm of hiding behind the blocks then ducking out to shoot.

It was working well until one of the blocks I was hiding behind completely disappeared leaving me exposed. I rolled across the floor, a flash of blue zipping right past my eyes, and ducked behind the next block. Within seconds, that one too had vanished. I was outnumbered and the hiding places were becoming fewer and fewer. Without being able to hide, I'd be a sitting duck, so I needed to think fast. I shot spells quickly without precision, hoping that they'd hit their target. Pings rang out every time they did. I almost threw up on the floor as I zapped Adam and watched him turn to blue smoke. I wouldn't win this way. I needed to concentrate. Taking a deep breath, I ran to the block at the very end of the tent, hoping it would be the last one to disappear. From there I peeked out and calculated my shot. Without wavering, I let a blast of magic out, getting two at once. The blocks began to vanish more quickly until there was only the one I was behind left.

Three of the competitors were still in except now they no longer looked like the people they had just moments before. In front of me stood pale versions of Rhi and Topher. As my eyes turned to the third figure I gulped back tears. My mother, or a pale, almost ghostly version of her smiled at me.

I swore loudly under my breath and tried not to let my emotions take over.

"They aren't real," I whispered to myself.

I closed my eyes again and shot at the Rhi figure. After the sound of her body exploding, I heard another ping.

The block in front of me paled and then vanished.

"Don't do this," My mother begged as I held my wand out in front of me, waving it between the pair of them.

"Don't shoot me, I love you." Topher added.

I gulped again and tried to quell the hammering in my chest. Neither of them tried to shoot me. Instead Topher looked at me with terror in his eyes whereas my mother crinkled her eyes and smiled widely as she held her arms out for me."

"Come to me, my darling. I can see you are hurting. Let mommy make it better."

This time the tears flowed freely down my cheeks. Both of them had regained some color and with each second that passed, they appeared more real.

Topher opened his arms too. "Yes, come to us. We'll take care of you."

It was so inviting. To hide in their arms, to pretend everything was alright. I took a step forward.

"We love you so much," they chorused as I stepped up to them.

"Come on Darling." I held my hand out to touch my mother. Her smile widened and inside I broke.

"You aren't real!" I screamed, hitting first my mother and then Topher. Blue smoke erupted and in the midst of my tears and the smoke, I heard the sound of two pings.

Wiping my eyes on the back of my sleeve and taking a deep breath, I headed through the tent and outside to the waiting crowd.

I tried to spot Adam or Jake in the crowd but didn't see either of them.

The need to see them, even Jake was overwhelming. I'd basically killed them inside and though I knew it wasn't real, it hurt enough for it to have been.

I found a spot by the front and stared at the leader board. The scores and rankings were yet to change.

"Attention, attention," the announcer called. "Thank you to everyone who has taken part this year. As always, there has been an exceptional show of skill today. The points are tallied, and now it's time for us to reveal the winner of this year's casting competition."

Murmurs traveled through the assembled contestants at that, despite the fact we all knew what was coming. I felt relief at seeing they were all alive and well, and none of them seemed in the least bit unhappy that I'd murdered their magical counterparts. They probably didn't even know. I wondered how many of them had killed a magical version of me. It didn't bear thinking about so I chose not to dwell on it.

I shuffled from side to side as I waited with bated breath. There was a chance this was going to be the worst part of the entire competition.

The announcer counted down the contestants, awarding them their places. If I thought I'd felt nervous while going through the contest, then I had no idea how to describe the intense feelings I was going through now. I hadn't realized how much I wanted to win. Or what I'd do if I did. Should I reveal who I was if I did? Or just allow people to recognize me if they already knew who I was?

I pushed that thought to the side. I could worry about it *if* I won. I could always keep my competition life separate from my princess one. Some people would figure out who I was, but so long as I wasn't using my status to rig them, I didn't suppose it mattered.

Somehow, Adam had managed to pull his score up so much that he finished eighth. He must have done really well in the third test to have done that. Hopefully, that meant I'd managed to pull my score up too.

"And now for the runner up..." the announcer said.

My stomach did a flip. There were only two names that hadn't been called—mine and Jake's. I was starting to understand why he was so bad at losing. I didn't want to come in second. Not when victory was within reach.

Jake side-eyed me, a hint of malice in his gaze. He gave me a spiteful grin that was so unlike the smile his magical counterpart had given me inside the tent. Only now did I wonder how it had taken me so long to realize the guy inside wasn't real. I grinned back, thinking of the way his head had exploded just ten minutes earlier. Ok, it wasn't really him, but a girl can dream right?

"Second place in this year's contest goes to Jake..."

I didn't even hear the rest of the announcement. Nor the one of my own name. The blood rushed to my ears. Was this real? It was hard to process what was happening. When Adam and his friends had first encouraged me to take part in the competition, I'd never expected to actually win it. But, despite ignoring it for most of my life, it seemed that magic came naturally to me. With some more training, I could get an even better score. And beat Jake when he wasn't hungover, I was sure that was a factor, too, as much as I didn't want it to be.

Cheers sounded all around me, and the whole place suddenly erupted into a cacophony of sounds and colors as people surged down from the stands to talk to the people they knew. It was good to know that these competitions weren't particularly rigid in the way they were run. It would make staying under the radar easier.

"Congratulations, cousin," Adam said, slapping me on the back. "I should have known you'd take the crown."

"Thanks," I responded, still in a little bit of a daze.

"Kelis, you did amazing," Rhi said as she approached from the stands, a wide smile on her face. "And so did you two," she added to Jake and Adam.

The latter laughed loudly. "Don't go congratulating me. We all know eighth isn't worth anything." From the way he spoke, it was clear he wasn't in the slightest bit bothered by the loss. Perhaps he'd expected it.

"I'm going to see Stacey," Jake muttered and walked off.

"Who is she?" Rhi asked.

Adam shrugged. "His most recent conquest. I think they met last night."

I waited for the pain to lance through me, but nothing happened. My crush on Jake was well and truly gone. I was a free woman. And I could spend my energy on someone who deserved my feelings.

But speaking of that, where was he? Shouldn't he be here with my friends now? He'd helped me so much, I was certain he'd want to celebrate with me.

I turned to Rhi. "Where's Topher?" She'd understand why I was asking and not need to ask a dozen questions about it.

"He got a message, and said it was urgent," she replied.

"Oh." I tried to stop the disappointment that flooded through me. Not being able to celebrate with Topher kind of took the edge off my win.

No. That wasn't fair. He wouldn't have disappeared if he didn't have a good reason. Which probably meant that he'd be getting more information from his contacts. I wasn't sure how any of it worked, but I suspected it was better if I *didn't* know the ins and outs of his secret meetings.

"He'll be back soon," Rhi promised me.

I nodded. "I hope so." Because I wasn't sure what I'd do if he *wasn't*.

No. That was a lie. I did know what I'd do. Exactly the same thing as I had for the past eighteen years of my life. I'd learn to be the best ruler Enchantia had to offer while helping my parents and as many other people as possible. If I got to do it with Topher by my side, learning with me, and offering the support I would need, then that was all the better. But if he wasn't as interested as I thought he was, I'd be all right. I was too strong for a broken heart to leave me useless.

## 2ND NOVEMBER

The dream was different than it had been for the past couple of nights, and excitement thrummed through me as a result. I *wanted* to see more things. I needed it to know more about what was going on, then I'd have something to tell Topher when I saw him again.

"Are you all right there, Kelis?" Azia asked.

I startled. She was talking to me? That hadn't happened before.

"Yes. I've just never seen Skyla before." The words came out without me having any control. Did that mean I was *actually* saying them in the future, not just in my dream? This was even better than I'd hoped.

"It's amazing, isn't it?" one of the others asked, but I

wasn't paying enough attention to work out who it was.

Nothing could distract me from the sights in front of me. Castles towered in the sky, peeking between clouds and going up even higher than I'd even imagined possible. The cloud walkways connected them, but from the dots in the sky, a lot of the people flew around instead of using them. The cloud walkways must be used for transporting goods or for people who didn't have wings. Visitors, mostly, I imagined.

I'd read about this place in books, but it was nothing like I'd pictured. It was magnificent—beautiful and unique in a way nowhere else in the world could be.

My gaze locked on a waterfall, cascading from behind one of the castles down to the ground. The water shimmered in the sunlight, creating a magical atmosphere that couldn't be recreated.

"It's beautiful," I whispered.

"It is," Azia agreed. "But we're not here to admire Skyla. We have something far more important to do here. Then we can get back to Urbis."

I nodded. As much as I wanted to stay and admire the natural beauty of this world, we had curses to break, and there was no time to waste.

The dream faded into darkness, letting sleep overtake me once more. I welcomed sleep, knowing that in the morning, I could see Topher and tell him about everything I'd seen. And find out where he went last night. I'd gone to his rooms once I'd returned from the competition, but he hadn't been back yet.

Before I told him anything about my dream or what I thought it meant, I needed to tell him something more important. If I went one more day without telling him how I felt, then I risked exploding. I *had* to tell him—the moment I woke up!

~

I threw on my clothes, not wanting to waste a single moment of my day. Not when I had so much I needed to get out of my mind. I skipped breakfast, grabbing a pastry to eat on the way instead. It wasn't something I'd do very often, but this was a special occasion. Besides, once I was at Topher's room, we could order some breakfast brought to us and share it.

That would be nice.

I bit into the pastry as I rushed through the corridors, being careful not to go too fast this time for fear of choking. The last thing I wanted was for something as embarrassing as that to happen.

Topher and Jake's door appeared in front of me faster than I'd anticipated. I must have been too lost in thought to realize how close I was.

I took a deep breath, steadying myself. I wanted this. More than that, I *needed* it. But that didn't mean I wasn't nervous still. I reached out and knocked, then waited for someone to answer.

There was nothing I could do to stop bouncing up and down on the balls of my feet. It was how all of my energy was making itself known.

Movement sounded on the other side of the door, and my heart rose into my throat. I should have thought through what I was going to say before arriving. I'd been too focused on getting here and hadn't even considered what to do once I was here. But it was the right thing to do. I'd find the words once I saw Topher's face. Or maybe I'd just kiss him.

The door swung open, and my heart sank.

Not Topher.

“Kelis,” Jake said coldly.

Ah. So he hadn’t forgiven me for beating him in the competition. Personally, I’d have thought running away from him trying to kiss me would have gotten more of a reaction, but apparently not. Jake didn’t make any sense.

“Morning, Jake,” I said brightly. “Is Topher around?”

His eyes narrowed.

Hmm. Maybe he *was* more bothered by the whole kissing incident than I thought. That was his problem, though. I hadn’t done anything wrong. Perhaps, I should have refused to go with him when he dragged me away from our friends, but I’d only done that to spare his feelings and to avoid a scene.

“No,” he said coldly.

“Oh.” I failed to keep the disappointment out of my voice. “Do you know when he’s going to be back?” I shifted on my feet before I realized what I was doing and put a stop to it. I didn’t want Jake to see how much I cared about what he said.

“He’s not going to be back. He’s gone.”

My mouth fell open. “Gone?” Without saying goodbye? Something didn’t feel right about the statement, but it didn’t stop my heart from splitting in two at the thought.

What was I going to do without Topher in the palace? In so little time, he’d become the person I came to rely on the most, and I wasn’t ready to change that.

“Gone,” Jake repeated.

He really must be mad at me.

“Did he say where he was going? Or why?” It felt so awkward to be asking those questions, but I knew I had to.

Jake shrugged. “He said something about a girl breaking his heart. I didn’t even know he’d been seeing anyone."

Oh no. What had I done? Had he not liked it when I talked to Jake while we were waiting to be called into the final test?

No. That didn't seem likely. Topher hadn't seemed like the jealous type at any other point, and he knew he was the one I'd chosen to spend my time with during the Fright Festival.

"Where did he say he was going?" I asked.

"Urbis."

I blinked a couple of times, trying to process that one. How could he go to Urbis? They'd told me last week that the gates into the city were shut and no one was getting in. Topher had been struggling to get news from his sources as a result. Going there would be a strange thing for him to do. Unless things had changed, and that was what he'd been called away from while the contest results had been announced.

"Are you sure?"

"Why wouldn't I be?" he snapped. "Topher said he was going home. This *girl* he's been spending a lot of time with chose someone else, or something like that. I wasn't listening properly. I didn't even know he was spending time with anyone but you." Venom dripped from every word. Clearly, I needed to fix whatever was going on here. While I didn't want a romantic relationship with him anymore, that didn't mean I wanted something strained.

But that could wait. Right now, the world was dropping out from beneath me. Because Topher *hadn't* been spending any time with someone other than me. Which meant he'd told Jake I'd broken his heart, and that couldn't be good.

"Thank you, Jake," I murmured quickly, already

forming a plan in my head. "Sorry to have bothered you."

He grunted, then shut the door with a little more force than was strictly necessary. I'd deal with that later. First thing's first, I had to get down to the stables and saddle up one of the horses. Then, I needed to try and use my powers to see where Topher had gone. It was a long shot, but the only one I had, which was why I had to take it.

~

I closed my eyes and focused on thoughts of Topher, trying to bring up a vision of him. I'd been trying to do it as little as possible, as each vision left me more and more exhausted. But sometimes, it was unavoidable, especially if I wanted to check whether I was going in the right direction of something.

Things began to grow hazy, and I relied on the strength and training of my horse to keep me upright. A glen I recognized sprang to mind, and while Topher wasn't in the vision, I knew that was the way I had to go.

I dismissed the vision and opened my eyes, tugging on the reins so my horse would head in the right direction. I was eager to find him, not only because it would put my mind at ease, but also because it would be better to have someone with me in case I fell off my horse in exhaustion.

The trees thinned the closer I got to the glen. I hoped once I got there that things would become more obvious. I wasn't entirely sure I had enough energy for another vision, even if I wanted one.

Except that I knew I'd manage. I'd come this far.

I wasn't going to stop at the final hurdle in finding Topher.

Sunlight streamed through the trees, dappling the green leaves on the forest floor. The birds tweeted from the trees, joining the rustle of the undergrowth as smaller creatures went about their day. It was beautiful. And peaceful. I'd spent too much time in the palace and the surrounding city recently and hadn't taken much advantage of going into the woods that surrounded us. At least, this journey could go some way toward making up for that.

I rode on a little way further, listening out for any indication that something bigger was passing through the trees.

"Kelis?"

My heart lifted at the sound of Topher's voice. I looked around for him, more energized than I had been before, despite nothing having changed.

He crashed through the trees opposite me on a horse I'd never seen before. It must have been his from Urbis. We'd never been riding together and had used the carriage when we went to the stadium.

"Topher." Relief tinged my voice as I said his name. He didn't seem angry with me. Or particularly sad either. Had Jake been lying about the whole thing? I didn't understand why he would when he had nothing to gain from it, but who knew as far as Jake was concerned.

"What are you doing on a horse? You look exhausted," he said.

"I am." I swayed a little as if to demonstrate my point, though it wasn't intentional. "I was seeing the future to find out where you went."

"By the spells, Kelis. Why? You could have hurt yourself." He jumped from his horse and tied it to a nearby tree, then pulled out a blanket and lay it down on the ground.

Next, he came over to my horse and walked it over so he could tie it up with his, then he held his arms out as if to catch me when I dismounted.

Also, not the actions of someone who'd had their heart broken.

"I had to find you," I said weakly as I slid off my horse.

"I guessed that much," he pointed out. "But why?"

A wave of exhaustion rushed through me, and I knew I didn't have long to get across what I needed to say.

"Because I love you," I murmured, before passing out into unconsciousness.

Though, before I did, I could have sworn, I heard him say, "I love you back."

~

I opened my eyes slowly, quickly realizing I'd somehow fallen into a dreamless sleep in the middle of the forest. I had to admit, that one had never happened to me before.

Slowly, I propped myself up and looked around. The horses were still tied to the tree, but Topher had removed their saddles and bridles, as well as rubbing them down and giving them feeding bags. It must have been from food he'd brought with him because I certainly hadn't stopped to think about anything like that when I was leaving the palace.

"Oh, good, you're awake."

I looked up to find Topher striding back into the glen with an arm full of small branches. He dropped them not far from the blanket I sat on but didn't do anything with them.

"I was starting to worry you'd sleep through the night."

"What would you have done if I had?" I asked. Judging from the sun in the sky, it was mid-afternoon now, which meant I'd had a couple of hours' sleep. That was good. I felt better for it.

"Built a fire, made some food, and waited until you woke up." He shrugged. "So, basically, what I was doing anyway."

As if triggered by the words, my stomach rumbled. "I am hungry," I admitted.

"I thought as much. Did you come straight from the palace?" he asked.

A blush rose to my cheeks. What should I tell him about why I came? Should I go with the truth and hope it didn't make me look desperate?

"Kelis?" he prompted as he crouched down next to the pile of branches and began building a fire.

"Yes, I came straight from the palace," I said. "I mean, I went to your room first. But you weren't there. And Jake said you'd left to go home to Urbis because someone had broken your heart and..."

"Whoa, wait, what?" He stopped what he was doing and turned to face me.

"Jake said you'd left to go home to Urbis," I repeated.

"Not that part. The other one."

"Oh, and that you'd done that because a girl had broken your heart." I bit my lower lip, not knowing what the best thing to add to that was.

"Kelis, I'm so sorry." He reached forward and took my hands in his, the warmth of them sending tingles through my entire body.

I cocked my head to the side as his words processed. "Sorry?" I echoed.

Topher sighed. "May I sit next to you?"

"Of course." What was going on? This situation was getting more and more confusing as it went on.

"I'm sorry that Jake did that to you. He lied, Kelis." He shifted so that he sat next to me on the rug, our knees almost touching.

"Ooh." Understanding hit me. "It didn't cross my mind that he might have. Which part was a lie?"

"All of it." Topher thought for a moment. "Actually, he did tell the truth about me going to Urbis, kind of. But I wasn't going *home*. One of my sources sent word that they'd been able to get some papers out to me today, but I had to leave right there and then if I wanted to make it in time. The window of opportunity was very small."

"I'm sorry I believed him."

"Don't be," he countered. "I think he's just sore that you beat him yesterday."

"And probably a little bit that I refused to kiss him, too," I muttered.

"You refused?" He raised an eyebrow.

"Yes. On Fright Festival night. He kind of dragged me off to a private place and then tried to kiss me. I pushed him away, and then...well, you know the rest."

Topher chuckled. "I think you must be the first woman to ever reject him."

"I highly doubt that."

"But why did you?" There was a hesitation in his voice that I recognized. It was the same way I felt when I was trying to process my feelings for him.

"Reject him?"

"Mmhmm."

"Because he wasn't who I wanted to be kissed by," I admitted before I could chicken out. I'd come all this way, I had to tell him how I felt.

"And who did you want to kiss you?" Topher asked, his voice rumbling through me as he leaned closer.

"I think you know," I whispered.

"But I need you to say it. I need to know you want this."

The promise of everything hung between the two of us, and somehow, I knew that if we closed the final gap between us, our lives would never be the same again. There'd be no going back. It wasn't as scary as I expected it to be. When Topher was around, everything slotted into place. He didn't produce the same kind of fire and passion I'd read about in books, but that didn't matter. He made me feel things that were far better than that. Safe. Secure. Supported.

This was someone who would listen to me no matter what I had to say, and I wouldn't want to change that for the world.

"You," I whispered, the word almost carried away on the breeze. "I want you to be the one to kiss me."

A wide smile spread over his face as if he'd been hoping that was the case but hadn't dared believe it would be.

"I can arrange that if you'd like?"

"I would."

But I didn't wait for him to make a move. I didn't need to, now that I knew he wanted this too. I leaned in and pressed my lips to his.

The whole world changed in an instant... kind of. Everything but the feeling of closeness I shared with Topher drifted away as we kissed. He was the only thing that mattered. In this situation, I wasn't a princess. I was nothing more than a girl, and he was a boy, and we fit together in a way everyone searched for.

His fingers tangled into my hair as he pulled me closer, deepening the kiss. I let myself get lost in him for the moment. There were still things I needed to say, as well as other things to update him on, but everything could wait. I wanted to savor this moment so I could keep it with me for the rest of my life. And longer.

Eventually, we broke away from one another and spent another moment staring into one another's eyes.

"I love you," I blurted out.

"You realize you said that already?" he teased, his bright smile reaching all the way up to his eyes.

"That's not how you're supposed to respond," I pointed out, not hurt in the slightest. The way he'd responded to me made me certain I'd heard him right before. He'd already said it to me too.

"Then what should I say? Thank you? I know? Great news?"

A loud giggle escaped me, and I moved to cover it with a hand. "Great news, definitely."

"Hmm, it doesn't have the right ring to it, I think."

"No, possibly not," I agreed.

He nodded to himself. "I think I'm going to go with, I love you, too, Kelis."

I beamed, the words making my heart soar and my soul take flight. He might not have been the person I used to imagine would say them to me, but there was no doubt in my mind that he was the *right* person to share this with.

"We should get back to the palace before it's too dark, though," I said, looking up at the sky. It was still afternoon, but we were still a long way out, and I didn't want to cause anyone back at the palace to worry about us. Father had enough on his plate without me making it worse.

"I'll fetch us some water if you saddle the horses." he suggested.

"Sounds good to me." I got to my feet, only remembering as I stood that I was hungry.

It seemed I wasn't the only one who thought of it, as Topher handed me some bread and cheese. It wasn't anything fancy, but it would stave off the hunger until we were back at the palace, which was the main thing.

~

"You said you went to meet a contact in Urbis," I prompted once we were underway. I swayed on my horse, leaning into her natural rhythm to make things easier for myself. "And why am I still so tired?" I let out a loud yawn as if to accidentally prove the point.

"Which of those do you want me to answer first?" Topher asked from beside me. He was riding his own horse as easily as I was. He must have learned at a young age.

"The tired one? That seems like it will have the shortest answer."

He chuckled. "It does. I suspect you've worn yourself out from using so much magic at the contest yesterday and then trying to see the future. What were you even trying to see?"

"Where you were," I replied quietly. "Though, I had a vision-dream last night too. I was in Skyla with the other people with golden eyes."

He perked up. "That's good news. You've only been able to see the near future so far, which means they'll be arriving in Enchantia soon."

I nodded. "Perhaps they're already there."

"Is that going to be a problem? I don't know how far the wanted posters got distributed."

"I don't know," I answered honestly. "But Father said he'd let them into the palace if they turned up while I wasn't there."

"Oh, good. That'll make it easier," he said.

"That was my hope." I pulled out my flask and gulped down some water. "Now, Urbis."

He sighed. "You're going to be disappointed."

"Tell me, anyway." I spied the palace through a gap in the trees. The trip back had seemed much quicker with his company. We still had a ways to go, but we were nearly back.

"I made it to the meeting point with plenty of time to spare. And I stayed longer than I should have. But my contact never showed up. I ran off for no reason."

"It made me come chase you, though," I pointed out to cheer him up. "Not many people can say that."

Topher let out a good-natured laugh. "Admittedly, most people chase the princess, not the other way around."

"I like to do things my own way."

"One of the many qualities that will make you a fantastic queen," Topher said.

Pride welled up inside me. It meant a lot that he thought that, even if he wasn't the first person to say it to me.

"Hopefully, not for a long time, though," I added quickly.

"Absolutely not. We'll get back to the palace, make preparations for the golden-eyed people to arrive, and then we'll work out how we're going to break the curse on your mother," he promised.

"I think they have the answers on how to do it," I said. I was growing more certain of that with every vision, and every moment.

I couldn't wait for the people with gold irises to arrive. Somehow, it felt like they were part of my destiny.

# 3RD NOVEMBER

I'd never had one of my dreams tell me what day it was referencing before, but I was certain this one was about what would happen when I woke up. Well, perhaps not straight away. But whatever I was about to see would be happening within the next few hours.

My vision swirled but cleared faster than it had before. The scenery was familiar to me, having only ridden through it yesterday. If Topher and I had lingered in the forest a little longer, we might have run into them. But this was better. I'd rather meet them in my own palace than in the middle of the woods. It wasn't exactly very princess-like behavior to be traipsing around a forest without a guard. But then, that was Encahntia. Because everyone could do magic, person-on-person crime was reasonably low.

It only took a moment more for the golden-eyed people to come into view. They looked a little tired, but there was some anticipation and nervousness added into the mix. Perhaps, they felt the same way about meeting me as I did them.

None of them said anything as I watched them reach the city gates. Judging from how quickly it had all happened, I was watching in some kind of fast forward. I wished I could control it, but considering I'd only known what was happening for about a week, that would probably be asking for too much. I was reasonably sure that time would give me the control I needed over the gift, and then I'd be able to do all kinds of things with it.

The vision faded as they entered the city, and I let it. There was no point in fighting it, and there was nothing else I needed to know about them. They were going to arrive today. And I had to be ready. Once I woke up, I'd have to send a message to Father about their arrival, as well as to the head of the palace guards. The last thing we needed was for anyone to be taken by surprise.

As the vision turned into the deepness of sleep, I relaxed.

The moment I woke up, I jumped out of bed and started planning what to wear. Out of habit, I glanced towards the mirror, only to find it covered by a sheet and unable to give a snarky commentary to go along with my morning routine. I couldn't believe it had taken me this long to stop it from talking, but I was already starting to feel better.

I debated between the clothes most people would expect an Enchantian princess to wear and what I'd prefer to put on, and ended up settling for the latter. Topher loved me for who I was, black clothes included, and the golden-eyed people probably had no idea about the intricacies of Enchantian fashion and what certain colors meant. I certainly had no idea what any of the other kingdoms' biggest fashion trends were. Then again, it wasn't as if I was into that kind of thing. If I was, then perhaps I would understand.

Dressed and ready for the day ahead, I went over to my wand stand and picked up my wand, feeling it in my hands. I felt more of a connection to it now that I'd won the casting competition. That was an unexpected, but also welcome, side-effect. I slipped it into my holster while wondering if I should work out another way of carrying it around while traveling. While people in Enchantia would understand that a wand was useless unless it was used by its rightful owner, I didn't know if the other kingdoms had such a grasp on wand lore. And should I find a spare one before I disappeared from the palace? Most people didn't bother, but that was because we took a lot of care with our wands due to them being so personal.

None of that mattered, though. All I was doing was trying to kill time until Topher got here for the breakfast date we were going to have. Now, I'd had my dream and was certain the others were heading towards the palace, I was glad we'd already agreed to it. At least this way, I got to see him properly before I left and didn't have to rush a goodbye.

I paced back and forth as I waited for Topher to arrive, feeling more and more impatient despite the fact it was still early. Perhaps, I should practice my gift to see when he'd arrive. That would put me at ease... probably. I supposed it didn't matter too much. Practice was practice, and I could use all of that I could get. Once I was with the golden-eyed people, I suspected I'd need to use my future-seeing gift even more than I had in the past week. Hopefully, I'd be able to stop visions coming in my dreams with time, too. It was easy to go through it, but kind of exhausting at the same time. Not something I wanted for the rest of my life.

I focused on Topher, asking when he'd arrive for breakfast. It only took a moment for my vision to blur, and I saw him approaching my bedroom door even before he did. I jumped to my feet the moment my mind had finished showing me what was coming. I rushed over to the door and pulled it open to find him standing on the other side with his fist raised and ready to knock.

"I guess I'm going to have to get used to that," Topher joked.

"Who knows. It could randomly stop working at some point," I countered.

"Somehow, I think your gifts are only going to get stronger."

He stepped inside and shut the door behind him before reaching out and wrapping an arm around my waist. He pulled me closer to him and planted his lips on mine, kissing me deeply.

I melted into him, enjoying his closeness. It was probably the last time I'd get to spend some private time with him for a little while, especially with the golden-eyed people coming today if my visions were to be believed.

We broke apart but stayed in each other's arms. Breakfast would be arriving soon, but I wasn't in a hurry to change where I was standing. There was something comforting about Topher's presence, and I wasn't ready to give it up.

"What's wrong, Kelis?" he murmured into the top of my head.

"Nothing," I assured him. "But I had a dream last night."

"Today's the day, isn't it?" he asked.

I nodded against his chest, causing him to hold me tighter. I didn't want him to ever let me go, even though I knew that wasn't practical.

"I think so. I've never had a clear time frame in one of my dreams..."

"Other than the one with the newspaper," he countered.

"Hmm. Yes, you're right. But that was different. This time, my dream started with the knowledge that it was going to happen today."

"That's good, though," he assured me, pulling back slightly so he could look down at my face. "That means your gift is progressing."

"I hope you're right. I'm completely in the dark at the moment. Did any of your contacts tell you anything about seeing the future?" I didn't find it likely, considering he hadn't been able to get hold of any of them for a while.

"I'm sorry, Kelis. I've been cut off from them since I asked them to look into it."

I sighed loudly. "That's all right. I kind of expected you to say that. If it was something people had common knowledge of, then I'd probably have heard some of it myself."

"Or I'd have been taught about it at the university. I imagine it would be very sought after magic if anyone knew it existed."

"You're right about that," I agreed.

A knock on the door sounded, and a moment later, a servant came bustling into the room with a trolley laden with breakfast.

Topher and I pulled away from one another and made room for the man to set things up on the small table. It only took him a few minutes to have it all off the tray. He bowed gracefully to each of us and then disappeared back into the hallway. Probably, so he could deliver Father his breakfast.

The two of us sat down opposite one another, unable to keep our eyes off each other. Topher poured us both some tea, while I buttered some of the toast and slipped it onto each of our plates. It suddenly felt very domesticated to be doing this, but I didn't care. Far from it, I found myself enjoying a moment of normalcy within our last few strange weeks.

"I take it you're going to be traveling with the golden-eyed people?" Topher asked, then took a bite of his toast.

I nodded and swallowed my mouthful. "I'm certain they have the solution to Mother's curse. And maybe they know something about my birth, too. I have to try and find out more about both of those."

"That makes sense."

"Are you going back to the university, or are you going to stay here?" I knew which I wanted. If he was here, then Father's men could keep him safe, and he could keep my parents safe in return.

"I don't think the university is open again yet," he admitted. "The Urbis gates are still shut."

Oh. Right. I'd forgotten about that somehow.

"So, that means I'll be staying here." He smiled at me reassuringly. "But I won't go back to university until you're back from your adventure. I promise I won't leave them to fend for themselves."

A warm wave of affection swept through me at his words. I genuinely felt better knowing he'd be here and helping.

I reached across the table and rested my hand on top of his, giving it a gentle squeeze. "Thank you. I really appreciate it."

"It's no problem, Kelis. So long as you're not going to run off with one of the golden-eyed boys and abandon me."

I chuckled. "I don't think that's likely," I assured him. "For one, you're the only person I'm thinking of like that. And two, the golden-eyed people feel more like cousins than people to fall in love with." I had no idea what made me say that, but it felt true.

"Is it bad that I'm relieved to hear you say that?"

"Not at all. We haven't exactly had very long to explore what this is between us." I picked up my teacup and took a sip. The hot tea both warmed and refreshed me. It was a shame I'd have to get used to tea made over a campfire while we were traveling. Unless there was a spell that could boil water I didn't know about. "Is there a book I can take with me that has instructions for spells like those to boil water?" I asked Topher, knowing he wouldn't judge me for not knowing how to do that.

I truly wished I'd taken more of an interest in magic at a younger age. But I supposed that everything happened for a reason. If I'd done that, then I wouldn't have gotten so close to Topher now and wouldn't have fallen in love with him.

"Yes. I can go find you a copy once we're done with breakfast," he offered.

"Thank you, I'd appreciate that."

"I'm guessing you'll want me to keep an eye on Rhi too? Though, I don't think she'll need it with Adam around to protect her."

I snorted. "Maybe she needs protecting from Adam." I had no idea what my cousin was like in romantic relationships. For all I knew, he could be like Jake and not take them seriously in the slightest.

"You don't have anything to worry about," he assured me. "Adam is loyal to a fault when he's seeing someone. I don't think he's ever broken up with anyone. The few girls he's actually dated got bored with him and ended things themselves."

"Hmm." Did Rhi need protecting from that? It was hard to tell.

"I promise to keep an eye on her," he said. "And to make sure Jake doesn't cause any trouble."

I grimaced. "I'm not sure he's capable of staying out of it."

"He definitely isn't. I keep hoping he'll suddenly grow up, and we won't have to worry about the womanizing, or the drinking, or the sore loser in him, but it never seems to happen. I live in hope." He drank some of his orange juice.

"I hope you're right. And that he doesn't stay too angry with me." My eyes widened. "Or you." It had only just hit me that perhaps his hostility the other day had more to do with Topher than with me.

"Don't worry, Kelis, I can deal with him. I promise."

"Thank you."

A knock sounded on the door. I was on my feet in seconds and making my way over there. Perhaps I should have checked with Topher that it was all right if I did this, but it was my room, and it felt rude to ignore whoever it was, especially when I was expecting the people with the golden-eyes today.

That reminder was enough to stop me feeling guilty about not telling Topher. He knew what today was, and that I couldn't ignore it. These people would have the answers I'd been looking for. They could help me cure the curse that was on Mother and restore her to the kingdom. That was more important than anything.

I pulled the door open to find one of the maids standing on the other side of the door, a worried expression on her face.

"Is everything all right, Harriet?" I asked.

She nodded. "His Majesty, the King, has sent a message, Your Highness."

I tried not to wince at the sheer amount of formality in her statement. "What is it?" I asked instead of commenting on it.

"He said that the people you discussed with him have arrived, and he's invited them to have tea in the private dining room of the royal family," Harriet said. There was the hint of a question in her eyes. She wanted to know if Father was losing it, or if that was a valid instruction.

"Good. Thank you. I'll be there momentarily," I assured her.

Harriet dipped into a quick curtsy. "Yes, Your Highness. Is there anything you'd like us to prepare?"

I was about to dismiss her when I had the realization that I *would* need things packed if I was going with the golden-eyed people and staying with them for any amount of time.

"Yes. Please pack traveling clothes and supplies for a month's journey for me. And see to it that the various heads of departments are aware of what duties need to be attended to in my absence."

Her eyes widened. She hadn't expected me to say

I'd be going anywhere. Perhaps I should have waited to announce it. For all I knew, the golden-eyed people weren't going to say any of the things I thought they were, and I would end up looking silly.

Topher's hand landed on the small of my back. "I can look after things while you're gone," he promised. "If you and your father would be all right with that," he added hastily.

It only took a second for me to nod eagerly. "Thank you, I think that's a great idea. I'll talk to Father before I leave and clear it with him first."

"Your Highness." Harriet curtsied again. "I'll go and get the maids and kitchen staff packing provisions for you."

"Thank you."

The maid didn't need any other dismissal and disappeared down the corridor to do what she'd said.

I turned to Topher, burying myself deeply in his arms.

"Do you want to come with me to meet them?" I asked, the words muffled by his chest.

"No. I think it's something you need to do on your own," he countered. "But I'll be here the moment you're done and need someone to talk to."

"Thank you," I whispered. I pulled my head back and looked up, my eyes locking with his.

Topher's wordless support filled me with the strength I needed. And, when he leaned down to kiss me, I knew I'd have the strength to face anything. His arms curled around me, holding me tight. He didn't want to let go, and a small part of me wished for the same. But that wasn't what was needed right now. I had to go meet the people with the golden eyes.

I pulled back, breaking the kiss, much to my own

disappointment.

"I love you," I whispered, not letting the words leave our comfortable cocoon.

"I love you, too," he responded, then leaned in to kiss me again. I melted into him again, wishing I didn't have to leave, even if I knew I had to.

I paused with my hand on the door handle to our private dining room, not completely sure what to expect when I walked in. Perhaps, I was about to find out that this entire thing had been an elaborate plan to make me seem crazy. I wasn't sure why anyone would *want* to do that, but the irrational part of me was scared of that right now.

*Stop this.* I had to trust my instincts. And my visions. They'd been right about so many other things, I just had to trust them about this too.

I pushed down the handle and stepped inside.

Everyone in the room stopped talking the instant the door opened, and they turned to stare at me. No doubt, each of them was assessing whether or not I was the person they'd intended to find, or if I was someone different. Considering I had no idea *what* they were looking for, I didn't know how that question would be answered. But I had the same rings around my irises as everyone around the room did, which was a good sign.

A light brown-haired girl I recognized instantly stepped forward and held out her hand to me.

"I'm..." she started.

"Azia. I know," I cut in.

Someone sucked in a breath, though whether it was

because I'd cut her off, or because I knew who she was, I had no idea. I suspected I'd learn things like that in time.

"I'm Kelis," I provided. Though I suspected they knew that too. They *were* in my kingdom. If they didn't know my name, then they hadn't done their research properly, which wouldn't be a good sign.

"How did you know her name?" Gaia asked.

"The same way I know the rest of your names," I responded. "I can see the future."

I waited for one of them to tell me that I was crazy, or that it wasn't possible, but the admonishment didn't come. Perhaps I should have expected that from people who traveled with wolves and dragons. Did each of the golden-eyed people have a skill? I doubted they could all tell the future if they didn't know how I knew their names. Which made me feel oddly special.

"That explains why your guards let us straight in," Castiel said.

I nodded. "Father agreed to tell all the staff to give you a safe haven when you arrived."

Azia sighed with relief. "I guess that means you've already decided to come with us."

"Yes. I've seen it." There was no point beating around the bush. I didn't know them, which meant I couldn't trust them. But I did know my own mind, and my visions so far had come true in some way, shape, or form. I had to believe that if these people were going to hurt me, then my gifts wouldn't make it seem as if it was all right to go with them.

"Good," Azia said.

"But I need to know before we go, will this help my mother?"

"Yes," Deon said. "If by that you mean something's gone wrong with her happy ending."

I nodded. "She's been in a coma for a couple of weeks. A magic doctor said she was cursed and that I was the key to breaking it. But, she didn't tell me anything more than that."

"I'm sorry," Azia said. "Things like that are happening all over the kingdoms. My own mother is cursed too."

"I know. I've had someone getting the papers for me. Though, we haven't had much in the way of news since Urbis shut its gates. Even the people from Urbis itself can't get back in," I told them.

"That's not good."

"No. Not with the Urbis guard after you all, too."

"You've heard about that, too?" Castiel asked.

I shrugged. "It came along with the newspapers. It's why I talked to Father about letting you in before the Urbis guard got here," I admitted.

I wanted to know what they'd done to end up on the receiving end of a manhunt, but it didn't feel like the right time to ask. I was sure I'd find out soon enough.

A slightly uncomfortable silence fell over the room. No doubt, it was because I was a newcomer, and none of them knew what to make of me just yet. That would change, but for now, it would mean I had to put myself out there a few more times. That wasn't a problem for me; I was used to taking control. I'd been training for it my entire life.

"So," I started. "Where are we going next?" Perhaps, it was a silly question, given what I'd seen in my visions, but I needed to check what I'd seen against what they wanted.

"We're going to Urbis. That's closest," Gaia said.

While she wasn't technically wrong, I knew from my vision that Urbis wasn't our next stop. But it probably was the one after that.

"No," I blurted out.

Multiple sets of golden-eyes turned to stare at me. It was a disconcerting sight. The only person I knew with eyes like that was me. With how odd they looked, I was surprised anyone ever looked at me directly.

I supposed when there were so many of them already, having the new person say no wasn't exactly expected. And yet, here I was, being stubborn.

"I mean, I saw where we go next, and it isn't Urbis," I amended quickly.

"Oh?" Gaia raised an eyebrow. "We've visited most of the kingdoms already, I doubt we need to go back to any of them."

"What about Skyla?" I asked.

"We haven't been there yet," Deon said from the back.

I was glad I'd seen them all in my dreams and had names to put to the faces. It made it easier now that I was face to face with them.

"That's where I saw us. My visions have only ever been of a couple of days ahead at the most." Not the most useful of traits for seeing the future, but my guess was that my gifts would get stronger in time.

"Then that's where we'll go," Azia said. "To Skyla."

I nodded. It felt like that was the right choice, even if I couldn't fully explain *why* I was so certain. What I did know was that I was looking forward to seeing the sky castles and waterfalls in person.

It was time to go travel the world and find a cure for Mother's curse in the process.

# LYRIC

DAUGHTER OF PETER PAN

**GRAB THE NEXT BOXSET IN THE KINGDOM OF FAIRYTALES SERIES**

# MEET THE TEAM

The Kingdom of Fairytales Series was a team effort. Below are the people that made it possible:

EQP Management: Rhi Parkes & J.A. Armitage

Our authors: J.A. Armitage, Audrey Rich, B. Kristin McMichael, Emma Savant, Jennifer Ellision, Scarlett Kol, Rose Castro, Margo Ryerkerk, Zara Quentin, Laura Greenwood and Anne Stryker.

Our Editor
Rose Lipscomb

Our Beta Team
Nadine Peterse-Vrijhof
Diane Major
Kalli Bunch
Stephanie Woodwood

Our Proof Reader
Tina Merritt

And to all the wonderful people who loved the world we created and reviewed our stories.
Thank you

# READING ORDER

SEASON ONE
SLEEPING BEAUTY
Queen of Dragons
Heiress of Embers
Throne of Fury
Goddess of Flames

SEASON TWO
LITTLE MERMAID
Queen of Mermaids
Heiress of the Sea
Throne of Change
Goddess of Water

SEASON THREE
RED RIDING HOOD
King of Wolves
Heir of the Curse
Throne of Night
God of Shifters

SEASON FOUR
RAPUNZEL
King of Devotion
Heir of Thorns
Throne of Enchantment
God of Loyalty

SEASON FIVE
RUMPELSTILTSKIN
Queen of Unicorns
Heiress of Gold
Throne of Sacrifice
Goddess of Loss

SEASON SIX
BEAUTY AND THE BEAST
King of Beasts
Heir of Beauty
Throne of Betrayal
God of Illusion

SEASON SEVEN
ALADDIN
Queen of the Sun
Heiress of Shadows
Throne of the Phoenix
Goddess of Fire

SEASON EIGHT
CINDERELLA
Queen of Song
Heiress of Melody
Throne of Symphony
Goddess of Harmony

SEASON NINE
ALICE IN WONDERLAND
Queen of Clockwork
Heiress of Delusion
Throne of Cards
Goddess of Hearts

SEASON TEN
WIZARD OF OZ
King of Traitors
Heir of Fugitives
Throne of Emeralds
God of Storms

SEASON ELEVEN
SNOW WHITE
Queen of Reflections
Heiress of Mirrors
Throne of Wands
Goddess of Magic

SEASON TWELVE
PETER PAN
Queen of Skies
Heiress of Stars
Throne of Feathers
Goddess of Air

## SEASON THIRTEEN
## URBIS

Kingdom of Royalty
Kingdom of Power
Kingdom of Fairytales
Kingdom of Ever After

## BOXSETS

AZIA
BLAISE
CASTIEL
DEON
ELIANA
FALLON
GAIA
HALIA
IVY
JAKON
KELIS
LYRIC
URBIS

www.ingramcontent.com/pod-product-compliance
Lightning Source LLC
Chambersburg PA
CBHW020452310726
48979CB00016B/2614/J
* 9 7 8 1 9 8 9 9 9 7 8 7 1 *